From Agatha Christie to Ruth Rendell

Crime Files Series

General Editor: **Clive Bloom**

Since its invention in the nineteenth century, detective fiction has never been more popular. In novels, short stories, films, radio, television and now in computer games, private detectives and psychopaths, prim poisoners and overworked cops, tommy gun gangsters and cocaine criminals are the very stuff of modern imagination, and their creators one mainstay of popular consciousness. Crime Files is a ground-breaking series offering scholars, students and discerning readers a comprehensive set of guides to the world of crime and detective fiction. Every aspect of crime writing, detective fiction, gangster movie, true-crime exposé, police procedural and post-colonial investigation is explored through clear and informative texts offering comprehensive coverage and theoretical sophistication.

Published titles include:

Ed Christian (*editor*)
THE POST-COLONIAL DETECTIVE

Paul Cobley
THE AMERICAN THRILLER
Generic Innovation and Social Change in the 1970s

Lee Horsley
THE NOIR THRILLER

Susan Rowland
FROM AGATHA CHRISTIE TO RUTH RENDELL
British Women Writers in Detective and Crime Fiction

Crime Files
Series Standing Order ISBN 0–333–71471–7 hardcover
Series Standing Order ISBN 0–333–93064–9 paperback
(*outside North America only*)

You can receive future titles in this series as they are published by placing a standing order. Please contact your bookseller or, in case of difficulty, write to us at the address below with your name and address, the title of the series and the ISBN quoted above.

Customer Services Department, Macmillan Distribution Ltd, Houndmills, Basingstoke, Hampshire RG21 6XS, England

From Agatha Christie to Ruth Rendell

British Women Writers in Detective and Crime Fiction

Susan Rowland
Senior Lecturer in English
University of Greenwich

First published 2001 by
PALGRAVE
Houndmills, Basingstoke, Hampshire RG21 6XS and
175 Fifth Avenue, New York, N. Y. 10010
Companies and representatives throughout the world

PALGRAVE is the new global academic imprint of
St. Martin's Press LLC Scholarly and Reference Division and
Palgrave Publishers Ltd (formerly Macmillan Press Ltd).

ISBN 0–333–67450–2 hardback
ISBN 0–333–68463–X paperback

This book is printed on paper suitable for recycling and
made from fully managed and sustained forest sources.

A catalogue record for this book is available
from the British Library.

Library of Congress Cataloging-in-Publication Data
Rowland, Susan.
    From Agatha Christie to Ruth Rendell / Susan Rowland.
        p. cm.
    Includes bibliographical references and index.
    ISBN 0–333–67450–2 (cloth)
        1. Detective and mystery stories, English—History and criticism. 2.
    Women and literature—Great Britain—History—20th century. 3.
    Christie, Agatha, 1890–1976—Criticism and interpretation. 4.
    Allingham, Margery, 1904–1966—Criticism and interpretation. 5.
    Rendell, Ruth, 1930——Criticism and interpretation. 6. English fiction–
    –Women authors—History and criticism. I. Title.

    PR888.D4 R68 2000
    823'.0872099287—dc21

                                                              00–042202

10   9   8   7   6   5   4   3   2   1
10   09 08 07 06 05 04 03 02 01

Printed and bound in Great Britain by
Antony Rowe Ltd, Chippenham, Wiltshire

For my mother, Mary Rowland, a courageous woman

Contents

Preface

Upon finishing this book I realised that its true subject is pleasure. These six authors have not only accompanied my own life for many years, but have enchanted millions of readers. Perhaps there has been an inverse relationship between their enormous popularity and serious critical attention. Their comparative neglect has been an additional spur to *From Agatha Christie to Ruth Rendell*. As well as inspiring such widespread delight in the reading public, Agatha Christie, Dorothy L. Sayers, Margery Allingham, Ngaio Marsh, P.D. James and Ruth Rendell/Barbara Vine have all made definitive contributions to the crime and detecting form. Christie, Sayers, Allingham and Marsh constitute the 'Four Queens' of the so-called English country house murder, which I will refer to as the 'golden age genre'. The novels of James and Rendell engage in a literary debate with the earlier form in order both to scrutinise its limits and to develop the representation of crime in the context of literary realism. The lack of critical engagement with the profoundly influential work of all six writers is astonishing. *From Agatha Christie to Ruth Rendell* aims to remedy some of this neglect and to suggest areas for future consideration.

My subject is pleasure: this book will concentrate on the deeply literate embedding of readerly pleasures in these crime and detecting stories. All six writers maintain their reputations because their novels are not only widely read but treasured and repeatedly reread. This suggests that the reader is engaged not so much by the 'closure' of these novels, the 'whodunit', but the 'process', the *means* by which the criminal is finally identified out of many narrative possibilities. It is, in fact, the *literary* qualities of these crime fictions, which sustain their popular and cultural significance, making the refusal to treat these authors as literary artists all the more glaring an omission. If the pleasure of these novels does not rely upon the final pinpointing of a single criminal, then it must also be found in their stories of social and self-discovery. This is not to deny the very real differences between them as artists, and as writers with differing social and political approaches. *From Agatha Christie to Ruth Rendell* pursues a dual purpose in evaluating generic developments in the light of exploring their individual artistic visions.

What this book does discover is that the pleasures of these novels are bound up with an interrelated set of concerns. Unsurprisingly, these crime stories are interested in society and its attitude to deviance, but they express their anxieties by strategies ranging from social comedy to tragic realism. The reader's sense of identity, both personal and national, is also debated. In responding to other literatures, the fictions of the six authors draw upon the pleasurable terrors of the literary Gothic. As might be expected of writers who are women, the changing roles of femininity and sexuality receive their conscious attention which, I will also demonstrate, affects developments in the genre.

In an age in which psychoanalysis has become such a widely disseminated cultural phenomenon, the six authors record thoughtful critical appreciations of its resources for portraying unconscious nightmares and irrational passions. By considering the function of unconscious fantasy in the detecting literary form, I shall show some of the pleasures of the genre's duel with death. Last but not least, these six writers explore the metaphysical dimension possible to a genre depicting the healing of a society through a redemptive detecting figure. Again, I will suggest that part of the reading pleasure lies in alternately secure and ambivalent supernatural echoes.

Crucial to the reconsideration of these writers as literary artists is the acknowledgement of the power of individual novels. Therefore all bar the first of the subsequent chapters contain analyses of one individual novel by each author. *From Agatha Christie to Ruth Rendell* provides 42 studies of key texts as well as detailed explorations of the novelists' work as a whole. Throughout the book, I detect the possibilities of pleasure in the 'playful' nature of the golden age form, part of which survives in the succeeding, more realistic authors. In wanting to emphasise 'process' over 'closure' I am, of course, disputing the dismissive reaction to most of these authors as unproblematically conservative. This work aims to initiate debate by opening these fascinating novels to new forms of scrutiny. It does so in the cause of re-evaluating the literary delights engendered by these authors.

My acknowledgements should properly occupy many pages, so I can only mention a few of the people who have been the most helpful in the making of this book. Without the support of Gerard Livingstone this work could never have been written. I owe him more than I can say. Evelyn Hewitt made the completion of this text possible by nobly volunteering to type most of it. In this onerous task Joan Livingstone ably assisted her. I am deeply grateful for their generous and unstinting efforts. Part of the structure of *From Agatha Christie to Ruth Rendell* is indebted to the pioneering efforts of Juliet John, and I am also indebted to Gill Plain for helping me to see the importance of also focusing on individual novels. Her own published work on Dorothy L. Sayers is an inspiration. Conferences of the Association for Research into Popular Fictions, based at Liverpool John Moores University, have proved to be valuable sources of ideas, and I would like to record personal thanks to Nickianne Moody for all her work. The support of friends, in particular Wendy Pank, Christine Saunders, Claire Dyson, Ailsa Camm, Wendy Young, Edmund Cusick, Janet and Frank Carter, Linda Gilman, Margaret Erskine and James Forde-Johnston, have made all the difference in the world. My family has, as usual, put up with me with great patience.

Greenwich University supported this work both financially and in providing a congenial teaching environment. Particular help was given by Peter Humm, John Williams, Ann Battison and Mick Bowles. My students' cheerful interest and ready sympathy has been invaluable.

October 1999

1
Lives of Crime

One of the welcome innovations in approaches to women's writing has been the possibility of a more nuanced consideration of authors' lives in the context of their work. Therefore this book embarks upon its re-evaluation of these novelists by considering the effects of biographical knowledge upon our understanding of their neglected art. This chapter is divided into two parts: brief biographical sketches of the six authors will be followed by an essay, 'Lives of Crime', which will look at themes closely connected to subsequent chapters, such as psyche and inspiration, families, artistic and generic arguments, religion and the vexed question of 'homes'.

Throughout this book I have taken the six writers in the order of the first appearance of their series detective. In this way Ngaio Marsh, senior to Margery Allingham in age, follows her because of her relatively later production of Roderick Alleyn in 1934.[1]

Biographical sketches

Agatha Christie, 1890–1976

Born Agatha Miller in Torquay, Christie was the third child of a family living the life of the wealthy upper classes, but whose income was rapidly diminishing. Her autobiography depicts a happy childhood of a peculiarly musical girl who had hoped to become an opera singer.[2] This work's insistence upon a life of 'fun' is not entirely convincing. As well as recording traumatic nightmares, there are also hints of insecurity in relation to her beautiful older sister, who not only married a rich man but was also an accomplished published writer. First prompted to write stories by her mother,[3] Christie never made bold claims for her art. She married Archibald Christie, a pilot, during the First World War after a passionate courtship. Archie survived the war a hero, and the couple experienced several impoverished postwar years in London while he sought establishment in the City. During this period Christie's only child, Rosalind, was born. At the same time, financial pressures stimulated the production of her first novel, *The Mysterious Affair at Styles*, which introduced Hercule Poirot.[4]

Much to Christie's distress, her marriage did not survive, leading to the media sensation of her 11-day disappearance (discussed later). An unhappy divorce was followed by her second marriage to Max Mallowan, an archaeologist 14 years younger than she was. This new bond established Christie's working pattern of winters on the 'dig' in the Middle East followed by summers in England, and the fitting of her writing around her husband's commitments. The marriage was happy for many years, but it is likely that after the Second World War Max entered into a long-term relationship which distressed his wife.[5] In later life Christie embraced her Christian faith even more deeply, perhaps to enable her to maintain a dignified stoicism. She had a passion for privacy, and the traumas of media scrutiny during her disappearance in 1926 cast long shadows during the next 50 years.

Dorothy L. Sayers, 1893–1957

The daughter of an Oxford clergyman, Sayers grew up in a comfortable country rectory in East Anglia. An only child, from an early age she composed poems and plays. From Godolphin School in Salisbury she won a scholarship to Somerville College, Oxford, and attended with enormous enthusiasm from 1912 to 1915. After Oxford she endured several years of financial insecurity including 'suffering' spells as a schoolteacher, until she achieved basic financial stability by obtaining a job as an advertising copywriter in 1922. She stayed at S.H. Benson until 1929, when her detective novels had secured popular success and sufficient monetary reward. By then, however, her personal life had been transformed. An unhappy love affair with fellow writer John Cournos was followed by a relationship with a mechanic friend, Bill White. This resulted in an unplanned pregnancy, which Sayers managed to conceal from both family and work colleagues. Her son, John Anthony, was fostered by one of the few privy to her secret during her lifetime, her cousin Ivy Shrimpton.

From this point, Sayers's life was dominated by the need to do right by her son, especially by providing a secure economic future. She married journalist Atherton Fleming, known as Mac, in 1926, and the couple, many years later, formally adopted John Anthony, although the child continued to be brought up by Ivy. Sayers's relationship with Cournos can be discerned in the history of Lord Peter Wimsey's future partner, Harriet Vane, in *Strong Poison*.[6] Despite describing Lord Peter Wimsey as a 'permanent resident in the house of my mind',[7] Sayers turned to the writing of religious plays and popular theology after 1936, winning a significant reputation in ecclesiastical circles. Her final years were devoted to the translating of Dante, interrupted by her sudden death in 1957. Her friend and later her biographer, Barbara Reynolds, completed this work.

Margery Allingham, 1904–1966

Allingham was the eldest child of a mother who perpetually declared that she had never wanted children. Her unloving mother remained a source of difficulty throughout the writer's life. The Allingham family made an increasingly precarious middle-class living from writing for popular magazines, and young Margery was given her own writing room at the age of 7. In later years, she felt that the early pressure of her well-meaning father, Herbert, had been unfortunate and had curtailed her childhood. Allingham's own adolescent ambition was to become an actress, and she performed in as well as writing plays as a student at London's Regent Street Polytechnic. Here she cemented her friendship with a family connection, Pip Youngman Carter, whom she married in 1927.

A family séance initiated Allingham's first novel, but Albert Campion did not arrive until the third, *The Crime at Black Dudley*.[8] Her writing life was overshadowed by financial anxiety as she was the main breadwinner of a group of friends living together until the Second World War. She was then expected to finance her husband's expensive London lifestyle after the war. Pressure was exacerbated by the purchase, in 1934, of D'Arcy House in the Essex village of Tolleshunt D'Arcy. This was the former home of the formidable character Dr Salter, once beloved by Allingham's mother. Dr Salter becomes Dr Bouverie in *Dancers in Mourning*.[9]

Allingham's life was also scarred by her chronic thyroid condition, and significant undiagnosed psychological problems. Only as she was dying was her illness named as manic depression. In 1955 she underwent a severe mental breakdown and was given electric shock treatment (ECT) which caused her to lose some of her memory. Lack of treatment for a lump in her breast precipitated her death from cancer in 1966. Her husband Pip completed her last Campion novel, *Cargo of Eagles*,[10] and proceeded to write two more.

Ngaio Marsh, 1895–1982

On a wet afternoon in London during 1931, gentleman policeman Roderick Alleyn was born, but not to a British subject. Like Sayers an only child, Marsh was born to a creatively thwarted amateur actress mother and a creatively stifled bank clerk father in Christchurch, New Zealand. She grew up planning to be a painter and studied at the Canterbury School of Art until 1919, but came to believe that she had never found her true vision in art. Instead, she created Troy Alleyn, who certainly did. Unlike Troy, Marsh never married. Meeting the aristocratic English Rhodes family proved a crucial influence on her life and work, for not only did they provide the models for the charming Lampreys in *Surfeit of Lampreys*,[11] but they invited her to England in 1928. Delighted by London and English country house society, Marsh only returned to New Zealand upon the news that her adored mother was dying. Thereafter she stayed at home for many years, caring for her father until his death and simultaneously developing a formidable reputation as a director of Shakespeare and promoter of university drama.

After the Second World War she embarked upon a dual life and almost a dual identity, as a theatre producer in New Zealand and as a far more glamorous author in London. Her contributions to drama were finally recognised with the opening in 1967 of the Ngaio Marsh Theatre at the new university campus at Christchurch. Aged 58, she fell in love with a married friend and maintained a harmonious friendship with both members of the couple. Family, friends and colleagues testified to her gift for friendship and also to her ambience of sexual reticence, which is reflected in her autobiography. Her dual life lives on in a dual reputation: New Zealand honours her for her dramatic career while England treasures her detective fiction. Some of the most memorable novels combine both worlds in theatrical crimes.

P.D. James, 1920–

Like Dorothy L. Sayers, whom she admires, Phyllis Dorothy James was born in Oxford. Her tax inspector father did not believe in educating girls, so her education at Cambridge Girls High School was terminated when she was 16. Like her later creation, Cordelia Gray, she regretted not attending university. During the Second World War James worked as a Red Cross nurse, and she married Anglo-Irish doctor Connor Bantry White in 1941.

The war had a profound influence on her life and her later writing. Immediate consequences included her husband returning home so mentally scarred that James had to become the family breadwinner and the working mother of two daughters. She began a successful career in the Civil Service, which included work as an administrator in the Home Office in criminal policy and the police department, in which she rose to a senior rank.

Her first novel, *Cover Her Face* (1962), was a deliberate attempt to engage with golden age 'country house' conventions.[12] Its introduction of poet-policeman Adam Dalgliesh was confirmed in later novels with both London and East Anglian coastal settings. A committed, though conservative, participant in the management of the Church of England, James was created Baroness of Holland Park in 1991 by the then Conservative British Government. This status gives her membership of the House of Lords. However, she regards any political role as very much subordinate to her life as an author. Her work's sense of tragedy and its criticism of secular modernity has made a profound contribution to the genre.

Ruth Rendell, 1930– ; Barbara Vine, 1986–

Ruth Rendell has a tripartite writing identity: her Wexford novels, the most beloved, contain an ultimately reassuring detective in traditional garb. Always alongside the Wexfords Rendell has produced crime thrillers lacking the secure moral focus of the questing detective. Additionally, since 1986 she has also produced literary, psychologically adventurous crime-rooted novels as Barbara Vine. This new identity, she has suggested, is essential to this expansion of her art. Rendell is very private about her personal history. Born in London to two unhappily married schoolteachers, she was a lonely child whose Swedish mother died when Rendell was quite young. As a young woman she became a journalist; she married political reporter Donald Rendell in 1950. Their one son later became a social worker. His discussions with his mother enhanced her already very active social conscience.

Ruth and Donald Rendell divorced in 1975 but remarried two years later. For many years they lived in a sixteenth-century manor house in Suffolk, and Rendell still owns property in the area as well as always having houses in London. Rendell was once active in the Campaign for Nuclear Disarmament. Her lifelong support for left-of-centre politics facilitated her elevation to Baroness Rendell of Babergh in 1997 by the new Labour Government. As a fellow member of the House of Lords to her friend Lady James, Rendell nevertheless sits on the opposite political bench and campaigns actively on issues of domestic violence, public libraries and public transport. Stories abound of Rendell's private generosity to writers and artistic causes. An avowed feminist and

Christian socialist, Rendell's political values have become artistically infused with her development of the crime and detecting genres.

Lives of crime

Family life is heavily implicated in criminal passions described by the six authors. While it is specious to look for direct correlations between a writer's life and her fictions, biographies of the four 'golden age' writers in particular reveal profound influences from early years, especially from powerful 'magical' mothers.[13] Agatha Christie credited her adored mother, Clarissa or 'Clara', with second sight, and recorded her constant experiments with religions including the occult, such as Spiritualism and Theosophy. Significantly, when her mother appears to initiate a convalescent Agatha into writing, it is an occult story that Christie at first produces. Very like Christie's remarkable parent, Margery Allingham's mother, Emily, was reputed to have clairvoyant tendencies (even to the reading of her daughter's thoughts!), and similarly dabbled in Theosophy. However, unlike loving Clara, Emily was uncanny and cold, frequently declaring in her children's hearing that she had never wanted them. Later in her marriage Emily formed a passionate bond with the neighbouring Dr Salter and suffered several mental breakdowns.

The mothers of Ngaio Marsh and Dorothy L. Sayers each fostered her daughter's talents in less psychically demanding ways. Both women, the mothers of only daughters, were unfulfilled artists who may have compensated by channelling their creativity into the next generation. Marsh herself attributed her mother's strong identification with her creative work as Freudian projection, indicating that the respect for Freud in her novels may have originated in her attempt to understand her own family dynamics. Upon her mother's death, Marsh suffered a nervous breakdown. Her biographer links Marsh's sexual reticence with her mother's early training to conceal deep emotions. Something similar may have been the case for Sayers, as it was her mother's potential shock, even more than her father's, that prevented her from ever revealing the existence of her son during their lifetimes.

If 'magical' or creative mothers may have had a formative affect, then relationships with men provided more overt structuration to the writers' lives. Only Marsh of all the six novelists never married. She did fall in love later in life with a married friend and entered a platonic relationship, but that seems not to have caused difficulties for his wife. Like Sayers, Marsh portrays an ideal companionate marriage in her novels, that of detective Roderick Alleyn and artist Agatha Troy. Yet Sayers's lovers, Lord Peter Wimsey and Harriet Vane, struggle harder to reach equilibrium, a fact perhaps linked to the gestation of the character of Harriet in the context of Sayers's own unhappy love affair. The sexually expressed but ultimately unconsummated relationship between young Dorothy L. Sayers and John Cournos is reflected in Harriet Vane's situation with her selfish lover, Philip Boyes, in *Strong Poison*. Cournos refused to commit himself to marriage and Sayers to contraception. Ironically, in Sayers's subsequent relationship the contraception failed, resulting in the birth of John Anthony, the major turning-point of Sayers's life. Thereafter, she was determined to meet her moral, financial and spiritual responsibilities for her son, perhaps at the cost of denying herself much of the emotional satisfaction of motherhood.

Christie is the only other author of the early four to have given birth, to a daughter, who remained a stabilising factor in her life. Greatly in love with her first husband, Archibald Christie, she was devastated by his infidelity. However, her second marriage to Max Mallowan not only provided affection but also satisfied her passion for travel, as she took a full part in her husband's archaeology as a traditional wifely helpmeet. Christie seems to be unusual amongst all the authors for regarding her writing as very much secondary to her identity as a 'wife'. Allingham's marriage, like the latter stages of that of Sayers's, was not of the happiest. Whereas Mac's ill health made him increasingly difficult to live with, Pip Youngman Carter continued to provide emotional support. Such positive contributions did not always outweigh his infidelities, expensive in both psychological and financial terms.

Of particular fascination in the personal lives of the four earlier novelists is that they all experienced significant moments of psychological trauma. These episodes provide deeply marked turning-points in their inner lives. Sayers's unplanned pregnancy and its transforming effect on her life has already been mentioned. From this point, Sayers put aside her passions for 'high romance' (exploring it instead in her writing) to conduct her emotional life in a tone of earthy realism. She was also a personal witness to Christie's far more public fragmentation, as Sayers actually took part in the Great Sunday Hunt for the missing novelist. Agatha Christie disappeared on a dark December evening in 1926. Her car was found abandoned, her unfaithful husband was publicly suspected of murder, and she was discovered 11 days later at a Harrogate hotel claiming amnesia. She had registered under the surname of her husband's mistress. Jared Cade's new biographical work makes use of recent testimony by the family of Christie's friend and sister-in-law, Nan Watts.[14] In desperation after the death of her beloved mother and the imminent desertion of Archie, Sayers's unpublished suggestion that her fellow novelist was seeking deliberately to punish those who injured her seems the likeliest answer to a long media enigma. Jared Cade is convinced that the disappearance was staged by Christie in collaboration with Nan Watts in order to punish Archie. Neither could have foreseen the resulting media frenzy. Certainly, the eruption of tabloid energy deeply shocked Christie, who never referred to the matter in public again.

Evidence of her vulnerability to psychological hurt can be gained from her description of a recurrent nightmare as a child. 'The gunman' was a figure of absolute horror who would appear in dreams in the guise of immediate family. It is not too fanciful to suggest that Christie's generic devotion to the menace behind conventional domesticity may have been fuelled by these terrifying dreams. Similarly, the break-up of her marriage and the way that press intrusion exploded the whole fabric of her personal life may have cruelly mimicked the childhood trauma.

Ngaio Marsh's breakdown upon the death of her mother led to no public retribution, yet her autobiography, like Christie's, similarly recalled a recurrent childhood torment. The terror was occasioned by the idea of poison, almost certainly from a play, a psychic disturbance that remained an 'aftertaste' to the author, who rarely featured poison in her novels.[15] Notably, this childhood trauma combined both of Marsh's subsequent careers: detective fiction and the theatre. Ill health marked Margery Allingham's life so deeply that it is unwise to isolate one psychological turning-point. A recognised sufferer from a thyroid deficiency, Allingham had the excessive weight gain and low energy associated with the condition. What was never adequately diagnosed in time was manic depression, despite earlier treatment with ECT which she had dreaded. This serious illness could be connected to her writing in that in her adolescence her family credited her with mediumistic powers and her first novel was composed as the result of a séance.

Allingham's life demonstrates a peculiarly intimate and painful link between the occult, psychiatric medicine and the woman writer whose mental struggles were not taken seriously enough by doctors. Her constant employment of Gothic tropes and occult religious practices can be seen as related to the profound psychic energies moulding her day-to-day existence. Also, Allingham does produce a recurrent (significantly masculine) villain: a megalomaniac killer who fragments into madness. He is perhaps a sign of incipient self-analysis of the dangers of the manic depressive's typical 'elated' state.

Another writer who particularly uses the Gothic is Ruth Rendell. Quite properly concerned to protect her own privacy, Rendell is very open about her interest in psychology, having read a great deal of Freud and Jung. She admits that a concentration on obsessive natures in her work is reflected in her personal make-up.[16] Unconscious traumas are frequently represented in both detective and victims.

An acknowledged turning-point in the career of P.D. James was her husband's mental illness after the Second World War, not her own. This family crisis precipitated James's need for full-time employment. It would also have compounded the profound impression left on her by the war itself, whose atrocities define a dark and Gothic corner of James's imagination. It is this shared historical experience that becomes the propelling force behind her characteristic conversion of the golden age genre to bleak, realistic tragedy. Further chapters will look at these psychic elements in the six authors' work.

In suggesting psychological relationships between lives and art, it is important not to neglect the commercial significance of writing in a popular form. All four early novelists wrote detective fiction because they needed the money. Agatha Christie's penury was relatively short-lived. Margery Allingham suffered financial anxieties the longest in needing to support a complicated household of adults in a large and expensive home. Although her husband earned some money, Allingham remained the main breadwinner and later became the sole support of elderly relatives. Marsh was required only to keep herself after the death of both parents and so finances did not impinge so much as they continued to do in the life of Dorothy L. Sayers. Her letters record anxious moments in her self-imposed task of providing the best for her 'adopted' son.

Commercial considerations have fictional consequences. Popular detectives have to outlive their author's enthusiasm, as in the case of Hercule Poirot, and the constrictions of the form must not be lightly violated. Allingham frequently found herself forced to write a more conventional novel when sales of her more imaginative renderings of the genre dipped. It is a distinction between the golden age and the later authors that the works of neither P.D. James nor Ruth Rendell have had to conform to a commercial format due to immediate financial pressure. James continued her Civil Service career precisely to protect her art's integrity.[17] The genesis of Ruth Rendell's first novel,

From Doon with Death, does hint at the difficulties of unpublished authors. A naturally experimental writer closest in impulse to Margery Allingham, Rendell was obliged to rewrite the pre-existing story as a detective novel in order to get it accepted. Inspector Wexford, invented as a generic device, proved popular and so had to reappear. Rendell developed him as a character once she realised that she was going to have to live with him. Yet unlike the early authors, Rendell did not need to retain Wexford to finance a household, however much his popularity emboldened his creator additionally to embark upon detective-less crime novels and, much later, to reinvent herself as Barbara Vine. This recently generated artistic persona implies the 'self-creative' nature of writing for Rendell.

It is possible distantly to link Barbara Vine back to Margery Allingham's 'authorizing' séance. Rendell has stated that she needs the writing identity of Barbara Vine in order to find the psychological freedom of Vine's distinctive works. We might discern a structural similarity between the apparition of Vine and Allingham's opening herself up to 'other' voices or spirits within, in composing her first novel. Such a shaping of creative energy recalls the Spiritualist narrative in the early career of Agatha Christie (embedded in her powerful mother). P.D. James reveals traces of a similar inspiration to a séance (though, of course, without the occult overtones), in also looking to 'voices' within to embody characters. These figures then frequently evade the expectations of the surface aspect of the author's mind. As far as the creative impulse is concerned, these six authors reveal links between occult practice, mental disturbance and the work of the woman novelist.

Drawing back a little from inner inspiration, the six novelists offer conscious analysis of the detecting and crime genres. All of them express a sense of the roots of the fictional detective going back to the medieval morality play in which a drama of good and evil is played out within a secure theological framework (see also Chapter 7). P.D. James is particularly insistent upon this, yet her novels, while retaining the conflict of vice and virtue, significantly differ in lacking the intimations of a just God behind it all, thereby moving her art into the realms of tragedy, not divine comedy. She has agreed with this distinction.[18] Christie's overt interest in the 'morality tale' aspect deepened as she became more concerned to protect innocence in later novels such as *Hallowe'en Party*.[19] Of course, it is Sayers who is the dedicated medievalist amongst the golden-age writers. In her two introductions to the Gollancz collections of mystery stories, she proposed mythical interpretations of the contemporary popular form.[20] The detective functions as a modern Arthurian knight in a secularisation of the sacred quest to restore and heal a wounded society. The crime story is old indeed, but the detective hero requires a society prepared to be on the side of the law. Sayers devises two categories and places the origin of both in the works of Edgar Allan Poe: detection and mystery as well as detection and horror. Later chapters of this book will identify both types in the range of the six authors.

Allingham and Rendell have an artistic alliance across time in that both develop the genres towards novels of suspense and obsession. Allingham's remark that the act of murder can be also, or even instead, a *metaphor* for psychological cruelty or social dysfunction actually anticipates much of the work of Barbara Vine.[21] Ngaio Marsh's autobiography reveals her deliberations over her own distinctive artistic problems as a colonial author. Even at an early stage she was aware of the complex issues involved in producing a novel adequate to the New Zealand landscape's non-European intensities with only Western literature as a model.[22] Such artistic consciousness, allied to her sensitive attempts to represent New Zealand's 'difference' in some of her detective novels, confirms Marsh as a 'post-colonial' writer as well as historically a colonial one. To Marsh, crime fiction provided an alternative to traditional realism because she regarded the genre as 'fixed' as metaphysical poetry. Her reluctance to experiment with the detecting form needs to be seen in the light of this way of responding to her colonial situation.

Apart from Christie, who was content to classify her art as secondary to her married life, the other golden age writers were all concerned both to develop their writing into crime *novels* and to be recognised as novelists and artists. In this they anticipate the careers of James and Rendell, who produce fascinating dialogues between golden age aesthetics and literary realism.

Before leaving the issue of genre, it is worth briefly revisiting the concept of the morality play with its metaphysical dimensions. Religion plays a part in the lives of most of the six authors, with only Ngaio Marsh a confirmed sceptic. P.D. James is active in the Church of England, Ruth Rendell links Christianity emphatically with her left-wing politics, both Allingham and Christie had a personal faith to sustain them, and Sayers is famous for taking theology into the heart of her identity as a writer, producing an influential work examining God in terms of the creative artist.[23] Alongside these orthodoxies, the golden age writers in particular depict occult influences in their works, reflecting early twentieth-century fascinations with Spiritualism,

Theosophy (which also engaged the likes of Yeats), and more folklorish manifestations such as witchcraft. Such fragmented and sinister forms of the metaphysical in the novels are also present in the writers' lives, such as in the enthusiasms of Christie's mother, Allingham's early propensity for séances, and Sayers, the vicar's daughter, comprehensively exploding Spiritualism in *Strong Poison*. This situating of an occult heritage in the writers' own histories complements the occult's generic function of reflecting the fate of the metaphysical in the secularised irrationalities of modern culture.

To take this further, one way in which the metaphysical can still inhabit the supposedly God-free space of crime fiction is in the 'playfulness' and self-referentiality of the golden age form. Twentieth-century crime fiction does not *become* self-conscious. Instead, in the golden age writers it always *was* self-referential, right from Christie's early works. Golden age crime novels refer repeatedly to their own genre, and this self-conscious artifice will be explored thoroughly in Chapter 2. Here I suggest that the 'performing' nature of these fictions interestingly coincides with the presence of the theatre in the lives of the four early authors. In youth, Margery Allingham received drama training and longed to become an actress, and her first mature attempts at writing were plays. Sayers not only became a writer of religious drama, but as an adolescent masqueraded in the role of Athos, the Musketeer, conducting a passionate mythical affair with her cousin, Ivy (who would later bring up her son!). While Christie's early hopes of operatic performing had to give way to the significantly ideal match between her novels and the stage, Marsh had an important and successful career in developing New Zealand drama.

P.D. James and Ruth Rendell have not followed their golden age predecessors into the theatre. Other popular mediums for drama have superseded the stage, and millions of fans have been drawn to their novels by television adaptations. However, in the 1990s both of them have taken on new roles as political figures with membership of the House of Lords. This body cannot initiate laws, but can modify or delay those produced at the seat of direct political power, the House of Commons. This move into the law-making process can be seen as highly appropriate for authors concerned to combine golden age characteristics with psychological and social realism. Their novels comment directly upon contemporary society, just as the House of Lords is a body concerned in the organising of society's laws and prohibitions. The theatrical nature of politics, particularly British politics with its ancient rituals, expresses neatly in these writers' lives the generic blend of their art. Where the golden age writers were engaged in the theatre and produced self-conscious 'theatrical' novels, James and Rendell partake of politics, and write works in which truthful representations of passion and society are enacted within, and against, golden age tropes. Of course, the fact that James and Rendell produce such different visions of society is also a sign of the different political and social 'truths' represented by differing political parties.

Contrasting social visions can perhaps be placed back into writers' lives in the material reality of the 'home'. Agatha Christie retained a lifelong attachment to her childhood home of Ashfield in Torquay. In later years she was also a seasoned traveller. Interestingly, her work comes close to that of Ngaio Marsh in her persistent exploration of the colonial politics of 'Home' in such novels as *The Hollow* and *Sleeping Murder*.[24] Allingham remained far more attached to the Essex countryside where she spent much of her childhood. This includes the nearby mysterious coastline of Mersea Island, the scene of smuggling stories and of Allingham's initiatory séances on a family holiday. Even the purchase of D'Arcy House in the village of Tolleshunt D'Arcy is intimately connected to her interior history, being the home of the formidable Dr Salter, the emotional focus of her mother's later life. The house continues to have significant effects on Allingham's adult life as it entails much financial struggle.

For P.D. James, of course, 'home' in her novels rarely lives up to the promises of order and nurture that the word may evoke. But in dialogue with the golden age, there is a certain self-consciousness about her employment of East Anglian landscapes, and in particular in the use of Allingham's Mersea Island at the violent conclusions of both *Original Sin* and *A Certain Justice*.[25] A great admirer of Dorothy L. Sayers, James refuses to find an earthly home to match her moral vision. Here she is unlike Sayers's development of potential homes of integrity and cosmic order in Oxford (in the healing resolution of *Gaudy Night*) and the Fenland great church in *The Nine Tailors*.[26] It is surely not coincidental that these places represented times of security and happiness in Sayers's own life.

In a later chapter I will suggest that the social vision of Ruth Rendell, alone among the six writers, looks forward to a utopian place – one which may never exist but which remains a quest object for liberal politics. Possibly this aspect of her art can be allied to her creation of a wholly fictional 'home town' of Kingsmarkham for Wexford. Kingsmarkham is not an earthly paradise, but it is repeatedly visited by the remarkable detective's resolutions of crimes that are, for this author, embedded in social issues. Barbara Vine is often concerned to explore some of the complex 'meanings' of London (Rendell's birthplace), in works such as *King Solomon's Carpet*, focusing upon the London Underground.[27]

Unsurprisingly, 'home' is always a post-colonial place for Ngaio Marsh. She was brought up to call England 'Home', and in later years she created a renowned English country garden at her house in the New Zealand hills. Marsh's devotion throughout her career to London models upon which to develop New Zealand theatre came to irritate younger colleagues. In her writing, her interpretation of the English detective genre into what I will call 'camp country house' reflects her intense attraction to a society in which she also remained well aware that she was a colonial outsider.

The following chapters will explore the work of the six writers in a vain attempt to give these authors their literary due. There can never be enough space in one volume to consider the hitherto neglected literary abundance represented by these fascinating writers. My aim is to provoke debate, in particular by moving away from the stale conception of these writers as unproblematically conservative. It is time to look at the *processes* of crime novels and not give too much importance to their endings, their 'closure'. To this end, Chapter 2 will discuss the topic of gender and genre and Chapter 3 will dispute the oversimplified conservative reputation of these writers and their genres. Chapter 4 will consider the unexplored arena of Englishness, race and colonialism in their works, while Chapter 5 offers a new perspective on the frequently linked fields of psychoanalysis and detective fiction. This chapter develops arguments about crime narrative, pleasure and the reader, as well as showing some of the responses *to* psychoanalysis by these authors. A chapter on the Gothic will continue the issue of the reader's suspense and horror while assessing the writers' treatment of this important literary legacy. This is followed by Chapter 7's delineation of the metaphysical dimensions of the genre, and discussion of how the authors each absorb the occult connotations into their art. The book concludes with a feminist perspective: Chapter 8 examines the changing portrayal of women in crime as well as the novels' structuring of a proto-feminist ethics. Chapters 2–8 are divided into two: a thorough exploration of the topic in the work of the six authors is followed by a close analysis of one novel from each of them. By such means, I hope to detect some of the remarkable literary achievements occurring *From Agatha Christie to Ruth Rendell*.

2
Gendering the Genre

In 1920 the character of the fictional detective changed.[1] For a fanciful moment, we could imagine the advent of a refugee Belgian at an English country house called Styles coinciding with the arrival of a deferential ex-soldier at a Piccadilly flat. Bunter's taking up his post begins the healing of the shell-shocked Lord Peter Wimsey into the socially active yet ambiguous role of the detective: one who uncannily succours the innocent and deals death to the guilty. More inferentially, it is surely now that a young diplomat embarks on mysterious adventures culminating in the switching of careers to the metropolitan police. Roderick Alleyn's devotion to law and the professionalisation of 'duty' is never suspect; but far more marginal (in all senses) is the pre-career of Albert Campion, who by 1920 is testing out his ambivalence towards the law. We might even extrapolate from the 1960s debut of those idiosyncratic policemen, Adam Dalgliesh and Reg Wexford. In about 1920 we envisage an obscure but respectable birth in a quiet Sussex town for Wexford and a marriage of Dalgliesh's clergy parents to be followed by the birth of their solitary child some 10 years later.

What we have, starting in 1920, is a literary event in which crime fictions by these six women come to dominate the genre in Britain. In the first place they constitute the early twentieth-century sub-genre of 'golden age' detective fiction. In the case of P.D. James and Ruth Rendell (not forgetting Barbara Vine), they transmit this heritage into an age when the fictional representation of crime is dispersed across a number of both 'popular' and 'literary' genres. This chapter will assess the extent and significance of this literary event in the matter of gender and genre. What has been the impact of hugely popular women writers on detective fiction? Despite the continuing stress on male

15

detectives in these mainstream authors, is gender a perceptible factor in the evolution of form?

A later chapter will examine the issue of feminism in relation to these works; but here I want to look at genre as a potential space where gender strategies may be tested, confronted and reconfigured by queens of crime. This is not the seeking out of an essentially feminine crime fiction to place against an essentially masculine predecessor. Rather, it is to explore how women writers may disrupt the ways in which femininity and masculinity have been previously construed as mutually exclusive and mutually constitutive. Such relative structures have historically taken the form of the masculine assuming culturally desirable qualities of reason, intelligence, objectivity, judgement, action and heroism, leaving the feminine, by structural definition, to signify irrationality, foolishness, subjectivity, passivity and the need for masculine guidance.

This is what feminist critics mean when they describe the feminine as the 'other' of the masculine dominant cultural structure. It is not just that the feminine is 'something else' but that it is defined as the 'not masculine' – as what has been cast out of masculinity in the very act of its formation as reason, intelligence and so on. It is certainly *not* that femininity really *is* like this, for gender cannot be represented as separate from the culture which construes it. Rather, the feminine has been the dark other to the masculine western tradition of privileging reason, intelligence, order and rationality; a tradition that has much to do with the generating of the fictional detective. No one bears the privileging of masculine reason more ambiguously than the literary detective Sherlock Holmes.

Holmes will, as is his wont, disappear and reappear in this chapter, but at a deeper level we may find gender and genre bound together already in a relationship to the law. As a simple historical matter, male culture has exclusively produced and administered the law as well as its attendant apparatus of police, lawyers and courts. Feminism has always argued that this has not resulted in a law of universal benevolence but a gendered product which has taken an active role in construing the feminine as other. Feminist psychoanalytic theorists have gone further in suggesting that the whole idea of law, with its fixed texts and belief in unambiguous language, is at a profound level associated with masculinity because of the way every individual infant learns about language and sexual difference as part of the same process.[2] To the developing child, so much depends upon possession or non-possession of the phallus as the sign of sexual difference that the small girl is assigned the role of disempowered 'other' to the masculine, who inherits linguistic and, ultimately, cultural privilege. This is what feminist critics call the law, as the paternal function that produces a privileged gender and its other. It is clearly connected both psychically and culturally to the body of written laws which are those documents supposed unambiguously to assign criminal status to their own otherness: that which transgresses or is excluded by them.

We need to return, with some relief perhaps, to crime novels. I now want to offer a definition of crime fiction: that it crucially supplements the culturally authoritative texts of the law. What I mean by this is that all crime fiction, when clearly defined *as fiction*, is offering a story that the laws cannot or will not tell. It is saying, in effect, that there is more to crime than the institutionalised stories told in courts and police stations; there is more to criminals, their motives, actions and lives that can be represented through the cultural authority of the legal system. Crime fiction is the *other* of the powers of legal institutions to *represent* crime to the culture. Perhaps the appetite for crime fiction is driven by the desire generated by a sense of cultural excess to the operations of the law. There is always 'more to it' than legal institutions can represent, so crime fiction comes to answer that excessive desire by evolving an aesthetic form. Paradoxically, its definition 'as fiction' means that crime fiction can happily occupy the role of other to the laws, so helping to constitute the laws' claims to be 'factual'. Yet, a characterisation 'as fiction' simultaneously guarantees that it can never satisfy that demand for the 'true excess' to the laws; a demand that, if met, would transform the role and power of the legal system by collapsing the binary opposition of law/crime fiction.

In this sense we could suggest that detective fiction is structurally gendered as feminine. Perhaps critics should rather be concerned to explain how anxious male writers may engender a fundamentally unruly femininity in the genre, rather than start from the position of women authors as anomalous. At this interesting juncture, enter the confident demeanour of Sherlock Holmes.

Holmes, as Raymond Williams suggests,[3] arrives at a crucial moment in the development of urban culture and of modernist literature's consequent attempt to understand the mass energies of the modern metropolis. In harking back to the free-floating super-intelligence of Poe's Dupin,[4] and by combining a lofty ratiocination with an aura of science and its reassuring narrative of progress, Holmes is a potent adjunct to the law. He functions as a kind of licensed masculine other who can embody near-mystical powers of reasoning as a way of shoring up legal institutions which seem less solid in the modern era. His very isolation and distance from the reader (emphasised by Watson's self-evident inadequacies) mystifies masculinity as a saviour-hero. As Stephen Knight points out,[5] Holmes, like all good mythical heroes, dies only to return, empowered by his mysterious triumph over death. Unsurprisingly, it is Sherlock Holmes above all, and often Holmes exclusively, to which the female-authored detectives refer.

In suggesting that Holmes and his male colleagues signify an attempt at a masculine heroic detective, I must refer back to my argument about crime fiction as structurally feminine. The Holmesian heroic and its indirect descendant, the male hard-boiled mystery, do not provide a monolithic model of heroic masculinity, but contain otherness and gender ambiguities within their masquerade of gender. They participate in the 'femininity' of their fictionality. My argument will be that the six authors 'play' with the Holmesian heroic *as if it was* a secure construction of masculinity which they can then disrupt. This textual 'play' is part of their characteristic self-conscious artifice.

In the task of gendering the genre, these six writers rewrite the figure of the detective in ways that directly address the Holmesian legacy. Such a project results in far-reaching transformations. These include the delineation of an anti-heroic detective as a 'playful' counter to Holmes, the exploring of gender ambivalence, the enacting of a more dispersed operation of detecting powers, the developing of what can be called a 'psychic construction through detection', and a re-situating of their detectives in relation to modernity. After the detective, the forms of narrative themselves can be seen to be energised by considerations of gender. Most crucially, the genre becomes highly self-conscious and self-reflexive as a form of fiction. Within this rhetoric of artifice, the stories of crime and detection are used to explore gender anxieties and boundaries. The Gothic also becomes a distinctive mode for representing conflicting structures of otherness. Lastly, there is a spectrum of generic 'outcomes' in these writers, rather than one repeated, compulsive and socially inflected conclusion. Such final configurations of characters and crime range from the comedy of Christie's remaking of social worlds to the lone, tragic heroes in the irredeemable universes of P.D. James. But first of all: the detective.

Gendering the detective

Both Alison Light and Gill Plain, in their valuable work on Agatha Christie and Dorothy L. Sayers respectively, have described an ethic of anti-heroism in the female-authored detectives in the traumatised aftermath of the First World War.[6] Protagonists such as the spherical, obsessively neat Hercule Poirot (whose name is mock-heroic in the combination of macho 'hercules' and 'poirot' – buffoon) and hysterical Wimsey both seem feminised, creating an ambivalence about gender which moves away from prewar styles of male heroism. Even Roderick Alleyn, who does not appear until 1934, has a postwar sensitivity and 'fastidiousness' about his job. His taut nerves are stressed when he has to arrest anybody.[7] Albert Campion's most characteristic quality is ambivalence, in particular in his liberal interpretation of his role as hero. Refusal to adopt the mask of traditional male heroism in *Mystery Mile* leads directly to the loss of his first love, Biddy.[8]

Fracturing the heroic mould of masculinity transforms both the detective's and the reader's relation to the novel. No longer exhibiting a mastery of events, the loss of Holmesian confidence democratises the form and allows the puzzle genre to become something the reader is invited to enter on more equal terms. The detective remains ahead (usually) but his efforts are imitable and his evidence is proffered to the reader. One of Harriet Vane's overlooked tasks is to get Peter Wimsey to tabulate his progress, for example in *Have His Carcase*.[9] Discussions between police colleagues after hours often fulfils this function in James and Rendell.

A particular factor in the anti-heroic detective is the way personal weaknesses and vulnerabilities are not external to the success of investigations but intrinsic to them. That which appears as 'excessive' or unnecessary to the detective function becomes a vital ingredient of success. Hercule Poirot is remarkable for wearing his weaknesses on his sleeve. He is frequently despised for his attention to domestic details and gossip, but his espousal of what are characterised as 'feminine' methods of investigation in *The Murder of Roger Ackroyd* proves crucial.[10] Similarly, it is Peter Wimsey's vulnerability to war trauma in *The Unpleasantness at the Bellona Club* that enables him to untangle the dynamics of a family dominated by ex-servicemen.[11]

If Albert Campion exhibits weakness, it is in his tendency to look foolish when engaged in fruitful speculation, a deliberately anti-heroic mask. For Campion, it is his ambivalence about the law and his perception of it as not unified but potentially incoherent that becomes a defining ingredient. This unspoken attitude is realised in Campion's engagement by other services or by friends who may be in conflict with the police. For Roderick Alleyn, the only policeman amongst the early detectives, it is his superior class position and excessive sensibilities that are continually defined as other or 'extra' to the all-male middle-class police force and then shown to be essential to his work. Alleyn's unfailing glamour to the monied classes allows him to penetrate their masquerades of respectability where subordinates are struck dumb.

This basic division is still to be found in Wexford and Dalgliesh, who are in fact hybrid policemen/private detectives on gender lines. In both series the police force is predominantly male and associated with masculine, often sexist values. Both Wexford and Dalgliesh combine inner qualities of a feminised unconventional 'other' with a deep loyalty to the male bonding of the police. For Dalgliesh, the gender disruption is significantly buried in his poetry, which we are told in *Death of an Expert Witness* contains a passionate outpouring at the murder of a child. Dalgliesh the policeman behaved with efficient detachment on that particular case.[12] Yet it is Dalgliesh's capacity for extra-professional pity that contributes to his success and the consequent aura of mystique with which his colleagues regard him.

Wexford's relation to the police force is more hot-headed. Loyal and even parental to his devoted authoritarian subordinate, Mike Burden, Wexford's imaginative excursions into the unusual or unconventional aspects of crime leads to frequent accusations of obsession. This may provoke him into taking expensive holidays just so that he can further a case outside official sanction, as in *Put on by Cunning*.[13] Wexford may not always be right in his intuitions, but these powers, explicitly structured as 'outside' proper detecting, do lead to a solution that would otherwise be unrealised. In this, both Dalgliesh and Wexford are the true inheritors of Miss Marple, an ironic creation of extra-legal methods. Cordelia Gray, interestingly, tries to reconcile Miss Marple's gossipy and unofficial strategies with what she takes to be an authoritative and authorising police method, which looks directly to Dalgliesh as a final masculine sanction.

The reason these detectives need the resources of feminised practises in addition to legal processes is the domesticated sphere of the emerging genre. The four interwar writers set murder in the home or in a work environment where men and women work together with strong domestic and erotic overtones. Yet the crimes are not just a matter of the potential destabilisations of family and class, they also involve specifically domestic crime scenes, places conventionally demarcated as feminine. Missing matches, a torn handkerchief, where a lonely female servant goes on her days off, a subtly changed domestic routine, are all characteristic clues to be decoded by a detective alert to gendered spheres of influence. Typically, only those male detectives most rooted in the gendered upper class need feminised subordinates to search for clues in female realms 'foreign' to them. Alleyn needs his sexless companion,[14] Inspector Fox, to haunt the pantries of female servants, while Peter Wimsey employs Miss Marple's near-relative, Miss Climpson, until Harriet can take over the role of a spy in female realms.

The detective is, of course, a paradigm of the reader who follows clues in order to arrive at a coherent story. The democratisation arising from the puzzle structure and the domesticity of the vital signs tends to offer the reader a more feminine position *vis-à-vis* the novel. Golden age detective fiction offers reassurance in being the promise of a rationally determined world. The reader is confident that the novel *will work* to offer a coherent solution tying up all loose ends: the detective is a kind of guarantee for the reader that narrative completion will ensue. So what happens if crime fiction omits the detective? Barbara Vine explicitly disrupts the detective form of the crime fiction contract in ways I will describe in later chapters. For now, the final anti-heroic flourish of the six authors' detectives is an ambivalence concerning the role of the criminal.

For the Holmesian detective, a secure master of detecting strategies (as posited in the 'play' of the six authors), the detective is unambiguously heroic in opposition to an unambiguously 'bad' criminal. Such demarcation produces a conservative genre by suggesting that traditional hierarchies are to be supported. By contrast, the anti-heroic detective can sometimes not be distinguished from the criminal, for example, in some of the adventures of Albert Campion,[15] can take part in a killing, as Lord Peter Wimsey does,[16] can decide that the true murderer was the victim, as Poirot does.[17] He can even abet a murderer as the only way of exacting a kind of justice, as Cordelia Gray does,[18] and can discover death-dealing crimes unpunishable by the current legal system, as Dalgliesh does.[19] What the anti-heroic feminised detective discovers is that the law is not a stable, infallible system for administering justice, and that its instabilities are often bound up with formations of gender. Interestingly, it is the most extra-legal detective, Jane Marple, who becomes most unambiguous and clear-headed about identifying and punishing murder. Her methods remain unrecognised and *unrecognisable* to the legal system until the final denouement, when legal proof or confession will be provided.[20]

If the detective is constructed against a posited traditional male heroism, he is not as isolated as he was either. In the role of lovers,

Harriet Vane, Agatha Troy and Campion's Amanda Fitton, there is a subordinate but contributing intellectual role far surpassing that of Dr Watson. Captain Hastings is, of course, an amiable neo-Watson to Poirot, but another Christie creation, crime writer Ariadne Oliver, contributes some useful insights in works such as *Dead Man's Folly*.[21] Jane Marple is able to work with energetic young subordinates in *4.50 From Paddington* and *Sleeping Murder*,[22] and a collective of police detectives, still headed by Dalgliesh and Wexford, disperses some of the solitary detecting charisma for James and Rendell. The most unassisted investigator is Cordelia Gray, but she still has to share with Dalgliesh the final intuiting of the crime in *An Unsuitable Job for a Woman*. The detecting function is more collective (while still retaining a single detective talent) and dispersed, allowing for what I will call a psychic construction of detection generated by these six authors.

What I have described as a limited dispersal of the detecting function is nevertheless still centred on the detective, and is held by a dynamic of energies which both challenge the limits of and reconstitute the detective's self. Psychic construction, in this sense, is the argument that the self of the detective exists in an interconnecting web of emotional energy within the novel. Much of the time the energy is overtly sexual, particularly for Peter Wimsey, Roderick Alleyn, Adam Dalgliesh and Albert Campion (a bit). These male figures are construed as eroticised beings from a feminine point of view whether by the narrative inclusion of lovers, or in relation to suspects, but always persistently to the reader by constantly reminding us how attractive to women these male detectives are. In other cases, the psychic construction – the self-making of the detectives through detecting – are relational or familial. The action of the narrative structures the detective's 'self' in an evolving identity connected to both colleagues and suspects. The detecting of the 'true' story, is itself an activity of self-making for these writers.

The Wexford tales suspend the protagonist between his relational familial identity to wife, Dora, and daughters, Sylvia and Sheila, and usually dysfunctional families focused through the murder investigation whose obsessive passions draw the narrative into the Gothic. Wexford's self is constituted within a familial construction, haunted by his intuitions of extreme and darker passions as an underside to the nuclear family. Where Rendell's work centres on obsession, often connected to the family, James's novels trace an absence of a governing metaphysical authority in contemporary culture. Yet even Dalgliesh, the most socially isolated of all the six writers' detectives, explores and expands the limits of his psyche within his investigations; for example, in detecting a mirroring self in the murdered politician in *A Taste for Death*.[23]

The employment of the detecting narrative to question and construct the detecting self is not only a vital part of the investigations. As well as being closely allied to the crucial role of the detective's so-called weaknesses or extra-legal qualities, it is also an exposition of gender strategies within the self. It is usually the intuitive, feminised aspect of the masculine detective that is most visible in the psychic construction of detecting, although that does not inhibit heterosexuality. Roderick Alleyn and Peter Wimsey are most empathetic, exposed and feminised when sexually entranced by future wives or potential suspects. A typical example is Alleyn flirting with suspect-actress Carolyn Dacres in *Vintage Murder*.[24] Campion's most sexually energised moments are when he loses his memory in *Traitor's Purse*, desperately requiring the devotion of Amanda to restore not only identity but some stable structures of masculinity.[25] Neither he nor the reader can tell whether he is a murderer or a saviour until a satisfactory erotic relation with Amanda (in all senses) can be achieved.

Above all, the psychic construction of the detective through detection includes the reader. The detectives' evolving selves draw the reading consciousness into the imaginary world of the novel: that is, we make sense of the story partly through making sense of, learning to trust, the detective as a reassuring stable identity. Even Poirot and Jane Marple, who seem the most self-contained, participate in a growing bond with the reader in which we overcome any sense of the ludicrous (in the case of Poirot) or marginality (in the case of Miss Marple) and develop an affectionate trust which is construed by the psychic construction of detection as *a form of knowledge in itself*. 'Psychic construction' as described here is thus another (an-other) form of knowing, a relational form in which self boundaries are permeable to others and knowledge ensues as subjectively understood. It operates with, and is not excluded by, the masculine stress on objectivity, clues and material evidence.

I must emphasise that I am not suggesting that a detecting knowledge gained through the renegotiation of the detective's self boundaries (or that of the reader) is an essentially 'feminine' form of epistemology. Rather, gender is structured into this mode of detecting by the socially contingent association of masculinity with reason, law, scientific and material evidence both at an institutional level and in terms of Western humanist philosophies. All these women writers in various ways include what might be called, in this context, a feminine structuring of knowledge, as a valuable and necessary mode of detection alongside the traditionally masculine gendered methods of the law.

The detective's relation to modern society is another factor where gender can be perceived to affect genre. Scott McCracken's work links, in particular, the masculine hard-boiled private eye to the alienated consciousness within the cityscapes of modernity.[26] I would want to put the six authors' detectives with their psychically reconstituting selves into the decentring mode of literary modernism. In female-authored modernist novels, it is possible to discern a positive inflection of modernist fragmentation as offering opportunities for the feminist writer.[27] Now free of a unified masculine model of identity, she can explore more relational and provisional modes of being, bringing the feminine out of the dark other of realist representation. I am suggesting a supplement to Alison Light's impressive study of Agatha Christie as a popular modernist (in which she does not consider issues of self-making), to situate all six writers in a tradition of feminine modernism. Psychic construction through detection, in this argument, is a feminine modernist strategy.

Gendering the genre

Having lifted the detective out of the limitations of the unified objective self of literary realism, it is time to do the same for the detective novel form. Julian Symons's comprehensive work on crime fiction, *Bloody Murder*, traces a narrative of progression from the formulaic crime story to the realist crime novel.[28] I want to radically modify this trajectory for British crime fiction by women. As Light argues, golden age crime fiction should be viewed in relation to contemporary modernist experimentation. I would additionally want to stress its highly rhetorical and artificial nature. The dominant tone is one of generic 'play'. It is this 'playfulness' with the inherited form, of course, that allows female golden age writers to construct fictions with and against a masculine Holmesian genre. In the play of the feminine works, the cited male novel becomes re-created as a fantasy of masculinity as a stable whole identity, ignoring any ambivalence within the antecedent works. Sherlock Holmes becomes not a masculine model, but a playful mask within a consciously self-referential novel. The genre becomes wittily artificial in its references to itself *as artifice* in an intertextuality of crime fiction.

Agatha Christie's early work is peppered with references to, and outright parody of, male precursors. Her later generic confidence is evident in the way that novels become more self-referential of the golden age, for example the murder game based on golden age aesthetics in *A Murder Is Announced*.[29] This self-referential irony indicates a novel perceiving itself at a double remove from the authorising texts of the law: once because crime fiction and twice because defining itself against (even as it so constructs) a masculine heroic tradition.

By the era of P.D. James and Ruth Rendell, female writers are in the ascendant, so these authors define themselves both with and against the artifice of the golden age. They make a conscious bid for realism (with its attendant status as literary writers), but also conspire to operate within golden age generic strategies of the domestic murder, the restricted group of knowable suspects and so on. Tensions between realism (with the obvious point that most murder is *not* like the genre) and golden age aesthetics is a fascinating dynamic within these novels. For instance, Wexford's investigation in *Road Rage* reads at first like crime realism in that it centres on the 1990s British phenomenon of eco-warriors in alliance with middle-class environmental campaigners. Yet the kidnapping of Dora and Wexford's intuitive tracing of a more intimate manipulation of the crimes around a restricted group of suspects means that answers are to be found by detecting golden age structures disguised within social realism.

Whereas the self-conscious artifice of Christie and Sayers is predominantly expressed as self-referentiality, for Allingham it lies in generic experimentations resulting in textual play with golden age expectations. The eccentric plausibility of the murder-haunted Victorian family of *Police at the Funeral*[30] offers a puzzle murder in Christie mode, while *Look to the Lady*[31] is a Gothic romance 'solved' but not contained by Campion's assumption of a detecting mask. By contrast, Ngaio Marsh's attraction to the genre from the position of an outsider, a colonial writer, is so intense as to produce what I call 'camp country house' in her domestic settings. These provide outrageously stagy set-ups, such as a host with domestic servants who are all convicted murderers,[32] or one who deliberately invites mortal enemies for the fun of it.[33] Her other favourite setting is the theatre, wherein a spectrum of 'acting' is introduced, from that involved in perpetrating the murder to the habitual and stereotypical masks of her thespian suspects. Unsurprisingly, theatricality is a mode which extends across all four early writers as one inflection of their embrace of self-conscious fiction. It even resurfaces in James and Rendell, as suspects or setting hover between the depiction of the 'realistic' and the generic. For instance, detective Kate Miskin in *Original Sin* is struck by her initial impressions of a crime scene as a film set.[34] Such a moment would be recognised by Alleyn or Poirot.

It is this theatricality and self-conscious artifice that constitutes one of the narrative functions of the golden age genre, which is to parody death. Crime fiction's otherness to the law becomes explicitly therapeutic when it is secondarily otherness to nineteenth-century realism. Golden age fiction is a deliberately unbelievable artifice which 'solves' death by absorbing it into a story which fully 'accounts for' it. Death is disposed of as unnatural, solvable, as a mendable tear in the social fabric. In this sense, golden age fiction is about the restitution of comedy in the face of tragedy. Only with a dwelling upon the execution of the murderer in such novels as *Busman's Honeymoon*,[35] or in the textual conjuring of death as totally un-accountable in P.D. James's repeated returns to the holocaust, does a leaking away of the reassuring parody of death occur.

Given this argument of parodying death, detective fiction can be said to have a religious function. It operates as a ritual to banish mortality: its artificiality in one sense is distanced from the ritual structure, and in another sense makes it possible (see Chapter 6). A tone of 'play' moves the novel away from ritual seriousness, but by parodying and solving death, by turning it into a self-consciously fictional narrative, it fulfils a ritual function.

James and Rendell, of course, being merely in dialogue with golden age artifice, have a different relationship to metaphysics. Indeed, I would argue that James's use of holocaust echoes is precisely a violent assault on those golden age conventions that threaten to overwhelm her claims to literary realism in *Shroud for a Nightingale* and *Original Sin*.[36] Without artifice as a dominant (which then serves as an other to the law as something stable), the law in James and Rendell is revealed as fallible. It follows that Dalgliesh and Wexford must 'act' confidently while being acutely aware of the psychic and cultural deficiencies of the police. The social authority of the police for these writers depends upon a masquerade of corporate masculinity; a masculinity pretending to be undivided and unproblematically upholding the law. Wexford manages to sustain an erotic community in family and work in which his masculinity and authority is continually renegotiated. Dalgliesh, on the other hand, becomes the sign of the absence of a trustworthy secure authority: he becomes the sign of the absence of a transcending stabilising force in society. In James's terms, he becomes the sign of the cultural absence of God. P.D. James's innate conservatism lies in her nostalgia for this god-function. A final consideration of gender and genre brings us to what I would characterise as the narrative 'destination' of these novels. The artifice and 'play' of the golden age writers, Christie, Allingham and Marsh, ally detective fiction with the comedy of manners. Murder becomes, paradoxically, a form of social restitution as the social group is purged and reconstituted at the end. This is often substantiated in the figure of the romantic couple whose courtship occurs via the detection. On the one hand, these lovers are a focus for erotic energy as both displacement and illumination of the detective's psyche, and on the other hand they are the crucial emblem of social healing on reformed lines. Sayers injects a tragic sense into the mix by showing that war trauma (as a metonym for war itself) is not finally solvable by the detective genre. Here, P.D. James is a direct descendant in her use of Second World War atrocities. Yet, whereas Sayers remains in tragi-comedy, James looks to the fully tragic with her depiction of an alienated consciousness in a godless culture. Rendell largely opts for a family Gothic in which Wexford's incipient Lear-complex is both evoked and thankfully banished. By en-gendering the genre, these six chroniclers of crime provide a surprising richness of consummations.

The Murder of Roger Ackroyd by Agatha Christie (1926)

Narrated by a suspect, Dr Sheppard, *The Murder of Roger Ackroyd* is Christie's most celebrated and radical treatment of the detective narrative form. The novel consciously problematises the detective as a masculine hero, which starts with the opening rivalry between Sheppard and his gossipy spinster sister, Caroline, over medical diagnosis. The parallel doctor-detective recurs later in Christie, notably in *Appointment with Death*, but not with the peculiar ironies of this doctor as narrator.[37] Early opposition between professional masculine science and feminine gossipy intuition is broken down by the arrival of 'feminised' Poirot. He defends Caroline's form of social detection by rationalising her uncanny traces of 'intuition' into acute skills of social perception. Some occult traces remain, however, and accrue to Poirot as he describes an interrogation of suspects as a séance (p. 219).

Unsurprisingly, the breakdown of gender polarity is replayed as Poirot's feminised psychic constitution through detection. At first despised by all male onlookers, Poirot continually wins hands down against the clumsy detective logic of the police. His term for his detecting strategy is 'psychology', by which he means an empathy with the passions of both victim and suspects in the close-knit village of Kings Abbot (the village name suggests that two forms of dominant institutional masculinity can no longer keep order).

Class viewed as theatricality drives the plot dynamics. Ackroyd's wealth is newly generated. His assumption of the position as squire gives him dangerous access to secrets and familial power over such as his wayward stepson, Ralph. Class as theatricality enables further deceits as the maid, Ursula, is discovered to be acting a part and concealing a far more intimate relation to the family. 'Theatricality' becomes a crucial object of Poirot's detection as he must trace the desire energising the social masks, even unto death and blackmail.

Self-referentiality becomes another way of structuring the interrogating of social masks as Poirot distributes the role of 'Watson' and even his own 'Hastings' to subordinate characters. Yet the role of Watson in particular is employed as a form of ironic commentary on the Holmesian tradition, as it proves one respectable mask among several for the guilty party. *The Murder of Roger Ackroyd* is a comedy in which the self-conscious artifice derives both from cultural stereotypes and from crime fiction. The heroic model of Holmes and Watson is comically parodied by the interchangeability of Watson and the blackmailing murderer. A detective/murderer ambiguity is thus displaced from Poirot, but still operates to radically challenge again the morally undivided model of masculine heroism.

Near the investigation's end the narrator announces that he had planned this account to be a record of Poirot's failure, but it was not to be. Therefore the reader is peculiarly enjoined to scrutinise the act of representation, to look for gaps, to distrust comic non-heroic signs, not to dismiss 'feminine methods' and to perceive 'writing' as potentially something problematic and open to multiple interpretations. Such a 'learning to read differently' must be seen as a gendering strategy in the novel because it is explicitly said to work against the assumptions of a heroic male model.

In learning not to dismiss the gossipy buffoonery of Poirot, the feminine intelligence network of the spinsters with their intuitive grasp of social interaction, the 'trivial' domestic clues in the Ackroyd house, and learning to *distrust* the confident narrative of professional males, the reader is alerted to feminine modes of knowledge traditionally marginalised by the law. *The Murder of Roger Ackroyd* both detects the excluded feminine and indicts the intertwined machinations of masculinity, money and power in its diagnosis of crime.

Strong Poison by Dorothy L. Sayers (1930)[38]

Strong Poison's plot centres around social constructions of gender and male–female relations. The question of both the crime and detecting narrative is whether gender politics can move on from the repressions of the Victorian marriage. Society finds crime writer Harriet Vane more emphatically guilty of poisoning her estranged lover, Philip Boyes, because of her sexual deviance: she consented to live with him outside marriage yet ended the relationship when he finally decided she was acquiescent enough to wed. Only Peter Wimsey, his mother and his spinster colleague, Miss Climpson, are able to detect Harriet's moral integrity. The legal system sees only criminality. Harriet is on trial for her life as the novel opens. However, the novel also records Wimsey's failure to reconstruct gender relations in the detecting narrative. Despite his parodic occupancy of the role the story assigns him of saviour-hero, he is found to be insufficiently distanced from 'knight errant' forms of masculinity for Harriet to accept him as a potential partner.

Intriguingly, the detecting plot of Wimsey's quest to convict the only other credible suspect is more conservative on gender than the crime plot, which is viciously contemptuous of Boyes's (note the name) pretensions to superiority, substantiated (he thinks) in his 'masculine' modernist writing. It is this disjunction of feminist energies which is unable fully to refashion Wimsey so that male–female relations can be re-formed. The detecting narrative traverses different social spheres of gender such as the masculine professions and a feminine world of spinsters and companions. It demonstrates no wish to undo such social structures, but it does aim to demystify. Where the crime dynamics contrast a misogynistic homoerotics of high modernism with a feminine popular fiction, it seems to require the charismatic endorsement of erotic hero, Wimsey, to support a feminine literally imprisoned under a threat of death from the law. The feminine cultures of office secretaries and domestic servants provide crucial evidence for a detective working against the male logic of the police, with only his stubborn desire for Harriet as 'evidence' at the start. In this Wimsey is a detective in the feminine and *for* the feminine, but his final success in terms of the law is not yet success in terms of romantic relations.

Nevertheless, detection in the feminine contains a number of criticisms of gender stereotyping. Significantly, in the detection, female cultures have to be penetrated by female subordinates, Miss Murgatroyd and Miss Climpson, who reveal intelligence and resourcefulness.

Despite operating under Wimsey's idiosyncratic guidance, both agents have to initiate their own plans of attack. There is also a sense of Sayers playing with role reversal in that much of the detecting *action* is taken by the spinsters, with Wimsey in a frustrated and passive feminine position. The feminine is explicitly demystified by Miss Climpson's firm exploitation (with the aim of eventual disabusing) of a female domestic's fascination with table-turning. Spiritualism as an occult practice is deliberately contextualised here as a sphere of the middle-class feminine. Miss Climpson is an unrecognisable detective to the suspect within the masculine culture of the law. Her activities demystify the feminine as occult to reveal the feminine as suppressed writer. Through mock séances she uncovers a concealed female will. Just as the feminine is here restored to legal recognition, the court action of the novel aims to recuperate the female writer as one whose 'will' to difference should be respected.

However, a final particular challenge to the detective as unambiguous masculine hero in *Strong Poison* is to be found in the denouement. Since much of the detecting has been done 'in the feminine' – not so much done by women as by extra-legal methods, a position is reached where the murderer is known, but legally acceptable proof is inadequate. Here the determined detective has to resort to tricks, including a claim to have fed arsenic to the suspect. Strong-arm tactics are not considered. Through his trickery, Wimsey situates himself as a potential murderer.

Strong Poison does not defy its gendered cultures of domesticity and male clubs, but it does construct gender hierarchy as both specious and perilous to the feminine. It problematises the gendering of the detective and seeks to recover feminine forms of representation. Only by gender strategies of psychic reconstruction, anti-heroism and even proximity to murder can something of feminine integrity be recuperated. This novel seeks a new romantic form in which detecting otherness is no longer a strong poison.

Death of a Ghost by Margery Allingham (1935)[39]

The ghost of the title is John Lafcadio, renowned painter, whose peculiar will and imperious personality dominate his female household for years after his demise. His elderly wife, Belle, lives with Donna Beatrice, a Theosophist, who claims to have been Lafcadio's chief inspiration. They are served by Lisa, once the artist's Italian model, and there are also a couple of artistic hangers-on. Trouble breaks out when Lafcadio's artist granddaughter, Linda, returns from Italy with her artist-lover, Tom, who has married an ignorant model called Rosa-Rosa. Max Fustian, art dealer, who has made a lucrative career out of John Lafcadio, completes the list of potential killers when Tom is murdered during a viewing. Friend of the family Albert Campion is also present, so this is one of the adventures in which he is 'personally' involved.

Never impelled by a simple desire to uphold the law, Campion's psychic construction through detection here is signified by his blend of deduction and intuition. The feminine occupies the sphere of the occult, with Donna Beatrice's form of sleuthing consisting of detecting blue auras, but this potential gender polarisation is gently ironised into comedy, not least by the intelligent but dismissive amusement of the sympathetic Belle. Femininity as extremity of desire, expressing itself as criminality, is a greater possibility, as Linda's uncontrolled passions make her an early suspect.

A sense of the uncanniness of gender propels the detecting story in both social and ghostly manifestations. Once the gender polarisation of feminine as occult 'other' to the masculine artist is overcome by comic deflation, feminine sexuality then becomes problematic. Finally, the answer is shown to lie *not* in the devious feminine but in an unstable 'doubleness' within the masculine. Answers are found in both Lafcadio's betrayal of his authorising function (the will is dodgy) and most dramatically in a male suspect's fragmentation. The murderer is at first a casting of gender ambivalence as theatricality, but eventually his ambivalence fragments into psychic breakdown. This is caused by his overwhelming desire for power over all otherness, as the feminine (both within and without) as the ghostly legacy of John Lafcadio.

The ghost himself does not remain unchallenged, either in gender or in his potency for dominance over his surviving household. Lafcadio as dead patriarch appears to dominate all: he is a kind of gendered god-figure in whose shadow and by whose will (literally, as his will governs their lives) this familial group is constituted. Yet much of his god-power, his art in his hidden paintings, is revealed as a scam. Similarly challenging is the way Lisa comes to be described as ghostly, a female embodied icon of past art and desire to counter the masculine disembodied 'will' – revealed as increasingly ambiguous and unauthorised writing.

Crucially, the ghost as dead patriarch can no longer protect. It is the ambiguous and unofficial detective, Campion, who must save Belle from the threat of murder in a narrative that will dethrone Lafcadio's ghost as masculine authority. Such a move will then enable Belle to reconfigure him as her beloved husband. Significantly, the true painting by the dead master is a self-portrait revealing him as 'half-genius, also half-buffoon' produced only for Belle, not for the adoring, money-driven art world (p. 253).

Therefore Campion's psychic investment in detection is motivated by a protective empathetic involvement, particularly with Belle and Linda. He explicitly refuses a heroic detecting model that would position him as trying to replace Lafcadio as patriarch. Campion's ambivalence evades the occult as displayed by Donna Beatrice, but it is detectable in his growing self-division. Not only does he feel his 'unconscious' trying to communicate vital facts to him, but he starts to form a mirroring or doubling relationship to the murderer. On the one hand, Campion decides that becoming a murderer himself by killing the criminal might be the only way to protect Belle, while on the other hand the murderer becomes his double by drugging him and leading him into peril through unconscious suggestion.

Although Campion succeeds in identifying the killer, he has to lapse into the protection of the law (as in the police), not to become just another victim. Rescued by the police, Campion fails to provide effective proof of the guilty party's wrongdoing. In failing to *account for* criminal otherness to the police who have similarly failed, both unofficial and official detectives are reliant upon the perpetrator's collapse into madness, a psychic fragmentation with no hope of a recovery. This is in itself an ambivalent form of otherness to the law in that it here allows incarceration, but not conviction. *Death of a Ghost* disempowers the mystification of masculine authority as artistic 'master', the lawyer's will, and the police, as upholders of secure social boundaries of law and crime. In this novel the detective is little removed from a victim and is far from a conquering hero.

Artists in Crime by Ngaio Marsh (1938)[40]

In this work the detecting plot is given a typical Marsh twist toward further self-referential artifice. It is a county house murder in which a nubile artist's model is killed while posing *as* a murder victim in an unnatural posture copied from a stylised painting. The elaborate crime premises restricts the suspects to artist Agatha Troy and her assorted artist friends and pupils. The tangled sexual passions and monetary misdemeanours of the group are unravelled by Alleyn as integral to the solution. Yet Alleyn's confident poise is crucially disrupted by his love for Troy, who remains a logical suspect until the end. Alleyn's vehement refusal to consider Troy as potentially guilty is the clearest evidence that the intense passion of his involvement in this case is imperilling his other detecting drive: the professionalisation of masculine authority into corporate police 'duty'.

The narrative is framed by two moments of Alleyn and Troy meeting. The opening, set on a passenger ship, suspends Alleyn between two models of femininity. A predatory flirtatious woman fails to draw him into her sexual theatre while signaling his attractions to the reader and, potentially, Troy. She, in turn, is a woman absorbed in her painting, and takes no notice of Alleyn until he can enter *her* world by providing a helpful suggestion. It is highly appropriate that Marsh's staging of the first meeting of these erotic partners should both distinguish Troy from sexual theatre and itself be focused upon the representation of foreign landscapes in art. Femininity and foreignness are juxtaposed, just as art and detection are aligned initially against each other in the detecting story. The initial exchanges between Alleyn and Troy both suggest a gendered opposition between police detective and artist and suggest its mitigation as Alleyn's specialist training aids Troy's artistic vision. It is typical of Marsh the (post-)colonial writer that difference (of gender or culture) is not simply eroded but can be negotiated.

The murder investigation is severely strained between masculine police procedure as erotically invasive – in his position as detective, Alleyn goes through Troy's clothes and reads her intimate letters which include her thoughts on *him* – and Alleyn's growing self-divisions which mean that he is less able to remain loftily detached from the passions of the artist group. At one point, Alleyn is drawn to the murderer's role by his identification with Troy's homicidal feeling at the victim's destruction of her best ever work. Again, art has the potential to negotiate difference, but not appropriate it. Troy and Alleyn meet at the conclusion as mutually involved, but Troy is unable to overcome her repugnance for the detective function which will send the killer for execution. Their final embrace is an acknowledgement of their difference, not its overcoming, despite the narrative's signalling of difference *within* Alleyn in the processes of investigation.

Alleyn has another erotic focus in this work in a harmonious semi-Oedipal relation to his craftswoman mother. Indeed, their courtship-like relationship acts like an analytic partnership in which the two can change places in the interests of intuitive insight. Alleyn can structure his 'feminine' otherness into a maternal relation to the case and can 'go broody' until he conceives the solution.

The psychic construction of detection here enables the detective to combine the objective weighing of material evidence (Alleyn and companion Fox search diligently for clues), with the subjective framing of knowledge via desire and intuition. The crime plot traces the ways in which desire has penetrated class barriers in the working-class model's affairs with two male artists and a female artist's desperation to conceal a socially shameful liaison in the interests of marrying above her station. Here, Marsh's respect for difference slides into social conservatism: the violation of class barriers leads directly to blackmail and murder, with the unfortunate victim referred to by all (including Alleyn) as an 'animal'. Alleyn's class status, of course, is always coded as superior to his professional position and as contributing to his sexual magnetism. Nevertheless, his destabilising otherness, so erotically charged in this investigation, must be recuperated into his detective role at the end of the work. Therefore, the final scene, where Troy displays revulsion and repugnance to capital punishment, serves to reconfigure difference as *between* genders, allowing Alleyn to retreat into his profession. Yet taken as a whole, the detecting story, in a circular movement between the two meetings, has proved that difference can be renegotiated through art and desire. It is not the end for these momentarily estranged lovers.

The acute self-consciousness of *Artists in Crime* as fiction in the imitation of art in the murder, the theatrical egos of the artists, and the references to crime novels provides a prime example of Marsh's 'camp country house' in the golden age genre.

Shroud for a Nightingale by P.D. James (1971)

P.D. James's novel, set in a home for nurses, combines a typical golden age scenario of murders within a restricted group of suspects in a neo-Gothic house, with a characteristically 'Jamesian' nostalgia for social and moral authority. The desired authority is perceived as ultimately absent in a culture that has rejected God. Those potential reassurances of golden age aesthetics and artificiality are finally dismissed by a link to Nazi crimes. Since these crimes involve hospitals 'curing' by killing mentally ill patients, this functions both as a monstrous other to the idealising of femininity in the training of devoted nurses (all female here) and as death which can neither be represented or re-solved in crime fiction.

Much of the power of the novel – as in all of James's work – lies in the tensions between the comforts of detective fiction as 'art' and its inability to restore a nostalgic social fabric, which demands a divine authority. In this Jamesian world of art and its limits, Dalgliesh acts as a sign of the absence of God. He is the representative of cultural authority plagued by his awareness of the inability of the police to substitute for God in healing pain and providing justice. Dalgliesh's metaphysical anguish offers one form of his otherness to the corporate masculinity of the law; engaging in self-construction through detection provides another. Socially more isolated than the other detectives, Dalgliesh's obsessive privacy is a necessary characterisation in his masquerade of authority. Yet this does not prevent a complex psychic self-reconstituting operating in his investigations.

In *Shroud for a Nightingale*, Dalgliesh is at first fascinated by the second victim, Nurse Fallon, perceiving a mysterious impenetrable femininity combined with his own reticence of self. Dalgliesh continues detecting a feminine erotic other in finding another psychic mirror in Matron, Mary Taylor, suspect and icon of maternal authority. Deeply attracted to Mary Taylor, Dalgliesh is forced to recognise his own hiding behind the rules and oaths of his profession, as a guarantee of integrity, in Mary Taylor's past career as a nurse within the Nazi system, similarly regulated by rules and oaths, which do not prevent killings. The issue motivating both crime and investigation is what makes a good nurse, and behind this, whether the feminine is naturally nurturing. Obedience to the rules is not enough to underpin moral integrity, as the Nazi experience demonstrates. Similarly, nurses who kill, both in Nightingale house and for the Nazis, can claim to be doing so for the 'good' of others or to 'cure' the patients.

The first Nightingale crime is committed with that ultimate fluid of feminine nurture: milk. *Shroud for a Nightingale* teaches that language is dangerously unstable: in certain circumstances killing can be redefined as 'curing' or as 'treating', and in such a world gender too is unstable and cannot be relied upon. In the developing mirroring between the feminine nurses and masculine police, Dalgliesh is shown that institutional authority cannot incarnate morality in any stable sense. The dialogue with otherness is inescapable, and there is no reliable fixed source of goodness without an acknowledgement of God to stabilise culture.

Another distinctive way in which gender affects the police investigation here is the use of the Gothic to destabilise realist assumptions. Nightingale House is a Gothic mansion surrounded by haunted woods where Dalgliesh finds a woman 'howling'. This setting represents spatially an uncanny other to the institutions of nursing and police which are meant to guarantee values of caring and justice. Significantly, the house is pulled down at the end.

Shroud for a Nightingale genders the genre through a continued refiguring of detection which places the novel both within and without golden age aesthetics. What golden age fiction could suggest in its self-conscious artifice is not possible for a writer seeking a place in the realist tradition. Therefore James's work becomes suspended in tensions between the possible consolations of genre and the acute melancholy nostalgia for order and authority which is impossible for this realist writer to depict in what she perceives as a wilfully godless society. That desired authority is gendered masculine, because it can then nostalgically evoke an imaginary past culture ruled by the Christian god. Masculinity is further coded as authority by Dalgliesh and the corporate masculinity of the police. The police as an institution can uneasily co-opt female officers as long as its values do not have to change. Nostalgic for an absolute authority without otherness, *Shroud for a Nightingale* is also nostalgic for a comforting fixity and polarity of gender values (nurse: feminine, mother, caring/police: masculine, law, justice) that it knows to be impossible.

Kissing the Gunner's Daughter by Ruth Rendell (1991)[41]

Ruth Rendell stages the tension between golden age domestic artifice and contemporary realism in a crucial ambiguity about the crimes. Both the bank hold-up in which a policeman dies and the murder of a whole family (bar the youngest, Daisy) at Tancred House bear the hallmarks of typical crimes committed by career criminals. It is Chief Inspector Wexford's emotional involvement with suspects (in a familial not a sexual sense), in addition to police sifting of material evidence, that pushes the novel close to the intimate domesticity of golden age deviance. Far from semi-random targeting, the murders at Tancred House are deeply bound up with issues of property, inheritance, sexuality and family dynamics binding together inmates and servants on the family estate.

Rendell's Wexford novels tend to move in the opposite direction to James's, in taking a modern-sounding crime such as an accidental murder during a robbery, via an often Gothic configuration of obsessive family relations, to arrive at a realisation of golden age domestic crime. Here, the narrative drive towards the golden age is counterpointed by Wexford's passionate dislike of the new lover of his favourite daughter, Sheila. Gus is an intellectual novelist who personifies 'high art' as arrogant and snobbish. He therefore provides an argument against the hierarchy of 'high' versus' low' literary forms, an argument more deeply embodied in this novel's traversing of literary realism to 'low' consolations of past detective genres. Gus, by threatening to remove Wexford's best beloved, demonstrates the spurious nature of literary snobbery inside a novel seeking to place the arts of realism within the artifice of golden age detection.

This can only be done by suspending Wexford in a complex psychic negotiation in which the victim, Daisy, temporarily takes on the familial guise of the lost daughter, Sheila. The detecting plot additionally has to mesh rhetorically the fictional genres of fairy tale, Gothic and theatricality with the crime plot. Such evocation of genres in a novel of psychological realism combined with golden age-inflected plotting works by making fairy tale, Gothic and theatricality keys to the crime itself. The trauma of the bloody crime scene and the waif-like pathos of the chief living victim are so powerfully affecting precisely because they have been rhetorically *staged* for the police and onlookers. Fairy tale, Gothic and theatricality are the imaginative modes by which the killers both stage the crimes and hope to evade detective penetration. It is precisely Wexford's vulnerability to imaginative genres versus 'dirty realism' that at first makes him the murderers' stooge and then enables him intuitively to reconstruct their modus operandi.

The 'artful' genres thus operate in a threefold manner: they feminise the crime in that what appears to be professional robbery gone wrong is (even in the bank heist) more to do with sexuality and domesticity; they serve as a form of mystification for the criminals; and they are a means of feminising Wexford. These non-realist genres structure Wexford's psychic construction through detection so that paradoxically, he dismisses the obvious (and accurate) deduction of an unimaginative subordinate, yet discovers more of the 'truth' in his solution than his colleagues, who remain devoted to masculine professional practices.

Wexford's blending of knowledge from police procedure and his subjective intuition results in a far more satisfactory outcome for the reader, but is explicitly in excess of the law's needs for conviction. The poetic uses of fairy tale, Gothic and theatricality point to this excess in suggesting the presence of unrepresentable desires. Wexford's psychic sensitivity increases his confusion when he misreads signs of trauma in the Gothic hauntings and psychic repetitions of the murder scene. He misreads signs because the trauma he witnesses in others is also his own, in his psychic self-making. Rather than being confused with the role of the murderer (as Dalgliesh is in *Shroud* by his mirroring of her), Wexford's almost uncanny empathy takes him close to the role of the victim as Gus's threatened snatching of Sheila leads him to identify his daughter more and more with Daisy. Only when he can renegotiate restoratively his relations to his daughter, his 'own' feminine, can he 'see' Daisy more objectively, but still informed by his previous near-obsession.

Kissing the Gunner's Daughter genders the genre by adding to masculine police procedure a feminising psychic construction through detection. Like *Shroud for a Nightingale*, it evokes golden age aesthetics as a literary form in which the feminine is not outside a masculine heroics of professional detecting, but inside, in the dynamics of money, sexuality and familial groups. As in *all* the previous novels, feminine stereotypes become problematised by the plot. Can the nurse, daughter figure, female artist, beloved female writer, harmless spinster, kill? All the novels discover through crime that gender is a spectrum containing its own contradictions and otherness rather than any fixed set of qualities. Golden age fictions gender themselves against what they structure as male heroism. The two post-golden age writers gender their work with and against the golden age as feminine. They combine generic self-referentiality with literary realism in further interventions of gender in the genre.

3
Social Negotiations: Class, Crime and Power

Popular preconceptions of these six novelists and, indeed, the whole detecting genre tends to associate their works with conservative politics and against the democratising forces of modern society. Crime fiction implies naming and capturing a criminal. This, in turn, suggests the restoration of both a moral and social order. Such a restitution can easily condense into a social conservatism which manifests itself as a nostalgic re-forming of social classes. The elements of such a structure are perceptible in five of the six authors, Christie, Sayers, Allingham, Marsh and James, but it is heavily compromised in the golden age quartet by their distinguishing self-referentiality. By portraying detecting as a self-consciously fictional 'game', golden age writers both democratise the form in promoting reader participation and, crucially, permit a *self-critical* depiction of social class embedded in the genre.

Such formal embellishments as the problematised distinction between detective and murderer challenge the social dimensions of this literary form with its peculiarly intimate connections between content and structure. If the *matter* of the detecting genre is the uncovering of crime plot and criminal through some socially acceptable questing figure, then so is its *formal* constitution. This alliance between content and form both suggests an intrinsic conservative social bias *and* provides the possibility of its criticism from *within* the genre.

On the other hand, the works of Ruth Rendell/Barbara Vine point towards later developments in the detecting/crime genre in a more liberal recasting of form. If the traditional closure of golden age writing suggested that the crime could be viewed as an aberrant outburst of antisocial desire, then crime in the Rendell/liberal canon proves to be connected to outmoded social conceptions, particularly those of class. Conservatism is thereby indicted as oppressive because it provokes criminal desire. Apprehending the criminal does not restore moral and social order; first because the criminal is in part a victim, but particularly because the conservative societal codes implicated in the crime are still operating. Instead the energy of the detecting narrative is directed towards a *utopian social order*, one not achieved or even coherently imagined, but characterised by social progressiveness and liberal tolerance. In effect, the social order that Rendell's works wish to imply is in the form of a hope for future reform.

The ironic result of the above argument is the implication that P.D. James is the most purely socially conservative writer of the six. Since her novels aspire more to literary realism than the overt self-fictionality of the golden age writers, her treatment of form would appear to confirm its conservative bias. True, she does largely substitute professional hierarchies for traditional social classes, but what really mitigates her undoubted conservative politics is her pessimistic and nostalgic metaphysics.[1] Her religious nostalgia uses the crime genre to lament the moral decline of a society which has rejected religion as a social mechanism. A novel such as *Devices and Desires* makes it plain that the social and moral cohesion that James desires through Christianity may be located in the past, but it is chiefly mythical.[2] James's detecting moralists know that past Christianity may have provided a social framework, but it was not without cruelty, incoherence and injustice itself. Religion represents a *dream* of order to James's crime fictions. It is time to look at politically conservative intentions in more detail as well as more liberal rewritings. What happens to social class in the imaginations of these six authors?

Social class: six novelists in a conservative genre

Conservative intentions and the detecting narrative

The five conservative queens of crime are not nostalgic for the social mores of the Victorian era. Indeed, the eventual argument of their fictions seems to be that social class needs to expand and mutate in order to survive in modernity as a stabilising social structure. Part of that expansion is a desire to relegitimise class by prescribing a moral dimension and a duty of consideration towards aspirants from below. Yet class itself, for these writers, should survive, or social chaos may ensue.

Ngaio Marsh exemplifies the fears of a classless society in a later work, *Hand in Glove*,[3] which portrays a backward-looking, class-bound village disrupted by a pair of delinquent lower-class petty criminals, one of whom has been misguidedly adopted by a lonely spinster.

However, it is significant that these obvious suspects are not the chief perpetrators of crime, and that much mockery is devoted to Mr Pike-Period, self-confessed snob and prospective author of a book on outmoded social etiquette. *Hand in Glove* portrays Pike-Period as ridiculous, but also as pathetic and essentially harmless; class needs to evolve, but not to be banished. This conclusion is embodied in the explicitly class-based admiration of that superb restorer of moral order, Inspector Alleyn.

As Alison Light has indicated,[4] Agatha Christie is emphatically anti-Victorian and anti-nostalgic, as is displayed in works such as *The Hollow*[5] and *The Mirror Crack'd from Side to Side*,[6] both of which include Tennysonian references to criticise desires for imaginary social pasts. *The Hollow* subtly condemns a whole generation of vapid gentry and colonial survivors, so unable to come to terms with contemporary Britain that murderous desires are generated. Most fatal is that desperation induced by class, gender and erotic submission in an unequal relationship. Most redeemable is the working woman who is able to nurture and save the scion of the declining country house.

Even Dorothy L. Sayers's entrancement with her detective, Lord Peter Wimsey (in part because of the glamour of his class), does mitigate social rigidity in the detecting story as early as *Whose Body?*[7] The novel starts almost offensively to the modern reader, in the class patronage of middle-rank Mr Thipps, who has the misfortune to discover an anonymous naked male corpse in his bath. Naturally falsely arrested by the police, the comic duo of Thipps and his aged, deaf mother feel safe in the hands of a 'real gentleman' when Wimsey formally takes up the case. However, the role of aristocrat-detective as redeeming hero becomes acutely problematised as Thipps and Wimsey appear to change places in the detecting narrative. It is Wimsey who panics and whose self fragments, as his attempt to cure society of a single murder exposes what is incurable to himself and his culture, the First World War. Stresses of detecting induce in Wimsey a recurrence of mental breakdown in shell-shock. When Thipps's aged mother compares Wimsey to her son, and Bunter, the former sergeant, has to nurse Wimsey, the former major, then class has moved beyond snobbery to a limited moral flexibility. *Whose Body?* ends with Wimsey announcing a dinner party for former suspects and the Thippses, a comedy and festival conclusion that emphasises both the class fluidity and the final restoration of the traditional hierarchy.

Such social comedy in the golden age writers is directly contrasted by Ruth Rendell's citing of class as the social problem liable to provoke disorder rather than maintain social stability. For Rendell, traditional class structures do not regulate desire but instead collide with it, often leading to crimes where individual murderous impulses cannot be isolated from more general social oppressions. *A Judgement in Stone*,[8] for example, is Rendell's most sustained critique of a social role that golden age writers took for granted as unproblematic, the servant class. In *Road Rage*,[9] what appear to be crimes emanating from the margins of society in radical ecological protesters prove to be firmly traceable to middle-class arrogance and greed over property values. Rendell is highly suspicious of the social dimensions of country house murders.

Social class and the self-referential genre

The intentional conservatism of the golden age writers is complicated by their use of self-conscious fictionality to criticise (as well as ultimately uphold) traditional class structures as they threaten to become outmoded and morally empty in modernity. These writers portray social status as theatrical and ethically vacuous unless reinvested by the drive to justice embedded in the detective. Christie early depicted the British establishment as decaying from within in her thriller *The Secret Adversary*.[10] Despite idly distributing accusations of Bolshevism, the novel locates the source of crime firmly in the heart of the masculine establishment. It is the middle-class impoverished outsiders, Tommy and Tuppence, who redeem England; first by solving the crimes, but also metonymically by providing moral success for their own rhetoric of patriotism and honesty. This serves to reinvent the class system within the post-First World War world. Even Lord Peter Wimsey needs to reimagine his class superiority by solving crimes explicitly *not* by the upper-class rules of cricket and fair play, as Parker points out in *Whose Body?*[11] and by his wooing of Harriet into an anti-feudal, modern partnership.

Margery Allingham seems the most polarised of the four early writers between an attraction to a rural feudal-cum-pastoral ideal and an ambivalent sense of its potential cruelty if actualised. Her ambivalence takes the form of occult and Gothic traces of witchcraft. Most enchanted by the potential seductions of English social class is the colonial Ngaio Marsh. In *Surfeit of Lampreys*,[12] a work intimately related to her own experience of a charming aristocratic English family, she subjects her fascinations to moral scrutiny. *Surfeit of Lampreys* provides a dual perspective upon the engaging yet financially irresponsible Lamprey family. First, we meet the central character, Roberta, an orphaned New Zealander sealing her love for the whole family by falling erotically for the heir, Henry. Alleyn, the second perspective on the Lampreys, arrives after the murder of an inconvenient wealthy relation. The detective severely criticises the moral failings of a family able to charm their way through society largely through their inherited class position. Unsurprisingly, the Lampreys' chief talent proves to be for charades, a metonym for their operation in the modern world. Roberta recalls a key past charade of 'Eden' in New Zealand, where the Lampreys again failed to gain financial respectability. The game-playing both suggests that Roberta's psyche situates a paradisal past in Lamprey familial relations and indicates its essentially artificial nature. By extension, the colonial aesthetics of the New Zealand landscape providing a fantasy return to innocence, an Eden for the (morally) bankrupt West, is similarly portrayed as an artificial fantasy.

The self-referential genre is effective in depicting the erotic and desiring components of class while simultaneously revealing it as an artificial and theatrical constraint. Even P.D. James, who reimagines class as professional hierarchies, does criticise the blithe assumption that moral value and social status easily correlates. This is done not so much by a self-referential genre as by examining professional ethics through the detecting story, such as those of nursing in *Shroud for a Nightingale*.[13] It is time to consider how that emblem of social stability, the country house, fares in the crime genre.

What happens to the country house mystery when capitalism makes worlds collide?

Despite the reputation gained by Christie, Sayers, Allingham and Marsh for providing unproblematically conservative country house mysteries, these rural economies prove surprisingly non-coherent and fragile. Christie's country estates generate their murderous desires from within, right from the opening *The Mysterious Affair at Styles*,[14] while Marsh perfects her 'camp country house' in which theatricality becomes the indices of class, gender and sexuality. Unsurprisingly, her work opens in true camp style when a murder 'game', based self-reflexively on the golden age genre itself, proves the vehicle for killing in *A Man Lay Dead*.[15] Allingham, too, starts in a country house in *The Crime at Black Dudley*.[16] Here, her trademark of colliding worlds in modern society starts in a criminal capitalism clashing with feudal survivals. Far more developed are the buffeting worlds of the theatre, the police and rural traditions in *Dancers in Mourning*, which is also a subtle blend of rural and urban mysteries.[17] Sayers's early country house in *Clouds of Witness*,[18] like Christie's, combusts from within. Yet, for Lord Peter

Wimsey, the social negotiations entailed in his romance with notorious middle-class crime writer Harriet Vane enable the ironic re-formation of the country house rural economy in *Busman's Honeymoon*.[19] Since P.D. James's country house is reinvented as the place of the rituals of work which aim but fail to substitute for the rituals of religion, her 'country houses' quickly became Gothic in works such as *The Black Tower*,[20] as did the London 'country houses' in *A Taste for Death*[21] and *Original Sin*.[22] Here James and Rendell briefly converge in providing a reimagined 'country house' as the generic destination for crime realism in such fictions as Rendell's *The Speaker of Mandarin*,[23] *Put on by Cunning*[24] and *The Veiled One*.[25]

What the 'country house' stands for in all six writers is a structure that can be opposed to the social instabilities created by modern capitalism. Conservative in intention five of the writers may be, but it is a social conservatism linked to notions of order and fearful of the fragmenting and destabilising effects of modern consumer society. Allingham and Rendell appear to be the extreme poles of attitudes to consumer capitalism. For Allingham the country house is the location of a myth of social stability beset by Gothic shadows of occult feudality and/or Victorian oppressions (see *Police at the Funeral* later).[26] However Gothicised and made even more fragile by transportation to the hungry metropolis (see the beleaguered house in *The Tiger in the Smoke*),[27] the country house stands for implacable opposition to the corporate capitalism of modernity. Such an opposition provides an arena for violent crime, either from the capitalist gangs of earlier novels or, in later works, from the insanity-breeding vacuum of morality embodied in individual criminals and linked to capitalist values.

Ruth Rendell, on the other hand, takes the country house as a dream of order and reveals it as embedded in economic capitalism. The country house thereby forms a battleground structured through economic instability, in turn inducing anxieties which contribute to the coercive strategies of outdated social class systems. Rendell's country house is no refuge from the cruelties of the modern world. Agatha Christie, unsurprisingly, is closer to Allingham in opposing the instabilities of consumer capitalism to the traditional gentry's country house in *Death on the Nile*, as American heiress Linnet Doyle buys her English 'kingdom'.[28]

Marsh's Alleyn marks both the excess and limits of her fascination with the English upper classes. Portrayed as an attractive icon of upper-class masculinity, Alleyn persistently limits his class loyalty in favour of his profession: he will *use* his class identity in detection but will not *be used* by it.

The detective: class loyalties and the law

Criminal justice presupposes that an individual is responsible for the crimes he/she commits, and that the duty to uphold the law is a moral absolute beyond other loyalties. It therefore entails a sense of a stable self (not mad or fragmented or programmed by other forces), and equal applicability of the law's demands to all in society. Such an ideology of the law places pressures on a detective who may not be wholly detached from the circle of suspects, and so is not a simple embodiment of the law's claim to neutrality and objectivity. Ngaio Marsh deals with the potential ambivalence between the law and social class by identifying her detective wholly with the police. Nevertheless, her work still contains frequent tensions between Alleyn's marking the limits of class loyalties and his more aristocratic suspects' expectations of 'special treatment'.

The greatest distance between the police and the detective is incarnated in Lord Peter Wimsey, who significantly needs his policeman friend, Parker, to mediate. The potential problem is identified in the very first novel, *Whose Body?*, when Parker has to spell out that the phrase 'gentleman detective' can become an oxymoron if the detective is to avoid sliding into abetting criminals.

> you want to swagger debonairly through a comedy of puppets or else to stalk magnificently through a tragedy of human sorrows and things...You want to hunt down a murderer for the sport of the thing and then shake hands with him and say, 'Well played – hard luck – you shall have your revenge tomorrow!' Well, you can't do it like that...You want to be a sportsman. You can't be a sportsman. You're a responsible person.[29]

Of course, sliding into abetting criminals is precisely the risk that Albert Campion is prepared to take, which perhaps explains why some of his adventures cannot be contained within definitions of the law and belong to romance or the Gothic. Guarding the sacred Gyrth Chalice in *Look to the Lady*[30] or searching for proofs of a princely inheritance in *Sweet Danger* are two such examples.[31] *Dancers in Mourning* devotes its psychological tension to Campion's tangled class and erotic loyalties to chief suspect Jimmy Soutane, whose wife also attracts Campion's passion and sympathy. Contrary to Campion's feelings and class identity is his policeman friend Superintendent Oates's sublime assurance that being asked to assist the police is the highest honour possible. *Coroner's Pidgin* makes such a conflict of loyalties even more acute by being set in wartime.[32] The criminal issue surrounding ace pilot and aristocrat Johnny Carados is that his class values may be so at variance with the law as to prove treacherous. Again, Campion is torn by his detecting of criminal desire within his own circle.

Even Adam Dalgliesh and Reg Wexford find it hard to reconcile some of their conclusions with the demands of the law, despite their police roles. Adam Dalgliesh carries the burden of P.D. James's anti-Enlightenment stance that the law cannot substitute for the justice of God in a society – in particular, in a post-holocaust era. Wexford discovers that the attempt to harmonise the law with a vision of justice embedded in the police-detective is only possible in his becoming eccentric in the performance of his professional duties. Mike Burden is a superb embodiment of the law who paradoxically serves to demonstrate not its 'absolute justice', but the way the law is often a codification of social conventions and may prove to succour privileged social groups at the expense of those more marginal. Wexford's interior life overflows his professional and social roles, and is condensed in the detecting narrative as a moral stance that points the way to a more utopian vision. The detective in conflict with the social codes of the law may also function as a vital questioning of the law's subject, the knowable, stable, bourgeois self.

Social constructions of self and identity

The detective in fiction embodies a promise of individual justice under the law and the resulting restitution of social order. However, we have already seen how detective identities of class (and of gender, sexuality and psychic constitution) are in excess of the demands of the law in the concept of the modern self. All six authors' detectives explore what has been repressed in the construction of the modern, post-Enlightenment self. Detectives unmask theatrical negotiations of social status and the formulation of identity as neither coherent nor stable but as in process *through* the detecting narrative.

A particular challenge to the ideal of the detective as an agent of rationality and law is the slippages between the roles of detective and murderer, with the consequent implications for social stability. 'I feel like a murderer,' says Wimsey in *Unnatural Death*,[33] in which his investigation appears to provoke the death of a suspect. In *The Nine Tailors*[34] he actually becomes a 'murderer', so exceeding his far more apparently fluid shadow, Campion, who frequently finds himself in murderous circumstances. Even Alleyn, willing to shatter his class identity on the altar of the law, threatens murder when a friend is killed in *Death in a*

White Tie.[35] Mike Burden's devotion to police procedure precipitates him into self-annihilating horror when he seems to have pushed an unstable character into killing.[36]

It is not only in the figure of the detective that these novels mount assaults on the idea of a stable, knowable self in modern society – a stability necessary to the fiction of a stable and coherent class system. Plots, criminals and crimes also dispute the apparent conservatism contained in the basic literary form. One key method of problematising the stable self is by the use of occult material (see Chapter 7 for a detailed analysis). Particular attention is paid to the psychic disturbances to identity in works by Christie, Sayers, Allingham and especially Marsh, who frequently links cult religions metaphorically with drugs to signify both assaults on identity and perversions of desire.

Other challenges to the notion of the individual as stable and knowable comes from the theatrical structuring of identity in the self-conscious golden age novels. Such moves can still be found in the hybrid golden age/realism works of James and Rendell. Not only do works such as Allingham's *Dancers in Mourning* and Marsh's *Final Curtain*[37] deal with theatre people who offer society only a series of masks, but self-referential works provide a theatre of ironic stereotypes in a more modernist take on the traditional novel form. What the detectives in both *Dancers in Mourning* and *Final Curtain* discover is true of the six authors as a whole: identity is not a mask concealing a truth but a series of social masks that are both genuine and inconsistent. The attempt to promote the detective as a more stable construct to contrast with his theatrical suspects is constantly undermined by his/her psychic reconstitution of identity through the detecting story. Revealingly, in *Surfeit of Lampreys*, colonial outsider, Roberta, has a moment of panic about her adored Lampreys as they engage in a charade of trying to conceal some events from the police. She momentarily finds them terrifyingly unknowable, while Alleyn optimistically expects to discover truths of personality in detection. Much of Alleyn's exasperation in the novel can be accounted for by his discovery, not of stable identities, but of the shifting charades that are the Lampreys' typical social dealings.

The six writers' depiction of criminals also fails wholly to endorse the generic cliché of individual evil, emanating from isolated selves free of social constructions. Both Sayers and Christie appear to provide isolated murderers, yet Christie develops an interest in a more sexual and Gothic notion of crime. This is particularly true of the Miss Marple books when Miss Marple's theology of individual responsibility for evil is not quite sufficient to dispel the Gothic atmosphere (see Chapter 6).

Similarly, Sayers's *Gaudy Night*[38] embeds the crime in issues of scholastic integrity, gender and sexual identity which demonstrate that conflicts of desire and eroticism cannot be confined to one deviant individual. Allingham's concept of criminality is never wholly located in a single being. Whether a master criminal, crooked businessman or pathological killer, Allingham's murderers represent the contaminations of corporate capitalism, unhinging the individual to prey on familial and rural dreams of order. For Marsh, property crimes in her 'camp country house' mysteries come overwritten with sexual excess. Deviant desires are never confined to one abnormal sufferer, but are implicated in a web of erotic identities. She even betrays an interest in sexual serial killers in *Singing in the Shrouds*.[39]

Adam Dalgliesh for P.D. James would certainly claim to discover moral evil in individuals, but the portrayal of sin is not isolated from the psychological agonies of a secular society, which has discarded its theological frame. Indeed, some criminals are motivated by the perceived inability of the law to deliver its promise of justice – a justice, for James, portrayed nostalgically in the myth of a homogeneous Christian society. Examples of such revenge killers can be found in *Original Sin* and *A Certain Justice*.[40]

Ruth Rendell has a more materialist and ultimately more utopian conception of crime. Rejecting a theology of individual sin versus the social body, Rendell exhibits a liberal condemnation of oppression arising from the conflicting structuring of identities within coercive hierarchies of power, sexuality and gender. Such social analysis is more apparent in her later works but is still traceable in her first novel, *From Doon with Death*, in which class frictions contribute to eroticism not containable within conventional social norms.[41] The desperate female lover, reduced to writing volumes of undelivered letters, may also function as a metaphor for the psychic frustrations of the woman writer in a less enlightened age.

Crime fiction without detectives: social negotiations and Barbara Vine

The distinguishing mark of the crime novels of Barbara Vine is the absence of a professional detective, leaving an 'insider' or several of the intimate circle to be both the observing and the detecting consciousness. A second feature is a lack of traditional 'closure': Vine novels leave some aspect of the crime as indecipherable, usually connoting something unknowable, even sublime, about human characters at the extremity of passion. *A Dark-Adapted Eye*[42] will be explored later in this chapter but in *Gallowglass*,[43] the ability of Joe to 'become' his beloved Sandor is suggested at the end. *Asta's Book*[44] concludes with the incommunicable passions of maternity, while Elizabeth's fate at the conclusion of *The House of Stairs* remains ambiguous in ways that link to unanalysable aspects of criminal Bell and her chief victim, Cosette (see Chapter 6).[45] In effect, this lack of the traditional closure of crime fiction mounts a more profound challenge not only to the stable, knowable bourgeois self, but also to the ideology of the law as an indivisible stabilising force in society.

Vine novels reveal the law as impotent to regulate desire: moral, erotic and social order is not restored by its operations. These novels open up questions about crime, desire and society without limiting the responses of the reader. Such a development of literary form is achieved by the lack of a detecting authority and the rejection of plot closure. Since there is no professional detective, the act of tracing patterns of crime becomes even more assimilated to fragile negotiations of self. This narrative drive becomes extended to the reader, especially in such works as *Asta's Book* in which reading *is* the form of detecting, wholly open to the external reader as we are given all the crucial documents.

These six crime writers inhabit a genre with broadly conservative social tendencies. Although five of the six could be described as right of centre in personal politics, their treatment of the genre reveals a complex negotiation and subtle criticism of modern society that cannot simply be assigned to reactionary nostalgia. Self-conscious fictionality in the golden age writers does not unproblematically support the status quo, much less hark back to the 'good old days'. Nevertheless, it is Rendell/Vine who most consistently develops the literary form in a liberal direction; first, by evolving imaginary utopian possibilities, and secondly, as Vine, by pushing the genre over the borders of the possibilities of secure knowledge and fictional authority. Crime fiction without detectives thrills because it hints at the possibility both of social chaos *and* of remaking the world nearer to the heart's desire.

The Murder at the Vicarage by Agatha Christie (1930)[46]

The first full-length Miss Marple tale, *The Murder at the Vicarage* establishes the rural English village as a kind of expanded country house with a traditional social hierarchy firmly in place. Narrated by the vicar as the spiritual authority, it tells of the detestable domestic tyrant and local magistrate, Colonel Protheroe, found shot dead in the vicar's own study. Medical authority is represented by the likeable Doctor Haydock, and the triumvirate of male social stability, vicar, doctor, magistrate, is leavened by the feminine and the domestic. Miss Marple appears as one of a stereotypical group of elderly spinsters entertained by the vicar's lively wife, Griselda. They gossip about Colonel Protheroe's family of sulky daughter, Lettice, and attractive second wife, Ann, both friends with charismatic painter Laurence Redding. Also introduced around the tea table is the appropriately named Mrs LeStrange, a mysterious new arrival who seems to have struck up an ambiguous relationship with Dr Haydock.

Colonel Protheroe's social function as local embodiment of the law and as familial patriarch means that his murder provokes a crisis in the social stability of St Mary Mead. Additionally, class rigidities are challenged by both social comedy and the detecting story, focused through the vicar. Plagued by Mary, the unservile servant, the vicar, Len, nevertheless demonstrates that his Christian principles have not been absorbed by blind class loyalties: he believes the lower-class murder suspect, the poacher, Archer, to be innocent, and sympathises with the poor who are cruelly patronised by do-gooding 'ladies'. Nevertheless, it would be wrong to suggest that the vicar is a potential social revolutionary. In fact, he proves to be a force for conservatism in that his profession enables him to re-invest his social status with moral worth. Significantly, his sympathy for the badgered poor cannot be expressed aloud: 'I am debarred by my social standing from expressing my prejudices in the forceful manner they do' (p. 96).

Vicar Len's ability to underwrite social class with moral behaviour also serves to emphasise the hollowing out of class certainties through the self-referential nature of the genre. Opening the novel as avid readers of detective fiction, Griselda and Len continue to compare the 'real' investigation with their extensive knowledge of crime fiction. However the vicar may, in himself, morally vindicate class, its social power is under attack both from the selfish pettiness of other village inmates *and* at the self-referential level, in the conducting of the novel as self-conscious artifice. Characters function as flat comic types rather than the particularised beings of literary realism. The use of realism would have given depth and support to the depicted social scheme. Instead, social relations and class itself become a ritualised game of theatrical masks, as the vicar notes when disputing the apparent stupidity of a low-class witness: the woman is no 'half-wit' but deploying 'the camouflage of the poor … They take refuge behind a mask of stupidity' (pp. 134–5).

As a social comedy of self-referential 'types', crime and desire can be detected in the deployment of social masks. Is daughter Lettice as dim as she seems? Does Griselda's levity conceal infidelity or adherence to the stereotype of a patient wife suggested by her name? Miss Marple is presented as 'the worst cat in the village' (p. 8), as one of a series of gossips, but this easy cliché is shown as liable to slippage into a detecting role. Unsurprisingly, Miss Marple's 'uncanny' powers rely on a theory of knowledge through types and analogy:

> One begins to class people, quite definitely, just as though they were birds or flowers, group so-and-so, genus this, species that. Sometimes, of course, one makes mistakes, but less and less as time goes on ... There's money, and the mutual attraction of people of an – er – opposite sex – and there's queerness, of course – so many people are a little queer, aren't they? – in fact, most people are when you know them well. And normal people do such astonishing things sometimes, and abnormal people are sometimes so very sane and ordinary. In fact, the only way is to compare people with other people you have known or come across. You'd be surprised if you knew how very few distinct types there are in all.
>
> (pp. 191–2)

Miss Marple develops this theory of knowledge, detecting by types and analogy, throughout her later adventures. On the one hand, she employs it democratically in comparing housemaids to ladies of the manor, gardeners to magistrates: her 'human nature' is not class-structured, with social status shown as irrelevant to crime, desire and moral value. On the other hand, her methods depend fundamentally on *classification* of relatively fixed human essences so is at a deep level, conservative of the idea of class as a viable social construct. In effect, Miss Marple's detecting practises are a personification of Christie's version of the golden age genre: a game of essentially comic stereotypes revealed as uncanny masks of deviant desires, but with social order re-formed in the act of securing the criminal. Therefore, Miss Marple as the detective assumes the position of 'omniscience explained'. Gaining the respect of a whole host of characters who once doubted and belittled, Miss Marple becomes a comic, self-consciously ironic version of a deity.

Murder Must Advertise by Dorothy L. Sayers (1933)[47]

A somewhat suggestively named Death Bredon enters Pym's Advertising Agency as a new copywriter. He starts asking awkward questions about the mysterious death of his predecessor, Victor Dean, who tumbled down an iron staircase. Readers familiar with Lord Peter Wimsey's insouciance will recognise his incarnation as Death Bredon and will not be surprised to learn that he has been engaged to investigate by the victim's sister, Pamela. The trail leads to the drug-fuelled Bright Young Things, headed by the disastrous Dian de Momerie, and back, to find drug-trafficking at the heart of the advertising agency. Chief Inspector Parker enlists police resources to aid Peter in tracking both drugs and murder. Yet while Parker concludes jubilantly by rounding up the drug gang, Peter ends in a sombre mood. He has sent the guilty yet sympathetic killer out to his death in a perverse act of class- inflicted solidarity, to protect the killer's young family.

As an advertising copywriter, Wimsey discovers that the language of his trade is slippery. The law tries to fix meanings of frequently used words such as 'pure', etc., but cannot succeed in making language transparent. Advertising depends on slippages of meaning driven by consumer desire: the gap between the product and its representation as an image of social desirability. Simultaneously, advertising fears the irrationality of public desire which may detect unintentional or disastrous connotations. Since Wimsey's experiences of advertising serve to uncover its role in constructing consumer identities by structuring desire for status, sexuality, and fulfilment of all kinds, we are unsurprised to discover advertising becoming a metaphor for identity as a series of performing masks.

First encountering Wimsey in the mask of Death Bredon, gentleman dispossessed, Peter then explicitly 'advertises' (p. 90) himself as another, far more occult image of desire, the Harlequin, in order to attract the interest of Dian de Momerie. In harlequin costume, Wimsey dives off a fountain into a fishpond at her party. The detective's identity becomes spectral, in the guise of a harlequin animated by the desire of the 'other'. To Dian's perpetually drugged consciousness, Wimsey-as-harlequin subverts the borders between reality, dreams and death. She gives him information that the police could never get from her, so demonstrating the limitations of social realism in crime at the extremities of identity and desire.

In reconstructing himself as an advertisement, first as Bredon, secondly over the borders of social realism as the occult harlequin, Wimsey reveals the limitations of the unified self under the law. However, the fragmentation of the detecting identity to map the borders of realism is not the sole focus of the novel's social criticism.

Advertising as both engine of and subject to the desires of consumer society is revealed as an addictive drug. By energising consumer passions, it hollows out social substance. As the key media of consumer capitalism, advertising destabilises society by making identities more fragmented and incoherent. Sayers puts this diagnosis in apocalyptic terms:

> Not on the wealthy … was the vast superstructure of industry founded and built up, but on those who, asking for a luxury beyond their reach and for a leisure ever denied them, could be bullied or wheedled into spend their few hardly won shillings on whatever might give them … a leisured and luxurious illusion. Phantasmagoria – a city of dreadful day, of crude shapes and colours piled Babel-like … rocking over a void of bankruptcy – a Cloud Cuckooland, peopled by pitiful ghosts …
>
> (p. 187)

Of course, this indictment of the social and psychological effects of consumer capitalism is literalised in the crime plot by making the advertising agency the actual dispenser of illegal cocaine. This literalising of advertising as the drug of consumer society in the crime plot matches the detecting plot's exploration of the fragmentation of self in such a society.

What the detective here discovers is that the only way of reconstituting both self and society is to work *with* the destabilising media to reconstruct subjectivity *as* series of social masks or fictions. Wimsey has a tripartite persona: his pompous aristocrat tells a drug baron of the evil propensities of his second mask, Death Bredon; these two are haunted by spectral, death-dealing Harlequin. This triune identity can only be re-formed fictionally by using the police as actors to stage for the newspaper media the arrest of Bredon and the wholly separate upper-class lifestyle of Lord Peter. As the press fictionally but successfully (re)produce a habitable social mask for the detective by advertising his presence in incompatible places, so does Wimsey reinvent Britain through advertising and capitalist consumption. Wimsey's final triumphant advertising campaign, 'Whiffling Round Britain' (p. 263), is a more comprehensive precursor of today's 'air miles'. By collecting cigarette coupons, the consumer can exchange them for travel, hotels, excursions in what is literally a remapping of Britain as a playground for leisure consumption. National identity is re-imagined as a matter of consumer-tourism.

Murder Must Advertise tries to suggest that the aristocracy, pompous and moribund, is nevertheless outside the social instabilities of consumerism. In economic matters the novel sustains this, but in the detective as a series of advertising signs, the public school honour code (associated strongly with class by debates in the novel) cannot be isolated from retribution and death. Despite his remaking of a social identity as meaningless aristocrat, Wimsey the detective fulfils his death-dealing harlequin role by suggesting the 'honourable' way out to the killer.

Police at the Funeral by Margery Allingham (1931)

The novel opens with the reader and an unknown man following Inspector Stanislaus Oates through the streets of London. The policeman arrives at a tiny courtyard wherein rests a Tudor knight's tomb, dwarfed by tall modern buildings. Repairing to an adjacent boiler-room, Oates discovers his comrade, Albert Campion, who is meeting a young female client, Joyce, the fiancée of an old lawyer friend. She tells Campion that she is distressed by the disappearance of her unpleasant uncle, Andrew Seeley, from the Victorian household of elderly relatives where she occupies the post of housekeeper-companion. Satisfied that this is not a police job, Oates leaves Campion and Joyce, only to reappear at the said house in Cambridge when Andrew Seeley is discovered murdered.

The stifling atmosphere of *Police at the Funeral* is generated by revulsion at the outdated Victorian family structures, here transmuted into fear of evil and madness in a decayed family mansion. Ruled by the relic of Cambridge academic John Faraday, the family consists of matriarch Caroline Faraday, her elderly impoverished children, Julia, William and Kitty, their cousin, Andrew Seeley, and somewhere just out of sight, black sheep George. The initial setting of the Tudor tomb, choked by modern London, is a neat encapsulation of Allingham's nostalgia embodied in Campion. While the whole novel emphasises a distaste for Victorian social mores, Campion's evasion of a fixed identity in the modern world (here he denies being a private detective, preferring the term 'adventurer') suggests the role of a knight errant out of his period. The Tudor survival almost buried by London (significantly a tomb) harks back to Allingham's desire for a near-mythical golden age of social cohesion, ironised by the self-conscious fictionality that Campion brings to his activities.

Within the Faraday establishment, Victorian class rituals are shown as both theatrical and deeply oppressive. The frustrated and ancient household then becomes brutally disrupted by the arrival of the dreaded cousin, George, who behaves 'like an animal' (p. 208).

Campion's detection reveals the family stain to be colonial: George is literally the 'black sheep', having a mixed racial inheritance. On the one hand, Great Aunt Caroline's 'shame' over George is racist, but on the other, George as the return of the (colonial) repressed indicates the buried violence of imperialism coming home to roost, even if Campion decides that George represents no viable future and has to be evicted.

Unlike George, Campion has been invited to the house as a 'gentleman', coded here as outside the law and the police. He engages in his typical struggle between the roles of investigator questing for justice and family friend. Just as typically, Campion's progress involves a struggle to come to terms with the moral and social legitimacy of the police. Although intimate with the family because he is *not* police, he is forced to impersonate a policeman in order to cast out cousin George and reimpose social stability, significantly the same moribund order as before.

In the end, *Police at the Funeral* utilises the self-referential 'theatrical' nature of the golden age genre, on one level to expose the emptiness of rigid Victorian class practises and on another to indict them by having such 'theatre' literalised in the crime plot. Campion comes to believe that the family is theatrical because divorced from the modern world, but also in the internal staging of the crimes. Such an insight easily identifies the killer, and the novel ends with a balance of ironies. A last gift to Campion is a miniature of Caroline Faraday as a beautiful, young woman. Having come to admire the matriarch despite the stultifying atmosphere of her home, Campion's final vision complicates his earlier revulsion towards a social setting dominated by old age, selfishness and crime.

Death and the Dancing Footman by Ngaio Marsh (1942)[48]

This novel is a prime example of Marsh's signature 'camp country house'. The host, Jonathan Royal, has invited for his amusement known sworn enemies for the weekend. As an additional observer, he has included his friend, playwright, Aubrey Mandrake, whose personal weakness is fear of exposure of his humble origins and true name, Stanley Footling. Set in the early months of the Second World War, the novel is dominated by anxiety about class, nationality and gender identities (especially of masculinity) in the face of wartime demands. The eponymous footman is about to join up, while the murderer turns out to be not the 'alien', Jewish Austrian Dr Hart, but an apparently charismatic soldier who demonstrates cowardice, sexual irresponsibility and greed.

Death and the Dancing Footman asks what needs to be cast out of, or renegotiated within, social and national identity to survive the profound crises of war. Aubrey Mandrake, the narrative focus, is significantly disabled, perhaps as a metonym for his wounded class persona. Unable to fight in the war, Aubrey is at first feminised and victimised by crime as he is thrust into a swimming-pool in the dead of winter, apparently in mistake for the intended subject, Nicholas Compline. Yet if the crime story further damages Aubrey's class and masculine identity (his true name becomes known), then the detecting process enables him to construct a more viable and courageous masculinity. This is then substantiated by forming a relationship with the feminine in the person of beautiful Chloris Wynne, sometime fiancée of both Nicholas and William Compline.

The Compline brothers are feuding, in part because their accompanying mother, Sandra Compline, appears to love only careless Nicholas while it is William who adores her. Sandra Compline has a hatred of plastic surgeons like Dr Hart because she is the victim of a botched operation on her once beautiful face. Dr Hart and Nicholas Compline are at loggerheads over the favours of Madame Lisse, who is cordially loathed by her rival in the local beauty business, Hersey Amblington. The presence of all these persons summoned by Royal is complicated by the discovery that Dr Hart is, in fact, the very surgeon who mistakenly destroyed Sandra Compline's looks. The house party becomes snowed in, and a series of attempts at murder begin, apparently directed towards Nicholas, but which finally succeed in killing William.

The 'camp' cast of this fiction is particularly highlighted by the host's pronouncement that he is a 'playwright', and that the weekend is his 'composition' with a 'cast' of country house guests. Whereas Royal's surname suggests an implicit criticism of the arbitrariness of royal power, Aubrey observes all as theatre, on one level because he is a playwright and a class outsider, on another, because social role-playing is a cover for crime. Yet another dimension to the novel's theatricality is, of course, its self-conscious fictionality, embedded internally in the 'author' figure of host, Royal. *Dancing Footman* also clearly reflects Marsh's attraction to English upper-class manners, but her criticism of its ruthless insensitivity (here in Royal) reveals a profound belief that class as a social system must mutate. Aubrey renegotiates his social identity so that by reconfiguring his sexuality, he can adopt a more coherent class position. Inspector Alleyn, of course, sets his seal of approval on Aubrey. He is no social radical, needing, as always, his determinedly lower-class subordinate, Fox, to interrogate the servants for vital clues.

In fact, the 'dancing footman', finally established as a key witness, could be regarded as metonym for Marsh's attitude to social class: he embodies flexibility and even playfulness (in the reordering of identity), but the basic structures are to be retained if they can adapt to modern conditions.

Issues of 'foreignness' and the social legitimacy of police and the law prove crucial in this setting early in wartime. The chief suspect, non-British Dr Hart, proves to be innocent despite mounting circumstantial evidence. Marsh almost always has one foreigner amongst her English groupings, although this can be a New Zealander. The foreigner is rarely guilty, and serves to examine English racist residues or colonial identities within the detecting narrative. Here, Dr Hart explicitly throws in his lot with British law, trusting in the police embodied in the sympathetic Alleyn because of the crucial national *difference* to the law under the Nazis.

> I have developed what I believe you would call a good nose for justice. Austrian justice, Nazi justice, and English justice. I have learned when to be terrified and when not to be terrified. I am a kind of thermometer for terror. At this moment I am quite normal. I do not believe I shall be found guilty of a murder I did not commit.
>
> (p. 209)

What must be renegotiated in Englishness in time of war is the need to construct the law as synonymous with justice, to combat racism, and to neutralise femininity's destabilising sexual power. The devious Madame Lisse is negated through the detecting, while sensible Chloris is firmly assigned to a sympathetic male and is to become a Wren. English masculinity is to be de-essentialised in ethnicity (so Dr Hart leaves as an 'ally' to become a field surgeon) and reordered to include the moral courage of disabled Aubrey. *Dancing Footman* suggests that the detective genre could become a self-parodic metonym for winning the war. Alleyn addresses the corpse ironically, as having suffered its own 'blitzkrieg' (p. 215). Naturally, Alleyn succeeds here in rolling back these Panzer divisions of death, 'solving' in this self-conscious fiction the traumas of war.

Death of an Expert Witness by P.D. James (1977)[49]

Abrasive forensic expert Dr Lorrimer is killed in his East Anglian laboratory, to the relief of many. These suspects include a bullied junior colleague, a cousin to whom he was denying vital financial support, other colleagues who found him impossible to work with and perhaps his ex-lover, Domenica, the especially beloved sister of his boss, Howarth. Crucially involved in Adam Dalgliesh's subsequent investigation is a child of the medical examiner, Nell Kerrison. She is desperately trying to attract her father's love since he is more devoted to her younger brother, William, after the desertion of their unstable mother. Nell suggests to Dalgliesh the essential Jamesian tenet, that justice is easier in a society that believes in God. Despite descending in a helicopter like a *deus ex machina* (a god to sort out all social disorder), Dalgliesh replies to Nell that fallible human justice is all we have. *Death of an Expert Witness* is a meditation upon the social consequences of this exchange.

The role of firm yet theatrical class structures is largely replaced by a work-based hierarchy in P.D. James's novels. Her association of traditional religion and social stability is a source of conservatism, and at first it appears that work rituals can take over the sacralising (and thus stabilising) of social relations. Murder proves otherwise. Professional communities are no substitute for the social morality and stability contained in James's dream of a religious society of justice, however mythical such a society is shown to be. When the ritualising of work fails, the relatively enclosed community slides into the Gothic. Such a threatening erosion of boundaries (of society and self) is anticipated by the portrayal of families as neo-incestuous and unstable. Howarth is aware of his passionate desires for his sister, Domenica, while the intense emotions of the fragile nuclear family, in particular Nell's crucial deprivation of love, prove the key to both the committing and solving of the crimes.

This is a more liberal novel on gender inequalities than might be expected from later James works. The difficulties of professional women are gently highlighted while not featuring as significant to the plot. However, two women existing in a loving relationship are presented positively, although the word 'lesbian' is never used. The protection of such happiness is cited as a motive for murder, but it is the desire to cherish a more conventional menage that proves the final spur to a killing.

It is interesting to compare middle-class Dalgliesh and his upper-class subordinate, John Massingham, to Roderick Alleyn and Inspector Fox in their reversal of class positions. Like Alleyn, Massingham is depicted as something of an anomaly in a middle-class service. Unlike Alleyn, Massingham's class training leads to emotional brutality when he 'breaks' Nell to gain key information. Dalgliesh observes this scene both feeling repelled and acknowledging moral responsibility for this sacrifice to the law's demands. Unsentimental about social class, James refuses Marsh's use of Alleyn to humanise the law, even as Marsh herself acknowledges the tension in Alleyn's class and professional roles. What the cruel treatment of Nell in the quest for police evidence also shows is the divorce between the law and an ideal of justice in a godless society.

If 'justice' under the law is highly compromised, then so is the concept of a stable, knowable self that the law requires if its operation is to be coherent. Dalgliesh reflects upon his detecting methods as dependent upon getting to know to the life of the corpse, when such knowledge is necessarily provisional and distorted (p. 86). With such a sense of the law's limitations in the pursuit of human truths, it is not surprising that Domenica ends by mocking the legal claim to comprehend and represent social reality: 'Longing and loneliness, terror and despair, all the human muddle, neatly documented, on one-and-a-half sheets of official paper' (pp. 340–1). As a result of such a critique of the law, it becomes clear that social stability is not restored but, on the contrary, is further rocked by the arrest of the criminal which will devastate a fragile family.

A Dark-Adapted Eye by Barbara Vine (1986)

A Dark-Adapted Eye begins where traditional detective fictions cease, with the family of a murderess, Vera Hillyard, on the morning of her hanging. Narrated by Vera's niece, Faith, the novel very gradually releases clues to the reader concerning the killing of Vera's sister, Edith, known always as Eden, an event provoked by a custody struggle over a young child, Jamie. Both women claim to be Jamie's biological mother, and *A Dark-Adapted Eye* ends with the undecidability of this question of maternity, leaving family passions as ultimately indecipherable: social-familial identity becomes a matter of construction as much as a biological given.

Unlike the traditional crime-detective genres and, indeed, Rendell's own Wexford books, the quest of the narrative is not 'who' but 'why'. Also unlike golden age fictions, the murder is revealed not as an anomaly within class structures of potential social order, but crucially implicated *within* social forms of class and gender. The passionate complexity of relations between Vera and Eden are the result of oppressive class structures of mid-twentieth century Britain: crime is the consequence of the *irrationality* of class which, far from stabilising social identity, breeds incoherence, conflict, anxiety and insecurity.

Eden is born late to a family that already straddles wide divisions within the middle classes. While Vera acts as a maternal figure to the beautiful child, Eden, she in turn is the beneficiary of well-intentioned patronage of her elder half-sister, Helen, of decidedly superior class position through their father's first marriage. Helen summons Vera to India, where she too makes a marriage 'above her station' but is never fully accepted by her husband's family, who feel that they have been misled by Helen's superiority. Vera seems little interested in the child of her marriage, Francis, less in her husband, and devotes her life to bringing up Eden in a mutual atmosphere of petty snobberies and the minutiae of middle-class femininity before the outbreak of the Second World War. All this is observed by niece, Faith, who is an 'internal' detecting figure to this family, and finds her own identity implicated in the intensities of her aunts' mutual obsessions.

A Dark-Adapted Eye is remarkably convincing in its wealth of social observations. Although, in this sense, profoundly a novel of realism, it is not so much a study in character as a study in a social period, so often depicted nostalgically as stable but in fact revealed as psychologically damaging. The bourgeois world of Vera and Eden is anatomised for its confinement, pettiness and narrowness, yet its seductions are recognised by presenting its impact on the child, Faith. Narrating from the vantage-point many years ahead, Faith's story is part family history and part analysis of the class and gender motives driving Vera and Eden – an analysis more urgent for forming part of her own evolving identity.

Constructions of the feminine in the 1940s are focused through Eden's sexual career during the war. Beneath the surface of the jealously guarded respectability of the family, Eden's 'boyfriend' Chad is both cover for her sexual adventures and the sympathetically presented lover of Vera's devious son, Francis. When Vera somewhat unexpectedly produces a second son, Jamie, it becomes very plausible, later, for Eden to allege that Jamie was hers, given to Vera to assuage the all-important family social position. Where it is undoubted that Vera passionately adores Jamie, Eden's later wishes for the child are social and snobbish, which accords with her upbringing by Vera. Having married into the gentry, she wants a son to secure her new social status. Eden has always shown signs of insecurity in the cross-class obsessions of the family structure. Driven near to madness when Eden gains temporary custody and starts telling all that Jamie *is* her son, Vera's desires spill over into murder.

The names 'Vera' and 'Eden' prove bitterly ironic: there is no truth or paradise to be found in this acute and persuasive history of British social class. Indeed, the ability of narrative form, and even of writing in general, to decipher the truth is deeply problematised. Provoked to her narrative by both 'official records' and a new so-called 'objective' study's failure to come close to the nature of Faith's family experience, Faith nevertheless is unable to present a definitive account. The lack of closure in this Barbara Vine novel is occasioned by the impossibility of detecting Jamie's biological mother.

On a deeper level, the inability to detect everything and solve all outstanding mysteries is an expression of the complexities of social identities, which cannot be isolated from forms of power in contemporary society. It is the novel's denial of the bourgeois self as a hermetically sealed entity, and as such is a profound challenge to the claim of the law to be the indivisible embodiment of social justice. The law demands that individuals be held wholly responsible for their actions. In depicting identity as subject to class, gender and sexual ideologies, *A Dark-Adapted Eye* criticises the law's claim to exact justice and structure social relations. By making maternity the mystery rather than criminal responsibility, Barbara Vine produces a Gothic reinterpretation of the borders of self and society.

4
Lands of Hope and Glory?
Englishness, Race and Colonialism

These six queens of crime are not chroniclers of Britain when it comes to the negotiation of national identity. The kingdoms of Wales and Scotland rarely merit a murder. Northern and western regions of England occasionally appear as remote areas in which wealthy southern settlers fail to evade nefarious pasts. These six novelists are artists of the dominant region of English political culture in the twentieth century, the southern and eastern lands radiating from London. The detection of crime in the English hearth and home almost obsessively concentrates on what are still known as the 'home counties'. Therefore this chapter will look at the novels in the context of the construction of a dominant form of Englishness, still deeply imbued with class structures (see Chapter 3), but nevertheless formed in tension with a constant preoccupation of twentieth-century Britain: race and the legacy of colonialism.

The post-heroic detective and his more intuitive style of operation is one mode of illustrating or even debating 'Englishness'. Psychic construction of the detective through detection can make use of cultural difference, with the detective functioning as a kind of post-colonial focus in the novel, seeking to unite (not always successfully) diverse ethnic and racial perspectives. The issue of racism within the writings needs careful evaluation, particularly with regard to the golden age authors. Do Agatha Christie and Dorothy L. Sayers, for instance, merely reflect their period's racism and anti-semitism, or does their work reveal something more complex and nuanced? Undoubtedly, some golden age writing does engage in what Edward Said has called 'Orientalism'.[1] Here a Western identity is psychically constructed by projection onto a homogenised Eastern 'other' of precisely what the occidental is supposed *not* to be: irrational, savage and dark. Such

Orientalism within detective fiction needs consideration, in particular for the way it interacts with the self-conscious artificiality of the genre which in turn extends to the parodic development of English stereotypes.

The play of artifice and self-referentiality, which I argue is central to these writers, leads to a theatrical notion of Englishness in the sense of national identity as 'made up'. Such constructions operate in tension with both the literary and the political: with traditions of literary pastoral as well as with issues of colonialism.

Detecting England

If we take the figure of the detective and his companions in what I have described as a leaning to a more collective mode, then we can see that Englishness and ethnicity is immediately brought to the fore in the novels. The exception to the roll call of indigenous detectives is most obviously a Belgian, Hercule Poirot. Not only is he not English, he is most determinedly foreign. An affront to English masculinity in his neatness, fussiness, demands for fine food and central heating, Poirot is frequently to be found reflecting negatively on English habits and sentimentality. His ultra-English companion, Hastings, faithfully conveys Poirot's continental mannerisms, spiced with his own comically presented narrow English outlook. Taking his surname from the greatest English military defeat prior to a successful invasion by a French-speaking people, Hastings's ironic double act with his stupendously more intelligent detecting friend is a comically bathetic repetition of the national defeat of English pride and aggression. Poirot always wins. It is frequently his specifically non-English habits which prove successful against Hastings's mundane taking of stereotypical characters at face value.

Interestingly, Miss Marple's first appearance in a novel is in a collective of stereotypical Englishness: as one of a selection of gossipy elderly women entertained by the vicar's wife to tea in *The Murder at the Vicarage*.[2] Nevertheless, this quintessence of middle-class English femininity is flipped into a conscious 'other' by the vicar's wife, (im)patient Griselda, who characterises the women as cannibals. Her musing on which object of village scandal would be consumed for tea is foregrounded further by her need to relieve her feelings at this trying occasion by concocting a fiction about missionaries and cannibals.[3] Naturally, it is Miss Marple who spots the untruth. The whole episode emphasises an awareness of Orientalising as a self-conscious device and the construction of English identity as overtly fictional in relation to the colonial 'other'.

For the later detectives, Wexford, Dalgliesh and Cordelia Gray, relationships with detecting companions (however distant and mythical Dalgliesh is to Gray), becomes a matter of debating whether an English identity can be coherently constructed in contemporary Britain. P.D. James's more recent creation of Inspector Kate Miskin, a young police officer who grew up on an inner-city council estate, seems partially designed to emphasis the difficulty of connecting to Dalgliesh's masculine solitariness, far more predicated upon English heritage traditions of architecture, art and religion. If the professional relationship of Kate and Dalgliesh fails at times to evoke a coherent sense of 'England' from within the corporate identity of the police, it suggests that the very institutional meaning of the police force in the genre is designed to make 'England' somehow possible. For P.D. James 'England' is only 'thinkable' through institutions. By contrast to James's pessimism, liberal Wexford and socially conservative Burden's chaffing yet affectionate partnership looks remarkably successful. Nevertheless, Wexford and Burden realise that their more coherent if not mutually identical Englishness often fails to account for the dark passions they detect. For Rendell (and Vine) the Gothic becomes an aesthetic reaction to the breakdown of ethnic identity.

Albert Campion and Peter Wimsey, those scions of English aristocracy, are in danger of becoming uncanny versions of ethnicity when detecting on their own. Minus Amanda, Campion can only succeed in constructing a frail narrative of English identity if his radical otherness can forge alliances with marginality within England itself. Hence his need for the material aid of the gypsies in *Look to the Lady*.[4] A later Allingham work, the Second World War tale *Coroner's Pidgin*, explores problems with English masculine heroism by showing that the contradictory forces shaping Johnny Carados's wartime role lead him to be suspected as a murderer and a traitor.[5] Campion needs Amanda in *Traitor's Purse* to escape such an identity for himself.[6] Wimsey risks turning his aristocratic Englishness into the feudal Gothic in *Clouds of Witness*,[7] or into fragmenting into a series of uncanny masks when he actually tries to do 'a proper job' in *Murder Must Advertise*.[8] Indeed, it takes several volumes of a complex love story to convert Wimsey from nerve-ridden 'other' to English stiff-upper-lip heroism to a country gentleman capable of a reinvention of a somewhat ironic pastoral in *Busman's Honeymoon*.[9]

In the sense that the detective's psychic construction through detection constructs a narrative for the negotiation of cultural differences, then the detective functions as a post-colonial vision. He is the focus of a novel which may explicitly cite or even include colonial or other racial characters such as black Cousin Hallelujah in Sayers's *Unnatural Death*.[10] Yet the post-colonial vision need not be literalised in events or characters. Instead, it may be traced in the rhetorical modes of presentation, such as Miss Marple's threatening old maid uncanniness as a cannibal. It may also, in James and Rendell, operate in the vision of England as a land of potentially alienated separate cultures existing in colonial relationships of power to each other. This is evident in James's recent work *A Certain Justice*, in which a villainous character, partially 'explained' by his origins from the heart of darkness within an inner-city council estate, is heavily ironised when this point of view is put to Kate, another 'emigrant' from that same estate.[11]

The writer for whom a colonial sense of Englishness must be acute is, of course, Ngaio Marsh, a New Zealander who grew up in a culture that regarded England as the 'mother country'. Marsh is a colonial writer in accepting the paradigms of Englishness and the English golden age genre as her 'norm'. She is also a post-colonial writer in her exploration of the incoherencies of colonial and English identity. For her, psychic construction through detection appears to centre upon Englishness with the homo-erotic bonding of aristocratic, nervy Alleyn recuperated by the unswerving devotion of unimaginative, lower-middle-class Inspector Fox. Their tender relationship is so deferential and imperturbable that Alleyn requires a more potentially destabilising erotic focus in artist Agatha Troy. Alleyn's travels in New Zealand are, significantly, usually without his psychic English stabilisers, and seem arranged so as to infuse him into the colonial landscape. These New Zealand novels thereby re-imagine the relations of the colony with the 'mother' country. Marsh deliberately challenges the typical gender paradigm. Alleyn visits New Zealand and finds it enlarging his values in *Vintage Murder* as he is taught respect for Maori beliefs.[12] In the more usual English country house or theatrical setting, it is typically a female colonial who is romantically re-initiated into Englishness. Additionally, the typical Marsh circle of suspects contains one or more foreigners. These figures invariably attract suspicion, so advertising English racism, but are very rarely guilty.

Ngaio Marsh's 'camp county house' fictions betray both an anxiety in identifying *with* 'Englishness' in her adopting of the golden age genre *and* the ability to criticise and dissect Englishness using the touchstone of foreigness. Marsh's stories provide not only a psychic construction through detection, but a psychic construction of ethnicity using the deliberate 'otherness' of foreigness or colonialism. In 1963, Marsh expressed the literary problem of representing New Zealand in more overt post-colonial terms when she spoke of settlers possessing 'no Victorian formulae to encompass the violent landscape' where whites were 'interlopers' amongst a Maori people who 'had their own involuted secret culture'.[13] Maori culture is always respected by Marsh as different, never to be completely comprehended by the whites, and *not* in an evolutionary relation to Western modernity. Maoris may attract racist suspicion in novels such as *Vintage Murder, Colour Scheme*[14] and *Light Thickens*,[15] but are never guilty. Their cultural integrity is such that they do not participate in murder, seen as a corruption of English ethnicity.

Racial difference

Golden age writers lived and wrote in a racist society. Characters in works by all four writers make unchallenged racist comments, and only Marsh emphatically addresses racism as a stain on English character. Her treatment of blackness, such as the abuse of murder suspect Dr Natouche in *A Clutch of Constables*, may seem heavy-handed today but she preserves a notion of 'difference', as Troy's announcements in the novel demonstrate, while always exposing racism as pernicious.[16] With Sayers and Christie, racism is more ambiguously depicted. Yet for neither author is racism endorsed by the detective or the detecting plot. Although capable of anti-semitic remarks, Sayers has Wimsey's friend, Freddy Arbuthnot, marrying a Jew and becoming enthusiastic about the culture.[17] The childlike naivety of Cousin Hallelujah in *Unnatural Death* looks like a racist creation in its condescension. Yet the pathological hysteria about possible black attackers of white women in the novel is definitely not shared by Peter Wimsey, who expresses no racist paranoia and defends Cousin Hallelujah as 'innocent'. Similarly, as well as Christie's constant debunking of pompous Englishness by Poirot, racism is to be found in appropriate English types and does not determine the choice of murderer.[18] Indeed, in *Appointment with Death*, the 'suspicious Arab' is a mask employed by a murderer wholly indigenous to the white upper-class tourists.[19]

By contrast, Allingham unthinkingly adopts a racist structure in *Police at the Funeral* when the family 'black' sheep, Cousin George, who desecrates a neo-Victorian household, is revealed as literally dark, a half-caste product of colonial expansion bringing the violence of imperialism 'home'.[20] P.D. James's characters are all properly non-racist in their attitudes, but her novels reveal a passionate dislike of multicultural education which records a nostalgia for a fantasy England, one without cultural difference. Never condoning discrimination against the other as black, James is nevertheless opposed to the integration of other cultures as the importation of difference *within* England. Rendell is far more aware of the liberal dilemmas about treating all the same while/or respecting ethnic and racial differences. *Simisola*, to be examined later, is a sincere criticism of attitudes to race and cultural difference in the late twentieth-century English 'home counties'.[21]

While noting the racist rhetoric of golden age fiction, it is important to register it as precisely that, rhetoric. A major characteristic of the golden age writers (minus post-colonial Marsh) is their self-conscious deployment of Orientalism in the construction of psychic Englishness. Miss Marple among the cannibals is one example. Another is Englishwoman Sarah King's exploration of her own capacities for murderous sacrifice in an alien desert landscape encoded with non-Christian religions in *Appointment with Death*. Cousin Hallelujah reveals Sayers's limitations on race, but he functions as the psychic other to the real criminal, secure in her class and English identity which has allowed her to kill without suspicion. Campion, on the other hand, functions as an other within 'England', particularly when without his erotic connection to English 'hearty' femininity in Amanda.[22] It is therefore unsurprising to find some foreign villains, such as Ali Fergusson Barber in *Mystery Mile*, serving structurally to reposition Campion as native to the home counties.[23]

Allingham's England is itself riddled with divisions, darkness and otherness. This is signalled in the early works by witchcraft and the occult, in late stories by crime and corruption. Only an ambivalent detective like Campion, who explicitly rejects a class destiny as a colonial governor, can construct frail narratives of detection across a self-divided ethnic England, which will only submit to his efforts in the form of a temporary alliance against some kind of 'invader'. Since England is so riven by 'differences' within, Campion is constantly finding that maintaining an awareness of what is 'England' and what is 'other', the alien invader, is the delicate task of his detection. (Post-)colonial Marsh is most aptly illustrated by the unjust hatred heaped upon foreign Dr Hart in *Death and the Dancing Footman*.[24] The murderer turns out to be his greatest accuser, a non-combatant flashy English soldier in wartime. Marsh recognises English racism and

Orientalising, but her novels are far more distanced from this tendency than those of the other golden age writers.

Masquerading England

If a characteristic of the golden age is the projection of Englishness through an overtly Orientalising psyche, then it becomes one method of destabilising and parodying English stereotypes. The result in the self-referential genre is to suggest a constructed and theatrical notion of Englishness rather than a self-evident given. Golden age fiction located crime at home. It is to be found amongst the colonels, spinsters, minor gentry, middle-aged businessmen, impecunious relatives and young feckless socialites. For James and Rendell, despite going beyond golden age conventions to link their novels to mainstream literary realism, their criminals are similarly detected within a domesticated workplace (James) or the family (Rendell). The self-referentiality of the fiction *as fiction*, which partially extends to the later writers, both sets up and undermines stereotypes of dominant Englishness. Locating crime amongst the stereotypes both serves to dethrone them as emblems of English complacency and functions as a critical commentary on Englishness in its mode of upper-middle-class cultural dominance.

In *Dumb Witness*, for example, Christie exploits cultural misunderstandings of a Greek husband to forment suspicion while the true culprit lurks among young socialites and middle-class English jealousy.[25] Allingham provides a near-parodic England to the rescue in *The Crime at Black Dudley* as the hunt, outraged by an attack on one of its hounds, saves the English heroes from a dastardly foreign gang.[26]

Allingham's early work appears to celebrate a rural English heritage at the expense of the foreign, yet the distinction is really more subtle. The foreign or internationally inspired gangs of *The Crime at Black Dudley*, *Mystery Mile*, *Look to the Lady* and *Sweet Danger* stand also for corporatism, big business and urban modernity.[27] They come to be pitted against a rural England of subversive and marginal energies characterised by arcane ritual, myth, superstition, witchcraft and the occult. In later works Allingham casts a more ironic if still affectionate eye on fantastically decaying aristocracies such as the indigent Palinodes in *More Work for the Undertaker*,[28] while business life, now located in London, remains capable of crime and/or of 'enslaving' its workers.[29]

The self-conscious artifice of golden age writing does celebrate a style of conservative dominant Englishness, but at the price of ironically undercutting its claim to be natural, genuine or stable. The self-conscious nature of these fictions is embedded in the articulation of a playful constructed Englishness. For instance, Ngaio Marsh has a double-edged colonial identification with England which simultaneously mocks by mimicking its stereotypical forms. She propounds an explicitly theatrical or masquerading Englishness both in her 'camp country house' fictions and in the frequent use of the literal theatre as setting. *Final Curtain* provides a particularly apt example of a theatrical family living in a country house whose very architecture speaks bombast and self-invention rather than tradition and heritage.[30] The Ancred family's overwrought emotions are proclaimed to be both theatrical and genuine. As in other golden age writers, there is a modernist distrust of the tradition and depth rendered in traditional literary realism. James and Rendell differ here. For these modern writers, Englishness is fractured rather than theatrical. The detecting narrative is unable to construct a frail edifice of English identity as continuous across society, so the novels are forced to retreat into pools of shared understanding, surrounded by the threatening unknowability of the Gothic. An example can be found in Wexford's Chinese journey in *The Speaker of Mandarin*.[31] While travelling, Wexford experiences hallucinations and at first the story seems to erode cultural differences when chemical and literary explanations are found: Wexford had been overindulging in green tea and M.R. James's ghost stories. Then it is revealed that some 'excess' or cultural differences remained, since Wexford really was trailed by an elderly Chinese woman.

Not all the apparitions can be traced to the detective's disturbed psyche, especially as crime has disrupted the overly controlled relationship between tourists and the alien culture. Ultimately, however, 'the speaker of "Mandarin" ' is not Chinese but English, adopting the word 'Mandarin' as a code-word to initiate murder – a code taken from a legend of Oriental despotism. Rendell's novel does make the distinction between respect for the differences of Chinese culture and the Orientalising practice of English subjects who thereby project their criminality as 'other' or foreign to their own psychic construction of Englishness.

As in Marsh's acting companies, P.D. James's Englishness is a matter of professional identities, in her case of the police, doctors and nurses, publishers, pathologists, psychiatrists and lawyers. Unlike Marsh, James deeply distrusts difference *per se*, and longs for an imagined land of Englishness undivided. Although against racism as discrimination, her plots are nostalgic for a Christianity of cultural homogeneity to provide moral authority and hence social stability. The loss of God for James is the loss of England as a coherent Christian society. Professional work cultures such as the police and the law supply impoverished substitute English cultures. These in turn, using traditional values of professional ethics, hierarchy and order, seek to colonise a surrounding landscape of crime, barbarism and decay. The rituals of the work cultures are supposed to re-sacralise secular society. Unfortunately, the rituals prove flawed and incoherent, and so internal conflicts result in murder. P.D. James's political vision is crucially ironised first of all by the disruption of the murder, and secondly, by both Adam Dalgliesh and Cordelia Gray's sense that the desire for a sacred past Englishness is a fantasy not borne out by history. These detectives know that England never was the ideologically whole, undivided nation they long for.

Pastoral England

All six authors express a nostalgia for England, but it is an imagined England of whole, sufficient, cultural peace. They do this through constructing a nostalgic relation to literary pastoral, the tradition of social imagining through rural landscapes that goes back to the Eden of the Bible and Arcadian Greek myths. Dorothy L. Sayers makes the most deliberate attempt to engender positive paradises in making the detective narrative purgative and re-sacralising in works such as *The Nine Tailors, Gaudy Night* and *Busman's Honeymoon*.[32] Despite the serpent-criminals in the peaceful countryside or in the maternal paradise of Oxford, these stories do suggest a redemptive relationship possible to a conservative vision of England in the shires, and to more progressive notions of femininity in an Oxford women's college. Margery Allingham's pastoral resides in the Gothic romance of her occult rurality. It encodes a perilous ambivalence about pastoral which prevents her work from simply sliding into an uncomplicated conservative aesthetic. Far more so than all the other detectives of the six writers, it is Campion's vocation to 'save England', but he can only do so within a frail and contingent detecting narrative that is overtly temporary in effect and cannot hope to weld a stable and permanent national identity.

Christie's pastoral perspective in St Mary Mead is more simply ironic. Miss Marple not only detects sin in rural life but uses her village to supply a series of analogous types to solve crime among the English anywhere in the world, as *A Caribbean Mystery* demonstrates.[33] For

Ngaio Marsh, pastoral is an artistic post-colonial literary tool, as her work returns regularly to the problem of representing the New Zealand landscape within a Western literary tradition. In P.D. James's work, on the other hand, nostalgia for the pastoral is also nostalgia for an ideological and metaphysical genre capable of homogenising disjunctions of ethnic identity. For James, any attempt to re-create pastoral, such as the writers' community in the rural fastness of *Unnatural Causes*, is doomed.[34]

Unlike the functioning church-based community of its near namesake, Sayers's *Unnatural Death*, which is easily penetrated by gossipy spinster Miss Climpson, James's Dalgliesh finds neither rural solitude nor literary solidarity. Instead the writing 'community' is riven by jealousies and conflicting desire. In the same way, *A Certain Justice* ends in Allingham's eastern coastal landscape around Mersea Island, but definitely *not* using the golden age author's tactic of providing a rural bulwark against city corruption. Pastoral is a dream which fails in P.D. James's perceptions of a de-sacralised England: the land is returning to barbarity now that the missionaries are withdrawing. *Devices and Desires* needs to situate a narrative of 'England' in relation to apocalypse in order to suggest anything more.[35]

Ruth Rendell's English landscape is more politically rendered as a site for competing social groups, especially those of class. In *Road Rage*, what appears to be a kidnapping by eco-warriors is revealed as closer to a coded civil war between classes over the fate of the land, with Wexford's cross-cultural sympathies strained to breaking-point.[36]

Colonial England

Interwoven with the evocation of pastoral is the examination of colonial relations within Englishness. As well as Christie's typical scene of English travellers realising their own otherness in foreign lands, plots can often rely upon anxiety over colonial relations of all kinds. From the simple expedient of the mysterious visitor from the colonies in *Why Didn't They Ask Evans?*,[37] Christie can shift sharply to colonial relations as trauma in *Sleeping Murder*.[38] In the latter work, what appears to be a mental breakdown in a young colonial is revealed as a repressed memory of a brutal killing of a sexually persecuted woman in wicked old England. Agatha Christie's articulation of Englishness, race and colonialism can be further understood by reading *The Hollow* as staging the English country house as the focus of colonial desire. This potent form of nostalgia is revealed as psychically as well as criminally sick.[39] The novel (concerning a household headed by an ex-colonial governor) subjects characters to a hypnotic enthralment to a past that is irretrievable and which most of them are unable to exorcise.

Allingham's typical early structure of foreign inflected corporatism versus rural Gothic is, in fact, an inverse colonial relation: 'England' functions as the threatened site of native cultures in an 'invading' world of big business. Later works develop this political trope as Campion's own otherness in detecting (an otherness to his class position) allows him to evade his family's planned destiny for him as a colonial governor, and he remains in 'colonised' England.[40] Ngaio Marsh persistently eroticises colonial discontinuities. In *Opening Night*, a colonial and destitute young actress is regarded with suspicion in a London theatre.[41] Martyn Tarne is first revealed as an uncanny double of the leading actor, then as a literal relation who saves the company from embarrassment. She is finally psychically reborn into the company in ways that preserve her colonial difference (see Chapter 5).

Dorothy L. Sayers is less preoccupied with the literal colonial (apart from Cousin Hallelujah), but shares with other golden age writers a sense of the feminine as a colonised other within English society. In fact all six authors are aware of the potent intersection of gender and colonial structures. In Sayers's *Strong Poison*, Harriet functions as the colonised outsider whose unconventional sexual behaviour condemns her as other in the eyes of England's establishment.[42] Even for P.D. James, the haunting sense of alienation within Englishness is particularly acute when gender provides an added complication. Kate Miskin, from the council estate 'colony', feels even more of an outsider to the corporate identity of the police when Dalgliesh prevents her from shooting a suspect in *A Certain Justice*.

Ruth Rendell's examination of colonialism is part of her more liberal interest in difference of all kinds, including that of gender. For Rendell, difference can be colonial and oppressive when it is that of class, such as the disastrous attempt of middle-class employers to patronise and 'domesticate' their servant in *A Judgement in Stone*.[43] 'Difference' also conditions desire which may be structured through colonial paradigms in England. In *Wolf to the Slaughter*, trees escaping industrial expansion are doomed 'aborigines' while desire 'enslaves' characters, uncovering a dark otherness to their middle-class English passions.[44] Colonial tropes are formative in notions of Englishness within the work of these six authors. Their novels bear traces of the woman writer's awareness of the interdependence of colonialism and gender.

Death on the Nile by Agatha Christie (1937)[45]

Agatha Christie's *Death on the Nile* takes issues of colonialism, consumer capitalism and Englishness to a point of crisis by assembling a party of upper-class English and American tourists on a Nile river-boat. The resulting manners and murders are observed regretfully by Hercule Poirot. The murder of honeymoon heiress Linnet Doyle proves to be intimately connected to most of the party. Also aboard are her husband and his vengeful spurned fiancée, representatives of her two sets of lawyers, members of a family once ruined by her father, a kleptomaniac old lady after Linnet's pearls, a communist agitator who is also a British lord, a professional upper-class jewel thief, and a dipsomaniac writer of sex stories with her increasingly desperate daughter. Significantly, the scene is framed by the presence of Colonel Race, known to Poirot and on 'imperial duty' in seeking a colonial agitator of 'mongrel blood' (p. 90).

The detecting narrative must negotiate an oriental setting, colonial politics and Anglo-American ethnicities all bound up with consumer capitalism. All the characters are feeling the effects of the 1930s stock market depression. Additionally, Egypt features here not as a mere landscape but as a self-conscious 'Orientalism' on the part of characters who construct identities by consuming the 'otherness' of the alien culture in a colonialism ironised in the novel by self-referential artifice. Although Rosalie Otterbourne suggests a classic 'Orientalist' attitude when she describes the savage landscape as releasing her inner passions – 'it brings to the surface all the things that are boiling inside one' (p. 45) – her real target is the fracturing of Western femininity in her mother's ideology of sex distorted by drink. She parodies Islam by describing her mother as 'the prophet of the god, Sex' (p. 65). Both Simon Doyle and his ex-fiancée, Jackie de Bellefort, mimic the cries of native children to signify their own distress. Englishness requires a native other for representation, but it mimics rather than appropriates the authentically other culture. Rather, psychic colonialism, depicted in the characters and through their crimes, serves to 'consume' Western English or American identity by showing that it is the otherness *within* this ethnicity that destabilises society and identity through crime and desire.

This delicate delineation of colonialism as a psychic component consuming identity is explored both comically and powerfully in the person of the drunken author, Salome Otterbourne. Her vulgar, neo-Freudian reduction of all human motives to sex and 'blood lust' is never directed towards the native other, but instead provokes a violent climax consummated by her own murder. When she announces her eyewitness account of Linnet's maid's killing as vindicating her theory of primordial urges, context and events confirm that she is accusing, with some justification, the monstrous other within the white suspects. While Mrs Otterbourne's crude simplifications of desire are not endorsed, her role is to bend an Orientalising aesthetic back within the consuming passions of the Anglo-American party.

The novel locates Englishness as beset by consumer capitalism and its international dimensions. *Death on the Nile* pitches an American heiress of business millions as a possible restorer of the grandeurs of the English country house with its potency for English aristocratic identity. Perhaps unsurprisingly, American capital and sexual politics prove unable to redeem the English aristocracy. By preferring the impecunious Simon Doyle to an established but impoverished lord, Linnet proves first an invader, literally taking over her best friend Jackie's fiancé, then oppressor, then murder victim. A rhetoric of slavery surrounds the feminine members of the Anglo-American privileged group. Firstly, Linnet is accused of having wealth funded by slave workers, then the dependent Cornelia and desperate Rosalie are described as slaves to their despotic relatives. Cornelia, revealed as pauperised by Linnet's capitalist father, is called 'a black slave', but is later able to choose between two suitors, a communist lord and a neo-Freudian Austrian, Dr Bessner.

Slavery is not only a subtle critique of gender relations here, it is principally a surprisingly fierce commentary on consumer capitalism at the level of high finance. Not only is Linnet's money surrounded by issues of pauperism and enslaved workers, but her American lawyer is prepared to kill over financial speculation and Tim Allerton's so-called stock market dealings are a code for a life of crime. Replacing the English country house aristocracy with an American heiress is to replace a defunct order with a valueless one. *Death on the Nile* uses colonialism to explore English and American cultural identities in relation to capitalism. It cites Orientalism as an overtly fictional strategy of self-expression and only endorses imperialism at the level of Colonel Race, whose 'mongrel' (not native) agitator is depicted as exploiting colonial subjects. Western identities in crisis are depicted as consuming any notion of a stable self through colonial aesthetics.

Busman's Honeymoon by Dorothy L. Sayers (1937)

Busman's Honeymoon shifts from parody to pastoral in its detecting story. The result is a novel interrelating but not homogenising the two modes of parodic self-referentiality, and re-sacralising pastoral. While *Busman's Honeymoon* depicts a masquerade of gender, nevertheless I would argue that it produces an ironic yet sustainable relation to a pastoral, stable, hierarchical England. The problem for the novel is the cross-class marriage of urban nervy aristocrat Lord Peter Wimsey to country doctor's daughter and detective novelist Harriet Vane. How can the narrative frame the marriage as an epithalamion reconciling the contradictions of 'Englishness' in modern society?

The answer to the conundrum appears to lie in the reversing of the dynamic of the typical country house mystery. Instead of a murder plunging an ostensibly coherent household into chaos, here the murder of Mr Noakes is revealed as the last act of the breakdown of the rural gentry-led economy: the detecting story will restore it. Upon arrival, the Wimseys are taken to be those most outlandish of impersonators, 'film actors', but immediately set about restoring the traditional household even before discovering the body (p. 43). After they re-establish, somewhat self-consciously, relations with the indispensable rural clichés of the vicar (Mr *Goodacre*), the sweep, and the stereotypical spinster, Miss Twitterton, the discovery of the murder threatens to fragment this nascent (re)construction of country house Englishness. Henceforward the drama of the novel lies in the erotic relation of Peter and Harriet. Is the structure of their marriage going to supersede the pursuit of justice as Harriet argues for Miss Twitterton's hysterical confidences to be respected? Can the relationship subsume the chaos of murder – here very much identified with post-country house modernity – and allow the (re-)creating of a country house rural economy as a pastoral vision of idealised hierarchical England?

If Peter and Harriet are to turn the detecting narrative into the re-creation of country house conservative aesthetics then it cannot be done without irony which in turn mitigates the political punch behind the vision. The honeymooning detectives are forced to face otherness within as they both reveal a primary loyalty to personal integrity which may appear to conflict with their mutual devotion. The otherness without proves to be a harsh version of the democratising forces of the modern world combined with capitalism stripped of ethics. The previous owner, Noakes, has despoiled the historic old house for money and failed business ventures. His murderer is not a native of pastoral lands, but is significantly 'from London' in a novel which establishes at length the rural origins of Peter and Harriet, overdetermining their mis-identification as 'film actors'. The murderer is motivated by the desire to move out of his subordinate class and is ready to exploit a vulnerable spinster in order to do so. Counterpointing the love duets of Peter and Harriet, more corrupt versions of romance lead to brutality and crime. The weapon of the hanging cactus plant is both comically playful and a sign of the un-English desert that Noakes has produced.

Erotic relations between Peter and Harriet can restore (and re-story) Englishness on conservative, but not reactionary lines. Class mobility is slapped down on the part of the murderer, yet Harriet's sister-in-law's class aggression is deplored. Peter exploits his protean nature to declare himself a fraud cosmopolitan. *Busman's Honeymoon*'s comic domesticity allows the reconstruction of Peter as an aristocratic country dweller, rooted by hearth and Harriet in ways not possible to the figure in the more Gothic *Clouds of Witness*. As a result, Harriet can say to herself, 'I have married England' (p. 98) and Peter tells her, 'I have come home' (p. 288). Together they represent a psychic re-formation of Englishness, continuous with country house nostalgia, yet crucially permitting both the novelist (Harriet) and the detective (Peter) to operate with integrity.

Total regression into pastoral located in an aristocratic past is prevented by the layering of the successful erotic pastoral with the tragicomic romance of Frank Crutchley and Miss Twitterton. The most passionate Wimsey love scene is preceded by Frank's brutal demolition of Miss Twitterton's 'romance' and is interrupted by the spinster's distress at the honeymooners' happy duet. As a whole, the novel is structured around two uninterrupted moments of union which are meant to redeem death. The wedding night is said to purify the house of the murder of Noakes, once the body is discovered on the morrow. In addition, the novel ends with the most extended treatment of Peter's neurosis as the death sentence is carried out on the unrepentant criminal. After the near-ritual quotation of the infamous words of the death sentence, Harriet's triumph in waiting for Peter to seek her out for comfort is reinforced by biblical citation. Validation via the sacred text is a stronger version of Harriet's earlier acceptance by the occult strain in Peter's aristocratic lineage at Duke's Denver (see Chapter 6).

What *Busman's Honeymoon* does is to re-sacralise the country house as a source of conservative and nostalgic Englishness by linking the political and literary traditions of pastoral to more progressive notions of marriage relations. It succeeds because the celebratory erotic structures retain a sense of otherness, in the first place in the cruel exploitations of sexuality. Counterpointing Miss Twitterton's experience of romance with the Wimseys' is a form of *overlapping* in the novel, a layering of heterosexual relations that prevents the re-sacralising from becoming unambiguous. Secondly, pastoral is renegotiated into a more critical and less conservative mode by Wimsey's neurosis as he feels himself to be what he structurally is, a kind of murderer. Wimsey, the reinvented restorer of country house values of a stable England, can psychologically imagine himself into the role of the 'other', the killer, the serpent in paradise. Significantly, his breakdown threatens to poison the house for the married couple. Only alliance with Harriet, with otherness as the feminine, can superimpose a delicate restitution of paradise.

It is wholly coherent with the six authors gendering of the genre that the execution of the murderer does not expunge all the darkness from pastoral England. As the traces of otherness re-appear in Wimsey, the trumpets that sound for Harriet do so for her psychic restructuring of Peter into signifying England. This 'England' is one in which self and cultural stability is depicted as a fiction to be constantly remade. Sayers crime writing is far less a matter of *discovery* and far more so stories of imaginative *re-creation*.

Traitor's Purse by Margery Allingham (1941)

Unlike other literary detectives, Albert Campion is regularly called upon to save England. *Traitor's Purse* is narrated from the point of view of a man who has lost his memory, is accused of murder, is haunted by some tremendous destiny he is neglecting and whom other people call Albert Campion. This figure learns that as Campion he may be a traitor or a potential saviour of his country. He may be an 'impersonator' of Campion in the sense of being a criminal, but he is certainly an 'impersonator' for most of the novel as he tries to trace his unknown identity in relation to an imperilled country in the early stages of the Second World War.

Traitor's Purse centres on one of Allingham's legendary landscapes with both sacred and nationalist functions. The Masters of Bridge are a secretive archaic and mercantile organisation in a position to financially aid England in war time. Their base is a neolithic fortress in the town of Bridge, so named for the legend that the land itself rose into a bridge to aid the endangered populace. What takes Bridge into a Gothic location is the growing realisation that from these Guardians of England may arise great national danger, intentional or not. Gothic ingredients of dangerously blurred boundaries are magnified through the consciousness of Campion as he tries to situate his unknown self in relation to England. Is he saviour or traitor? This existential enquiry becomes experienced as a psychological division as Campion feels alternately mad or ghostly.

Like Wimsey, Campion needs an alliance with the feminine in order to stabilise his otherness. Amanda is explicitly named his 'other self' in the novel, but is lost romantically early on to the figure of Aubrey Lee. Amanda loves Lee, ironically, because he is like Campion, except that he seems to love Amanda. This situation is described to Campion at the point when he discovers his love and need for her for the first time (p. 51). Without Amanda, Campion has to make do with his feminised, monstrous servant Lugg to aid his rebirth and to try to construct his destined erotic relation to England, as Gill Plain has argued.[46] Whereas Wimsey is allowed to stand *for* England in an erotic relation with otherness which cites him in ironic pastoral, Campion must become the heroic saviour-lover *of* England. While still dispossessed of memory, Campion is told that only he can save the situation which depends upon the knowledge which he cannot remember and England's faith in herself. Explicitly, nationality must become whole and undivided, and as part of this process Campion must become whole and undivided to face the external threat. Campion's psychic conflict must no longer signal his ambivalence, but must become an undivided bond with England.

Unsurprisingly from Allingham, the threat comes from corporate big business. The plan is to put 'the British Empire on a company footing, with a personal invitation to every tax-payer to invest his all in it' (p. 157). The prospectuses prove a convenient route for the traitorous other, now forged money, to be sent to every household in a move which will destroy the British economy. There is a sense in which this Hitlerian weapon is described bitterly as a precursor of the welfare state: it forms a modern corporate attack on nostalgically described economics.

Fortunately, fragmenting Campion's self in memory loss becomes a means of resolving his ambivalence when his memory is restored in the face of national danger. Campion is stabilised both by recovering Amanda and by having his internal otherness reconfigured into his double, the true villain and mad traitor, who sought fascistically to 'restore decent order' to England (p. 197). Through Amanda, masculinity, identity and fidelity to England are finally remodelled in ways designed to prevent self becoming other, saviour into traitor. Campion admits to being 'nuts' in several senses, so indicating his doubling relation to the mad villain. *Traitor's Purse* enacts nostalgic drives for a reactionary notion of England fearful of contamination by modernity, commerce and welfare. Yet it demonstrates that traitors and otherness lurk within the desirable sites of Englishness within a continuum of betrayal from the corrupt, the mad or the merely unwitting. Therefore identity becomes as much a psychic battle within as a thriller narrative without. In this intriguing novel, to detect the self is to (re)construct national identity.

Photo-Finish by Ngaio Marsh (1980)[47]

Photo-Finish takes Alleyn and Troy together to New Zealand near the close of Marsh's career. Both are engaged in professional duties: Troy is to paint Sicilian opera diva Isabella La Sommita amongst her entourage; Alleyn is ostensibly to be consulted about a photographer stalker, but in reality seeks a drug gang. Country house aesthetics are replicated by the operatic gathering taking place on a remote lake island owned by La Sommita's consort, enigmatic businessman Montague Reece. Artistic and sexual passions conflict over the semi-professional staging of a juvenile opera specially composed for the diva by her new young lover, the vulnerable Rupert. It is aptly, we are told, called *Alien Corn*. The novel allows Marsh to stage post-colonial anxieties about constructions of ethnicity, sexuality and gender, all in relation to her persistent artistic problem of the depiction of the otherness of New Zealand in Western literary forms.

In the first place, the term 'primordial' is repeatedly and obsessively applied to the landscape. It is not so much 'primordial' in suggesting an evolutionary colonial aesthetic, but instead situates the land *outside time*, specifically the Fallen time of the Westerners and their murder. The landscape is allied with Maori culture in the evocation of the legend of the sacred creation of South Island, and in the Island murder setting as 'tapu', a sacred burial site now violated by the Europeans. With the New Zealand wilderness and Maori legends, Marsh's novel delicately establishes her post-colonial position of respecting difference while not appropriating it. The pristine and archaic power of the landscape and Maori culture remain 'other' to the murder plot yet not absolutely external to it, as the act of respecting otherness sets up echoes in the psyches of the suspect group. The country house motif of isolation is cemented by a storm on the lake known as the Rosser after a Westerner who died as a consequence of violating Maori tapu. Not respecting cultural difference leads to a narrative not of social but of 'natural' violence from a culture where nature and narrative cannot be easily distinguished. The storm becomes an actor in the murder drama; but more than just a practical instrument, it becomes a motif of violence, of the exposure to extreme otherness recorded in the spectral-isation of Alleyn:

> The voice of the wind, which he was always to remember as a kind of leitmotif to the action, invaded their room. The window pane…was a black nothing with vague suggestions of violence beyond. When he leant forward his ghost-face, cadaverous with shadows, moved towards him.
>
> (p. 141)

New Zealand 'natural' violence, transformed into a legend of white colonial violation, brings the otherness of death and violence to Alleyn after the discovery of La Sommita's body.

What is also noticeable here is the use of art, here opera, as a metaphor to structure a meaning out of alien nature. Troy functions in this story as a post-colonial artist who respects difference and who can also represent it without devouring its otherness. It is she who intuits a 'consonance' between the 'dramatic' effect of the landscape and future murderous events. Later she considers it 'brave' of painters to try to cap-ture the land, and hints of some future artistic work using metaphors not unrelated to Maori legends of making, in 'bones' and 'anatomy'. Yet Troy ends the novel by reconfiguring post-colonial difference, empha-sising the alien nature of Western intrusion in a final statement that is explicitly *not* conversation with other characters: 'This landscape belongs to birds: not to men, not to animals: huge birds that have gone now, stalked about in it' (pp. 217–18). That art is not a facile tool for colonial representations is demonstrated by the failure of *Alien Corn*, Rupert's opera. Its title alerts us to the potential for artistic *exploitation* of cultural difference and it is the novel's attempt to dis-tance itself from such a possibility.

Troy is not only a sensitive artist of the post-colonial, she is also posi-tioned differently in relation to differences of all kinds due to her gen-der. The murder plot comes to focus upon Sicilian ethnicity, and in particular sexuality, since a feud fusing sex and murder between two families is discovered to be the key. (Post-)colonial rhetoric portrays Isabella La Sommita, murder victim, as other in terms of gender, eth-nicity and voracious sexuality as she is termed 'cannibal' in a house of 'slaves'. 'Gargoyle' is repeatedly used to describe her, suggesting also her masquerade of diva-dom in terms of gender and power, a masquer-ade significantly penetrated by Troy who 'translates' her into art.

Photo-Finish has pushed Marsh's self-referential camp country house form to its limits and beyond in ways that are in danger of over-exposing the constructed nature of gender and ethnicities. It marks the end of an outmoded literary genre. Simultaneously, the novel tackles what it discerns as more fundamental post-colonial issues of New Zealand art. In the portrayal of New Zealand 'difference', the exploration of the potentials of art to work with 'the alien', Marsh has her New Zealand novel.

Devices and Desires by P.D. James (1989)

P.D. James's conservative nostalgia concentrates upon lamenting the consequences to modern English society of the decline of Christian faith that ought to provide an ordered governing authority. In *Devices and Desires* she suggests that a religious vision has returned in demonic form: nuclear power provides a material narrative of apocalypse to rival and echo the Christian one. Although the novel opens with a serial killer stalking his victim, this dallying with crime realism blends subtly into golden age aesthetics as it is discovered that one of a group of suspects all associated with the power station has killed in a way imitating the now dead serial killer. Such a beginning establishes the 'Fallen' nature of rural England, here located in East Anglia.

Despite the opening note of random violence, *Devices and Desires* is strongly related to pastoral in that the nuclear complex (psychological and literal) allows a Protestant vision of Englishness in relation to faith, martyrdom, landscape and time. Failure to remain a unified society (without cultural difference), James seems to suggest, opens England to a demonic other not only in nuclear power, but also in terrorism dreaming of apocalyptic consummations. Faith in science can function as a psychological substitute for God in some characters, but its boundary with the demonic is frail as science fanatics destroy for their god or science apostates come to feel that the power station is apocalyptic.

What particularly ties this novel to pastoral is the use of metaphysical landscapes of nostalgia. The nostalgia is for a unified English religion which would guarantee (for James) a unified English cultural identity. This desire is embedded in the novel's landscape of the natural beauties of the headland: a ruined abbey used for lovers and political trysts and the sinister lights of the nuclear power station. Yet what prevents James's conservative nostalgia from sliding into purely reactionary art is the sense that a religious vision of unity and order cannot be simply identified with the past. A vital ingredient to the metaphysical landscape is Martyr's Cottage, so named for a female Protestant martyr whose violent burning is not only evoked in the novel but used to counterpoint and to suggest structures of understanding for the murder plots' martyrs to faith in science. Even the killer is a possible martyr to love for kin and to past sexual oppression. James's distrust of 'difference' within England is shown by the martyrdom of sympathetic Meg, a school teacher banished to the headland by cruel applications of multicultural education.

Martyrdom seems to work two ways in the novel: on the one hand it is an attempt to sanctify and unify the diverse cultural energies the novel discerns in modern England, an attempt to find a religious narrative to mitigate difference and subsume cultural diversities under a construction of Englishness. On the other hand, the martyrdom narrative encodes terrifying violence and prejudice within Christianity. It is a narrative of national disintegration, of the other within, imaged in the metaphysical landscape here in the Protestant martyr's cottage and the ruined abbey whose Catholic associations are substantiated by being the object of pilgrimage for bereaved Catholic, Theresa. The forlorn abbey stones stand as a motif of a time of one faith for all England, yet also incarnate the realisation that their first despoliation was likely to be at the hands of Protestant fervour. The pastoral of *Devices and Desires* is one of a complex relation to a religious past.

The novel's implicit recognition of the dangers of identifying the past with a dream of cultural homogeneity finds further realisation in the treatment of time as not always linear. The theology of religious martyrs places them outside time which is the curse of the Fallen world. Therefore, the potentially sacralising structure of martyrdom can be revisited as the plot appears to return to the original legend of Martyr's Cottage at the end; although the possibility of contemporary martyrs flipping over into demonic 'others' is not negated. The headland, similarly seems to be without linear time in ways that dwarf human concerns. The martyred teacher, Meg, finds her final comfort in this sense of a landscape outside of time, so outside narrative and culture: it is the novel's only alternative to the pastoral of martyrdom – as the fate of the faithful of all kinds in divided England – and to the pastoral of apocalypse.

As in the majority of James's works, the narrative is diffused through many different characters to emphasise the discontinuities in English cultural identity. This leads to suprisingly acute examples of 'gender martyrdom', as in Amy, the single mother who thinks she is engaged

in secret animal rights subversion but is, in fact, employed by terror-
ists, and Alice, who has a secret history of abuse. Both these characters
die mis-labelled by the authorities as feckless single mother and frustrated spinster respectively. Adam Dalgliesh may achieve his usual
function of providing a connecting conscience in intuiting truths he
does not directly know, but here he may equally well fail, leaving a
sense of Englishness as irredeemably discontinuous, traversable by no
one narrative form.

This is a pessimistic novel of Englishness as only imaginable in relation to apocalypse. 'Martyrdom' provides a structure flexible enough to
drive landscape into metaphysics and pastoral, to problematise James's
nostalgia for an imaginary religious society in the past. As well, it can
represent heterogeneous passions because of the otherness of violent
hatred contained within the sanctity of religious martyrdom. In *Devices
and Desires*, martyrdom is a structure of both likeness and difference. It
provides a fictional construction of Englishness that does not want to
be so self-evidently a fiction.

Simisola by Ruth Rendell (1994)

Simisola could be read as an answer to *Devices and Desires* on the need
to construct a place for racial and ethnic otherness within Englishness.
It is a warning not to try to cast difference outside, where it may recur
as a demonic other. The novel follows Wexford as he learns what
Photo-Finish already knew, that difference needs to be respected and
not appropriated.

In a work devoted to the exploration of colonialism, racism and
ethnicity, the crime plot progressively indicts middle-class white
Englishness. The disappearance of middle-class black Melanie Akande
comes to be linked to the murder of a white woman treated as a sex
slave and then the murder of an African girl who had been living invis-
ibly as a tortured slave in a wealthy white family. Much of the power of
the analysis comes from the detection that violence against blacks
exists in a complex continuum with the racist assumptions made
partly in ignorance by well-meaning whites, including Wexford and
Burden. The professional relationship between the two men brings to
consciousness unrealised racism in the white middle-class dominant
English culture. Ignorance becomes racism when it leads to the
assumption that all blacks are alike, therefore interchangeable.
Wexford falls down badly when he asks the Akande parents to identify
their dead daughter only to discover that not only is the victim not

Melanie, but that their distress is the direct result of his neglect of his professional duty. The neglect would not have occurred for a white victim.

Differences between middle-class Melanie and the enslaved girl prove significant despite their common racial origin in Nigeria. The power relationship of slavery is shown to interact with blackness, but not be identical to it. The slave girl is found dumped in an archaeological site linked to an English heritage of slavery, when the Romans enslaved the Celts and may have practised female infanticide, reminding the reader of connections between gender and colonial power here. Indeed, slaves are more uniformly female than black, since the first discovered murder victim is a middle-class white woman sexually enslaved to a coldly professional married man, aptly named Snow.

The novel investigates the condition of slavery in relation to race, colonialism and servants. Several households possess servants, mostly Filipino and all women. Wexford explains to sceptical Burden the potential for exploitation of servants brought in from abroad with limited immigration rights. Weird hostess Cookie Dix proves a relatively enlightened employer of a Filipino maid, but conservative electoral candidate Anouk Khoori, who pretends to the Akandes that her 'soul is black' (p. 268), is justifiably accused of treating her maids as slaves. The argument that the objectionable Khoori needs to be supported to keep out a far right candidate completes *Simisola's* presentation of cultural identity as also a political matter. Without legal safeguards, ethnicities perceived as other, especially darker-skinned Filipinos and blacks, are vulnerable to class and power exploitation which may culminate in murders such as that of the slave girl.

Wexford's cruel mistake with the Akandes indicates what Anouk Khoori's crass adoption of a 'black soul' confirms, that to crudely homogenise or appropriate difference is as racist as the opposite danger of defining the ethnic other as so 'other' as to be outside human standards, the 'other' who can be made your slave. Burden maintains a distrust of cultural difference, so that Wexford has to return home in search of his familial psychic construction as healing. Here he finds it is his 'other' daughter, the less sympathetic, less beloved Sylvia, who can help him understand the dangers of 'purity' in regarding otherness. She describes a theory of negritude that seeks to account for the systematic degrading of another human being. It is therefore significant that the slave girl victim does not remain unnamed in Wexford's investigation. Slaves were deprived of their names as one means of erasing their identities. Wexford calls his slave Sojourner, and tells

Burden (and the reader) that she was a slave who became an artist, who found her voice as a poet of protest. Yet the novel does not cease with the bestowal of a name of potential liberation. Virtually the last word is the revelation of her true name, Simisola, which simultaneously solves the riddle of the title. It is now revealed as signalling the restoration of a black slave's identity.

There is a sense in which the artificiality of the golden age genre seeks parodically to account for death (see Chapter 5). Ruth Rendell is too attached to realism to account for, or to solve, the brutality of the death of Simisola. Indeed, here realism makes a moral claim as it clothes the generic detecting structure of the crimes with a far more politically motivated detecting of racism and colonialism within Englishness. However, *Simisola*, the novel, does reflect Rendell's faith in literature, to restore, if not the victim's life, then some awareness of her identity which would liberate her from the role of nameless slave.

When Wexford retreats to his healing familial setting, he quotes Tennyson's languishing Arthur setting sail for 'Avilion, where I will heal me of my grievous wound' (p. 164).[48] Returning to solve the case, Wexford is Arthur, an English monarch, come again. Tennyson's Arthur vanished defeated by the break-up of a unified culture organised through a nationalist and religious hero myth. Wexford returns able to learn a different kind of Englishness: one that needs to renegotiate the legacy of colonialism and respect a diversity of ethnic cultures living within England.

5
Detecting Psychoanalysis: Readers, Criminals and Narrative

Like detective fiction, psychoanalysis is a narrative art. Both function as a literature of crisis in looking for clues to previously unsolved traumas and in seeking secure boundaries to fix knowledge and desire in a social context. Sharing not only methodology but also tropes of analysis, plotting and deciphering, both detective fiction and psychoanalysis promise popular culture certainties which they cannot ultimately deliver. Psychoanalysis is often cited as a form of secure knowledge of human motivation and desire, but it reveals a double nature, simultaneously suggesting the impossibility of a firm grasp on what is, by definition, unknowable, the unconscious. Similarly, detective fiction offers a narrative guarantee of answers as solutions, but, as Scott McCracken points out, individual novels raise more questions than they are able to satisfy.[1]

It is traditional for critics to seize upon the multiple parallels between detective fiction and psychoanalysis in order to use the psychological theory to interpret the fictional form.[2] I want to go further in suggesting more complex intimacies between the generic development of the six authors and a psychoanalytic model of understanding. At the margin where psychoanalysis and feminist theory collaborate, psychoanalysis can also help to situate the social implications of these feminine fictions. The reader's pleasure and investment in the work, narrative processes and ideologies of crime and desire are all susceptible to psychoanalytic interpretation. I will also describe a more complex relationship between the psychology and golden age writing in the genre's explicit commentary on psychoanalysis as a cultural phenomenon.

Psychoanalysis and the crime fiction reader

The term 'psychoanalysis' typically refers to the theories of Sigmund Freud and his intellectual successors, in particular Jacques Lacan. However, it can also refer to both Freudian and other constructions of the unconscious, so this chapter will include some of the relevant work of C.G. Jung, specifying where the theoretical ideas are native to one theorist. Freud posited an unconscious, structured as a result of repression when the sexual desires of the infant for the mother become reconfigured as forbidden. The male child's desire to continue the passionate bond to the nurturing (m)other through his discovery of genital pleasure is interrupted by his intimation of the role of the father. At first loathing and desiring the removal of the father, the child comes to fear retribution from him in the form of castration. This nascent tragedy is resolved by the child identifying with the paternal function and repressing prohibited desires for the mother, so creating a sexual unconscious.

Female children have a more tortuous route to the necessary repression of desire for the maternal, according to Freud. This dramatic process of guilt, forbidden desire and criminal fantasy Freud called the Oedipus complex. Lacanian theory takes the Freudian formation of subjectivity and uses it to understand the acquisition of language and the child's place in the social world. What Lacan calls the 'symbolic order' is the laws and conventions of a particular culture. In Western societies this is organised around the phallus as a symbol of male power. The phallus does not simply equate to the fleshly penis, but is a symbol of the significance attributed to masculinity in society. A child enters the symbolic order through entry into language. This occurs at the Oedipal stage, when subjectivity is split through fear of castration and the resulting repression into the unconscious. Where Freud stressed the importance of the biological penis, Lacan argued that the phallus would operate as a symbol of cultural power, but would always be seen in relation to a 'lack' since it is predicated upon repression and splitting. The centrality of the phallus to the symbolic order needs to be seen as a cultural sign of the valorisation of masculinity rather than any biological inferiority of the feminine. In Chapter 2 I linked the symbolic order to the law and the detective genre. Now I want to consider notions of the Oedipal unconscious and reading processes.

Peter Brooks has produced a theory of narrative using a Freudian model of the appeal of stories and of the reader's engagement with them.[3] Essentially he provides two related schemes from Freudian case history: on the one hand narrative literally *embodies* in the reader the two great Freudian unconscious forces, that of Eros and the death drive. On the other hand, the reader's relationship with the novel can be understood as a form of analytic transference. Freud believed that the self was subjected to the sexual energy of the unconscious desiring ever greater connections and relationships with the 'other'. This 'other' is often understood as other people, but it could also function in objects, activities, and forms of knowledge – in effect a drive towards participation and 'life'. But this creative energy is always in tension with a drive towards stasis and inertia, which Freud understood to be a desire for death.[4] Brooks takes these two mutually implicated forms of unconscious energy and shows them operating in narrative plotting.

Then he goes on to argue that reading plots which enact these Freudian dynamics must be understood as a form of transference, in that the reader's unconscious patterns and motivations are being channelled through the operating framework of the literary text.[5] Narrative is structured upon erotic energy and the drive to death. In this way, reading reformulates subjectivity in that transference acts out unconscious desires. Readers experience their sense of self through the process of understanding the novel. Such an absorption of Freud into narrative analysis ties in neatly with the reader-response theory of Wolfgang Iser. One of Iser's notable ideas is that reading provokes a stream of images in the reader which are subject to influence from unconscious structures and drives. He too, argues that reading reconstitutes subjectivity through contact with a Freudian unconscious.

Since two of my six writers, Margery Allingham and Ruth Rendell, deal explicitly with Jungian psychology, it is worth considering how the Freudian model might be modified by Jung's rather different conception of the unconscious. Jung does not reject the Freudian Oedipus complex or repression, but his unconscious is distinctively creative and autonomous due to inherited structuring principles called archetypes. Archetypes are not inherited ideas or concepts, but are the potentials for image formation and meaning. They are androgynous, plural and multiple and can only be represented by their culturally inflected derivative,   archetypal images. The Jungian model of subjectivity is goal-oriented; the unconscious is proactive in creating more and more complex connections with the ego. Yet what might appear to be a psychic process of ever greater unions is complicated by the 'shadow', an archetypal process of undoing and destruction. The shadow is the opposite of how the conscious ego tries to define itself, so it is often imaged as darkness, evil or death.

Through these theoretical divergences, we could see a Jungian model of narrative desire taking a familiar Freudian structure, but with significant differences. The goal-directed nature of unconscious activity strengthens the notion of reading as intimately pleasurable because it is contributing to the evolution of the subject. Eros and the death drive are better described in Jungian terms as subjective patterns of romance partnered by tragedy, as the unconscious becomes a more creative partner in the dialogue with the ego.[6] Similarly, reading can be linked to analytic transference as with Freud, but the unconscious is understood to take a more active and playful role.

An example of the application of these psychoanalytic conceptions of narrative and the reader can be found in what I have described as the romance or comedy element in the golden age writers. The reconstitution of society that concludes Christie's and Marsh's work in particular, usually symbolised in a projected marriage, can be understood as the prevalence of Eros even within the literal enactment of the death drive. Indeed, I think it is even closer to a Jungian notion of romance inseparable from tragedy, where a creative *romantic* restitution must accompany the tragic shadow's murderous shattering of established social and familial relationships. Now to a psychoanalytic consideration of 'death' in crime fiction.

The psychoanalytic model: parody and death

Parody, it has been noted, seems intrinsic to golden age detective fiction.[7] I want to link this insight to the Freudian-Jungian psychoanalytic model to argue that the golden age crime fiction of Christie, Sayers, Allingham and Marsh parodies the death drive. Death in these fictions is a problem that is 'solved'. It is re-solved, re-narrativised as unnatural. The un-beloved victim whose death is revealed to be not inevitable, as 'artificial', stands as a metonym for death itself. Golden age fiction *accounts for* death in its parodic form that operates here through unconscious fantasy. Many of the novels betray a sense of that fantasy in their self-referential or 'playful' tone. For example, exhumation to prove that death is, in Sayers's *The Unpleasantness at the Bellona Club*,[8] unnatural, *solvable*, is called 'resurrection'. Of course, there is no total closure in these parodic fictions. There always remains some motivation or passion not wholly accounted for. The fantasy of overcoming death can only be maintained *as a fantasy*, as 'play'. We remember that fantasy is structured in relation to a 'lack'. Here the lack of closure in these parodic novels; the inability to tie up every narrative possibility, is the precondition for the fantasy of overcoming 'death'. Parody, self-referentiality and conscious artificiality are necessary, since inter-pretations cannot be fixed.

These novels do not allow psychoanalysis itself to be a consistent and complete explanation for desire and crime. Their 'playfulness' is at the same time a challenge to claims of secure knowledge of human motivation. Parody of death fulfils a readerly fantasy of simultaneously enacting and overcoming the death drive. Sayers places Peter Wimsey at the margins of this narrative in that Wimsey's war neurosis is unable to banish the death drive for long. This aspect results in the tragi-comedy inherent in Sayers' work.

P.D. James and Ruth Rendell place their writing in a dialogue between golden age referentiality and realist fiction, evident in their suspension between a fantasy of overcoming the death drive and its fulfilment. Here also, romance partnered by tragedy can be an apt motif. Wexford manages to sustain the psychic romance of his familial relationships by separating them out from the tragedy that he finally structures through his investigations. The murder stories he uncovers offer the fantasy of 'solving' death, but the fantasy is unsustainable within the arena of revealed Gothic passions. Rendell deploys the Gothic to bridge the divide between golden age parody and a realistic depiction of death as irretrievable. James, on the other hand, tends to limit the way romance can connect characters to an internal psycho-logical dynamic. For her, the consolations of psychoanalytic romance are explicitly and overwhelmingly countered by death in metaphorical as well as literal forms. Instead of a murder investigation operating as a fantasy to close off this death from society and history so making it (and metonymically death itself), solvable, James opens up the murder through the investigating process to narratives of social breakdown, conservative theologies of intrinsic evil, and historical atrocity. James's fiction forces the reader to acknowledge as unsustainable the fantasy of 'accounting for' death in detective fiction, and serves to reify the death drive or tragedy at the expense of eros or romance.

The psychoanalytic model: the reader's self

In Chapter 2 I suggested that a crucial factor in the work of these six authors was a psychoanalytic structure of reading in which the detec-tive operates as a focus in guiding the reading consciousness through-out the novel. To look at this further we can make use of another psychoanalytic and specifically Lacanian term, the mirror stage. This occurs when the child is discovering his/her own boundaries by reflect-ing a developing sense of him/herself as separate from an-other. This complex process of self-construction can be understood as identifying bodily limits through an image in a mirror, or though something or someone acting in a 'mirror-like' way for the evolving consciousness of the child. Reading a detective story is to engage in a conscious search for knowledge with which to orient oneself to the world of the novel. In this way the reader, already heavily involved in transference in the release of unconscious desires, is re-enacting the mirror stage. Through the person of the detective, the reader searches for clues and signs, leading to criminal and innocent identities to 'make up' the boundaries of a meaningful world in the novel. Through processing the detecting story the reader experiences the construction of boundaries of self, in the interpretation of signs as well as in the fantasy of overcoming death, and in the limitation of that fantasy.

Detective fiction allows the exploration of unconscious fantasy, so providing the addictive pleasures of re-imaging, re-imagining the mirror stage. The pleasure of constructing provisional selves through seeking and testing clues allows the reader to experience identity as unfixed and playful because these novels cannot produce totally closed and secure forms of knowledge. Some questions of motivation or desire always remain provisional. Indigenous to Barbara Vine's crime fiction is the exacerbation of the lack of closure in the types of knowledge available to both reader and her detecting figures. *A Dark-Adapted Eye* ends with the reader offered mutually incompatible histories of murderer and victim where the mystery is not 'who?' but exactly what forms of mothering murderer and victim competed for over the same child.[9]

Let us now look at psychoanalytic models in more detail, if not as *closure*, then as a shaping of narrative form. We will see psychoanalytic theory affecting the depiction of passion, crime, the detective's methodology and social and gender strategies.

Psychoanalysis in crime

Characters of all six authors suffer from Freudian or Jungian 'relations' in the sense that these theories offer the most satisfying models of the intensity and desire to be found in these novels as trauma and crime. Peter Wimsey's shell-shock has already been alluded to. More ominous forms of relationship seem susceptible to Freudian understanding in Christie's *Appointment with Death*, where a truly 'terrible' mother inspires atavistic notions of human sacrifice.[10] Like Christie here, P.D. James appears concerned to limit the possibly radical implications of psychoanalytic theories of desire. Yet the moral scrupulousness of James's work does entail an exploration of familial intensities and a portrayal of desire as complex in the generous Freudian sense, not limited to the crudely sexual. Two 'incestuous' families in *Death of an Expert Witness*[11] contribute to the murderous matrix of personal, professional and familial relationships without being a simple 'cause', while an erotic but unsexual sibling relationship in *Devices and Desires*[12] contains a similarly delicate provocation to murder.

Ngaio Marsh is the most convinced adherent of Freudian theory, and even parallels Inspector Alleyn with a female Freudian children's therapist in *Final Curtain*.[13] Although the novel and Alleyn belittle Caroline Able's efforts, her diagnosis of father fixation and Oedipality afflicting the murderous yet outrageously theatrical Ancred family is finally conceded. Both Margery Allingham and Barbara Vine dip into Jungian theory to portray irrational, dysfunctional families. An eccentric uncle erotically obsessed with a niece he wrongly accuses of obscene letters is described as having 'anima' problems by Albert Campion in *More Work for the Undertaker*.[14] The 'anima' is Jung's term for a male's unconscious feminine side, here clearly sexual and wanton, as the underside of the restricted scholarly life led by the elderly man. Vine's *The House of Stairs* builds its Gothic plot on Jungian theory: Bell functions for narrator, Elizabeth, as dark shadow and erotic trickster, initiating unconscious desires. Maternal, loving Cosette is explicitly said to be the 'self ', the Jungian archetype of wholeness, fulfilled identity and desire.[15] The 'house' of the title is dominated by a massive spiral staircase, a typical Jungian mandala form, suggesting both unconscious initiations and the potential to reach the unconscious 'self'. Typically, Vine takes a Jungian structure of subjectivity and views it through Gothic passions by accentuating the interweaving of romance/tragedy: the dangers of erotic desire mingled with the pleasures of criminal fantasy.

In effect, psychoanalysis can be used to help understand crime and murder in these novels, but for no one author is it a full and sufficient explanation: it cannot provide that form of closure. This reflects the tension in psychoanalytic theory itself between its 'popular' consumption as a narrative decoding all deviance as merely sexual, as simply *caused* by incestuous fantasy, and the conception of psychoanalysis as a radical form that problematises such simple deciphering. Interestingly, the six authors reflect this dynamic, in that popular versions of Oedipal anxieties explicitly infuse some family narratives but are never used as forms of narrative closure, as pure and complete motivations for crime. Criminal desires are shown principally to be structured around material gain, lust for power, fear and revenge, and, particularly for Ruth Rendell, are crystallised through class deprivation.

The closest the six novelists come to accepting a popular Freudian motivation for murder must be *Singing in the Shrouds* by Ngaio Marsh. Here a male strangler of women is diagnosed by the young romantic doctor as having suffered a traumatic Oedipal moment in early childhood.[16] Yet this doctor, however briefly, has been a suspect, while the detective, Alleyn, maintains a thoughtful detachment from this 'solution'. If psychoanalysis is a possible but never a wholly sufficient narrative to map desire and crime, then maybe the methodology of the 'taking cure' might aid the beleaguered detective?

Detectives: analysts, mirrors and doubles

In Chapter 2 I suggested that these six authors' detectives combined two forms of detecting which were structurally but not intrinsically gendered. Collecting of material evidence and formal interrogations are structurally associated with the masculine because of their embodiment in the law and police force. 'Other' unofficial forms of knowledge are more relational in that they not only partake of desire between detective and suspects but are also intuitive responses which could be linked to the detective's own unconscious processes. Conventional culture has constructed relational, intuitive forms of knowledge as feminine. In this sense the detective becomes paralleled to the analyst, typically a 'masculine' medical role of power, but making use of subjective models of knowledge traditionally assigned to an inferior, feminised position.

All six authors offer suggestive examples of the psychoanalyst in the detective. This may occur through the detective's own methods of questioning, his 'talking cure' for crime, his own self-analysis of internal trauma, or his own transference to victim, suspects, or even murderer. Even a mutual transference may occur. Such mirroring or doubling problematises the binary structure of the detective as promoter of law and stability versus the criminal as harbinger of chaos.

Christie, Allingham and Marsh all explicitly parallel their detectives to psychoanalysts as investigators of criminal desire. In both *Appointment with Death* and *The ABC Murders*,[17] Poirot is aided by an analyst and demonstrates his detecting methods to be complementary but not identical. Like an analyst, Poirot finds talking to suspects the key, and also seeks inconsistencies and slips of the tongue. Unlike the fictional analyst he is not restricted to popular conceptions of Oedipality with which to pinpoint guilt. Albert Campion frequently tries to practise analysis upon himself, sure that his unconscious has grasped more than he himself knows. *Death of a Ghost* finds him indebted to his unconscious as it tries to protect the drugged investigator.[18] Marsh's Roderick Alleyn, gains much from feminine suspects' erotic attraction to him but also practices word association in works such as *Artists in Crime*.[19]

Like Albert Campion, Adam Dalgliesh and Reg Wexford often have to analyse their own psychic traumas as part of sleuthing. In *A Taste for Death*,[20] Dalgliesh's detecting motivation is psychically represented by his involuntary subjection to a mental image of the bloody chaos of the murder scene. This traumatic symptom haunts his psyche, superimposed upon his recollection of the measured beauty of the chief victim's Soane house. Dalgliesh's determination to decontaminate the lovely building by finding a crime narrative to separate the two settings cannot succeed, since the Soane household proves intimately involved. James's pessimism that romance can suspend the death drive as destruction and chaos is again fulfilled. Wexford in *Kissing the Gunner's Daughter* is also haunted by traumatic repetition of the murder scene.[21] Like Dalgliesh he seeks a narrative explanation to exorcise its hypnotic power, but unlike James's hero he does not aim to eradicate its disturbing influence on an emblem of conservative social order (see Chapter 2).

Detectives complicate their analytic roles when involved as mirrors or doubles of suspects or victims. As well as Gill Plain's valuable exposition of Wimsey's doubling relation to both Bunter and Harriet Vane,[22] we have in *Clouds of Witness*[23] his 'mirroring' of chief suspect-cum-victim, his brother Gerald, Duke of Denver. This doubling complicates the distinctions between detective, police and suspect on both plot and psychic levels. Campion's later police colleague, the charismatic Charley Luke, is significantly doubled in the equally fascinating master criminal Jack Havoc in *The Tiger in the Smoke*.[24]

Campion possesses a double as a sign of an unconscious alter ego in the magnificent Magersfontein Lugg. This beast of a man clearly represents Campion's repression of aristocratic identity, physical refinement and ambiguous relation to the law in being physically gross, a lower-class snob and an ex-con. Sign of excess in all directions, Lugg remains a key player in Campion's detecting, and is a nurturing figure when Campion is maimed. Another figure of detecting 'maternity' is Roderick Alleyn, who needs no double as he is persistently mirrored erotically by female suspects. Sustained by romantic energy, he speaks of 'going broody on the case' with his 'other' in detecting, Inspector Fox, whose only permitted eros is in questioning female servants too low-class for

Alleyn. As a figure of maternity, Alleyn again returns to the role of analyst, here as receiver of transference. He is able now to decipher the evidence as forms of analytic talk in which true motivations are veiled. The crime becomes a traumatic symptom traceable to concealed desires. Alleyn gives birth not only to the 'solution' but to new erotic relationships structured through his transferential investigations (see *Opening Night* later).[25]

It is typical of Adam Dalgliesh that he exhibits fastidious moral evaluation when finding himself mirrored in such investigative subjects as the chief victim of *A Taste for Death*. Investigation here not only indicts rather than 'cures' modern society but also delineates Dalgliesh's psychic flaws.

If psychoanalysis illuminates some of the relational forms of knowledge engendered by the detectives, then it is time to consider the social implications of such psychic investigation.

Psychoanalysis in society

In the first instance, the six novelists' works are critically concerned with the exploration of the feminine in society through psychoanalysis. In demonstrating awareness of Freudian theory, these crime fictions often provide challenging rereadings of psychoanalysis's construction of gender. Secondly, psychoanalysis can demonstrate how criminality could be linked to a disruption of a psychosocial contract, or, to put it another way, the inability of an individual to operate psychically in the symbolic order of his or her culture.

Regarding the feminine, Agatha Christie can be more radical in her use of psychoanalytic tropes than Alison Light allows when she notes accurately the political pessimism evoked in descriptions of the unconscious in *Appointment With Death*.[26] As well as Poirot's valuing of female intuition as sensitivity to unconscious observation in *Dead Man's Folly*[27] and in *The Murder of Roger Ackroyd*,[28] the battle between sceptical Miss Marple and apparently gullible Carrie Louise in *They Do It with Mirrors*,[29] is highly suggestive of feminine power in the symbolic (the social codes of society). The plot of *They Do It with Mirrors* appears designed to ridicule nurturing feminine Carrie Louise's belief in the devotion of her family. However, Miss Marple's discoveries not only validate Carrie Louise's assurances of love but prepare the reader for an eerie and phallic description of Carrie Louise's voice going 'through you like ... a sword'. Miss Marple's vindication opens up a feminine space in the symbolic of the detecting story (see more in Chapter 6).

If the 'lack' in psychoanalysis of a female phallus clarifies processes in *They Do It with Mirrors*, then *Sleeping Murder*[30] is built upon a woman's initial trauma, diagnosed by Miss Marple as a repressed memory based on violent events rather than as any hysteria based on a fantasy. This act of detection puts Freudian theory in reverse by going back to Freud's original conception of feminine trauma in *Studies on Hysteria*.[31] Where Freud redefined hysterical symptoms not as the scars of real abuse but as unconscious fantasy, Miss Marple refuses to follow the masculine authority's change of diagnosis. Hysteria can also be a matter of 'history', such as the concealed murder that Miss Marple goes on to uncover. For Dorothy L. Sayers, Freud in *Gaudy Night* can only pathologise the feminine and is not a useful guide to isolating criminal abnormality, as Peter tells a distraught Harriet, who fears that she is staying in a 'Freudian University'.[32]

More specific to cultural implications is the interweaving of the symbolic, society and desire in both crime and detecting plots. Not only does Ngaio Marsh depict desire as intrinsically 'theatrical', but her detecting plots almost invariably culminate in a police reconstruction of the crime which reveals the murderer in a form of traumatic re-enactment. Not for Margery Allingham, however, Christie's marginal, momentary emergence of a feminine phallus as beneficial. *Look to the Lady*[33] is driven by the necessity to eradicate a phallic woman. Her usurpation of masculine powers is incarnated in the plot in her role as the leader of a criminal gang dedicated to stripping England of the nation's occult feminine powers in the form of a sacred chalice.

P.D. James describes two conceptions of time in *Devices and Desires*: first, linear time linked to technology, phallic power and the role of nuclear energy on the lonely headland, and secondarily, circular time linked to female martyrdom. The murderer violently combines a 'circular' perception (in the sense of owing a death for a past rescue from a sexual trauma) with the linearity of killing in time and history. Such a psychic gendering of time is reminiscent of Julia Kristeva's argument in 'Women's Time'.[34] Kristeva links the feminine to an understanding of time as circular, eternal or monumental due to women's intimate involvement with reproduction, while the masculine symbolic is focused upon historical linear time. Similarly, in Ruth Rendell's *A Judgement in Stone*,[35] a female killer is dislodged from historical time and unable to manage a psycho-symbolic contract with society, here because she is illiterate. Her incomplete entry into the symbolic order means that she is unable to comprehend social relationships and is, ironically but terrifyingly, not subject to 'normal' class oppressions.

For Dorothy L. Sayers, Peter Wimsey encounters the criminal interpenetration of the social symbolic in *Murder Must Advertise*[36] when narcotics, by law distinct from legitimate business such as advertising, is discovered to be continuous with it. In plot terms, an advertising agency is revealed as cover for a drug ring. Wimsey simultaneously diagnoses the inflaming, narcotic effect of advertising on desire in the social-symbolic.

Reflecting upon psychoanalysis

As part of their rhetorical and playful nature, golden age writings comment explicitly on the arrival of psychoanalysis as a cultural phenomenon. Since psychoanalysis is never allowed to dominate totally in any one novel (or closure would result), it produces a theatrical language of desire. It is one mask (perhaps an apt one, but still a mask) which characters and detectives use to both represent and decipher strong feelings. Alleyn detects 'Freud without Tears,' punning on a popular comedy of manners,[37] Christie's Miss Marple proves correctly sceptical of the Freudian Dr Maverick's facile identifying of Oedipal crime in *They Do It with Mirrors*, while Sayers mounts a campaign against the potential of psychoanalysis for abusing the feminine in both *Gaudy Night* and *The Unpleasantness at the Bellona Club*.

What golden age crime fiction does is to question the legitimacy of psychoanalysis functioning as a cultural authority claiming to explain all crime and deviance. Roderick Alleyn puts it succinctly in challenging the hermeneutic methods of Freudian Caroline Able:

> Your professional training teaches you that behaviour is a sort of code or cryptogram disguising the pathological truth from the uninformed, but revealing it to the expert. Mine teaches me to regard behaviour as something infinitely variable after the fact and often at complete loggerheads with the fact.[38]

It is undeniable that psychoanalysis offers valuable training for the detective as well as the literary critic in deciphering tales of fantasy and deviance, and in tracing readerly pleasures. These six authors need also be situated in the tradition of women's writing commenting critically upon the influence of psychoanalysis in culture. As narrative arts searching for boundaries to identity and desire, detective fiction and psychoanalysis share the need to forge dramas out of their own sense of knowledge in crisis.

The Hollow by Agatha Christie (1946)[39]

This novel provides an instance of a classic country house mystery intimately bound up with desire, time and nostalgia. 'The Hollow' is the house inhabited by Sir Henry and Lucy Angatell, to which they invite soon-to-be-victim John Christow, his drab wife, Gerda, and his mistress and sculptor, Henrietta. Also included in the house party are Edward, who pines for Henrietta, and Midge, an impoverished relative who pines for Edward. During the weekend, an old flame of John Christow's arrives to 'borrow matches'. After escorting Veronica home, John is discovered shot and dying by the swimming-pool the next morning, just as Hercules Poirot arrives for lunch.

All characters, including the victim, are revealed to be so psychically bonded to the past that it constitutes a traumatic threat to their sense of identity. Sir Henry is an ex-colonial governor who discovers that his wife is prepared to kill John in order to secure the male line at the beloved ancestral home of Ainswick. The Angatell family, including Lucy, Edward, Midge and Henrietta, are emotionally and psychically bound to the country house era idealised *as past*, as Ainswick, which formed a setting for a golden childhood. The past as desire is the 'problem' that the novel tries to address. 'The Hollow' is revealed *as* 'hollow,' as a mere echo of Ainswick hollowed out by unsatisfied desire. Psychic conflict becomes metaphorically represented by murder in a novel which explicitly cites Tennyson's Maud.[40]

Artist Henrietta condemns her relations as mere 'echoes' of that country house childhood dream. She prefers the vitality of John Christow, a research doctor devoted to his career in London. However, John starts the novel afflicted by traumatic flashbacks to what he involuntarily calls 'home'. Despite Henrietta functioning as his psychoanalytic mirror and analyst by assisting him through 'a talking cure' for his research problems, John remains psychically in thrall to his unresolved affair with Veronica until the night she arrives at The Hollow.

John's erotic return to the past heals his psychic wound, but initiates his murder. The matrix of desire, nostalgia and trauma which becomes realised in the crime can be most clearly articulated by referring again to Julia Kristeva's description of gendered relationships to time. John Christow admirably demonstrates the masculine commitment to time as linear history in his devotion to science and 'progress', but he needs to develop an unconscious relationship to what Kristeva calls 'women's time', the reproductive sense of time as both circular and eternal or monumental. Both Henrietta and Gerda exhibit a traumatic confinement to women's time only. Like Lucy, Edward and Midge, Henrietta's psyche is damaged by her bonding to the past as Ainswick and childhood, but she is also a creator of monuments of art. Her final action of mourning for John is to embark on a sculpture; an activity depicted as a neurotic inability to enter linear time and move forwards. For Gerda, the mother of John's children, he functions (we are told by the novel) as her god, suspending her in reproductive and monumental time. She is similarly unable to encompass the linear and cope with John as unfaithful because that would mean envisaging a past different from a possible future, and the severing of her idolatrous passion.

The romance of Midge and Edward is a more fortunate therapeutic counter to the murder of John via unresolved gender traumas in relation to time. Although Midge starts paralysed in desire for Edward as an emblem of Ainswick as golden childhood, her position as a downtrodden working woman at least gives her the strength to be exasperated by Edward's psychic confinement in past social realities. They become engaged, but Midge then breaks it off, fearing the erotic persistence of Henrietta for Edward. The novel makes it clear that Henrietta stands for imprisonment in the past for Edward, not a possible entry into linear historical time nor any possibility of re-producing himself. Trapped in women's time, Edward's masculinity is so devitalised by comparison to vibrant John Christow that he attempts suicide. Midge saves his life, not only physically, but explicitly by structuring a psychic rebirth for him. Both enter linear time by being enabled to envision a transformed *future* for themselves at Ainswick while Edward, reborn as Midge's child, reconfigures their traumatic temporal relations. Edward looks up from the gas oven to see Midge as past, present and future for him (p. 177).

The Hollow represents the investigation of desire as nostalgia, where the past is the psychic 'home'. In revealing nostalgia for colonialism and the aristocratic country house as socially and psychically dangerous, murderous, suicidal and enervating, the novel has it both ways by being deeply critical of the social worlds it depicts. However, the exploration of psychic bonds to time and history show the interpenetration of gender, desire, art, colonialism, ambition and sexuality, all in the proximity to criminal fantasy. Murder, of course, repositions the victim. No longer the energetic inhabitant of linear existence, John *Christ*ow becomes an imitation of 'Christ', as a sacrifice to the psychic conflict between gender and time.

The Unpleasantness at the Bellona Club by Dorothy L. Sayers (1928)

The Unpleasantness at the Bellona Club opens with Captain George Fentiman describing the club to Lord Peter Wimsey as a 'morgue'. This proves more than usually apt upon the discovery that George's aged grandfather, sitting in an armchair, is in fact dead. It is the evening of Remembrance Day, and First World War veteran George betrays his war hysteria at the end of the chapter.

> 'Take him away!' said Fentiman, 'take him away. He's been dead two days! So are you! So am I! We're all dead and we never noticed it.'
>
> (p. 9)

This is a novel about the dead hand of the past suffocating the living. The past is war in George Fentiman's shell-shock and, behind him, that of the sleuth Wimsey. During the course of investigations George suffers breakdown, a split personality and hysteria, causing him to assume the guise of his grandfather's murderer. Old General Fentiman could be a war casualty in this sense. Additionally, the first mystery is that of the moving of the corpse after death, again early assigned to George's war neurosis. In fact, the deed is traced to his phlegmatic war veteran brother, Robert, who is sufficiently hardened by his traumatic experience to make use of the sacred two minutes' silence.

The novel centres on this question: can the detective narrative free the living from the grasp of the dead; metonymically, can it free them from death? Embedded in this narrative drive is the subsidiary question: can psychiatry and Freudian analysis free the living from the dead?

To take the detective plot first of all, the threat is encapsulated by the narrator's comment on the presumed natural death of the General: 'The planet's tyrant, dotard Death, had held his grey mirror for them for a moment and shown them the image of things to come' (p. 12). So can the detective narrative redeem death and offer a more consoling, if parodic, mirror? Why, certainly, the General is metaphorically and explicitly 'resurrected' in the novel's term for exhumation. With the resurrection of the corpse comes the discovery of murder and the removal of death from the mirror of grim necessity to parody. On one level, the word 'resurrection' is Sayers's citing of her Christian 'explanation' (of which more later); on another it is an emblem of the parodic nature of the genre.

Yet, this is no simple redemption. George Fentiman's neurosis is inflamed by the investigation, and he nearly fulfils his role as war casualty. Fortunately, he survives to allow the critic to redefine his experience as traumatic re-enactment which may prove therapeutic. The real murderer nobly commits suicide rather than entangle the innocent Ann Dorland. Wimsey, therefore, escapes the role of executioner (a spiritual Fall into becoming a killer), but his repeated identification with George suggests that the psychic burden has been displaced onto the suspect, just as the role of war victim is displaced onto a carefully staged corpse in a gentleman's club. There is one further point where the detective's powers threaten to fail, and that is the matter of the feminine. Ann Dorland remains the unquestioned suspect for much of the novel; the object of the detective's quest to know and solve. When it appears by logical deduction that she must be part of the murder plot, Wimsey demurs on the grounds that it is 'too mechanical'. It is Ann as the feminine who is similarly problematic for Freudian theory.

George Fentiman is threatened by the detecting activity as far as his sanity and his life is concerned – should his hysteria be interpreted as guilt? Fortunately, he is recovered by an alternative narrative of psychiatry. He is diagnosed as ill rather than guilty or suffering from diabolic possession – all possibilities mentioned. His repeated identification as 'hysterical' links him to Freudian ideas, whereas Ann Dorland is subject to 'misrepresentation' through Freud. The doctor uses Freud to accuse Ann of 'a mania about sex' (p. 219), where she is said to be 'gibbering', a contrast to George's more dignified description of 'muttering'. Whereas Wimsey before accepted a vague designation of Ann as having 'complexes', he now decides that Ann has been cruelly exploited by a doctor employing Freudian terminology to misrepresent female sexuality as pathological. The murderer as doctor is a direct challenge to the cultural power of Freudian theory substantiated in the male analyst/female patient structure. The novel reflects critically on psychoanalysis' diagnosis of femininity.

In fact, it offers three possible explanations of criminal deviance: the murdering doctor's biological 'glands', Christian original sin, and Freud. Significantly, none are wholly endorsed. 'Glands' are marginalised by the uncovering of the murderer with economic motives; original sin is not the diagnosis for George (he is not possessed); and Freud is not safe for the feminine in a society with too many opportunities for patriarchal oppression. Yet the reader might well conclude that, properly applied, Freud could have some value, especially for hysterical George. Death's grey mirror gives way to the mirror of the detective narrative, which allows the reader to form a constructed but not fixed identifying of knowledge and truth. No one explanation is shown to be wholly satisfying. *The Unpleasantness at the Bellona Club*'s defining feature is the transformation of the narrative structure of death into parody: death from old age into 'resurrection'. The endorsement of and challenge to Freud is intrinsic to the parodic nature of the novel, since it needs to convert Freud's death drive to one narrative possibility amongst others. Psychoanalysis can illuminate energy in the plot and the pleasure of reader while being itself the object of the novel's critical scrutiny on social and gender grounds.

Flowers for the Judge by Margery Allingham (1936)[41]

Margery Allingham anticipates P.D. James's *Original Sin* by setting her murder at a publishers.[42] The death of partner Paul Brande is revealed to be both traumatic repetition and plagiarism. The method is copied from a manuscript and the novel is eerily haunted by the unexplained disappearance of another partner, Tom Barnabas, 20 years before.

Albert Campion's task is to shore up a society whose phallic symbolic conventions are shown to be crumbling. Not only is the social order corrupt in the form of the publishing firm (for one of the inmates must be guilty of the poisoned corpse in the locked strongroom), but the law here is fallible since it devotes all its official energy in this novel to the trial of the sympathetic young lover, Mike Wedgwood. He is the beloved of the victim's wife, Gina, and is believed by Campion to be innocent. Finally, 'the Word' itself has been hollowed out by crime to an empty sign. First the murder is shown to be a form of plagiarism, so breaking down the generic boundaries between a fiction novel and society's conventions. Secondly, the motive is revealed as bound up with the founding text of the whole firm. Their one treasure, a handwritten, unpublished manuscript by Congreve, is revealed by the detecting plot to be a worthless fake. The Congreve manuscript is the founding phallus that has failed. Like the fantasy phallus in the symbolic of society, it existed in relation to a lack (as long as it was unread), as a fantasy. When disturbance in the symbolic, here crime, leads to the need to invoke the phallus as a stabilising power, it remains a fantasy but now is *known* to be a fantasy. The word as book and authority has vanished. What remains is the fake, now without social potency.

Campion's detecting career in *Flowers for the Judge* functions within the gaps in social-symbolic as a co-opted member of the commercial family. Campion is a friend and supporter of Mike and Gina, and is therefore shown to have more aptitude in detecting the psychic complications of this crime than the detached policeman relying on the 'neutral' gathering of material evidence. One problem with Campion's intimate emotional relation to the suspects is that he risks changing places with the murderer. Once he identifies the true criminal, Campion's intuitive detecting leaves him with insufficient evidence to satisfy the law. Only the death of the murderer will provide proof, so will Campion take on the murderous position in order to restore the social-symbolic contract? Campion is apparently saved from what Freud might argue would be a re-enactment of the founding of society by the murder of the primal father,[43] by the apparently fortuitous death of the perpetrator.

Yet what is finally revealed to have occurred is the re-investment of the symbolic from its most despised margins. Richie Barnabas is the most humble member of the firm and family, dysfunctional in social role, unambitious and unassertive in sexuality. It is he who articulates a frequent Allingham motif that the corporate life of business and capitalism is a form of slavery. When Richie disappears after the death of the murderer and the romantic restitution of Mike and Gina, he is unmourned. His evacuation from the symbolic proves a true repetition of Tom Barnabas's vanishing, for Richie has joined his relative in the circus, where he is witnessed by Campion in the clown's role of Lord High Executioner. The true defender of the social-symbolic has been marginalised. Campion has solved the murder but Richie has solved the social 'problem', by killing the murderer before vanishing to the circus. Richie has carried out his repressed role of Executioner of Paul's murderer at the price of relinquishing symbolic identity altogether. The circus where Richie has no stable name or identity functions as a semiotic pre-Oedipal structuration, excluded from the social-symbolic, but which nevertheless shores it up, as the narrative demonstrates in this crime plot. Always marginal to masculinity, Richie sacrifices his tenuous relation to the phallus.

Flowers for the Judge depicts the symbolic order as unable to guarantee subjectivity (the wrong man is condemned for much of the novel), without violent sacrifice from the extra-symbolic. Despite the condemnation of capitalism as slavery, the novel is uninterested in reconfiguring history (as progressive 'left-wing' desire for change), but dips into a semiotic realm to re-invest a patriarchal order simultaneously portrayed as oppressive. This oppression is integral to Campion and his anti-Bunter butler, Lugg, as well. Both Campion and Lugg are characterised as hysterical in this novel, due to the social pressure of Campion's potentially aristocratic entry into the symbolic. There is a constant threat that Campion's family is going to force him to take up a purely upper-class non-marginal role. Campion's ambivalent detecting persona is clearly designed to evade an aristocratic 'birth' that will fix his identity in a carapace of status and phallic power.

Opening Night by Ngaio Marsh (1951)

Unlike Allingham, who stresses the death drive and sacrifice, for Marsh the psychoanalytic initiation into the symbolic is dominated by the erotic and is viewed as a beneficial *theatrical* staging of identity.

Opening Night begins with its protagonist, Martyn Tarne, wandering alone in London. She is introduced as a placeless, historyless, moneyless, gender-ambiguous character. The reader's orientation in the story is structured through Martyn's developing self. We trace not only the murder's crystallisation of patterns of desire, but also Martyn's own history and her psychic reconstitution of her identity through her encounters with a theatre company. She (and the reader) will experience detecting Alleyn as (m)other figure in birthing her identity in relation to murder suspects. This is followed by Alleyn's role as phallus in assigning 'secure' knowledge and loss in naming the murderer. It is significant that the murderer is an author as well as authority figure. As in *Flowers for the Judge*, an authorising text (the company's new 'play') is under threat from charges of plagiarism. Martyn, a New Zealander newly robbed of all her funds, functions also as a metonym for the colonised consciousness in relation to the (m)other country in London.

The detecting plot of *Opening Night* is a metaphor for desire articulated through the staging of the self as theatre. Near starvation, Martyn is taken on at the Dolphin Theatre as a dresser to leading lady Helena who is at the end of a long-running love affair with leading man and director Adam Poole. Martyn's uncanny resemblance to Poole provokes comment. She is really an actress and, it becomes obvious, is far more suitable for the key role of Poole's twisted young relative in a forthcoming premiere than the current incumbent. This unfortunate lesser talent is the hysterical niece of Helena's drunken, jealous husband. The metonymic continuity of surname, 'Poole' and 'Tarne', gives credence to the thinly veiled accusations by other actors that Martyn may be Adam's illegitimate child. Martyn finally admits that she is a cousin of Poole's and has not wished to presume upon their relationship. Her talent is recognised and she is given the understudy of the crucial role, only to have to perform when the other actress breaks down on the opening night. Martyn's triumphant entry into the symbolic order of the acting company is marred by the simultaneous murder of Helena's abusive husband and the arrival of Inspector Alleyn upon the disordered stage.

The crime plot deploys Martyn, her name significantly gender-ambiguous, to play out a Freudian version of her desire which will gain for her an explicitly constructed and theatrical identity in relation to a masculinised symbolic. Her first initiation into the theatre is spectral as she sleeps alone in the eerie building, but for a watchman who is ambivalently positioned as both paternal guardian and possible sexual threat. However, Martyn's eros is soon engaged by Adam as a potentially satisfying mirror. At first, she is a ghostly revenant beside his portrait, then she engages in Oedipal playing when she may be (to the reader as well) his illegitimate daughter. Finally she enters legitimacy and the symbolic as a fellow actor and lover. Adam functions as the erotic mirror, or pool(e), to constitute Martyn's entry into the symbolic and to gender her as sexually feminine in relation to his position as the representative of phallic power. Significantly, in the company's 'play', Martyn has to embody a perverted feminine 'mirror' to Poole's character on stage.

Yet entry into the symbolic involves psychic splitting and repression. The liberation of psychoanalytic eros into sexual romance between Martyn and Adam simultaneously constellates the death drive in the form of the murder. Drunken Clark is murdered just as Martyn becomes her 'self' in taking up her desired social role on stage. Thereafter, the detecting narrative is required to complete the negotiation of Martyn (and also the reader) into the symbolic. Alleyn will operate as the (m)other who explicitly goes 'broody' over the case and who will at last enable Martyn to complete her Oedipal relation to the appropriately named patriarch, Adam, as her father/lover.

Any potential hysteria in the detective is of course displaced onto the narrative focus of Martyn, allowing Alleyn to migrate seamlessly from broody (m)other to phallic functionary in assigning guilt and innocence. Although Martyn seems to conduct her mirror and Oedipal machinations with aplomb, the plot bestows upon her the failing actress, Gay, as a disintegrating double whose rapid psychic decline is the precise reverse of Martyn's construction of self. Another dark side to Oedipal romance is embodied in the murder victim, who becomes the lover as rapist threatening the psyche of the older woman, Helena. Indeed, feminine vulnerability seems neurotically insisted upon by the novel. Is the sexual assault on Helena a negation of any possibility Martyn might have of structuring a self in relation to the feminine as well as, or instead of, the masculine? The star actress as potential mother is violently displaced in favour of Alleyn as (m)other. *Opening Night* is a novel aware of patriarchal violence, but still erotically entranced by phallic power. Only its portrayal of identity as theatrical, erotic and psychic is suggestive of 'other' fantasies of crime and desire.

An Unsuitable Job for a Woman by P.D. James (1972)[44]

Like Marsh's Martyn Tarne, P.D. James's protagonist Cordelia Gray is the reader's narrative focus substantiated by a psychic connection to a police detective, Adam Dalgliesh, and to a figure in the case, here murder victim Mark Callender. Unlike Marsh's novel, *An Unsuitable Job for a Woman* records the failure of the police to restore the symbolic order of society. Social-symbolic recuperation requires the resources both of the crime fiction genre and of Cordelia as a *private* detective, who becomes the feminine agent of the fallible phallus embodied by the police. The reiteration in the novel of private detection as 'an unsuitable job for a woman' makes gender a recurrent issue, but paradoxically Cordelia's final position is to fulfil the role of her Shakespearean namesake at the outset of King Lear, to 'love and be silent'.[45] Her most potent action with regard to the symbolic of the police is to keep family secrets in the interests of a love and justice that the law is shown not to comprehend.

Cordelia Gray is contracted by Sir Ronald Callender to investigate the apparent suicide of his ex-student son, Mark. Uncovering the traces of murder, Cordelia pursues investigations amongst his student friends in Cambridge and within the Callender family. She discovers that Mark has suffered a double maternal deprivation, once in the early death of Ronald Callender's wife and twice in his recent realisation that she was not his mother after all. Cordelia's detecting becomes a narrative of dual identification: she finds her orphan self increasingly mirrored in sensitive Mark as she wears his clothes and sleeps in his bed, but her detecting methodology is taken more and more from the lore of Adam Dalgliesh, the mentor of her unsuccessful partner, Bernie Pryde.

The suicide of Bernie Pryde opens the novel, reinforcing the failed paternal function in Cordelia's life. Through her detecting, Dalgliesh takes on this role. Cordelia inherits from Bernie not only the detective agency but his gun, as a metonym for detection wedded to the symbolic phallus. The subsequent murder of Mark's killer with this gun results in Cordelia's loss of the weapon, but she gains instead her first face-to-face confrontation with its symbolic power in the person of Dalgliesh. Through identification with Mark, Cordelia realises that the crime victim has been the casualty of economic patriarchy; his castration has been literalised as murder. Can Cordelia redeem Mark by making good his double loss of the maternal, by saving his biological mother as she comes to realise he would have wished? Cordelia ends up in opposition to Dalgliesh because she is trying to embody the role of Mark's (m)other while phallic law demands revenge for the death of his father. This is not the action of the feminist in a simple literal sense, since Cordelia protects the mother through psychic identification with Mark, by becoming *his* (m)other, not through sisterly loyalty.

In order to restore phallic potency, *An Unsuitable Job for a Woman* then has to fall back on the generic preference for murderers not to go free. The plot disposal of Cordelia's protégé forces her to complete her Oedipal stage. She moves from a rather negative identification with the castrated mother (in her assumption of the position of (m)other to a dead child) to an emotional identification with the father as Adam Dalgliesh. His role as the legitimation of her professional identity as a detective is brought into the open and mutually acknowledged. However, the novel does not completely eradicate a feminine disruption of the phallic symbolic: the disruption is transferred to the psyche of Dalgliesh. Cordelia satisfies the phallus in the corporate body of the police in that as a feminine detective she has comprehensively failed. The reader knows better, and Dalgliesh intuitively realises that Cordelia has used his own methods to seek out and preserve the erotic crimes of the Callender family. Cordelia reveals to Dalgliesh his own potential doubleness, his gendered self-divisions from the patriarchal requirements of his job which here seeks vengeful answers about the death of a powerful yet brutal man. Although Cordelia is dismissed by the social symbolic as inept, the resources of fiction and femininity have undermined the claims of the phallic function to control and secure all meaning: knowledge is also feminine, psychically constructed, relational. It may be located in those who can only 'love and be silent.'

The Veiled One by Ruth Rendell (1988)[46]

This novel deals explicitly with Jungian theory and the social-psychic intensities of the psychoanalyst. Not only is an analyst a significant character in the plot, but the analytic relation is structured as intimately connected to criminal fantasy and so contingent to crime.

After the murdered corpse of a female home help is found in the multi-storey car park of the new imitation castle shopping centre, Wexford and Burden's investigations focus on a dysfunctional mother and son, Dodo and Clifford, both proximate to the crime scene. Wexford becomes distracted by a serious injury when his favourite daughter's car is blown up with himself instead at the wheel. Burden unsuccessfully interrogates Cliff for the murder, which initiates a further killing. Such a violent repetition unveils a family dynamic of Gothic proportions and enables Wexford to solve a further series of murders.

The novel is obsessed with the term 'client', which stands both literally and metaphorically for a series of social and professional relations. These are gradually revealed to be open to exploitation and corruption. Wexford worries about the evacuation of meaning of the word 'client', for instance, when the failing client relation between Cliff and his Jungian analyst, Serge Olson, has a degraded counterpart in the activities of a magazine agony aunt, providing opportunities for blackmail. Wexford's legendary 'otherness' to the phallic function, his intuitive questioning of convention and unthinking police methods, is also corporeally represented in the plot when he becomes a feminised injury victim, a literal substitute for the perennially rebellious Sheila. This temporary 'castration' perilously leaves upright Mike Burden to pursue his excessive desires of becoming identified with the paternal phallus as the law. His excess of zeal so destabilises the interrogation of the 'other' as suspect that Burden becomes an analytic mirror to unstable Cliff. Indeed, once he senses that he has become a psychic mirror for Cliff, Burden feels himself psychically fragmenting, in danger of *becoming* Cliff in a paranoid dissociation from the symbolic-social contract.

Analyst Olson is able to explain to Burden, Wexford and the reader that Cliff has formed a transference relation to Burden as interrogator-cum-analyst. Despite Olson's attempts to reclaim his professional role with his 'client', Burden the policeman cannot restore his detective-social relation to the suspect. Denied psychic transference to Burden, Cliff enters the symbolic order of police law by killing his (m)other – he really does murder his mother. His literal interpretation of the Oedipal metaphorical exchange will brand him, will *name* him in the social symbolic forever. Horrified, Burden realises that Cliff's psychic identification has caused him to assume the role of murderer that Burden's own obsessive desires have constellated. The intolerable 'burden' of guilt is somewhat shifted by the novel refocusing on relations to the feminine or Jungian anima, 'the veiled one', as the novel describes her.

The Jungian anima is not an objective portrayal of femininity, but is the projected feminine of the masculine psyche. She is veiled because she is the unknowable other as a blank screen upon which the masculine images his desire and terror. Wexford fears that the bomb attack on Sheila is for her *performance* of a patriarchal (m)other, an anima of adulterous, murderous deviousness in her acting role in a play. For the hapless Cliff, the veiled anima is his mother, the (m)other he kills for the paternal function, incarnated for him in Inspector Burden. This threatened breakdown in the symbolic relations with the feminine is what, fundamentally, the detecting narrative has to encompass and try to limit. Wexford discovers that the apparent violence directed towards Sheila as anima is, in fact, an attack upon the law. Sheila's barrister boyfriend was the intended target. The death of the anima in Dodo is narratively and generically 'solved' by converting this failed Jungian romance into a Gothic family saga.

The Veiled One makes use of Jungian romance where Jungian theories of transference, counter-transference and the anima literally *animate* the plot. Dodo's past history as a servant marrying into an upper class family is seen through this veil as a 'romantic story'. However, the failure of the analytic relation to operate in its allotted place in the social-symbolic means that Jungian theory stops functioning as a *container* of desire in therapy. It operates instead as a means of *representing* desire as deviant, erotically murderous and Gothic. Jung wrote: 'through our unconscious we live naturally and unconsciously in a world of were-wolves, demons, magicians.'[47] Jungian theory becomes a means of re-investing the symbolic in Gothic terms: Dodo's 'family romance' is unveiled as a Gothic plot of revenge, desire and murder in a sinister, blood-splattered dwelling.

6
Gothic Crimes: A Literature of Terror and Horror

Why does Roderick Alleyn refer to himself as a werewolf?[1] How can we understand Reg Wexford's claim to be possessed of near supernatural powers,[2] and why do both Lord Peter Wimsey and Adam Dalgliesh appear to re-enter the terrifying machinery of *Wuthering Heights*?[3] To track these uncanny spectres in the writings of the six authors, it is necessary to explore the twilight territory of the literary Gothic.

The Gothic tradition is both a specific event in literary history, stemming from the novels of horrifying apparitions in the late eighteenth century, and the characteristics of a response to literary problems of boundaries and taboos, the borders of knowledge, belief, representability and culture.[4] As a literature of excess, the Gothic problematises knowable categories of law and transgression. Although Gothic texts usually offer forms of closure that recuperate social norms and conventions, they are nevertheless bound by their intrinsic exposure of the terrifying contingency of social fictions. The Gothic shadows modernity in that it explores what is repressed or ignored by the social privileging of reason, consciousness, masculinity, materialism and the law. Therefore, the Gothic is a literary inheritance of anxiety concerning transgression and cultural limits, including issues of class, sexuality and definitions of the 'real'. It is a perpetually insecure attempt to 'map' unfixable borders of desire, identity, psyche and knowledge.

From their initial location in late eighteenth-century novels, Gothic terrors were imagined through wild mountainous landscapes, decrepit, haunted castles, evil aristocrats, mysterious spectres and a chorus of monks and nuns. Through the virtuous endurance of a pair of innocent lovers, evil and chaos could be finally banished and externalised through the restoration of a conservative social order. In the nineteenth century, the Gothic travelled more to the interior: to 'England' in both moorland and the metropolitan city, to domesticity in its eruption within the bourgeois family, to the feminine in fears of gender and sexuality, and to the psyche itself in the horrific productions of doubles and internal spectres. As the fear of modernity extended to science, technology and the city, so the nineteenth-century Gothic breeds a new kind of ambivalent hero in the detective as a frail phantom of potential social order. This figure focuses the narrative desire to construct a path through the terror and horror of Gothic transgressions.

Native to eighteenth-century Gothic aesthetics are notions of terror and the sublime.[5] Terror, in the Gothic sense, signifies the psyche-enlarging fears engendered by notions or events that are unrepresentable in full, or which evade classification and 'mapping' in the human mind. This is the Gothic sublime, in which terror expands the sense of self and the sense of what potentially can *be*, or what potentially can be known. Nineteenth-century Gothic writings, Fred Botting argues, are more characterised by 'Gothic horror' in which there is an aghast recoil effecting the erosion or near-annihilation of the sense of self. Horror is particularly occasioned by dead bodies, by the conception of death as the absolute limits of the human. Gothic horror functions as the negative sublime.[6] Both terror and horror work in a complex manner in Gothic fictions. The sublime is the possible annihilation of categories, as the permeability of limits of the self. In this, the sublime is suggestively subversive of cultural norms, but can also be employed to mystify and reinforce conventional powers. Horror, similarly, can mark the borders of ideas and beliefs in ways that can be progressive or reactionary. The six authors produce a literature that bears a strong imprint of nineteenth-century Gothic horror, but which also seeks out the resources of the Gothic sublime. They also use the fully Gothic methods of parody and intertextuality (the conscious reference to other literary works), which are embedded in the genre from its genesis. If the Gothic deals with the terrifying possibilities of the collapse of boundaries, then novels themselves are no longer virginal bodies.

Additionally, one anxiety-provoking destabilisation native to Gothic is the social and psychic representation of the past or history. The past, presented as nightmare, needs to be understood in the context of fears of rapid social change, of revolution, modernity and technology. Where once the divine or demonic threatened the individual self, now modernity or technology is an alien invader. Botting argues that twentieth-century Gothic attempts to affirm the individual, to make it sacred in a horrified reaction to scientific encroachments. This drive is certainly perceptible in the writings of these writers, but the Gothic is also used to represent a haunting ambivalence about the detective as an individual agent of justice.

Parodic castles and Gothic settings

The scenes of crimes for the six authors often evoke a Gothic lineage, which serves to destabilise the belief that conventional social norms will be sufficient to restore order. Even Agatha Christie suggests the mysterious moorland territory of *The Hound of the Baskervilles* in her short story 'The Idol House of Astarte', a very early case for Miss Marple in *The Thirteen Problems*.[7] Dorothy L. Sayers makes a London club into an eerie morgue when its most ubiquitous inhabitant is discovered dead in very strange circumstances.[8] More sustained is the thickening atmosphere of Harriet Vane's college at Oxford with its 'poltergeist' and anxieties about 'walled in women'.[9] *Busman's Honeymoon* is set in a feminised country house described as having 'a lovely body inhabited by an evil spirit' (p. 82).[10] Once detecting and the Wimsey marriage have banished this 'spirit', then Harriet is taken to the ducal home, Denver, when she meets friendly ghost, Old Gregory, and hears of other domestic spectres.[11]

At this point *Busman's Honeymoon* enters what Avril Horner and Sue Zlosnik have defined as the 'comic Gothic', in which the supernatural 'other' is recuperated into the text to foreground laughter and sexuality.[12] After the uncanniness of Talboys is revealed as the residues of crime, the Vane–Wimsey marriage is sacralised within the aristocratic family by Harriet (but not the snobbish duchess, Helen) being permitted to share its otherness. Here, aristocratic otherness as domestic ghosts is momentarily comedy. Earlier detective novels record, with Gothic unease, reactions to Lord Peter's aristocratic literary heritage.

For Margery Allingham, early works openly deploy Gothic aesthetics in a horrified reaction to corporate modernity. *The Crime at Black Dudley* takes place in an ex-monastic 'ghostly old house'[13] in which a scholarly heir introduces his guests into an aristocratic ritual that assigns guilt and blood. Unsurprisingly, the Gothic trappings destabilise the boundaries between archaic warrior identities and a modern gang of corporate criminals. This occurs before the Gothic proves to have been on the side of justice and individuality, firmly allied with conservative social values. Later, Allingham often transports the Gothic to a city setting. *The Tiger in the Smoke* confronts an efficient killer, Jack Havoc, with an unworldly clergyman, Canon Avril, in an echoing city church.[14] Here the architecture comes to stand for the canon's spiritual authority, which significantly mitigates the brutal material power of a serial killer.

Ngaio Marsh is a devoted exponent of the parodic Gothic as theatre. In *Final Curtain* a theatrical family dwell in an outrageously over-the-top nineteenth-century parodic edifice, named 'Katzenjammer castle' by its most camp inhabitant.[15] Even in her country houses, the overtly artificial gatherings of mutual enemies are often confined by inclement weather that suggests the collapse of 'natural' categories. In *Death and the Dancing Footman*, the winter-bound inmates are confronted by a 'vast nocturnal whispering' and snowflakes like 'fleets of small ghosts' (p. 62).[16] Barbara Vine is similarly fond of the Gothic in nature. Those driven by extremes of desire in *Gallowglass* hurry through a countryside where trees 'were skeletons with blue bones'.[17]

Most deliberately referential with her Gothic settings is P.D. James, with her cloister-like Victorian Gothic house in *Shroud for a Nightingale*,[18] the horrifying re-invention of the evil castle as the nuclear power station in *Devices and Desires*,[19] and the sustained examination of Gothic architecture in *The Black Tower*.[20] In this latter work, the tower is first referred to as a phallic symbol, and hearing of its gruesome history in the horrifying self-immolation of its progenitor, we are told that the tower stands for the persistence of suffering and death.[21] While the tower functions as the laying bare (unveiling) of the significance of the phallus in the symbolic order (the structuring of time, limits, death), such a textual unravelling of the sources of Gothic horror does not prevent it from retaining a position as the point of threatened collapse of boundaries (see Brontë Gothic later). In fact, the citation of the Gothic is the most literary strain in James's dialogue between nineteenth-century novel realism and the golden age genre. Ruth Rendell is also deeply indebted to the Gothic, but her settings such as the mock Gothic castle in *The Veiled One*[22] (see Chapter 5 above) are particularly implicated in her critical concern with class and power. It is time to look at the uncanny nature of the detective him/herself.

Gothic detectives: the spectral and the horrified

Hercule Poirot's obsessive tidiness defeats the Gothic. His well-groomed boundaries permit no excesses, unless his spherical shape and luxuriant moustache can be viewed as comic transgression of the limited English prejudices which his expertise constantly defeats. Miss Marple, on the other hand, is introduced to us in *Murder at the Vicarage* as 'uncanny'.[23] Her narrative impact never loses a Gothic polarisation between icon of overlooked elderly femininity and avenging 'nemesis', the title of one of her later adventures.[24] The portrayal of Lord Peter Wimsey needs to deal both with an ambivalence towards an individual dispenser of justice and death (in an era of capital punishment) and with the Gothic stain of the aristocrat. There are, I would suggest, two layers to Wimsey's Gothic inheritance: first, the Gothic warrior/killer is articulated through Wimsey's war trauma and secondly, there is a deeper layer of knight erranthood and the legacy of feudalism. Such potential darkness has to be worked out in relation to the feminine, and it takes several detections with Harriet Vane to do so. However, the process of exorcising Wimsey's feudal Gothic inheritance is also anticipated and encapsulated in the relatively early *Clouds of Witness*, as I shall show later.

The urbane Roderick Alleyn would appear to be an unlikely candidate for monstrous incarnation, but his detecting intuition is described as a 'familiar demon' in *Vintage Murder*.[25] Here also, he proclaims his identity as a werewolf by telling an astonished porter, 'It's my night to howl'. Alleyn is additionally subject to out-of-body experiences in moments of detecting stress. At these times he feels himself to be his own ghost, and this uncanny experience is crucially linked to the expansion of his powers of mind in detection. The transgression of physical boundaries formulates the Gothic sublime *within* the act of detecting, as here in *Overture to Death*:

> His body was a stranger to his mind and he looked at it in wonder. He stood as if in a trance, alarmed at meeting himself as a stranger, yet aware of this experience which was not new to him. As always, some part of his mind tried to step across the threshold of the unknown, but was unable to give purpose to his whole thought. He returned to himself...
>
> (p. 271)[26]

Albert Campion's Gothic disguises are less spectral and more determined by his ambivalent identity with regard to the law. The early novels refuse to place Campion within secure limits as either villain, saviour or potential killer in the causes of his friends. Later novels show the detective's Gothic identity through doubles.

Ruth Rendell's Reg Wexford comes intriguingly close to Roderick Alleyn in the spectralisation of his detecting powers. In *A New Lease of Death* Wexford is credited with 'an extra uncanny sense that almost amounted to telepathy',[27] while in *No More Dying Then* Wexford tells Burden of his detecting intuitions as 'almost supernatural sensations'.[28] These intimations of the Gothic sublime in the detective are developed most elaborately in *The Speaker of Mandarin* when Wexford, travelling in China, is haunted by the apparition of a little old Chinese woman.[29] Fearing for his sanity, Wexford is later relieved to attribute some of his psychic disorder to copious amounts of green tea, some to reading M.R. James ghost stories, and later still, some to illegal activity in his travelling party. Here, the terrifying Gothic sublime lies in the temporary annihilation of categories of knowledge. Detecting does restore the categories, but this sublime is not simply the 'other' to be excluded from the detecting narrative. Rather, the Gothic persists *within* the detective's superior mental powers to both collapse and reorder categories of knowledge and belief.

If some of the six authors' detectives penetrate the Gothic sublime in their efforts, then others are peculiarly subject to Gothic horror. Even Reg Wexford experiences the archetypal horrific situation of being '[b]ricked up ... like a bloody nun'[30] when trapped in a police station lift; surely a metonym for how police rigidities may stifle him. This momentary feminisation of Wexford as Gothic victim also stresses his border transgressions in gender terms. His less imaginative and determinedly conventional colleague, Mike Burden, violates typical Gothic boundaries of life and death when subject to peculiar horrors that defeat his professionalism. Tormented by grief for his dead wife in *No More Dying Then*, Burden is described as 'like a Zombie', while his role in provocations to murder in *The Veiled One* similarly collapses borders between his inner self and outer events.

> Burden's face had that look of a man who has seen indelible horrors. They are stamped there, those sights, but showing themselves in the staring eyes and taut skin as the skull inside the flesh reveals itself, a symbol of what has been seen and a foreshadowing of the future.[31]

Cordelia Gray is another detective horrified in ways that demonstrate an erosion of boundaries between a professional detachment and her investigations. As part of her growing identification with the victim in *An Unsuitable Job for a Woman*, she experiences 'fascinated horror' when confronted with a hanging effigy *because* it elides linear time by conjuring up the original murder scene with a new immediacy to her psyche.[32] P.D. James's works prefer Gothic horror to sublime terrors because her art is concerned with human limitations in a godless society. For other writers, the sublime is not only a possible mode of representation in the detective's quest for knowledge, but may also be inherent in desire and its plots.

Looking for the Gothic sublime: plots of terror and horror

The lack of closure in the crime plots of Barbara Vine novels allows a sense of the Gothic sublime to haunt these novels. Vine's sublime is not unmixed with horror, and is intricately concerned with family dynamics and obsessive passion. *Asta's Book* centres on the attempt by a descendant to reconstruct the story of Swanny, mysteriously adopted daughter of the prolific diarist, Asta.[33] Swanny's sense of identity is heavily compromised by the late and incomplete revelation of her adoption. In old age, the disturbed Swanny unconsciously simulates the imagined personality of a possible origin: that she is the child who disappeared after the murder of one parent, probably by the other. This expansion of self is described as both horrific and sublime in being a reaction to even greater unknown horrors. Yet the novel closes with a more typical Vine sublimity concerning motherhood. Swanny's origin and the ancient murder case are solved by close reading of the diaries. The final, unknowable, unrepresentable moment is that of Asta's maternal joy at Swanny's arrival. Writing down such feelings is essential to Asta, but so is the destruction of these pages to signify the ultimate incommunicability of such intimacy. Both *A Dark-Adapted Eye*[34] and *A Fatal Inversion*[35] end with a similar sublime mystification of motherhood, tinged with terror at the murderous impulses engendered by its passions.

For Agatha Christie, the Gothic sublime can be a threatening state which detecting is meant to map and recuperate. *The Sittaford Mystery* is dominated by the initial séance held by the suspects which seems supernaturally to announce that a murder has occurred.[36] Such a sublime spiritual intervention in crime is kept as a narrative possibility until late in the novel. In the short story 'The Idol House of Astarte', the sublime is never entirely dissipated, for the down-to-earth explanation given by Miss Marple still allows the narrator to ascribe evil influences to the eerie grove where the imitation of pagan rites appeared to conjure up occult powers.

In Dorothy L. Sayers's *The Nine Tailors* the mystery of the means of murder, coupled with the corpse's reputed aspect 'as if he'd looked down into hell', structures a terrifying sublime which slides inexorably into horror as Peter Wimsey experiences for himself the frail limits of the human frame in nearly meeting the same fate.[37] More complexly, Peter Wimsey enacts an ironic sublime detecting identity in setting up his own ambiguous double, Death Bredon, in *Murder Must Advertise*. Here, the expansion of self is refracted into near-disintegration before the detective can 'advertise' his selves and invent new borders in society.[38] Wimsey takes on the spectral identity of the harlequin in order to investigate the drug trade. He enters a Gothic world of horror in which all boundaries threaten to collapse into death: 'a place of bright flares and black abysses, whose ministers are drink and drugs and its monarch, death.'[39]

Like other writers, Margery Allingham's plots slide most typically into Gothic horror, particularly in her distaste for modern capitalist society. Nevertheless, the sublime can be found in the neo-comic plot of *The Case of the Late Pig* in which a corpse is buried twice and twice strangely disappears.[40] However, comedy is banished by the criminal revelations pushing the novel into Gothic horror.

The Gothic sublime can be traced in the plots of Ngaio Marsh in her attraction to otherness as occult or non-Western religions. These feature strongly in novels such as *Death in Ecstasy*,[41] *Dead Water*[42] and *Spinsters in Jeopardy*[43] as points of contestation between sublime psychic energies and horrific assaults on the self through drugs or bogus beliefs. Only when the religious sublime is 'colonially' non-Western, in particular the New Zealand Maori, does the sublime come to persist as territory in which the detecting restitution of conventional anglocentric boundaries may not trespass. Additionally for Marsh, Troy Alleyn's art functions as the sublime other to her husband's investigations. Her skills are depicted as unexplainable uncanny insights into characters and events. Troy's sublime role and the post-colonial Gothic sublime chime together at the conclusion of *Photo-Finish*, when she is given the evocative lines assigning the landscape to non-human paradigms (see Chapter 4 above).[44]

Although P.D. James's work is characterised by a devotion to Gothic horror as a representation of psychic sterility in a society which abandons the divine, she does allow a moment of the Gothic sublime to a motherless child in *Devices and Desires*. Catholic Theresa summons the spirit of her dead mother by candlelight in abbey ruins that 'looked unreal, ethereal, an insubstantial edifice of light which would dissolve at a touch'.[45] Tenderness for bereaved or unhappy children is a feature of James's work, softening her pessimism about human relationships. This rare moment of Jamesian Gothic sublime is a point of stillness, a benign fusion of categories in a novel threatening to erode linear time in the repetition of horrific martyrdoms.

Use of the Gothic to destabilise categories of time and history is a device of all six authors, but a particular preoccupation of James. The Gothic ambivalences of the detecting process now needs to be considered in relation to the past.

The nightmare of the past and history

The major task of the Gothic for P.D. James is to allow representation of past atrocities in the detecting genre, in particular those associated with the Second World War and the Holocaust. The Gothic achieves this by collapsing categories of history, and of past and present, until such unmappable horrors become part of the psychic residues of the crime immediate to the investigation. *The Skull Beneath the Skin* offers a peculiarly clear model of Jamesian Gothic and Second World War horrors.[46] Cordelia Gray arrives at an innocent-looking castle on an offshore island to guard a threatened actress.

The castle possesses a truly Gothic, dual-layered past. In the first place, the original feudal family died out after contracting the plague in an act of revenge from the father of a girl brutalised, raped and murdered by the lord. Rising from the sea like a monster, the father, deformed by the disease, stormed the banqueting-hall. Skulls from these plague victims adorn the underground chambers like 'a descent into the hell of the past', Cordelia thinks.[47] Secondarily, in the depths of the castle there is a ladder leading down into the sea where a German prisoner of war was left to drown horribly by his fellows after accusations of collaboration. This immersion in Gothic horror serves as a prelude to murder that features the usual golden age restricted group of suspects. Fearfully gathered at night, suspects and detective are transfixed by the traumatic repetition of the vengeful beast from the sea.

> Silhouetted against the moonlight reared an immense form…As they gazed in fascinated horror…The gaping mouth, raw as a wound, seemed to suck at the window…Then the creature gathered its strength and heaved.[48]

These echoes of Frankenstein's monster signal the return of the Gothic: it is Munter, the butler, revealed to be the son of the very same tortured prisoner of war. Gothic literary conventions allow the representation of Second World War atrocities through a repressed, psychic return. Most often for James it is the Nazi Holocaust that returns; in the euthanasia policies Gothicised in *Shroud for a Nightingale*, in a killer driving a van around Cambridge 'as if he were transporting recalcitrant students to the gas chambers',[49] in *An Unsuitable Job for a Woman*, and in a museum mummy recalling the dead at Belsen in *A Taste for Death*.[50]

None of the other writers develops a Gothic aesthetic of history so passionately. Allingham conjures up Victorianism and colonialism as Gothic horror in *Police at the Funeral*, when the past as Victorian family mores is oppressive and crime-ridden, while the past as colonialism returns as a 'simian' half-caste invader.[51] The racist structure underlying the actively repressed but inevitable return of the 'colonial' family member in *Police* emphasises the way the Gothic destabilises boundaries between subversive protest and reactionary (here racist), demonisation. For Dorothy L. Sayers, Gothic realisations of the past and history centre on Wimsey's war hysteria and feudal overtones (see later on *Clouds of Witness*). Ruth Rendell's persistence in Gothicising the bourgeois family serves to examine family histories as an unstable arena in which borderlands between past and present, as well as those between genders, sexualities and class, become psychically renegotiable in Gothic forms of representation. Both Rendell and Vine use literature to insert the Gothic into conceptions of class and desire. In *The Best Man to Die*, the male corpse is discovered as a grotesque return of a Tennysonian 'Lady of the Lake', anticipating the detective's investigations of the passions of masculine comradeship.[52]

Since Ngaio Marsh's relation to British history is complicated by her colonial identity, it is unsurprising for her Gothic to take on an aura of self-conscious mimicry. For Marsh, Gothic pastness resides in theatrical camp, perfectly encapsulated by the outmoded self-conscious theatricality of the Ancred family in *Final Curtain*. The murder of Sir Henry, a hyper-theatrical actor in all his most genuine emotions, allows a self-referentially 'fictional' Gothic past to be celebrated in the investigation of camp emotion. The parodic and camp young heir tells Alleyn: 'Observe the peculiar flavour of Katzenjammer Castle ... The terrifying Victoriana within. The gloom. Note particularly the gloom.'[53] Past aristocratic manners are mocked, seen to be a matter of 'theatricals', and thereby are reinstated in conservative comedy. The Gothic's famous ambivalence proves capable of simultaneously signifying the self-conscious artificiality of golden age crime fiction and serving as a means of conventional recuperation.

It is now useful to consider how Gothic parody can become a more direct re-imagining of key Gothic female writers.

The Gothic feminine: six queens and Brontë Gothic

Five of the six writers deliberately re-investigate and restage the female Gothic novels of Charlotte and Emily Brontë. Agatha Christie, Ngaio Marsh and Ruth Rendell rewrite *Jane Eyre*,[54] while both Dorothy L. Sayers and P.D. James explore *Wuthering Heights*.

Dead Man's Folly is Christie's offering to Brontë Gothic by reconsidering the position of Bertha Rochester in a novel which pre-dates Jean Rhys' *Wide Sargasso Sea* by ten years.[55] The murder plot allows Gothic forms to re-imagine the boundaries between the mad Creole wife and gentle Jane by portraying her as either victim or killer. Not only is the detective fiction made Gothic, but it reconfigures Brontë's work in ways that self-consciously examine feminine 'otherness' as oscillating between angelic and demonic.

Ngaio Marsh's *Death in a White Tie* focuses alternatively on the 'Jane' character as a 'haunted' society hostess is blackmailed by murderous figures who have proof of her bigamous marriage.[56] The blackmail victim tells Alleyn that her story has the Jane Eyre theme but 'I hadn't Miss Eyre's moral integrity'.[57] Instead, the sexual politics of the Jane Eyre–Rochester romance became displaced onto Alleyn's wooing of Troy. Others urge Alleyn to take a more aggressively 'masculine' attitude to Troy's diffidence, but he distances himself from 'a bit of Rochester stuff'.[58] A later hint of Alleyn trying the mode of the sexually dominant male leads him to draw back in a self-parody of masculine heroics: 'Your most devoted turkey-cock.'[59] It is Troy's 'moral integrity' which will be the principal means of their union. *Death in a White Tie*'s acute re-examination of *Jane Eyre* both criticises Rochester's 'Gothic' masculinity and endorses Jane's choices through the suffering of the deviant blackmail victim as well as in the moral strength of Troy.

Unsurprisingly, given Ruth Rendell's social concerns with class, her recasting of *Jane Eyre* in *A Judgement in Stone* focuses on Jane as *servant*, in the psychic damage of servitude and unequal access to education.[60] Rendell's Jane is Eunice: deformed and atavistic through illiteracy, she murders her social superiors at the significantly named Lowfield Hall, in an eruption of violence that is the Gothic shattering of seemingly impenetrable barriers of class and education. Eunice, 'like a great white ghost'[61] and nicknamed 'Miss Frankenstein',[62] is a truly Gothic product of both her social deprivation and her employer family trying to live in a past of leisure and servants. Similarly, Wexford momentarily dips into *Jane Eyre* when he is asked in *Simisola* whether he is looking for a 'mad woman in the attic' in his pursuit of an incarcerated black slave.[63]

Rendell's Brontë Gothic is deeply critical of class and racial oppression, in ways that both dispute Brontë's work and diagnose the subversive possibilities in the female Gothic itself.

As I shall show in my consideration of *Clouds of Witness*, Dorothy L. Sayers sends Peter Wimsey into a double visitation of Gothic literature: into Conan Doyle's eerie *The Hound of the Baskervilles* and Emily Brontë's *Wuthering Heights*. Like Wimsey, Adam Dalgliesh strays into *Wuthering Heights* from the point of view of Brontë's Lockwood, the urbane stranger keen to decipher romantic and murderous passions of a claustrophobic household. *The Black Tower* depends for its resonance on re-investing a self-conscious 'knowing' Gothic with horrific power through the crime plot. As I suggested earlier, the black tower setting functions as the phallus unveiled or as Gothic horror 'explained' as its signifying potency of suffering and death is openly debated.[64] However, Dalgliesh can still experience a moment of Gothic sublime in relation to the tower when he thinks he hears the scrape of bone against stone, the ghostly, self-immolated founder trying to escape: 'for one second he had crossed the border into the unknowable world.'[65] Realising a moment later that the sound is merely a bramble in the wind, Dalgliesh is nevertheless able to use this brief entry into the Gothic sublime to save his own life. He simulates terror to destabilise the murderer who has him at gunpoint. 'It came again as he prayed it would, the bone ends, piercing the torn flesh, scrabbling frantically against unyielding stone.'[66]

This repeated immersion in Gothic terrors is strongly reminiscent of Lockwood's dream in Chapter 3 of *Wuthering Heights*, when fear of a child ghost shut *out* causes him to rub her wrist on the window pane. The stone tower walls are no window, Dalgliesh is a Lockwood who is both *outside* and a far better detective, but I would contend that this scene functions as a truly Gothic re-imagining of the Brontë. It retains the 'ghost', the urbane stranger penetrating murderous horrors, the Gothic building in open country, the Gothic horror of the rasping bone, the divisions between inside/outside, psyche and material reality, life and death all made momentarily unstable.

It is highly appropriate to the differing imaginations of the two authors that whereas Brontë's spirit is 'outside', suggesting possibilities of a sublime expansion of self, James concentrates on a figure 'walled-in' an image of horrifying self-suffocation. In effect, James's collapses Brontë's own Gothic structures to re-imagine them in a detective fiction that wants to support the urbane visitor in his quest to reorder a Gothic-infused landscape. James makes Dalgliesh a Lockwood who succeeds by drawing upon his own and another's Gothic imagination.

The Gothic erodes the borders between detecting order and criminal chaos. The Gothic is also integral to the detective: it is part of his *means* to triumph and not just the external chaos he addresses.

The horrors of modernity

If the Gothic genre shadows modernity, then Margery Allingham is the writer of the six who most overtly embraces Gothic forms to repel and criticise modern capitalist society. Not a liberal author, Allingham often uses the Gothic to re-invest feudal motifs with uncanny, sublime powers. These ultimately serve to endorse, or at least nostalgically evoke, a more feudal aristocratic society in direct opposition to modern capitalism that is associated by her with corporate slavery and crime. The early *The Crime at Black Dudley*, *Mystery Mile*,[67] *Look to the Lady*[68] and *Sweet Danger*[69] all deploy Gothic representations, at first to evoke mystery and finally to endorse the 'magic' of the aristocracy, ultimately triumphing over criminal gangs as emblems of modern capitalism. Even when later works acknowledge the decline of aristocratic society in the modern city, such as the Gothic eccentricity of the Palinodes in *More Work for the Undertaker*, detecting locates essential corruption in the capitalist banking system promoting the horrors of atomic technology.[70] More comically, Charlie Luke serves as another attempt to Gothically invoke a feudal order in modernity when his marriage to a desiccated aristocrat is explained as suitable because he too 'has a manor' in his own metropolitan police district.[71]

Gothic spectres representing the horror of modernity and the fear of the extreme destructiveness of technology can also be found in works by the other writers. An horrific corpse in Marsh's *Dead Water* is imaginatively yoked to a nuclear battlefield,[72] while even Christie includes atomic spies as possible killers in *Dead Man's Folly*. Peter Wimsey is, of course, constantly haunted by the horrific actualities of technological modern warfare; a Gothic mode intensified in P.D. James's holocaust-Gothic art. Ruth Rendell, by contrast, seems to locate Gothic horror more in class than in reactions to technology. Her modernity is one in which outmoded class and gender structures make horrific and psychic returns through Gothic means of representation. The Rendell horror of modernity is of the persistent haunting of the present by the oppressive, exploitative past. These six authors demonstrate both the potency and ambivalence of the Gothic literacy tradition in their varying political and artistic attitudes to its spectres, its sublime horrors lurking in unmappable borders.

They Do It with Mirrors by Agatha Christie (1952)[73]

In this Miss Marple novel appears the ghostly outline of the mock-Gothic *Northanger Abbey*.[74] Austen's novel provides a naive reader of Gothic fiction, Catherine Morland, whose common sense is overcome by the Gothic architecture of the title setting. Unlike Catherine Morland, Miss Marple appears to travel sceptically to 'a sort of Gothic monstrosity...Best Victorian lavatory period' (pp. 28–9), but she resembles the much younger Austen heroine in misreading the Gothic indications surrounding the possible murder of the mistress of the house. Like Catherine Morland, Miss Marple's task is to disentangle Gothic fiction from a Gothic-inflected actuality.

Miss Marple visits elderly school friend Carrie Louise, now married to a patron of juvenile delinquents, Lewis Serrocold, and her family, truly Gothic in its excess of social conventions. Carrie Louise is an uneasy parent of her own daughter, repressed, widowed Mildred, but also possesses a stepson, a child of her adored dead, adopted daughter who has married a lower-class American, yet remains beloved of Carrie Louise's two 'sons'. These 'sons' are, in fact, also no blood relation but are the abandoned children of an earlier husband who deserted her. Such neo-incestuous passions are compounded by the presence of a disturbed young man, Edgar, periodically convinced that Lewis Serrocold is his father. Although the opening reference to architecture suggests parodic Gothic, this entangled ménage demonstrates a dangerous collapse of familial boundaries of identity and passion.

Unsurprisingly, theatre (the profession of several family members) becomes a means of animating Gothic potentials and staging a mystifying murder. After the unexplained arrival of financier stepson Christian, the disturbed Edgar threatens Lewis with a gun and appears to shout at him in a locked study. Although inclined to ignore Edgar's 'ham' performance as the desirable granddaughter, Gina, puts it, the police have to be called in when it is discovered that Christian has been murdered at that very moment. The Gothic staginess of the crime in the fog-shrouded mansion induces a Gothic atmosphere of fear and horror. Gina's ability to inspire uncontrollable sexual desires is particularly signalled in Gothic terms, in the 'Gothic gloom' as she is interrogated in the library and then outside when she meets her estranged husband in 'that eerie half light when objects lose their reality and take on the fantastic shapes of a nightmare' (p. 193).

In fact, the feminine as Gothic femme fatale in film noir mode proves not to be the key to the murder. *They Do It with Mirrors* is one of many novels where Christie's plots detoxify feminine sexuality as the unproblematic spur to crime. However, the resolution does turn on two feminine relationships to the Gothic. Carrie Louise, apparently all sweetness and gullibility about her tempest-tossed family, is proved to be a 'Catherine Morland' figure who, like her fictional predecessor, has some vitally correct intuitions about the true Gothic nature of her household. She not only proves right about the threats to her life but, seen through Gina's impressionable eyes, becomes suddenly expanded into a formidable Gothic personage at the tragic conclusion of the detection.

> Aunt Mildred said, 'They'll drown – they'll drown … and Grandam just said 'Yes' … I can't describe to you just how she made that one word sound. Just 'YES' and it went through you like – like a sword.
>
> (p. 208)

By realising that Carrie Louise's 'feminine' intuition is a sign of authentic powers (represented as uncanny and Gothic through Gina), Miss Marple learns to trust feminised Gothic insights in preference to the masculine order which keeps insisting on patronising and 'protecting' her friend. Miss Marple's late appreciation of Carrie Louise's feminine Gothic allows this detective to separate the previously eroded boundaries of theatre and crime. Again, the Gothic is both interior to the ratiocinative powers of the detective (even if displaced onto Carrie Louise) and the means of crime to be dissipated; categories of knowledge and illusion need to be re-founded through investigation. The chief criminal had wanted 'to be God', a bishop solemnly pronounces at the end. Such a monstrous usurpation of divine authority is represented as a perversion of masculinity through a Gothic theatre of crime. It is countered by Miss Marple's necessary animation of her own uncanny ambivalence as a detective. Her friend Carrie Louise functions as a theatrical spectre of Miss Marple's equivocal participation in a Gothic femininity.

Clouds of Witness by Dorothy L. Sayers (1926)

Peter Wimsey's geographical progress in *Clouds of Witness* is from a typically eighteenth-century Gothic setting in bandit-strewn Corsica to the more domestic nineteenth-century Gothic situated on the Yorkshire moors. Alerted by newspaper reports of the arrest of his brother, the Duke of Denver, for the murder of Denis Cathcart, fiancée of his sister, Lady Mary, Wimsey speeds to the moors to find familial bonds of desire in a dangerous state of complication and collapse. Unsurprisingly, the threatened family disport themselves in Gothic terms. Lady Mary is both theatrical and 'haunting' (p. 115), 'white as a ghost' (p. 109), and hysterical when Wimsey challenges her unconvincing alibi. Even the traditional distinction between detectives and suspects is under threat. Not only are Peter's emotions intimately bound up in the investigation, but his psychic involvement is Gothically displayed by a narrative threat of doubling between himself and his imprisoned brother. When Wimsey is vainly trying to persuade the duke to account for his whereabouts on the night of the murder, the two brothers confront each other in a momentary destabilisation of divisions between detective and chief suspect: 'It was as though each saw himself in a distorting mirror' (p. 157).

Such a Gothic erosion of boundaries in the detecting identity proves intrinsic to the crucial solution of the duke's alibi, not an exterior distraction. Wimsey's pursuit of clues is not scientifically rational, but rather here a Gothic meandering down 'an entertaining labyrinth of side issues' (pp. 79–80). It takes him to the farmhouse of Grider's Hole, where a stunningly desirable and abused wife ignites Peter's erotic desires in explicitly feudal terms: 'even in that strenuous moment, sixteen generations of feudal privilege stirred in Lord Peter's blood' (p. 83). The mystery of the 'Medusa' woman's intimate address to the bemused detective is not solved until Peter's second visit after his rescue (by first Bunter and then farm workers) from sinking into the local bog. After a night at Grider's Hole, Peter discovers an important letter of his brother's wedged in the window, so indicating both the duke's extramarital affair and the fact that family likeness had momentarily deceived the terrified woman. Gothic doubling in *Clouds of Witness* allows the detecting plot to explore fears of aristocratic feudality as sexual and class exploitation. Mrs Grimethorpe, the focus of masculine feudal desire, occulted by references to her as Medusa, does escape her violent husband, but Wimsey fails in the role as her knight errant. In fact, feudal sexuality imperils her and the pressure on the woman to come to the duke's aid in court nearly proves fatal.

Wimsey's double visit to Grider's Hole recalls both Conan Doyle's *The Hound of the Baskervilles* and Emily Brontë's *Wuthering Heights*. In Sherlock Holmes's adventures on a spooky moor, however much Gothic trappings haunt the tale, Holmes retains his scientific approach and avoids immersion, particularly in Grimpen mire, the bog which finally swamps the villain. By unfortunate contrast, Wimsey's tramp on the moors is less confident, beset by detecting impasses, and results in him getting lost and nearly meeting Holmes's villain's fate in the aptly named 'Peter's Pot'. The destabilisation between detective and main suspect is reinforced by Wimsey's near-imitation of the villain's fate in *The Hound of the Baskervilles*. In fact, Peter's progress is closer to Brontë's Mr Lockwood's mistakes, accidents and erotic musings than that of Sherlock Holmes's confident, rational detachment. It could be argued that *Clouds of Witness* disputes both earlier Gothic fictions, but in ways that prefer female Gothic problematisation of masculine heroism rather than the Gothic devoted to the eventual recuperation of a masculine and conventional social order. For Peter Wimsey's encounters with the Grimethorpe menage could be read as both a criticism and a re-imagining of Lockwood's introduction to Heathcliff and young Catherine.

While writing *Clouds of Witness*, Sayers denied aspirations 'to be the new Emily Brontë'.[75] This could suggest a scepticism of Brontë's Gothic masculinity at the back of her mind while composing the novel. Grimethorpe's blind, jealous violence is a highly critical version of Heathcliff's more complicated ferocity. Peter, in a Lockwood role, is both a vindication of the sophisticated stranger, bringing more civilised social possibilities, while being simultaneously a criticism of the urbane detective whose casual stirrings of desire may endanger a vulnerable woman without being able to effect a rescue. Like Lockwood, Wimsey considers himself as a potential saviour of the abused victim (when urging her to testify on his brother's behalf), but is similarly unable to do so. Instead, Wimsey himself (like Lockwood) is subjected to rescue from the metonymic and Gothic violence of the moors.

Clouds of Witness addresses the Gothic heritage of the detective in three ways. The doubling of suspect/detective allows a feudal stain of exploitative class and sexual predation to be explored and neutralised by the restoration of boundaries between Peter and the duke. Then the interrogation of the Gothic in detective fiction in *The Hound of the Baskervilles* with its superior sleuth, and *Wuthering Heights* with its incompetent bungler, places Wimsey on a sliding scale more towards the critical feminine Gothic of the Brontë work. Lastly, comparisons and contrasts with Lockwood offer an alternative model of masculinity to Brontë's bleak vision while also casting a sceptical eye on the role of male knight errant. The Harriet Vane novels will develop Sayers's critique of sexual relations based solely on the male as saviour-hero.

Look to the Lady by Margery Allingham (1931)

This novel is a bold blend of modern capitalist criminal gangs intertwined with a 'holy grail' Gothic romance. Its aim is to restore the Gothic sublime as an energy behind a conservative social order. To achieve this, the plot needs to neutralise the destabilising and subversive energies of the Gothic, which it does by clothing the distasteful criminals more and more in images of Gothic horror. In this way, the feudal order identified with 'England' can be stabilised with its sublime energies directed outwards to corporate crime as the perceived threat.

The story turns upon a ritualised feudality in the service of the state which sacralises the monarch at one remove through the aristocratic Gyrth family. The Gyrth Chalice is a sacred relic kept by the family dwelling in the aptly named Sanctuary village. Upon coming of age, each male heir is initiated into a secret ritual concerning the Chalice which also provides a concealed ritual dimension for the reigning monarch. Unfortunately, Albert Campion discovers that an unscrupulous criminal gang has been paid large sums to steal the Chalice, and they can only be stopped by the killing of their chief protagonist, soon revealed as a brutal woman, Mrs Dick.

The narrative of *Look to the Lady* works by separating out Gothic strands. At first, Sanctuary village appears as the undifferentiated abode of terror and horror. Gyrth heir, Percival (Val), is aghast at Campion's assessment that securing the Chalice means murdering the chief thief. Val's aunt, Diana, has provided cover for criminals by initiating a new age cult around herself as 'Maid of the Cup'. She soon dies mysteriously of fright. Lugg is precipitated into hysterics by meeting a 'monster' in the woods that he thinks is a guardian of the Chalice. Sanctuary proves to be a Gothic realm where boundaries of gender, class, sexuality, the natural/supernatural, and psyche have truly collapsed. Campion's pursuit of the criminals necessitates disentangling the Gothic traditions. It is significantly not his aim to banish the Gothic, but to secure and stabilise the Gothic sublime of the Chalice in order to shore up a neo-feudal social order in defiance of modernity. Lugg's 'monster' proves to be appropriately plebeian Gothic in the practices of a village witch provoking 'elemental horror'. Witchcraft is frequently Allingham's more subversive instance of the Gothic, since it is characterised as indigenous yet potentially dangerous to the aristocratic central family.

Gothic horror mutates into the horror of modernity as Campion is left with the gender-defying Mrs Dick at the head of the criminal gang.

Campion's task is to exploit his lack of absolute social definition (his own Gothic spectralisation), so that he can unite feudal England against the horrific capitalist forces of modernity personified in Mrs Dick. Monarchy in *Look to the Lady* is sublimely non-present in direct form. Instead, it is metonymically evoked in the Gyrth Chalice, itself transcendentally concealed until the end of the novel (but signified through impersonation by a fake). Additionally, monarchy is conjured up by Campion's enlistment of the gypsies through their royal chain of command.

Nevertheless, Campion's excursions into sublime manifestations of feudal power means that he cannot employ that creature of modernity, the law, against Mrs Dick. He is forced to contemplate 'execution': his Gothic activities prove unable to provide him with a secure identity as saviour of the Chalice that will not collapse him into a murderer. Fortunately for Campion, Mrs Dick, as representative of corporate modernity, is killed by her own Gothic horror when she, at last, glimpses the Gothic sublime of her goal: 'her lips drawn back over her teeth, her eyes wide and expressionless with fear' (p. 256). Horror at realities beyond her limited comprehension (of money and crime) defeat her boundaries and plunge her to death from the tower which she is climbing. Campion is therefore saved from killing. He is rewarded by a rare glimpse of the sacred Chalice and its mysterious guardian, gone beyond the borders of life and death. 'But there had been something more than mortal about this ageless giant, something uncanny which filled him with almost superstitious awe' (p. 275). The horror of modernity is literally expelled by both Campion's Gothic identifying of feudal, neo-occult forces and by the resources of the Gothic sublime assimilated to, and simultaneously sacralising of, the monarchy. Campion is a detective in the Gothic who mobilises its sublimity against modernity, capitalism and the city as the breeders of Gothic horror.

Off With His Head by Ngaio Marsh (1957)[76]

Like Campion, Roderick Alleyn can prove a Gothic detective. Investigating the inexplicable beheading of the chief actor, the Old Guiser, in a mummer's play performed at the winter solstice, Alleyn makes use of his favourite trick of re-enacting the crime. Just as the murder proves to be a simultaneous gruesome violation and fulfilment of the drama (since the old man is supposed to be symbolically beheaded and rise again), so the investigation's reconstruction detects the killer by completing the ritual. Alleyn puts in a substitute victim who does 'rise again', shocking revelations out of murderer and accomplice.

The mumming play, the 'Dance of the Five Sons', is performed annually by the Old Guiser, William Anderson, and his five sons with other local players. It is explicitly described as the survival of a pagan fertility ritual and remote prototype for Shakespeare's *King Lear* and is, therefore, a Gothic space. Here boundaries between theatre and religion, masculine and feminine in the man/woman figure the Betty, animal and human in the bird/horse 'actor', and familial bonds are re-negotiable. Marsh's achievement is to reinvigorate the Gothic potentialities of the mummer's fertility ritual through both murder and detecting plots. Borders between theatre and crime are blurred by the actual murder forming part of the dramatic action while Alleyn travelling through frozen England likens detecting to 'produc[ing] a thaw' (pp. 71–2). His reconstruction of the crime dramatically 'resurrects' the victim and restores social order through revealing the murderer. Detecting fulfils the dramatic ritual and so satisfies its fertility myth function of banishing winter: the thaw. The Gothic destabilisation between detecting and theatre, typical of Alleyn's methods here, becomes the collapsing of borders between detecting, theatre and sacred fertility myth so that the investigating plot reconstitutes the Gothic sublime.

Such a reinvigorating of the sublime in theatrical ritual is deemed necessary because the pre-murder story demonstrated the loss of potency of the 'Dance of the Five Sons' under pressures of modernity, although these are not formulated with the distaste of Allingham. Femininity and foreignness threatens both the indigenous secrecy and masculine purity of the ritual in the sympathetically yet comically portrayed person of a German folklore specialist, Mrs Bunz. Class complexity also complicates the conservative social order of the village of South Mardian which the mumming ritual seems designed to preserve. The daughter of the plebeian patriarch William Anderson previously disgraced the family by marrying above her class and producing actress Camilla, newly arrived for a family reconciliation. Her position, described as a 'half-breed', is even more erotically complicated, since she is beloved by one of local gentry, Ralph Mardian, heir to 'Squire' Dame Alice. Ralph is another actor/suspect in the mumming play. Lastly, the potential sublimity of the fertility ritual is directly threatened by modernity in the shape of mummer Captain Begg's desire to turn the ancient forge, owned by old William Anderson, into a petrol garage. Most of the sons support Begg, an ex-serviceman whose wartime heroism allowed him to rise above his station.

Powerful domestic, social, familial and sexual turmoil re-invests the mummers play with a moment of Gothic sublime when disturbed son Ernie stands on the ancient sacrificial altar in the frozen landscape at the climax of the play. Real gore stains the snow: 'What price blood for the stone! What price the old man's 'ead? Swords be out chaps, and 'eads be off. What price blood for the stone?' (p. 71). Of course, this Gothic sublime transmits quickly into Gothic horror at the realisation of human agency in the murder. Camilla expresses the sense of horror engendered particularly by the theatrical nature of the crime, the collapsing of drama into murder: 'It's the awful grotesquerie that's so nightmarish. It's like something out of Webster or Marlowe: horror-plus' (p. 95).

Alleyn can reinstate the Gothic sublime by his detecting as ritual enactment which symbolically resurrects by 'solving' the crime, the 'solution' making death unnatural and solvable. Solution divesting death from the 'natural' provides fertility and 'the thaw'. Part of Alleyn's Gothic powers here lies in his own potency against the rigid class boundaries in South Mardian. Mistaken for a gentleman *rather* than a policeman, Alleyn's traversing of the aristocratic/professional boundary means that the sublime he enacts is not wholly a conservative recuperation. True, the murderer proves to be a violator of class, but Alleyn's erotic destabilisation of unyielding class barriers proves a nurturing influence on Camilla and Ralph's class-complicated romance. The restoration of the sublime through assimilating detection into ritual allows conservative modernity to be renewed through adaptation to pressures of sexuality and technology. The sons will get their petrol station, Camilla is admitted to the Great House and the mummers' play will continue to affirm a relatively unchanged class structure. The union of the lovers, also by means of Alleyn's detection, serves as a narrative substantiation of the embodiment of the fertility myth in the detective fiction.

Ngaio Marsh's typical mode is one of self-conscious theatricality within conservative gender and social aesthetics, complicated by post-colonial instincts. In *Off With His Head* she reveals the Gothic potentiality of theatre as a sublime textual space.

Original Sin by P.D. James (1994)[77]

London is a Gothic city in P.D. James's *Original Sin*. Clouds over the metropolis are 'stained pink like a lint bandage which had soaked up the city's blood' (p. 91). Multiplying stories of violence and death are associated with accounts of the lonely childhoods of both Adam Dalgliesh and Frances Peverell, suspect in the murder of a publisher found apparently strangled by a cloth snake at the firm's riverside headquarters. For Frances, the Thames is a 'dark tide of horror' where gulls sound with the screams of drowned children (p. 96).

Innocent House provides the traditional Gothic mansion, fusing eighteenth- and nineteenth-century horrors by bringing the 'haunted castle' to the spectral city. Named after its location on Innocent Walk where freed criminals left the local law courts, the neo-Venetian palace on the Thames doubly ironises its name in a novel whose title, *Original Sin*, comes more and more to stand for crimes that the law and contemporary society cannot purge. For Adam Dalgliesh, the house represents a 'potent amalgam of beauty and horror' in the legend that it was built with the money of a neglected wife who committed suicide in despair. Late in the novel, documents suggest that the crime was, in fact, murder by the husband, mad to complete his fantasy edifice with his wife's money.

The present Peverell Press is run by Gerard Etienne, the son of a French Resistance war hero. Gerard's brutal attempts to capitalise on business opportunities violate familial bonds within the firm as well as the old-fashioned traditions of literary publishing. Suspects for his murder include rejected lover Frances, his sister, Claudia, who needs his help to raise capital for her selfish lover, a brutally treated elderly secretary, James, a gentle admirer of Frances, and Gabriel, elderly poet and archivist. Investigation of the killing takes *Original Sin* into the fully Gothic tradition of literary self-consciousness. Temporary typist Mandy can enjoy a literary sense of Gothic horror in her attendance at Innocent House that 'had assumed some of the terrifying potency of a child's fairytale … the forbidden territory' (p. 388).

Yet true Gothic horror is constructed for Mandy and the reader by fear defeating the categories of literature to contain it. Even golden age crime fiction is cited as a literary form that tames desire and crime as one disturbed suspect stares into the domestic hearth, 'from which the image of Miss Marple seemed to rise … assuring her that there was nothing to be afraid of' (pp. 259–60). The depiction of golden age detective fiction as a literature of certainties defeated by modern Gothic horrors in an unstable society, culminates metaphorically in the murder of 'cosy' crime writer Esme Carling. Mandy's refuge in literary Gothic is finally eroded by her discovery of Carling's corpse as a monstrous collapse of human boundaries, made more horrific by simultaneous likeness and distinction from the romantic 'lady in a lake':

> beneath that surface, something was just visible, something grotesque and unreal, like the domed head of a gigantic insect...And as she gazed down in horror, the body shifted in the tide and a white hand rose slowly from the water, its wrist drooping like the stem of a dying flower.
>
> (p. 398)

The Gothic fusion of categories becomes even more pertinent to the detection when the grotesque murder of Gerard, apparently strangled by the draught-excluder snake, proves instead to be a gassing in an enclosed room. Again, Gothic blurring of borders allows Holocaust horrors to be represented. The snake, sign of 'original sin' in the biblical sense, signifies here the irredeemable stain that Gerard and Claudia Etienne were born carrying, as children of a so-called war hero who deported Jews under the Nazis, in particular, the family of the killer. Even Gothic London comes to represent this original twentieth-century sin that the law and current social conventions cannot erase or contain, according to this novel. Frances's Thames as a dark tide of horror explicitly comes to represent the dark tide flowing into the gas chambers in an erosion of categories that allows the Holocaust to be indirectly represented in Jamesian Gothic (p. 164).

As the story reaches its climax, the detective genre itself threatens to collapse with one of the detecting team, the Jewish Daniel, drawn so far into the passions of the case that he loses his police professionalism. The final revelation is that the victims, Gerard and Claudia, were adopted, so the biblical promise of the inherited stain of sin and the murderer's revenge on the children of the man who killed his family no longer operates. With this threatened loss of meaning, the murderer strides out to sea, sinking in the marshes of Mersea Island.[78] Significantly *not* captured by the police, the murderer becomes 'a stumbling figure...looking immense as a giant, arms raised as if in a curse or a last beseeching gesture...He had become part of the marshland and of the night' (p. 547).

The original sin of the Holocaust is shown to defeat the conventions of the police procedural genre, culminating in the Gothic sublime. The murderer within the Gothic sublime is the momentary erosion of boundaries between detective as agent of justice and killer. Distantly recalling Sherlock Holmes and Lord Peter's adventures with bogs, this conclusion of a crime fiction in the Gothic sublime swallows up the tragic killer-detective: it is a sign of the novel's Gothic belief that no law or courts can adequately contain such horrors.

The House of Stairs by Barbara Vine (1988)[79]

Rendell's typical narrative is to show conventions of romance as inadequate to contain the extremities of desire, so the Gothic emerges in the modification of generic boundaries. In Barbara Vine novels, the absence of a detecting figure external to the family Gothic allows more open endings in which Gothic horrors can also conceive of the Gothic sublime.

The House of Stairs provides a cursed narrator, a 'heir of madness' who we eventually learn lives with the threat of developing the terminal Huntingdon's Chorea in middle age. The narrator, Elizabeth, is invited to live at the House of Stairs with her aunt, Cosette, who in mid-life is seeking a new existence of passion and authenticity after suffering the stifling respectability of a middle-class suburban marriage. Elizabeth's story of the large bohemian household and particularly her introduction of the enigmatic killer/lover, Bell, seeks boundaries and definitions through the citing of literature, in particular Henry James's *The Wings of the Dove*.[80]

Bell operates as the focus of narrative speculation just as she is the object of the narrator's desire. Told the story of *The Wings of the Dove* by the infatuated Elizabeth, it appears that Bell may be trying to re-create that novel's conspiracy for financial gain by introducing her so-called brother, Mark, to Cosette, who instantly adores him. Bell seems to believe that Cosette will die soon and leave Mark her money. First introduced as an ex-convict, for a long period it seems as if Bell has murdered Cosette. It is finally revealed that after Mark and Cosette become lovers, Bell pushed Mark out of the window to his death. Cosette blamed Elizabeth for the tragedy as she introduced the killer/lover Bell to the House of Stairs. Vine's novel ceases with Bell installed in Elizabeth's house. Having made a will in Bell's favour, Elizabeth listlessly waits for a resolution that the novel does not define. She may be dying now from Huntingdon's Chorea, or Bell may kill her for her money, or Cosette, whom Elizabeth truly loves, may come to her rescue.

Despite the evocative name, *The House of Stairs* has less a Gothic setting than a Gothic plot of desire in which doubling and mirroring destabilises borders of identity. Cosette and Bell mutate into doubles as Cosette seeks the emotional freedom that Bell apparently represents. Bell is a protean trickster figure revealed as Gothic when she acknowledges no moral boundaries to acting to obtain her desire. Elizabeth, the narrator, is doubled both by Bell and Cosette as the object of her passion shifts between the two. Whereas loving Cosette is finally said to be her 'self', a self that cannot be preserved without the older woman's forgiveness, Bell and Elizabeth as authors of crimes also threaten to change places. Bell's refusal to be categorised means that even the key narrative of *The Wings of the Dove* cannot securely pinion her as either lover or killer. Bell accuses Elizabeth of moral responsibility for Mark's death and Cosette's estrangement by being the occasion of her meeting Mark, and the importer of both the Henry James story and the misleading information that Cosette was dying. At first the use of 'literature' serves to introduce and limit Gothic passions; then the protean Bell proves the embodiment of uncontainable Gothic energies by breaking down barriers between the roles of exploiter/killer and lover or family member. Overcome by the sense that her position of narrator has collapsed into that of *author* of crimes, Elizabeth is truly beset by Gothic horror, unable, without Cosette's regard to save her 'self'.

> ...I am awake again and in such a panic of horror, such an indescribable fear of life itself, of reality, of my black-dark surroundings, that my body jerks and twists with it and my eyes...stare in terror to the empty darkness.
>
> (p. 796)

The House of Stairs concludes by modulating Gothic horror into the Gothic sublime as three alternatives await Elizabeth: murder, death by disease or a rescue that is also a reconstitution of a secure identity in loving familial bonds. Barbara Vine offers the Gothic sublime as the expansion of narrative possibilities beyond the traditional generic categories of crime fiction.

7
The Spirits of Detection

Are the crimes to be real sins, or are they to be the mere gestures of animated puppets? Are we to shed blood or only sawdust...? If we wipe out God from the problem we are in very real danger of wiping out man as well.[1]

(Dorothy L. Sayers (1935))

The sense of the crime and detection genres as inherently metaphysical is important to the novels of all six writers. A religious dimension is a persistent expression of the form, from Agatha Christie's invocation to the 'Immortals' in *The Mysterious Mr Quin*,[2] to Lord Peter Wimsey suddenly acquiring a god-like perspective, and to Adam Dalgliesh's intimations that professional routines aim to substitute for sacred rituals. As argued elsewhere in this volume, the native self-referentiality of the golden age genre enables a fantasy of overcoming death to be included in the rhetorical 'play' or, as W.H. Auden put it: 'The fantasy...is the fantasy of being restored to the Garden of Eden, to a state of innocence, where he may know love as love and not as the law.'[3]

In particular, I suggest, the fantasy of a return to Eden is of a regressive return to an innocence before the knowledge of death. Therefore, it is unsurprising that the self-conscious artifice of the golden age genre (and its continued existence within the works of James and Rendell) should construct the detective as a metaphysical figure whose potency for restoring social order is reinforced by the trappings of neo-divine power. Of course, such an elevation of the detecting persona needs the self-referentiality of the genre in order to permit the visibility of such metaphysics. Specifically, the linking of the detective with divine powers of justice is frequently shadowed by Gothic traces of horror as the negative or demonic possibilities of the supernatural become manifest.

Chapter 6 describes some of these possibilities. Nevertheless, these six authors knowingly operate in a genre that itself believes that justice is possible, however fallible its human representatives prove to be. This entails the literary form endorsing a construction of 'knowledge' as accessible, fixable, stable and traceable through 'signs' or clues. Ultimately, this presupposes some kind of stable universe and ties the crime genres back to an earlier literary embodiment of human sins and divine justice: the medieval morality play.[4] However, before considering the 'divinity' of the detective, it is worth looking at the novelists' historical sense of 'spirits' and the feminine.

Female novelists and spiritualist detection

The development of the detective genre in the nineteenth century occurs at the same period as the emergence of a new religious movement of Spiritualism, the contacting of the deceased by means of a medium in a trance.[5] Nineteenth-century Spiritualism was distinguished by the prominence of female mediums. It seems to have gained resonance from the contemporary cultural definition of the feminine as 'other', so in extreme form as 'occult'. Where the detective genre reflects the secularisation of crime in the rise of the police force and recourse to the law (as a human system rather than a direct expression of divine justice), the detective, in turn, becomes the secularised knight on a quest. Like the divinely endorsed knights of medieval legends, the detective seeks that object which will redeem 'his' community. The knight on a Grail quest sought that which will bring the human world into divine communion. His literary descendant, the detective, seeks a secular truth to redeem by restoring the social law, supposedly connected to, but at one remove from, an abstract concept of justice.

While the detective genre describes the growing 'humanism' of justice as it becomes popularly conceived as socially centred rather than divinely centred, Spiritualism offered an alternative narrative of knowledge and signs. The 'clues' embodied by the (female) medium direct away from the human and secular to the metaphysical; an explicitly non-human centred knowledge in which the strong feminine presences suggest that it could be constructed as a non hu-*man* way of knowing. This is not an essentialist argument about women being necessarily 'other' to secular law, but a characteristic of the construction of the feminine in the nineteenth century. If masculinity claims exclusively to occupy the territory of reason and science, then the feminine becomes, by default, suspect, deviant and uncanny. What is significant for the six authors is the way that the four earlier writers enter the debate about Spiritualism and the supposedly occult nature of the feminine. Arthur Conan Doyle, creator of Sherlock Holmes, is the prime example of a giant of the genre who was simultaneously an enthusiastic participant in Spiritualism and the occult. Chapter 1 also suggests ways in which some of the six writers mirror this aspect of Doyle, but the golden age writers, in particular, *consciously* address the spiritualist challenge to the secularisation of knowledge in their novels.

In Christie's *The Sittaford Mystery*, the first intimations of murder actually occur within a séance, prompting a concerned friend of the named victim to embark on a journey which will lead to the discovery of the body.[6] This supernatural intervention in crime detection is allowed to stand for much of the novel, and the adventurous young female detective, Emily Trefusis, even plans to consult Conan Doyle about it.[7] The séance is finally redefined as part of the theatre of crime rather than of its detection.

Christie also wrote a volume of stories, *The Hound of Death*, in which there is no 'closure' excluding occult explanations.[8] Most eerie is the story of a séance given for the benefit of a bereaved mother, in which the materialised spirit of the dead child is seized upon by the fanatical parent, thereby causing the death of the medium. Her dead feminine form is revealed as shrunken as if her substance had been drained away.[9] Particularly interesting also is the trio of roles that recurs in the volume between male occult practitioner and investigator, male psychiatrist (often in one person), and female patient or medium subject. This re-enacts the late nineteenth-century transition between regarding female 'otherness' as metaphysical symptoms (hence mediumship and Spiritualism) to re-configuring them as medical, as hysteria interpreted by a male doctor.[10] The 'theatre' of psychonalysis comes more and more to replace the séance as the display of femininity.

Mediums and hysterics produce narratives that were often defined as 'unreliable' by male authority, or 'fictions'. Margery Allingham's initial work, *Blackerchief Dick*, plunges her straight into this occult stream, arising as it does from a family séance.[11] Even the more orthodoxly Christian Dorothy L. Sayers is aware of the occult traces threatening definitions of the feminine. Both *Strong Poison*[12] and *Gaudy Night*[13] demonstrate the need for the feminine to be purged of the uncanny before Peter can achieve a companionate marriage of equals with Harriet. Disposing of the female poltergeist in Shrewsbury College marks Harriet's and Peter's triumph over the occult feminine, a process which begins significantly with Miss Climpson's assault on classical feminine Spiritualism in *Strong Poison*. It is Miss Climpson's greatest detecting triumph to seize upon vital evidence to save the life of Harriet Vane by means of faking a series of séances with a gullible, lonely female employee of a rich, dying woman.[14] Despite the firm refutation of Spiritualism here, it is also portrayed as a specifically feminine method of detection, one closed to Lord Peter yet crucial to his investigation.

What could never be acknowledged by Sayers, but is implicit in *Gaudy Night*'s 'dread of Artemis', is the need for a female writer to seek out an alternative metaphysical language or to challenge biblical stereotypes.[15] If we take Christie's Miss Marple of St Mary Mead, she proves not to live up to her setting, neither as a Virgin Mary nor even as a contaminating Eve. Instead, as Marion Shaw and Sabine Vanacker[16] show, she evolves into *Nemesis* or an 'avenging fury', a classical divinity providing posthumous justice for the vulnerable and innocent.[17] In *Hallowe'en Party*, Hercule Poirot is summoned by Ariadne Oliver, shocked at the murder of a child while she was 'bobbing' for apples.[18] Famed as a great lover of apples, Ariadne can no longer consume them. She becomes an alternative Eve by renouncing the apples of the knowledge of good and evil. It is Poirot who discovers a beautiful garden, explicitly a man-made 'Eden', to be the key to the crime. Here the 'Adam' of the garden proves not to be the Creator's helpmeet, but Narcissus. His self-absorption leads to another classical legend as he seeks to murder his own daughter, citing the sacrifice of Iphigenia.[19]

Even P.D. James is aware of the temptation to 'other' metaphysical narratives when she has Cordelia Gray overtly reject a shrine to maternity in *An Unsuitable Job for a Woman*.[20] Ruth Rendell calls Wexford 'Silenus' to express his 'otherness' to the police force, but points out that his wine-imbibing is limited![21] Significantly, the Wexford novels continue the narrative of Spiritualism. In Rendell's work, Spiritualism becomes a metaphor for an ultimate impenetrability of human passion yet still associated with the feminine. A desperate mother is described as medium-like in *Murder Being Once Done*, 'awakened from a strange and transcending communion',[22] or a childhood trauma recalled by a disturbed young woman in *A New Lease of Death* is 'reminiscent...of a mediumistic revelation'.[23]

We need to turn now to the detective's trailing of divine clouds of glory.

Divine detectives

To a greater or a lesser extent all of the six authors' detectives partake of the secular form of the divinely sanctioned knight errant on a quest for metaphysical justice. Yet the detectives' relationship to conceptions of divine justice varies enormously. We could, if we wished, place the detectives on a sliding scale from Christie's as the most intimate with metaphysics to the works of Rendell/Vine as the most secular.

Starting with the most 'godly', Agatha Christie provides Mr Harley Quin, who appears spookily to collaborate with a Mr Satterthwaite on investigations, reminding him: 'I must recommend the Harlequinade to your attention…the Immortals are always Immortal.'[24] Satterthwaite, once 'always in the front row of the stalls of life',[25] becomes, through Harley Quin, an actor in dramas designed to achieve justice. Here, not only does the self-referentiality of the genre take on its familiar theatrical metaphor, but the presence of Harley Quin defines it explicitly as a *sacred* drama of divine justice. Harley Quin is not a *deus ex machina* utilising supernatural methods. He embodies a greater knowledge than the merely human characters together with a divine purpose, yet functions by prompting Satterthwaite's human investigations. In effect, Harley Quin and Satterthwaite represent a division of divine and earthly justice that Christie incarnates in the single figures of Hercule Poirot and Miss Marple. Like Miss Marple, who makes the police force 'just' and is a vehicle of divine fury, Poirot's investigations almost always combine the justice of God with the justice of the social law in an unproblematical manner. *Murder on the Orient Express* represents an exception in which the demonising of the victim as *outside* the human community, an 'animal', means that Poirot can allow cosmic justice to be in the hands of the killers.[26]

Sayers's Lord Peter Wimsey is far more self-conscious about the metaphysical implications of his role. Wimsey's self-doubt about the morality of his use of his social privilege to pursue murderers represents generically the tension within the detective function between metaphysical fantasy and secular realism. In Wimsey in particular, the struggle forms an arena for his characterisation. As early as *Whose Body?*, Lord Peter has a sense of solving the mystery as if he possessed the eye of God: 'as if he stood outside the world and saw it suspended in infinitely dimensional space…He knew it.'[27] Parker is accused of being the doubting Thomas to Wimsey's detecting Christ,[28] but this divine expansion of the detecting self is inevitably followed by the psychological horrors of retraction into war hysteria. What is on one level Wimsey's realistic reaction to moral stress is on another the return of the psychological to pollute the metaphysical vision embodied in the detective.

Sayers herself evolved a theology of 'making' which is clearly detectable in her fiction. She believed in the possibility of work as a sacrament, that truth to one's 'proper job' is an integrity that permeates to the divine and creates something sacred and enduring outside of oneself.[29] Such arguments become part of the discussion of the role of women in society in *Gaudy Night*. It is also possible to see many of Sayers's murderers offending against this 'sacrament', such as the killer lawyer and nurse in *Strong Poison* and *Unnatural Death* respectively.[30]

Despite very different relationships to the law and police, the detectives of Margery Allingham and Ngaio Marsh have a similarly self-consciously theatrical inflection of the notion of the detective as vehicle of divine justice. Albert Campion is never simply identified with the police. Even in *Traitor's Purse*, when he is directly working for the police, he is hampered by his loss of self.[31] Eccentric to the human law, Campion oscillates between a guardian angel figure and the role of killer in his desire to restore a moral metaphysics. On the other hand, Roderick Alleyn is a means of identifying the police with divine justice. No corruption or miscarriage of justice is imaginable in Alleyn's force. Marsh's writing is designed to endorse Alleyn's early assertion that no one is ever wrongly hanged in England, an idealisation, perhaps, only possible to a colonial writer.[32] Nevertheless, Alleyn himself is keen to dissociate his professional practice from divine pretensions, exhibiting acute embarrassment when a priest and fellow sleuth calls himself 'a spiritual policeman' in *Singing in the Shrouds*.[33] Yet, whatever Alleyn may himself prefer, his tag of resemblance to a 'monk and grandee' expresses his 'excess' to his secular job, in religious and class terms. Such extra emblems of authority act to bolster the claims he implicitly stands for regarding the infallibility of his profession.

Campion and Alleyn, so varied in their positioning to the law, are alike in the way the explicit theatricality of their mysteries promises, in fantasy, a metaphysical redemption. By contrast, James's detectives are one step further from the divine in that secular law cannot represent cosmic justice for this writer. James depicts a society where the secularisation of justice is characterised as a deliberate rejection of religion with its dreams of moral perfection. For James, the modern state has repeated the error of the Fall in cutting itself off from the promise of justice (from Eden), contained in Christian narratives. Her 'Adam' Dalgliesh stalks a post-lapsarian society, his alienation itself is a symptom of the loss of paradise.

Part of James's attraction to golden age writers and Dorothy L. Sayers in particular is her sense of the form as expressing an anguished and social need for a sense of the divine. Unfortunately for James, her attachment to social realism as well as her conservative pessimism cuts her work off from much of the metaphysical 'play' of previous writers. James pays particular homage to Sayers in *An Unsuitable Job for a Woman* when Cordelia Gray, like Harriet Vane in *Gaudy Night*, is so overcome by the beauty of a university city as to imagine it as Eden, a paradise of divine justice. Both Harriet in Oxford and Cordelia in Cambridge are reminded that 'there was a way to hell even from the gates of heaven', but Cordelia, significantly, hears this as one who has never been admitted to this particular 'paradise'.[34]

Ruth Rendell, as might be expected of a writer most inspired by social injustice, is least concerned to reflect the genre's metaphysical implications. Although a certain uncanniness does surround Wexford's intuitions, he is highly dubious of the social dimensions of religious belief, explaining his dislike of the clergy as '[m]ost of them expected you to worship God in them' in *A New Lease of Death*.[35] He is especially grumpy when professions pretend to semi-divine authority, as demonstrated by his disputes with Dr Crocker on the priest-like confessional role of the doctor.[36] Where James laments her portrayal of the inability of the professions to embody religious authority, Rendell deploys a lively scepticism about authority in general and religion in particular. Crucially, Rendell uses social injustice as a kind of alternative metaphysic to structure her work. In *Simisola*, Wexford's relief at his illness being diagnosed as a virus leads him to discuss a medical and secular interpretation of St Paul's conversion.[37] This forms a potent prelude to his own later 'conversion' experiences over his racial awareness involving the same Nigerian doctor. It is time to consider the darker side of the metaphysical traces within the detecting genre.

The heresy of detectives

The sublime nature of detectives in occupying a neo-divine position representing a dream of cosmic justice is inevitably haunted by the negative sublime as the occult or demonic. Such a shadowing often takes textual form in the presence of the cult practices, sometimes coded as extra-illegitimate by the use of narcotics to signify 'unnatural' assaults upon the liberal, individual self. In metaphysical terms, the negative sublime, eroding self-agency in 'horror', is the result of detecting in a Fallen world where truth is obscure and signs or clues tricky to follow. If 'divine truth' is opaque, barely reachable or barely conceivable, then detecting as/for God can lapse into the heretical through an almost inevitable transgression beyond the boundaries of a sacred narrative which can never be fully understood. Therefore, in generic terms, the negative sublime is a sense of the unknowable nature of the metaphysical transmuted into the fear of it as alien. In terms of secular modernity (the culture of the detective genre), it is the return of the repressed metaphysical as horror.

Agatha Christie's detectives' intimacy with divine authority allows a unique 'play' with the boundaries of a supposedly secular genre. Harley Quin or *The Hound of Death* can use narrative to refine occult horrors into instruments of divine justice while her more human heroes, Hercule Poirot and Miss Marple, are confident about naming metaphysical evil. This is due to the fact that they contain within themselves the role of divine instrument. Lord Peter Wimsey, as stated, experiences the negative sublime as psychology. The possibility that his role as dispenser of cosmic justice may falter or transgress is psychically coded into the horrors of his war trauma. For Margery Allingham, occult horror is bound up with her narrative of social authority. It represents the dark side to her fascination with a mythical, feudal rural hierarchy, inimical to corporate modernity. In early novels, Campion's role is to penetrate occult horror, which in one sense demonstrates his eccentricity to conventions in demonic form. In another sense he has to discover the social dimensions of the rural occult, whether it is continuous with feudal manifestations of social power, as in *Look to the Lady*,[38] or potentially subversive of it, as in *Sweet Danger*.[39]

In Allingham's later work, the negative sublime metaphysic is condensed into a theology of sin and madness. Both Jack Havoc in *The Tiger in the Smoke*[40] and Gerry Hawker in *Hide My Eyes*[41] are portrayed as serial killers with metaphysical dimensions. Jack Havoc's climactic scene occurs in an echoing London church with elderly Canon Avril who diagnoses his vaunted 'science of luck'[42] as 'the pursuit of Death', invoking 'Evil be thou my Good'.[43] This theology of crime is a structure of negative sublime horror that annihilates the self, as Avril explains: it is the 'only sin which cannot be forgiven because when it has finished with you you are not there to forgive'.[44] Avril serves to map horror onto a stable metaphysical scheme despite succumbing to a violent assault. Much of the 'horror' of *Hide My Eyes* resides in the absence of a similar figure of metaphysical authority.

The work of Ngaio Marsh is distinguished both by a persistent attraction to depicting crime through cults and by a post-colonial respect for other religions, in particular the Maori of her native New Zealand. Works such as *Spinsters in Jeopardy*,[45] which metonymically links orgiastic rites with illegal narcotics, demonstrate an interest in the occult as a sign of Western folly and moral exhaustion. Such implied social criticism is wholly distinguished from the integrity of non-Western religious beliefs. In terms of Marsh's entire oeuvre, the interest in cults that operate by assaulting the frail Western self is entirely continuous with her concern with the theatre. Alleyn is the most theatrical of the detectives, who must negotiate the negative sublime of the horrific, drug-fuelled cult staginess. He must substitute a sublime drama of detection producing justice through neo-sacred ritual (self-referentially presented as fantasy). His typical denouement through re-enactment of the crime is the emblem of his transformation of police procedure to dramatic and ritualised justice.

P.D. James has no such literary faith. Her detecting figures tend to be *subject to* negative sublime horror *because* they are irretrievably cut off from representing the dream of divine justice. Horror at human selfishness and evil is James's formal mode of representing her metaphysics of the genre. Part of the function of frequent references to the Holocaust is to provide an atmosphere of horror as a most acid form of pessimism about secular societies.

Ruth Rendell's fiction is most detached from metaphysics because she fears its potency to embody reactionary forms of social authority. Interestingly, the negative sublime accrues more to Mike Burden than Reg Wexford, as his determinedly conservative conventions, reaching deep into his sense of self, are brutally smashed by extremes of irrational desire in *The Veiled One*.[46]

Barbara Vine: losing the metaphysics of form?

Barbara Vine's novels are characterised by the absence of an external detecting figure. This entails the loss of the metaphysical intensity surrounding the detective and the consequent exploration of the difficulty of demonstrating objective, secure and unified knowledge. However, the loss of knowledge in the detective is met by a subsequent return of the numinous, the mysterious and the neo-mystical in the very unfathomability of human desire. Such a 'theology of un-knowing' explicitly counters the social conservatism embedded in conventional crime fiction where the detective is a dimension of a divine *narrative*, however ineffable in aspects. In *A Dark-Adapted Eye*, for example, the narrator, Faith, is a seeker rather than a detective, since she searches for understanding rather than the secure knowledge of cousin Jamie's maternity. The identity of his biological mother proves impossible to ascertain.[47] Such understanding will contribute to Faith's sense of herself as part of a quest for self-construction and self-acceptance. So when she dreams of Vera suckling Jamie 'Madonna-like, tranquil and splendid, her breasts bare',[48] it is not a clue to an objective 'fact', but a sign to be decoded as subjective emotional truth, directing the reader to a conception of human desire as ultimately unknowable, and sublime.

Explicitly, Vine's rewriting of the metaphysics of form can be considered as an attempt at a more progressive and liberal structuring of ethics. W.H. Auden wrote that 'the job of the detective is to restore the state of grace in which the aesthetic and the ethical are one'.[49] Barbara Vine's use of Gothic fable and a sublime mysticism of human desire opens up the crime genre to radical possibilities. It is her novels' achievement still to produce the aesthetic and ethical as one.

Appointment with Death by Agatha Christie (1938)[50]

This novel exhibits acute metaphysical tension between Christie's very rare *Orient Express* model, in which divine justice is finally assigned to the ostensible killers, and the more typical identifying of cosmic justice with the human law. Significantly, two-thirds of the way through the novel, Hercule Poirot tells a sympathetic suspect that this murder of the gorgon-like Mrs Boynton is *not* to be compared to the Orient Express case. Nevertheless, the early part of the story is devoted to describing the psychological terrorism inflicted by Mrs Boynton on her adult American family, now travelling in the perilously evocative middle Eastern landscape. The tortured family party encounters Sarah King, a newly qualified doctor, who becomes attracted to the vulnerable Raymond Boynton. Also travelling are Dr Gerard, a psychiatric practitioner, who becomes seriously concerned for the mental health of the youngest Boynton, Ginevra, and Lady Westholme, another forceful woman who is devoted to politics and women's rights.

In the events leading up to Mrs Boynton's death by lethal injection on a desert campsite, the novel's anxiety centres around the potential perversion of the Christian narrative. Can Christianity provide a stable and metaphysical morality in the face of Mrs Boynton's monstrosity? She is significantly evoked in 'heretical' terms: 'like an arch-priestess of some forgotten cult, like a monstrous swollen female Buddha, sat Mrs Boynton' (p. 76). Sympathetic Sarah King feels tempted to consider expedient death as a sacrifice for the good of the community. Her confidant, Dr Gerard, dryly points out Christian parallels in quoting the specious justification for the 'sacrifice' of Jesus for reasons of social stability. In particular, the temptation to take justice into one's own hands, however provoked, is associated with the temptation of Satan in the high place, offering worldly power to Christ. Christie's detectives (unlike Allingham, for example) always consciously counter the criminal's claiming of the role of God in deciding that some abstract notion of justice can be absolutely severed from human law in the matter of murder. Taking justice into one's own hands is regularly deplored. *Murder on the Orient Express* is the closest exception, but crucially, the final 'suspect' to appeal to Poirot speaks of the conspiracy as being 'mad'. She does not claim elevation beyond human law in the matter of a criminal whom all agree has escaped 'legitimate' justice.

Appointment with Death pins its faith finally on Christian humility as the ingredient of the religious narrative to be taken as a moral guide. The engaging theological debates of Sarah King and Dr Gerard seize upon humility as a possible point of stability amongst the material evidence of clashing religions and warring sects in their Middle Eastern tour. Interestingly, Christian humility is translated by Dr Gerard as contentment with one's station in life and contrasted with the truly terrible lust for power exhibited by Mrs Boynton. Such humility, which entirely endorses Poirot's and Miss Marple's attitude to the law (no one should take 'justice' into their own hands), becomes a neat demonstration of the social conservatism inherent in Christie's metaphysics.

As the crime and detecting plots work out the novel's metaphysical anxieties, the Christian references give way to those of the theatre, in particular those of Shakespeare and Hamlet. Hercule Poirot becomes identified as an external and detached figure who by detecting can heal the corrupt family dynamics of Hamlet. The feared model, that of Hamlet as internal family member trying to restore moral order by revenge killing, is gradually reduced to a merely theatrical possibility. This is embodied in the final pages by Ginevra, *acting* tragic Ophelia to great acclaim but in fact healed by the detective of mental illness, Dr Gerard. She is married to him and now a successful actress, so spared the literal 'acting out' of her excessive desires.

Detecting and psychiatry explicitly overlap in *Appointment with Death*. In fact, both Dr Gerard and Poirot are granted parallel and distinct successes that contribute to the moral healing of a distressed community. The novel endorses Dr Gerard's diagnosis of the pernicious effects of Mrs Boynton and his later assessment of her mental condition. It is similar to that of her daughter, Ginevra, but open to positive expression in the younger woman. Poirot's methods are even closer to the psychoanalytic 'talking cure' than usual and include an almost priestly mode of guilt and absolution when he describes to most of the suspects how they *could* have murdered and *why*, but how, in fact, they did not.

Poirot is also concerned in a neo-priestly role, to exorcise the 'demonic' power of Mrs Boynton. Using psychoanalytic terms to de-mystify the uncanny nature of her dominance: 'She neither sublimated that intense craving for power – not did she seek to master it' (p. 209), Poirot repeats the late nineteenth-century transition from constructing the 'otherness' of the feminine in neo-religious to medical-psychoanalytic terms. Although femininity and social power is anathematised in Mrs Boynton, the novel moves to a language of gender and identity which will prove more productive for the feminine and at least, here, gives us Ginevra, the *actress* of feminine, if tragic, potency.

The Nine Tailors by Dorothy L. Sayers (1934)

In this most rural of country house mysteries, the country house itself becomes a church: the great medieval edifice at Fenchurch St Paul in a mystery embedded in the rural church calendar. As John G. Cawelti describes,[51] the action follows the church year enacting a sacramental drama which seeks to heal a community fractured by disruptive contamination from specifically metropolitan criminals. From Wimsey's 'providential' (p. 17) arrival at New Year so that he can be persuaded to replace a sick bellringer to the 'resurrection' of an extra corpse discovered in Lady Thorpe's grave at Easter and the final destructive yet cleansing Flood, the crime and detecting stories become fused into a sacred ritual.

This time Wimsey, the urbane stranger, is not securely identified as a redemptive figure. His first action is to renew social hierarchies by joining the bellringers, so re-investing his class privilege with social utility (a similar role in village life is performed by the patrician but impecunious Thorpes). However, Wimsey does not become merely the detecting force for good in countering the crimes of the London jewel thieves.

Years previously the Thorpe's butler, Deacon, engineered the theft of valuable emeralds from a house guest with the unwitting aid of his wife, Mary, and the complicity of a London jewel thief, Cranton.

The emeralds were never found, resulting in financial distress for the Thorpe family. Both Deacon and Cranton were jailed, but Deacon appeared to die shortly after escaping so that the honest Mary Deacon was free to marry a local man, William Thoday. When an extra corpse, apparently mutilated, is discovered in Lady Thorpe's grave, Lord Peter Wimsey is summoned back to investigate. He finally identified the body as Deacon, who has been living under an assumed name in France. A riddle is discovered concerning the powerful presence of the church bells which finally leads to the recovery of the emeralds. Yet the mystery of the death of Deacon, whose battered corpse is traced to the bell tower, is not solved until the disaster of the floods drives the whole community to take shelter in the church.

The Nine Tailors demonstrates Sayers's belief that 'work' can function as a sacrament. It is most overt in the hard-working vicar, Mr Venables, who makes no distinction between his earthly parish duties and his Christian principles, for instance in ringing bells for all the dead be they Catholic or battered corpses. In a deliberate linking of the final flood with the biblical deluge, Venables becomes a literal Noah in organising the rescue of the community as the church becomes the Ark. At first, Venables signals the harmony between the work of Wimsey the detective and his own godly devotions in his summoning of Lord Peter and frequent references to the authority of Sherlock Holmes. However, the plot slowly distinguishes human detection from divine justice. Wimsey, baffled for most of the novel about the means of killing Deacon, comes at last to be identified with both murderer and victim, whereas it is the slightly comic Venables who pronounces that God's justice has been done. Almost falling victim to Deacon's fate by being in the bell tower when a peal is rung, it is Wimsey's minor triumph to realise that the New Year peal that he himself took part in was the death of Deacon. 'Perhaps God speaks through those mouths of inarticulate metal,' says Venables in response (p. 298). The sublime detective and judge here is God, with Wimsey falling into the negative sublime of horror in the bell tower.

In contrasting Lord Peter to both the masculine heroic model of detecting in Sherlock Holmes and the divine detective in part summoned by, and in part incarnated in, Venables, detecting becomes again a mode of self-discovery and self-identity. The flat fenland landscape is portrayed as 'a world of mirrors' in which a linear detecting narrative of clues leading inexorably to a stable truth, is not yet possible. Wimsey says: 'It's like Looking-Glass Country. Takes all the running we can do to stay in the same place' (p. 186). In such a pre-symbolic

world, Wimsey's detection feels stuck in a mirror stage where he is trying to trace the limits and limbs of the crime in which names and legal
identities prove fluid. Here the bells, described as like cats or mirrors
(p. 245), are semiotic, the voice of the 'other'. The bells' 'language' of
sound or riddles has to be decoded in order for fixed knowledge and
identities to be constructed. It is Wimsey's experience in the raging bell
tower which causes his detective self to enter the symbolic in the discovery of the knowledge of death. Such psychological splitting between
murderer and victim restructures the semiotic (feminine) other of the
bells into the symbolic as the voice/instrument of divine justice.

The bells as the solution to the mystery plot become the signs of the
Mystery, a sacred plot that the detective becomes subject to, not dispenser of. The transition of the bells from the pre-Oedipal (m)other
voice, pre-gender and prior to the knowledge of death, to their symbolic re-configuring in *The Nine Tailors* as divine other represents an
incorporation of gendered otherness into the Christian narrative. They
may hang in a patriarchal monument, re-invested with sacred power
through its functioning as the Ark, but the bells are still a re-engender-
ing of the divine.

Sweet Danger by Margery Allingham (1933)

In a typical early Allingham scenario, *Sweet Danger*'s criminal problem
is modernity, as might be guessed from the self-consciously ironised
Ruritanian opening. Amiable young Englishman Guffy Randall discovers Albert Campion posing as the hereditary Paladin of Averna in a
European hotel. Campion is accompanied by his entire court, consisting of more pals of Guffy, Jonathan Eager-Wright and Dicky
Farquarson. It is entirely typical of Campion that Guffy and the reader
need time to work out whether the principality of Averna is another,
hitherto unrevealed aspect of Campion's never-clarified identity or a
deliberate impersonation.

Campion's state-sponsored mission turns out to be to recover legal
proofs, consisting of a crown, a charter and a receipt that would confirm British title to a tiny central European territory. Averna has
recently acquired political importance by gaining a minute coastline
after an earthquake and by the discovery of an oilfield. The treasure
quest swiftly moves to the Suffolk village of Pontisbright and centres
upon the Fitton family, residing in genteel poverty at the Old Mill.
The Fittons, consisting of snooty young Hal, gentle Mary and the
redoubtable young engineer, Amanda (her first entry into Campion's

life), claim to be the legitimate heirs to the earls of Pontisbright, who in turn inherit Averna.

Urgency attends Campion's searches, since the adventurers, endorsed by the hereditary principle, aristocracy and patriotism, are competing with a dangerous criminal gang headed by financier and big businessman, Brett Savernake. *Sweet Danger* provides a rhetorically self-conscious conflict between a 'romance' plot of feudal knightly values and the corruptions of corporate modernity. The aged mill house in the pastoral setting of Pontisbright is described as repelling the disruptions of modernism in terms reminiscent of Yeats,[52] having 'a certain drowsy elegance that was very soothing and comforting in a madly gyrating world' (p. 71). Nevertheless, *Sweet Danger* is not a simple rejection of all aspects of modern England, but seeks to recuperate some of the energies of modernity to reinvigorate class values.

In part, the novel is able to stage a successful renegotiation of rural stability and urban 'progress' by the highly ambivalent manifestations of Campion. No other detective of these six novelists would be portrayed to the reader as a potential traitor, disguise himself as a woman and produce, without warning, a double to distract the criminal gang. Similarly, Pontisbright may be pastoral, but the potent sense of a dark side to the mythologising of feudal values is a legacy of evil and the occult. As the knightly band enter the village, the first 'clue', a mysterious mark, is identified as an ancient sign of fear, while the suspicious doctor tells them that the land is accursed for strangers and that they will succumb to a terrible skin disease if they do not leave at once. Part of Campion's quest is to identify and neutralise the sources of evil indigenous to this paradise.

Just as the self-conscious romance plot blends pre-modern and modern strategies in the aim to legitimate British imperial expansion by mingling the hereditary principle with laws of purchase, so Campion discovers in Pontisbright that an alliance with the feminine can bring him the resources of modern technology. As an accomplished engineer, Amanda's skill with the modern media of the radio means that limitations imposed by the destruction of the ancient Pontisbright Hall can be overcome. One of the proofs can only be discovered through the tolling of a now destroyed bell, so Amanda rigs up a broadcast of its sister casting from Europe. Modern technology is thus feminised and imported into the archaic treasure hunt plot.

If Campion's growing friendship with Amanda allows him to reinvent the Allingham mythical rurality with technological support, his knightly quest identity is reinforced by the need then to rescue

Amanda from the occult powers of Pontisbright. Amanda is vulnerable to the black magic of the doctor because she half-believes his Gothic theologies. From this oppressive aspect of a pre-modern rural world, Campion must save Amanda from becoming a literal human sacrifice. Yet, as well as protecting the heroine from pre-modernity, the defeat of the doctor's summoning of pagan deities is a re-establishing of social boundaries. In taking Brett Savernake's stooge, Peaky Doyle, to be 'Ashtaroth', the doctor's Gothic swaps positions of master/servant just as he also blurs boundaries of healer/sacrificer in his own activities.

Sweet Danger rewrites imperialism as romance with the power to vanquish the Gothic and occult and repel the criminal horrors of corporatism. Allingham's rural-based myth of class stability is allowed to gain strength from technology and a more adventurous femininity. Campion's famous ambivalence allows the self-conscious reinvention of tradition in an essentially comic form.

Death in Ecstasy by Ngaio Marsh (1936)

Here we have a story in total contrast to Sayers's *The Nine Tailors* in a rivalry between the detective and the 'priest' in embodying the justice of God. It is a contest where the outcome is overdetermined by the obviously bogus criminal nature of the figure claiming spiritual authority.

Journalist Nigel Bathgate calls upon his friend, Chief Inspector Alleyn, when his curiosity about a London cult of the House of the Sacred Flame causes him to witness the poisoning of an attractive initiate, Cara Quayne. This occurs mid-ceremony during a parody of the Christian Mass. Alleyn soon realises that Father Jasper Garnette's orgiastic cult is literally the opium of the people, as it also operates as a means of addicting its adherents to narcotics. Suspects include neo-parodic American Samuel Ogden, sexually voracious Mrs Candour, bitter spinster Miss Wade, worshipper of Cara Quayne M. de Ravigne, opium addict Maurice Pringle and his concerned fiancée, Janey Jenkins. Typically for Marsh, the self-referential nature of golden age fiction unites with a rhetoric of theatre surrounding the cult. The fact that the theatricality of this pseudo-religion may prove dangerously continuous with the drama of legal proceedings (where the inquest is described as 'a sort of curtain-raiser to the murder trial' (p. 204)) perhaps accounts for Alleyn's insistence that the law *never* makes mistakes where hanging is an issue. Alleyn's law must not be theatrical in the bogus sense. The story of *Death in Ecstasy* teaches the reader to trust

Alleyn's judgement as he proves the aesthetic and the moral to be undivided in their condemnation of the House of the Sacred Flame. The 'theology' of the cult works by exploiting divisions between world religions, in claiming to be a narrative of spirit and ecstasy combining all, and by parodying well known sacraments. On the one hand, Alleyn's aesthetic (soon moral) distaste distances the cult from readers' perceptions of Christianity. On the other hand, within the self-conscious play of the genre (conflated here with theatricality), religious authority *as such* is made Gothic. Religion in self-conscious fictional mode becomes the subject of the detective's quest, since there is a need to restore boundaries that have been transgressed in the Gothic collapse of sexuality and religion, crime and worship, authority and exploitation. Religion as theatre thereby surrenders to the secular authority of the police. *Death in Ecstasy* revisits, with self-conscious artifice, a vital tension in the evolution of the modern law and hence of detective fiction itself: the transition between religious and secular legitimation.

However, it is only Alleyn's hybridity that allows such a transition to the satisfaction of the reader. In this very early Marsh work, Alleyn's charisma is strongly inflected with social authority. He is liked to an Oxbridge 'don', with a suggestion of the 'army', and of course is far superior in class position to his professional role. Such indications make Alleyn both excessive to, and a bolster of, the professional authority of the police. But he is also here likened to a 'faun', and eroticised by being the unwilling recipient of overt attentions from suspect Mrs Candour. Astoundingly, Alleyn reveals that he once became a member of a Protestant sect, the Plymouth Brothers, for two months as an undergraduate (p. 66). His detecting exploits his uncanny 'otherness' to the law in order to provide a narrative of the detective's extra-legal engagement with the crime. This functions, in Marsh's case, to recuperate the surplus energies within the legal system. The creation later of Troy, artist and squeamish dissenter on the topic of capital punishment, shows the difficulties inherent in absorbing narrative and social tensions into a police dominated structure.

Here, Alleyn's priestly rival for authority over knowledge, the hypnotic Father Garnette, is quickly shown as to be an emblem of theatre sliding easily into crime. He is initially described as druid-like, an actor, a saint, a Midwest purveyor of patent medicines whose ability to drug with words is literalised into drug dealing. It is Alleyn's task to defend the modern secular and individual self from such bogus psychic assaults.

More emphatically than in later novels, the social order restored by Alleyn is the patriarchal sexual order. *Death in Ecstasy* is an instance of overt homophobia in Marsh's work. Distaste at the sexual exploitation of Father Garnette's initiation of attractive women is extended to indict the unpleasantly portrayed homosexuality of two young male acolytes. Fortunately, the homophobia remains incidental to the murder plot, which is traced to the commercial exploitation of drugs, but much of Alleyn's energy goes into the restoration of the conventional heterosexual couple, Maurice and Janey. This novel demonstrates the golden age linkage between moral order and conventional sexuality in acute form. Sayers may manage a limited lesbian portrayal in works such as *Unnatural Death*,[53] but we remember how Alleyn disrupts the relationship of Troy and her devoted more 'mannish' companion, Katti Bostock (painter of plumbers), in *Artists in Crime*.[54]

A Taste for Death by P.D. James (1986)[55]

Written at the height of British Conservative triumphalism in the 1980s (the era of Mrs Thatcher as prime minister), the crime plot centres on the discovery of two corpses in a neglected London church: that of a tramp and a prominent government minister. The murder of Sir Paul Berowne proves not to be a random killing, but conforms to golden age crime in being bound up with his household. Its members consist of his unfaithful wife, Barbara, her lover, surgeon Stephen Lampart, her brother, Dominic Swayne, Berowne's mother, Lady Ursula (desperate to secure the inheritance of the child Barbara is carrying), Berowne's estranged daughter, Sarah, now embroiled in far left politics, neglected spinster-housekeeper Miss Matlock, Halliwell, the soldier-chauffeur and other acquaintances.

A *Taste for Death* resembles a country house murder where the edifice is not only transported to the modern and political pressures of the capital city but is symbolically divided between the empty Victorian church where the bodies are found and the architectural glories of Berowne's Soane house. Much is made of the beauties of the house, described as a blend of the classic and Gothic (p. 109). It is the task of Adam Dalgliesh's detection to eliminate the 'Gothic' from the Soane household, even if he cannot remove the stain of crime. Unsurprisingly, he does locate the murderer within incestuous familial passions. Additionally, the final showdown in the flat of his new working-class subordinate, Inspector Kate Miskin, serves to purge her fears for her own moral integrity. Taking Kate's aged and dependent grandmother hostage, the murderer taunts Kate by suggesting that eliminating the sick old woman would solve Kate's current domestic problems. In response, Kate discovers anew her familial love and gratitude towards her grandmother, so confirming her ability to have a viable secular morality.

If Dalgliesh is able to purge the Gothic from the Soane house, represented psychically by his contaminating vision of the corpses superimposed upon its architectural perfections, he is quite unable to heal the split between religious and secular authority substantiated in the two key settings. Unlike Ngaio Marsh, James will not concede the legitimacy of the divorce between religious and secular authority. She situates in the consciousness of Dalgliesh both the painful division and the limiting inability to reconcile state and church that she perceives as the key to the 'Fallen' nature of modern Britain.

Much of Dalgliesh's interior meditation upon secular and spiritual authority is played out in his psychological relationship to the victim, Paul Berowne. In many ways Dalgliesh recognises himself in Berowne, whom he knew slightly. Through the victim, Dalgliesh traces the outlines of his own sensibility and failures in love: 'if he had a splinter of ice in the heart, then so have I' (p. 260). Yet Berowne's transportation from a Soane House to obscure unvisited church is more than physical. As a result of what he calls 'an experience of God' (p. 262), the politician is prepared to renounce his worldly power and live a more spiritual existence in ways that lead directly to his killing. When the unimpressive vicar, Father Barnes, tells Dalgliesh that he thought he saw holy signs of stigmata on Paul Berowne, Dalgliesh is shocked at 'the bizarre intrusion of irrationality into a job so firmly rooted in the search for evidence which would stand up in court, documented, demonstrable, real' (p. 55). By refusing to engage with spiritual signs, Dalgliesh turns away from the option that Berowne comes to represent for him: he refuses to become Berowne, concluding: 'Whatever Berowne found in that dingy vestry, it isn't open to me even to look for it' (p. 296). Consequently, despite Dalgliesh's strong sense of police professionalism striving to perform a *ritual* function in modern society, the narrative moves towards a sense of tragedy in which modern work rituals largely fail to redeem a social order.

In addition, the detecting strategies serve to demonstrate the limitations as well as the sublime potentiality of the crime genre. That icon of iron-willed conservative nostalgia, Lady Ursula, succeeds in her aim to foster the Berowne dynasty by retaining control of the wayward Barbara. This faithless widow is known to be pregnant with a male

Berowne heir. Lady Ursula points out to Dalgliesh what he has already discovered, the poverty of police rituals in the penetration of moral truth. Police reports cannot possibly encapsulate the intensities of human relations: 'you're a poet ... You can't possibly believe that what you deal in is the truth,' she says (p. 413). Just as Berowne's religious experience proves unrepresentable and thereby incomprehensible, so the detecting genre itself (in James's employment of literary realism) is forced to retreat from the claim to represent truths of crime and desire. Only in the sublime retreat from representation can religion and detective writing be momentarily reconciled.

Golden age fiction never claimed to be realism: its 'truths' are consciously artificial and ironised. It can, therefore, 'play' with detective fiction as a 'solution' to the social trauma of crime. For P.D. James as a deliberate novelist of literary realism, the limits of representation are tragic indeed.

A Judgement in Stone by Ruth Rendell (1977)[56]

The opening sentence of *A Judgement in Stone* gives the reader the 'what', 'who' and 'why' of this detective-less crime fiction: 'Eunice Parchman killed the Coverdale family because she could not read and write' (p. 7). Here we have no godlike detective to solve the crime and metonymically heal the trauma in society. The motivation of illiteracy locates deviance within social and material conditions, but the attempt of the novel to trace the outlines of stable knowledge surrounding the crimes will lapse into the Gothic as desire proves sublime. The novel depicts with intensity a social deprivation that proves explicitly impervious to the resources of the British welfare state and middle-class do-gooding.

The story of Eunice's crimes is that of a servant revenging herself on well-meaning but unintentionally cruel class superiors. The Coverdales' fatal flaw is to dream of living in some past age of live-in servants at the same time as thinking well of themselves. Consequently, they persist in trying to ameliorate Eunice's lot while she is desperate to conceal her illiteracy. Working-class deprivation condenses into educational deprivation in Eunice's background. *A Judgement in Stone*'s achievement is to portray a tragedy of social class without relinquishing individual portrayals of a complacent middle-class family totally unaware of the socially conditioned limitations of their perceptions. The Coverdales, unfortunately, are an extremely literate lot. Giles, studious son of wife, Jacqueline, spends much of his days in literary fantasy. He adores his stepsister, Melinda, in what he likes to imagine is a Gothic incestuous passion drawn from reading Edgar Allan Poe or Emily Brontë. Such self-conscious Gothic indulgence is explicitly contrasted to the far more elemental Gothic presence of Eunice. It is she who is truly marginal to society, excluded by class deprivation, repressed by social forces she cannot comprehend. Such deprivation is unwittingly, but not innocently exploited when the Coverdales take her on as a servant. It is Eunice whose desire is potent with Gothic horror as her deprived and unformed self erupts into violence.

A Judgement in Stone is not only a study of educational and class intersections but of literature and literacy structuring the social. On one level, the Coverdales' love of literature is fatally contaminated by class complacency as they try to live out a fantasy of a Victorian novel with deferential servants. Their home is Lowfield Hall, a name resonant with *Jane Eyre* references of Lowood and Thornfield. However, Rendell's novel is a rewriting of *Jane Eyre* that liberates the violence repressed in the madness of Bertha Rochester and the long years starved of human affection suffered by Jane. As a combination of Bertha and Jane, Eunice's story takes 'literature' beyond the class fantasies of the Coverdales and into the symbolic of society as a whole. For 'writing' is here portrayed as the currency of human society. If 'literature' provides a unifying set of cultural references (even if subject to lapsing into dangerous class fantasy), then being *literate* is portrayed as the ability to use symbols, not only the ability to communicate, but to be defined as a separate self among others in a social context.

Eunice's exclusion from reading and writing is not only, then, an exclusion from most social transactions, it means she has never become a socialised self. She is morally uninitiated: she resides, terrifyingly in the semiotic, excluded from the symbolic of society. As an unformed being, it is unsurprising that the husband of Joan, her insane co-killer, calls her 'Miss Frankenstein' (p. 107), a 'name' that brings her into the representation of literature, but only as monster. More typically, Eunice is 'a stone age woman petrified into stone' (p. 160), Gothic and pre-human.

Eunice can only be truly comprehended by society after her violent assault upon it. As a murderer, she and her illiteracy are recognised by society as she is forced to reveal that illiteracy in court. She has to fulfil the literary and violent destiny of her literary reference as 'Miss Frankenstein'. In fact, Eunice's 'mirror stage' occurs when the official representatives of the social power, the police, name her as the killer. Illiteracy means that she has misconstrued incriminating evidence and so the police discover a tape recording of herself and Joan in the act of shooting. When she hears herself as separate from herself on the tape and simultaneously sees herself in a mirror, she faints. At last, she experiences her subjectivity as split and enters the symbolic as a murderer. In a harsh but apt image of social conventions for deprived Eunice, her birth into the symbolic is her entry into prison.

The accomplice, Joan, is driven by religious mania shown to derive from a past of sexual and gender oppression. Joan's dangerous embrace of madness takes the form of metaphors of mediumship and possession. The traces of religion (and in particular Spiritualism), that accrue even to Rendell's detectives have been excluded from this novel's form only to return as crime. Secular modernity, portrayed in the realism of *A Judgement in Stone*, is shadowed by irrationality, superstition and religion. Religious mania becomes another of Rendell's Gothic powers of desire.

8
Feminism Is Criminal

> Surely if a woman committed a crime like murder, she'd be suffi-
> ciently cold blooded to enjoy the fruits of it without any weak-
> minded sentimentality such as repentance.
>
> (Agatha Christie, *The Murder of Roger Ackroyd*[1])

A writer need not call herself a feminist nor be female for her writing
to be concerned with 'feminist' questions of power, gender and the
social roles of women. Although of these six novelists, only the later
writers would accept the label 'feminist',[2] all six authors, as professional women in a century of rapid social change, are inevitably fascinated by tensions over female participation in society. Unsurprisingly,
given the focus on the domestic as the location of crime, the nature of
marriage, mothering and single women proves significant sources of
passion, conflict and familial drama. Feminist critics traditionally
employ a three-pronged approach to imaginary works: they examine
the representation of women and the feminine in literature; with
women writers they explore factors such as gender, writing and genre;
and they increasingly probe and question structures of gender themselves. Many of the foregoing chapters have considered the latter two
aspects, gender and genre (see Chapter 2), and the construction of gender itself in such contexts as the Gothic, psychoanalysis, the metaphysical, Englishness and social hierarchies.

This chapter will concentrate on the direct representation of women
in the novels. It will move from the depiction of women in the traditional family to women and work, to questions of sexuality, power, and
ultimately to how and when the authors' shaping of the genre portrays
women as victims, criminals and detectives. Lastly, I consider whether
the writers' representation of the feminine suggests (perhaps without

intending to) a feminist ethical attitude. Should contemporary feminism re-evaluate authors habitually considered conservative on gender? But first, to the perennially vexed topic of women in employment, in marriage and as parents.

Suspect women (1): work, marriage and mothering

> The best remedy for a bruised heart is not, as so many people seem to think, repose upon a manly bosom. Much more efficacious are honest work, physical activity and the sudden acquisition of wealth.
> (Dorothy L. Sayers, *Have His Carcase*[3])

Work, marriage and mothering provoke distinctive responses from all six writers. From Margery Allingham's rather strained portrayal of a long-term marriage in *The Beckoning Lady* to Barbara Vine's fascination with mothering as a source of intense, even sublime emotions, such bonds provide sources of dark passions.[4] Agatha Christie's habitual portrayal of robust jollity surrounding her heroic women tends towards a renegotiation of traditional roles. Her works promote female self-expression, but finally do not trouble conventional social structures. The playful exuberance of Tuppence in *Partners in Crime* explicitly rejects the closure of traditional romance in declaring herself dissatisfied with the mundane 'happy ever afterwards' of her marriage.[5] Nevertheless, her energies remain contained within matrimony as she embarks on a series of parodic detective quests with her husband, Tommy. What marks the cessation of this narrative of marriage-as-detecting partnership is the wholly conventional advent of maternity. Yet even here, Tuppence's vigorous personality allows the novel to represent pregnancy as a continuum of self-fulfilling adventures within traditional feminine domesticity. Announcing her news to Tommy, Tuppence says that motherhood will be '[s]omething ever so much more exciting... something I've never done before'.[6]

Similarly, the potentially disturbing impact of professional women on conventional family patterns is typically resolved by the forthright independence of Christie's women finding true happiness within the world of family rather than employment. Midge Hardcastle of *The Hollow* takes an unpleasant job rather than be financially dependent upon her relatives.[7] Although her beloved Edward appears as knight errant to rescue her with an offer of marriage, it is she who proves the stronger hero, subsequently rescuing him from a suicide attempt. Like Lucy Eylesbarrow of *4.50 from Paddington* (who significantly puts her university education into a successful career as a new blend of servant-housekeeper),[8] Midge finds her only true happiness in marriage. Christie's typical strong heroines resemble Miss Marple in reinventing existing conventions to their own advantage. An implicit libertarian on a woman's right to happiness, Christie remains instinctively conservative on erotic and professional social arrangements.

Here she is in direct contrast to Dorothy L. Sayers, whose works increase in clarity on two related feminine issues: the importance of professional work for personal integrity and the necessity to renegotiate power within traditional and 'romance' conceptions of marriage. In *The Documents in the Case*, an unimaginative husband falls prey to a bored wife who manipulates romantic notions of feminine vulnerability until she provokes murder.[9] *Have His Carcase* is a fascinating study of the limitations of 'romance' for both masculine and feminine genders. Rejecting 'repose upon a manly bosom', Harriet Vane's scorning of the appointed position for the rescued female (after *Strong Poison*)[10] is confirmed by the portrayal of Mrs Weldon, pathetic elderly fiancée of the young corpse discovered by Harriet, Paul Alexis. However, the detecting story shifts from the cruel exposure of 'feminine romance' to an indictment of masculine fantasies of Ruritania. Paul Alexis has been duped by a 'masculine romance' woven around his dreams of royal Russian descent. It will take the further novel of *Gaudy Night*[11] (see later this chapter) for Peter and Harriet to construct a partnership where professional integrity can become endorsed by, and not mystified by, the erotic.

Margery Allingham's anxieties about sexuality, gender and power will be considered later in this chapter. Not particularly interested in women as wives or mothers (even in Amanda Fitton), she does have a curious portrayal of a marriage in *The Beckoning Lady* in which artist Minnie has to cope with the fantastically devised parties of her husband, Tonker. These festivals do not help at all with her looming problems with the Inland Revenue. It is Campion and Amanda's son who perceives the aggression entwined with sexuality in the marriage, saying of his own prospects as a husband:

> I shall shout at her and put her across a bed and smack her until she cries, and then I shall kiss her until she laughs, and we shall go downstairs and pour out drinks for a lot of visitors.[12]

Unlike Allingham, Ngaio Marsh is interested in the emotional depths of mothering when Troy and Alleyn's son is temporarily kidnapped in

Spinsters in Jeopardy,[13] and in mothering as pathology in both *Death and the Dancing Footman*[14] and *Final Curtain*.[15] In matters of marriage, Marsh approaches Sayers's concerns with Troy's fear of a loss of self if she submits to her passion for Alleyn in *Death in a White Tie*.[16] However, Alleyn's successful marriage does differ from that of Peter Wimsey and Harriet in achieving partnership through separation of spheres rather than a renegotiation of romance and power. The supreme importance of Troy's art and its essential role in her selfhood guarantees her survival in works where passion tends to be pathologised in other sexually active women. Troy is depicted as an *exceptional* woman with a husband who exceptionally realises her artistic greatness: she is not Sayers's argument for all women to pursue professional integrity.

The work of P.D. James has always perceived social and moral tensions between professional women, eroticism and mothers. Indeed, *Cover Her Face*, her first novel, located criminal desire as centring upon a woman who deliberately blurred categories of deviant unmarried mother, wife and single woman.[17] Typically, James depicts professional women as suffering because of their gender and/or sexuality in male institutions. Her novels are also characterised by a recurrent concern for lonely, inadequately mothered children. James' social conflicts over mothering become more Gothic and sublime in the work of Ruth Rendell/Barbara Vine. More so than James, Rendell is interested in intense relationships that do not fit traditional social patterns, such as Joe's unequal, non-sexual passion for Sandor in *Gallowglass*.[18] She is also particularly concerned to explore shifting constructions of marriage and sexuality throughout the century. Like Sayers, Rendell can be specifically critical of gendered versions of romance, but unlike Sayers, she usually expresses such criticism through readings and misreadings of literature. Ursula's mistaking of future husband Gerald through her reading of Jane Eyre in *The Chimney Sweeper's Boy* is a recent instance.[19]

Suspect women (2): maidens, spinsters and crones

Miss Marple on Macbeth's Three Witches:

> I would have them three ordinary, normal old women…They would look at each other rather slyly and you would feel a sort of menace just behind the ordinariness of them.[20]

Women alone – as marriageable ingénues, the confirmed single and the elderly – have frequently engendered fear in conventional societies concerned to keep female 'otherness' bound up in patriarchal structures. Does the occult, spectral legacy accruing to femininity linger in crime fiction?

For Agatha Christie, any potential 'occult' in the feminine is usually reserved for crones. Miss Marple (a single woman) is the most metaphysical of detectives, announcing herself as 'Nemesis' in the novel of that title. Christie's habitual tone of domestic cheerfulness gives way to her characteristic aesthetic of the 'menace just behind the ordinariness'. Such a technique is at its most eerie in the depiction of elderly women such as the victim finally unmasked as killer in Tommy and Tuppence's neo-Gothic adventure, *By the Pricking of my Thumbs*.[21] Dorothy L. Sayers devotes an early work to the problems of maidens, spinsters and crones in *Clouds of Witness*.[22] Mary Wimsey's spinsterdom is fraught because her author does not share her political views. The young woman's valiant attempt at occupation in left-wing campaigns is doomed to result in her gender exploitation. Yet the alternative of marriage within her class to card cheat Captain Denis Cathcart is equally sterile. Sexual women outside the upper class, represented by the Medusa-like Mrs Grimethorpe and Cathcart's French mistress, are occulted and harbingers of doom. Only the dowager duchess, the crone as mother, makes a success of her class and familial roles.

Most of Margery Allingham's women tend to be single and come trailing occult, even threatening manifestations. References to witches abound, with the appearance of the genuine article in *Look to the Lady*.[23] Devoted spinsters can exist within masculine establishments such as legendary secretary Curley in *Flowers for the Judge*,[24] but are quite likely to reveal pathological or even criminal passions, such as in *Dancers in Mourning*[25] and *Coroner's Pidgin*.[26] Marriageable maidens can be reduced to docility, as in *Mystery Mile*,[27] or possess an ethereal sexual magic, as in the significantly named Clytie of *More Work for the Undertaker*.[28] Even Amanda narrowly escapes being turned into a human sacrifice because she has been educated partly by the local wizard.

In the work of Ngaio Marsh, Alleyn functions as an erotic touchstone for the depiction of women, whether single or attached. Spinsters of a certain age are a particular object of suspicion for this author, frequently succumbing to hysterical sexuality blamed on repression. If a suspect woman can form a relation of respect with Alleyn, then she is retrievable, such as the much put-upon Penelope Garbel in *Spinsters in Jeopardy*. Other spinsters literally 'rampage' in the pursuit of male victims as in the victim Miss Cost in *Dead Water*[29] and those spinsters feuding over the vicar in *Overture to Death*.[30] Marsh's spinsters also have a propensity to fall victim to esoteric cults as yet another channel for their threatening sexuality.

Ruth Rendell subjects the issue of spinsters, sexual attractiveness in women and social responses to crones to a devastating examination in *A Sleeping Life*. Here, a lonely single woman masquerades as a man and becomes a successful novelist.[31] Wexford only succeeds in solving this murder by re-examining his attitudes to elderly women (the crone here holds the key), and by reconsidering sexual desire in young women as problematic, not a conventional given. Rendell's work is prepared to rethink women outside of traditional romantic trysts in more sweeping ways than the other writers. She often uses the Gothic to do so.

P.D. James, on the other hand, frequently borrows spinsters of an earlier era and shows unhappier consequences for them in her frag-menting contemporary society. Particularly sustained is the sad story of devoted secretary Blackie in *Original Sin*.[32] After the death of her beloved elderly employer, Blackie's spinster ways are ridiculed in the new dispensation of modern cut-throat publishing. Even her domestic arrangements with a spinster cousin become unsatisfying. Golden age crime fiction itself proves an illusory comfort. Miss Marple may rise from her fire, 'handbag protectively clutched to her bosom, the gentle wise old eyes gazing into hers, assuring her that there was nothing to be afraid of,'[33] but this peculiarly generic self-referential virginal apparition (from St Mary Mead) will prove an icon of difference for James's work *vis-à-vis* the earlier writers. It is not going to be 'all right' for spinsters deprived of love in Jamesian England.

Suspect women (3): gender and sexuality

> You're a cannibal, Mary, and it's high time somebody had the guts to tell you so.
>
> (Ngaio Marsh, *False Scent*[34])

A fascinating aspect of the golden age genre's self-referentiality is that gender, and in particular the feminine, tends to be inscribed as a mas-querade. Sexuality, on the other hand, becomes the sinister aspect of a society of social masks. It is both shaped by gender and simultaneously challenges social forms, becoming concentrated into irrational, some-times criminal, passion. With Agatha Christie's aim to reinvigorate conventional gender and sexual arrangements, it is unsurprising that lesbian desire becomes 'the menace behind ordinariness' of *Nemesis*. This work contrasts significantly to Sayers's treatment of lesbians in

Unnatural Death.[35] While the ruthless Mary Whittaker 'preyed upon' Vera Findlater according to Miss Climpson,[36] finally extinguishing the younger girl, this portrayal of a pathological lesbian killer needs to be read against the same novel's depiction of a happy couple, 'old maids' Agatha Dawson and Clara Whittaker. Peter Wimsey hears testimony of their mutual devotion: 'Now Miss Dawson...bein' that fond of Miss Whittaker and not wanting to let her out of her sight.'[37] In fact, the poisonous aspect of Mary Whittaker's relationships seems to be that perennial Sayers bugbear, an imbalance of power between passionate companions.

Interestingly, Margery Allingham's works do not, as a rule, cite sexuality and passion as criminal. Even where it seems a likely source of murder in the example of 'elemental' Linda whose lover is killed shortly after he marries another in *Death of a Ghost*, even here the true motive is mercenary, egotistical and *masculine.*[38] A significant consequence of Allingham's refusal to investigate female sexuality (outside of *The Fashion in Shrouds* – see later)[39] is that for her, female sexuality is not criminal. Here Allingham is in complete contrast to Ngaio Marsh, who typically places one of her characteristic female figures at the heart of the crime whether it proves to be for passion or lucre. This figure of a stagy, larger than life, egotistical sexual woman I will call the diva. Marsh's divas are the flowering of the golden age genre's masquerade of femininity. Usually leading actresses (or opera singers – see *Photo-Finish*),[40] they could also be women of property, such as Sybil in *Grave Mistake*,[41] and are greedy for male admiration and sexual attention. Although 'good divas' do exist in the Marsh oeuvre, such as Caroline Dacres in *Vintage Murder*,[42] the diva typically represents a related fear to that represented by the hysterical spinster: the fear of female sexuality as aggressive.

Mary Bellamy, ageing actress of *False Scent*, is a portrayal of a predatory diva as pathological. She is significantly called a 'cannibal' by her oldest female friend. This demonising of Mary in Marsh's typical colonial rhetoric is offered rather horrifyingly as some justification for the reaction of her masculine 'keepers' now unable to control her rages. With true dramatic irony. She sprays pesticide upon herself, instead of cloying scent. Thus excessive female sexuality is reduced to an animal pest in favour of the docile maiden actress, Anelida, who is preferred by the theatrical establishment surrounding Mary.

Lesbian desire is similarly criminalised in Marsh's *Hand in Glove* after being ridiculed as the cross-class passion of an ageing spinster in adopting a worthless young woman.[43] However, Marsh does offer the reader

Troy's great friend, Katti Bostock, painter of working-class males, as a devotee of Troy who tellingly does not affect her heterosexual availability. Katti remains as a friend in Troy's life after her marriage (see *Final Curtain*), and is no criminal.

P.D. James presents lesbian passion as tragic but not pathological both in *Shroud for a Nightingale*,[44] in which the suspect lesbian Sister is unhappy in love, but not guilty, and in *Death of an Expert Witness*,[45] where the truly happy lesbian partnership becomes caught up in crimes of passion rather than initiating them. Ruth Rendell's interest in unconventional relationships and women's changing roles is signified in her first novel, *From Doon with Death*, in which lesbian desire is the concealed mystery behind the killing of an apparently dull married woman.[46] Barbara Vine's recent *The Chimney Sweeper's Boy* turns upon the pain and loathing inflicted upon homosexuality in an earlier era.

Rendell/Vine comes close to the golden age gender masquerade in that her novels are conscious of gender as socially inscribed. P.D. James sees both gender and sexuality as potentially tragic in secular modernity. Her conservatism, however, refuses to relinquish a sense of the persistent legacy of gender inequality, even as her novels tend to distrust difference, fearing its potency to further fragment society.

Suspect women (4): women and power

> Her potential dangerousness grew at every moment. She was like a beautiful, high-powered car driven by an engaging maniac.
>
> (Margery Allingham, *Coroner's Pidgin*[47])

The four golden age writers all variously exhibit unease with the concept of women *in* power but are critical of women *under* arbitrary power. Christie's attitude can be seen in the contrast between the female tyrant of *Appointment with Death*[48] and the cool, efficient Nurse Leatheran of *Murder in Mesopotamia*.[49] While all deference is to be given to the male doctor in the latter novel, Nurse Leatheran vigorously defends the professional authority of *her* sphere. Dorothy L. Sayers's novels are energised by a passionate concern about unequal power in sexual relations. Her detecting works could be read as a single narrative project devoted to allowing women to express themselves as sexual beings in a partnership of mutual respect. *Thrones, Dominations*,[50] the uncompleted Wimsey manuscript finished by Jill Paton Walsh, endorses the Wimsey marriage by contrasting it with an ill-fated but superficially similar union. Wealthy Lawrence Harwell marries impecunious

Rosamund after the financial disgrace of her father. Unfortunately, the Harwells base their intense eroticism upon the dynamics of conquest and surrender. This is made less of a game by its manifestation in a marriage where the woman is shamed by her past and has no meaningful work upon which to base her integrity. The perversions of sexual power lead to murder, also serving to illuminate the intense but symbolically fecund partnership of the Wimseys.

As *The Fashion in Shrouds* will show, Margery Allingham needs to separate issues of power and sexuality in women. Permitted to be authoritative in spheres that do not touch Campion's activities, in Val's fashion and Amanda's engineering, Campion's essential ambivalence (extending to gender) can tolerate no significant female force in his sphere of action. Women pretending to some power in Campion's world are either securely 'other', such as the Queen Gypsy in *Look to the Lady*, or are occulted or demonised, such as the witch and the masculinised master-criminal, Mrs Dick, in the same novel. Feminine power within the social hierarchy results in the mad crone of *Coroner's Pidgin*, or at best in the repression caused by the impressive Caroline Faraday in *Police at the Funeral*.[51]

For Ngaio Marsh, such is her fearful preoccupation with female sexuality that issues of power usually become collapsed into always perilous (for her) sexual allure. Troy remains Marsh's ideal female because in her emphatic sexual reticence, she never tries to exert sexual dominion. None of Marsh's divas, on the other hand, remain in their dominant positions by the end of the detecting story. Caroline Dacres of *Vintage Murder* comes closest to retaining erotic influence, principally because of her dalliance with Alleyn, but she is still relegated from wandering sexuality to maternity. Sympathetic diva Helen, in *Opening Night*,[52] is more horrifically punished by marital rape, while predatory divas are typically murder victims.

P.D. James's distrust of difference can be seen in the ways in which female power is more properly to be exercised *within* male institutions. Hence the transition in her works from independent detective Cordelia Gray (but still imagining Dalgliesh as a masculine authority) and Dalgliesh's actual subordinate, Inspector Kate Miskin. Biology in the form of motherhood, or loneliness in the form of sexually unequal relationships, can compromise women in the professional world in ways viewed tragically by the novels. Hilary, desperate for a child in *Devices and Desires*, abuses her professional position.[53] James's version of a Marsh diva, the sexually predatory actress of *The Skull Beneath the Skin*, is more harshly condemned in her depiction as a callous employer who prevented her dresser from attending her dying child.[54]

For Ruth Rendell/Barbara Vine, power is not monolithic, but is socially inflected and capable of analysis through crime fiction. Rendell/Vine uses the Gothic to investigate power structured through domesticity: the varying, often oppressive constructions of the feminine throughout the century, result in forms of domestic feminine power and assertiveness frequently contingent to irrational, even criminal urges. Even *Simisola* is a political study of women and power in the home sphere, as well as being bound up with issues of race and slavery.[55]

The six authors share an acute awareness that women's changing social roles produce tensions around issues of the feminine and power. Such a mutual realisation should not obscure the real differences in approach, from Christie's and Allingham's need to believe in a traditional gender hierarchy (for which Christie demonstrates a more willed optimism) to Sayers's personal–political renegotiations. Also distinctive are Marsh's fear of feminine sexuality as dominance, James's tragic sense of gender and sexual conflict, and finally Rendell/Vine's liberal and Gothic reconfigurings of desire and narrative.

Now to women, not just as 'suspect' but as the 'objects' of the genre; as victims, criminals or detectives.

Generic women (1): detectives, victims and killers

> And at the heart of the mystery, the clue which would make it all plain, lay the complex personality of Sally Jupp.
>
> (P.D. James, *Cover Her Face*[56])

How far does the 'placing' of female characters in the crime genre reflect or debate feminist concerns about women and gender? Does the writers' articulation of form suggest attitudes to changes in women's lives?

Agatha Christie's treatment of mothering finds generic expression in a repeated oscillation between victims and killers in works such as *The Mirror Crack'd from Side to Side*,[57] *By the Pricking of my Thumbs* and *Murder on the Orient Express*.[58] A mother may appear as a victim of a murderous conspiracy, but is later unmasked as menacing. This is in total contrast to Allingham's work, where mothers are marginal and benign, such as depicted in *The Mind Readers*.[59] A female killer is similarly untypical for Sayers, with the likelihood of female sexuality contributing to criminal deviance comprehensively exploded in *Strong*

Poison. Harriet Vane's exoneration from murder leaves her free to flirt with the role of victim in both *Have His Carcase* and *Gaudy Night*, but be narratively promoted to detective-helpmeet by the conclusion of the latter novel. There is an amusing and key scene in *Have His Carcase* when Harriet deliberately masquerades as a 'fluffy' and available feminine potential victim to the crude charms of suspect Henry Weldon by vamping him on a picnic. Her willingness to adopt a sexual masquerade receives a jolt that confirms her participation as a detective when she recognises a snake tattoo on Henry's arm as identifying him with an earlier suspect.

Discovering a 'snake' in the theatrical Eden of a family picnic reinterprets the Fall for women and sexuality. Brutally hurt by society's criminalising of female sexuality forcing her into the 'murderer' role for much of *Strong Poison*, Harriet in *Have His Carcase* employs a gender masquerade to be simultaneously victim and detective, becoming wholly detective at the discovery of the snake. In this already Fallen world, Harriet's recognition of the serpent is an acquisition of sexual knowledge that will reveal the cynicism and frequent victimising of women behind the accepted manners of courtship. The plot's restaging of the drama of Eden enables the novel to demystify gender roles and point out the dangers of conventional romance for women. Harriet's progress is one enabling women to be freer agents and 'detectives' of their own destiny.

Allingham's habit of marginalising women from the generic key roles is not as challenged as it might be by the advent of Amanda Fitton. Capable of independent adventuring, Amanda tends to operate separately where she is fully present in the plot. Significantly, in the novel in which she plays the most active role in Campion's self and detecting, *Traitor's Purse*,[60] she is physically little present and wholly ignorant of his struggles. By contrast, Ngaio Marsh's typical concentration on female sexuality as dangerous results in diva and spinster victims galore. Sexuality can be a sufficient drive to murder for both the deprived spinsters in *Overture to Death* and the sexually voracious ones such as in *Artists in Crime*.[61] What Marsh's women do not do is detect. Alleyn admits to wanting Troy to exist in a wholly separate sphere to his job in *Final Curtain* and enlists no female helpers. When she does coincide with his work, Alleyn manifests anxieties going beyond chivalrous concern.

P.D. James, on the other hand, is content to sprinkle female figures into generic positions because the tendency of her writing is to distrust 'difference' and so cast it as an ingredient of a disintegrating secular society. As well as transferring her female detectives to the masculine institution of Scotland Yard, James is keen to erode stereotypes of difference. For example, the disabled female so-called 'victim' of *Unnatural Causes* is revealed as calculating and murderous.[62] Whereas James challenges feminine types through generic positioning out of a tragic conservative nostalgia, Ruth Rendell has more liberal aims in dismantling stereotypes that have disadvantaged women. In *Wolf to the Slaughter*,[63] *A Sleeping Life* and *Kissing the Gunner's Daughter*,[64] the criminality of women also refutes the sentimentality which contributes to female disadvantage. Female detecting figures (apart from Wexford's Karen Malahyde) are more to be found embedded in familial structures in the Vine novels such as Elizabeth of *The House of Stairs*[65] whose final generic destination is to blur the boundaries between roles of detective, victim and killer. The refusal to easily assign guilt and virtue becomes part of Vine's feminist re-evaluation of literary form.

Generic women (2): criminal feminism and the ethics of aesthetics

> Paul, Paul, think how many men would be made happy by keeping a sleeping beauty in an impenetrable wood.
>
> (Barbara Vine, *Gallowglass*[66])

It is my belief that just as these important women writers have developed the artistic form of crime and detective fiction, so their aesthetic re-imagining makes ethical demands and vice versa. The claim that detecting and crime fiction is an essentially conservative literary art rests upon the privileging of 'closure' over 'process' in storytelling. Because, traditionally, crime fiction ends with the identifying of the criminal and the subsequent restoration of social order, it is said to be a genre that collaborates with conservative social forces. Society 'should' be returned to a past state of social order reinvented through the plot as a moral structure.

However, this book's exploration of innovations in gender and the generic, social and ethnic plots, psychoanalysis, the Gothic, the metaphysical and, finally, women has demonstrated that the literary arts of these six crime writers have re-plotted the *process* of crime novels in ways that profoundly affect the reading experience. The ethics of aesthetics lie in the transformation of the narrative structures. For instance, Christie's fascination with masks and social types embodies an aesthetic of 'the menace behind ordinariness' of traditional social structures, not at all dissipated by the neat endings. Sayers's works are more overtly concerned with the power relationships expressed in the genre and gender inequalities. Her novels produce a commanding aesthetic of 'Woman' stripped of occult otherness to gain social validation as an artist and a professional within existing class arrangements. Allingham's art approaches rapprochement with feminism in refusing to criminalise female sexuality and by sceptically investigating the feminine occult. Women artists and professionals can function effectively, if a little distanced from the adventurous masculine embodied by Campion.

Ngaio Marsh tends to represent an aesthetic of fear of female sexuality. Nevertheless, given sexual reticence, women are promoted as artists in painting, writing and theatre, but there is no ethical demand for their participation in upholding the law.

Both James and Rendell effect in different ways a formal hybrid between the literary realist novel and the golden age genre. James likes to define her works against the earlier genre such as the citation and refutation of Miss Marple in *Original Sin*, mentioned earlier. The adoption of literary realism as well as the repeated reference to, and distinguishing from, golden age forms, means that James's novels can more self-consciously concentrate on 'process' over closure. It is the revelation of the tragic nature of human consciousness within fragmenting secular modernity that is the object of representation to James. Her novels do not believe that capturing the criminal restores order. If the art is nostalgic and conservative, it also mounts a dialogue with feminism in the demonstration of feminine suffering within male establishments. Unfortunately, this suffering is not perceived as open to remedy, unlike Ruth Rendell's more directly feminist sense of the possibilities of a utopian ethics. The Wexford novels seek to detach a liberal ethics from social traditions of gender and class, often portrayed as oppressive. Barbara Vine's experimentation with detective-less crime novels aims to reinvigorate literary structures on more profoundly progressive and feminist lines. The investigations of gender, authoring and familial power in *Asta's Book* and *The Chimney Sweeper's Boy* are examples.

In a literature devoted to society's organisation of transgression and punishment, the aesthetics of crime writing are inevitably also ethical commentaries. Feminism, similarly, has concerned itself with transgression and punishment as part of the social construction of gender. Although five of the authors may disavow campaigning feminism, all six know that feminism has been found amongst society's definition of the criminal, and that some varieties of the criminal and the crime genre are also feminism.

Sleeping Murder by Agatha Christie (1976)[67]

In this, the official 'last case' of Miss Marple, written in the 1940s, the crime story continually tries to ascribe madness or deviant sexuality to the feminine. It takes the efforts of the good (non-sexual) crone, Miss Marple, to rightfully assign the pathology to male sexuality within a domesticity in which the feminine is victim.

Sleeping Murder traces the progress of young New Zealand colonial, Gwenda Reed, who buys an uncannily appealing house in advance of her husband's arrival in England. While staying with friends, she breaks down at a performance of *The Duchess of Malfi* upon hearing the lines of the murdering relative: 'Cover her face, mine eyes dazzle, she died young' (p. 23). Fearing a descent into madness, Gwenda is relieved by Miss Marple who suggests the true explanation: a repressed memory from Gwenda's early childhood, when she was living in the same house that she has just unwittingly bought. Gwenda recalls hearing those evocative lines spoken over the murdered body of 'Helen', who proves to be her young stepmother. History records only Helen's mysterious disappearance, but Gwenda's father soon after died, plagued by dreams of having strangled his wife. Gwenda and her husband, Giles, refuse to 'let sleeping murder lie', so Miss Marple determines to aid them in investigating the traumatic past. The inexperienced detectives quickly gain the impression that Helen was a man-hunter whose sexual appetites provoked her sorry end. More sceptical, Miss Marple is able to exonerate Helen from sexual guilt and detect masculine incestuous violence closer to home.

The relationship of women to the 'home' becomes a moot point in the detecting plot. Starting as a colonial subject brought up to call England 'Home', Gwenda's initial madness proves a repressed memory that England *is* literally her forgotten 'home'. The colonial feminine possesses a traumatic relation to 'home' that becomes staged throughout the story as the dangers for women lurking within apparent domestic security. Colonial identity becomes re-imagined as a traumatic and violent relation to domestic, 'Home', structures of power.

Again the novel draws upon Christie's sense of the uncanniness of ordinary familial living. Gwenda's disturbing experiences within her 'new' house repeat the past as Helen gradually realised that menace surrounded her home. Gwenda's father, Major Halliday, reports wife-strangling dreams to his doctors and Freud is cited to substantiate the ambiguity teasing the detectives: are the dreams the truths of guilt or appalling fantasies? In fact, sexuality is portrayed in the novel as irrational *and* theatrical in ways expressed formally through the self-referential genre. The use of the play *The Duchess of Malfi* both encodes the self-conscious nature of golden age detective fiction and proves a vivid illustration of the masking of chaotic familial desire.

Psychic connections between past and present thicken as past relationships are reactivated with attendant dangers. Victim Helen and proto-detective Gwenda become increasingly linked until Gwenda risks the same fate. 'Is Helen using me for justice?' (p. 114) she wonders to Miss Marple. A 'feminist ethics' can be discerned in the drive to 'rescue' Helen and by extension female sexual desire from condemnation as deviant. Of course, it is an ethics devoted to supporting the traditional heterosexual couple whose final freedom from the psychic legacies of the past is signalled by a pregnancy. However, the narrative process is so dominated by the menace of domesticity, that I would suggest that the resulting unease is not to be so easily neutralised by the apparent tranquil closure of the plot.

Also, the subtle paralleling of Gwenda and Helen means that the accusation of deviant female desire running in the crime story (only entirely refuted with the final unveiling of the murderer) does not remain the dominant impression. Initiation of the detecting by Miss Marple's sane banishing of Gwenda's fear of madness serves as an example of the dispelling of the fear of the feminine as 'other'. This opening move has a profound effect on the 'reading' of later reconstructions of the past. Miss Marple proves a defender of women within the domestic sphere without wishing for meaningful alternatives.

Gaudy Night by Dorothy L. Sayers (1935)

Gaudy Night concentrates on Sayers's heartfelt meditations on the position of women in society as beings with 'minds and hearts', both intellectual and passionate needs. It represents her most sustained argument for the necessity of useful work for personal integrity in women as well as men, and the need to purge the feminine of any occult 'otherness' in order to construct a viable partnership with the masculine. As part of the exploration of anxieties about the feminine, claims of female sexual pathology and the deleterious effects of popular Freudianism are exposed.

The novel focuses on the 'further education' of Harriet Vane as she re-enters her old Oxford women's college of Shrewsbury to (in effect) learn about women in society. Initially believing Oxford to be a paradise, a refuge from the corruptions of the world, Harriet is disabused of this illusion at a college reunion, a 'gaudy', in which she discovers a malicious letter. Later appealed to for aid by the female dons when a 'poison pen' becomes a vicious prankster, named the 'poltergeist' or later 'ghost', Harriet comes more and more to question the apparent female solidarity of the college. Does the cloistered femininity of these unmarried dons breed sexual repression, even madness?

Finally, badly frightened by one persecuted undergraduate's attempted suicide, Harriet asks Peter Wimsey for help. After attacks escalate to an assault upon Harriet herself and the smashing of a beautiful set of chessmen given to her by Wimsey, the noble sleuth is able to reveal the culprit to be a widowed college servant. She has become embittered by her husband's suicide following his deserved scholarly disgrace at the hands of one of the female dons. Most importantly, Wimsey is also able to restore the morale of the college. The dreaded sexual pathology of the unmarried woman is found to be bogus, the value of sincere work affirmed and Harriet finds that she has at last discovered how to reconcile the demands of her intellect and passions. She can now accept marriage with Wimsey as a partnership. The spectre of conventional 'romance', in which the masterful hero rescues the demure and grateful heroine, no longer haunts the couple.

In the first place, the re-entry to Oxford teaches Harriet that paradise cannot be gendered or based upon a total separation of the sexes. Shrewsbury College proves no refuge from the problems of women in the world, and its restoration depends upon the advent of Peter Wimsey as a sleuth who crucially respects the institution of female learning. Oxford may not prove wholly separate from the world but it retains a certain 'otherness' to it as a place where Harriet and Peter can meet as equals, as scholars, thus evading the fatal (and, to Sayers, degrading) patterns of traditional erotic romance. In Oxford, Harriet can complete her transition in the Sayers oeuvre from killer to victim to detective, begun in *Strong Poison*. Generically speaking, this movement of the feminine from criminal, to oppressed to detecting agent, is Sayers's riposte to what 'romance' does to female representation. It serves in a feminist ethical manner to pluck the feminine from pathological otherness to a partnership that erodes mystifying differences without extinguishing them. The fact that Wimsey remains the superior detective is a sign that Sayers is concerned to integrate the feminine *within* existing structures of power. Harriet therefore needs the integrity of her separate sphere of 'work' to guarantee her selfhood.

The combined prowess of Harriet and Peter serves to strip the feminine of occult Gothic powers as the poltergeist ghost is revealed as a pathological assault on unmarried women scholars. The perpetrator is not an indicator of deviant sexuality in *all* women or single women, but her criminality results from the obsessions of the traditional loyal wife. The fear of predatory, sexually unhinged spinsters proves groundless, unlike some conclusions in Ngaio Marsh novels. Popular Freudianism and its effect in indicting female sexuality is similarly countered. Harriet imagines a 'Freudian University' that becomes progressively more nightmarish as suspicions condense around the college (p. 264). As in *The Unpleasantness at the Bellona Club*,[68] Wimsey proves adept in challenging Freud's more reductive implications for female sexual abstinence. *Gaudy Night* proves to be a novel supporting expanded possibilities in society for women, no longer to be feared as occult. Its ethics are a progressive feminism eschewing the radical.

The Fashion in Shrouds by Margery Allingham (1938)

The only novel in which Allingham examines female sexuality with sustained narrative focus, *The Fashion in Shrouds*, depicts feminine eroticism as needing to be in relation to a dominant male. Women who use their sexuality actively are shown to be dangerous and ultimately theatrical and hollow. The novel appears to urge women to abjure sexuality in order to be active in professions: there is a need for separation between feminine sexuality and any social expansion of women's roles in society.

We are introduced to the most successful businesswoman in Europe, dress designer Val, who happens to be Albert Campion's sister. She is in love with aircraft designer Alan Dell, whose lack of sophistication about women leads him to be enchanted away from Val by her chief customer, actress Georgia Wells. Lady Amanda Fitton arrives upon the scene determined to rescue Alan Dell and put him back to work in his engineering team, of which she herself is now a valuable member. She announces her engagement to Campion, much to his surprise, as part of an attempt to defuse an explosive social situation when Georgia's husband, Ramillies, encounters Georgia and Alan Dell in a night club.

Ramillies, a colonial governor with a brutal reputation, is about to fly to Africa in a gold-painted aeroplane as a gift for the African leader of his new posting. At a great ceremonial send-off, Ramillies is discovered dead, the second of Georgia's husbands to die conveniently. Georgia happily announces that his demise occurred just after taking a medicine that Val had given to her for her own use. Terrified for his sister, Campion and Amanda investigate. True to Allingham form, the motives for killing prove not to be female sexual jealousy or sex at all but yet another masculine power-crazed manipulator: naked 'power' corrupts in Allingham's world with her love of traditional structures set up as a bulwark against crazed would-be 'dictators'.

Georgia Wells is a character closer to Marsh's divas than Allingham's usual stable of female characters. Unable clearly to distinguish reality from fiction when ensnaring men, her imperilling of Val is not malice, but her self-obsessed masquerade of feminine charm. It has become so habitual that her artificial spontaneity is now 'natural'. She seems designed to endorse Campion's otherwise misogynist remark that she is a woman bred to need a keeper. Val, on the other hand, is made unhappy by her superiority over most potential male partners. 'Female women love so abjectly,' she tells Campion (p. 67), and the most important businesswoman in Europe acquiesces joyfully to Alan Dell's proposal that she become 'my possession... It means the other half of my life to me, but the whole of yours to you' (p. 288).

Amanda represents the other side to this depiction of feminine sexuality as either initiating chaos or requiring subordination. Contrasting erotic obsession and more companionable affection in typical terms as 'cake love' or 'bread and butter', she champions the latter in becoming Campion's helpmeet in detection and finally his genuine fiancée. In order to trap the killer, Campion and Amanda mimic 'cake love' and a passionate break-up. A masquerade of sexual pain in the detecting story increases the sense of ambivalence about Campion's concluding proposal when he predicts that 'cake love' will come to trouble them.

The novel as a whole seems to fear sexual passion as a loss of control. In an explicitly sexual woman, Georgia, sexuality is inseparable from artifice, chaos and cruelty. However, the novel's ethical stance is not limited to the need to confine female sexuality as the bullying masculinity of Ramillies is thoroughly deplored. His fear of flying contributes to his death. Similarly, the 'peculiarly masculine' (p. 26) Alan Dell is easily duped by Georgia. It is the far more gender-ambivalent Campion who sees Val as an 'aspect of himself' (p. 65) and who will come to need Amanda in a similar fashion in *Traitor's Purse*. He alone retains his dignity and function as the ambivalent hero.

Singing in the Shrouds by Ngaio Marsh (1958)[69]

Singing in the Shrouds represents a rare example in Marsh's work of the murderer as a pathological serial killer. He is believed to be travelling amongst a small group of passengers on a ship heading south to the tropics. The killer strangles women and leaves flowers strewn on their corpses. Roderick Alleyn joins the ship incognito and seeks his man amongst a gathering of potential male neurotics. These range from a celibate priest, Father Jourdain, a waspish retired schoolmaster, Mr Merryman, the pathetic Mr Cuddy (travelling with Mrs Cuddy), psychiatrist Tim Makepiece, bachelor Mr McAngus, and Aubyn Dale, a chat-show host suffering from a psychiatric disorder. Potential victims range from ingénue Jemima Carmichael to coded lesbian Katherine Abbott, Mrs Cuddy, and one of Marsh's more sympathetic divas, the flamboyant Mrs Dillington-Blick. However, it is the homosexual steward, dressed in a costume copied from a doll given to Mrs Dillington-Blick, who becomes the murder victim in a move that is simultaneously homophobic *and* demonstrates the theatrical nature of gender and sexuality in Marsh's work.

Although the crime narrative would appear to indict masculine heterosexuality as pathological, two factors mitigate such an easy interpretation. In the first place, stress is laid upon the dysfunctionality of the potential suspects, with a firm heterosexual normality maintained not only in the young doctor Tim's wooing of Jemima but particularly in Alleyn. His frequent missives to Troy are a narrative device that genders the reader as feminine in a secure erotic relation to the trustworthy detective. Secondly, the stress of the detecting story is focused upon the need to protect the women and upon the thickening atmosphere of fear onboard ship. If the *closure* of the novel is to isolate the dysfunctional male as 'other', to restore 'normality' to heterosexual relations, then *the process* is to portray women more and more as potential victims. It is necessary to be in a conventional heterosexual relation such as that of Jemima and safe Tim or to renounce sexuality altogether, such as lesbian Katherine (who has lost her companion to marriage), for a woman to be secure.

The shipboard setting is described more and more as its own hermetically sealed world, with its own absolute governance in the alcoholic Captain. Yet the Captain proves to be a masculine authority who fails to prevent murder. He is a failing of social power that leads to chaos. Gender and sexuality become more Gothic and disembodied as boundaries appear less and less secure. Sexuality is presented initially as a masquerade in the explicit advances of diva Mrs Dillington-Blick, and is metaphorically condensed in the Spanish-dressed doll as a gift from erotically entranced Mr Cuddy. The large doll squeaks 'mama,' emphasising the sterility of this masquerade of gender. The Captain's deliberate refusal to accord official authority to Alleyn as well as himself enables gay steward Dennis to masquerade in Mrs Dillington-Blick's Spanish doll robes and reap the murderous consequences of sexuality becoming theatrical and Gothic.

Denied his usual role of eroticising masculine authority to make connections over barriers of gender and class, Alleyn has here to be more of a trickster: in disguise and cultivating multiple relationships for concealed purposes. As well as the homophobic eradication of Dennis, which also encodes the theatricality of sexual and gender identity, Alleyn comes up against conflicting metaphysics. When forced to enlist Father Jourdain and psychiatrist Tim as helpers, he encounters the priest's desire to exorcise devils out of the murderer and Tim's Freudian enthusiasm. Typically for Marsh (and in contrast to Sayers), Freud comes close to being wholly endorsed as Tim uncovers a childhood trauma when the killer's love for his mother is interrupted by the father's desire. Yet, as in previous instances, Alleyn retains a little scepticism, much like Wexford at the end of *The Veiled One*.[70]

Despite the superficially pro-feminine direction of the crime story, *Singing in the Shrouds* principally demonstrates the need for the detective to hold conventional powers if females are not to be victimised. The name of the killer suggests that relaxation of authority results in a carnival of killing rather than more liberal and exuberant possibilities for renegotiating power. A Gothic atmosphere of menace directed towards women pervades a ship ineffectively 'mastered'. Again, Alleyn represents traditional values and order made *desirable*. Troy's absence becomes a literal version of the need for separate spheres for the genders that do not challenge the masculine potency of the law.

A Certain Justice by P.D. James (1997)[71]

Venetia Aldrige, successful lawyer and divorced mother of Octavia, enjoys advantages of wealth and professional power, but not the esteem of her creator, P.D. James. The impression gained by a first reading of *A Certain Justice* is that James's tragic sense of the professions failing to assuage the social fragmentation of secular modernity, is finely honed here to criticise working mothers. The sense of a crisis in maternity in the modern world is very conservatively rendered, but what saves the novel from a purely reactionary feminist stance is that the detecting plot's critical focus extends to 'traditional' feminine roles and to the continuing 'masculine' nature of the professions.

Self-confident, professionally ruthless, Venetia would consider herself an unlikely murder victim. Yet she is found killed in her Chambers after a series of events initiated by her successful defence of the pathological Gary Ashe. He then insinuates himself into the life of Venetia's daughter, insufficiently loved Octavia, becoming her 'fiancé'. Venetia has also used her power brutally at work, threatening the livelihoods and futures of employees and colleagues. There is even, deep in Venetia's childhood, a connection to a family tragedy, perhaps caused by a lapse in the duties of love, that will haunt a particular lawyer colleague for the rest of his life.

Many people whose lives are injured by Venetia's unfeeling struggle for power prove to have had a hand in her demise. Punished through her inadequacies as a mother, Venetia is nevertheless willing to use her gender in court to gain personal advantages. This exploitation of gender is first displayed to the reader in the service of dangerous criminal Gary Ashe, and brings about terrible retribution. In contrast, Kate Miskin is shown to *suffer* her gender differences. She resents her lack of integration into the male camaraderie of Adam Dalgliesh's team, and provokes a final confrontation with him over why she was prevented (as a woman) from shooting the killer. Femininity seems doomed to suffer in masculine professions in the person of Kate, since differences remain and seem little negotiable. Meanwhile, the suffering of children is largely attributed to neglectful professional mothers. Kate feels moral revulsion over council estate dweller Enid, who fends off attacks from the young by exploiting a child's death. She pretends to be a witch in an arena of social breakdown in which only the occulting of the elderly feminine (by cursing a child who subsequently dies) gives her any protection.

Although depicting individual selfishness in working mothers, *A Certain Justice* more deeply diagnoses a social crisis in maternity, which goes beyond individual choices. Similarly, traditional female roles are shown not to provide easy answers: from the loyal wife terrified of her husband's retirement to the fecund, apparently 'ideal' mother who cares only for her own children and is indifferent to the sufferings of her husband's child, Octavia. Most pointed is the exploration of an apparently benevolent, 'Barbara Pym' woman, supposedly an emblem of 'feminine' virtues, but who is revealed to be driven by revenge.

Dalgliesh appears more shadowy in this novel which gives prominence to his subordinates, particularly Kate. Again, he fulfils his role as the professional detective who should restore moral order but cannot, an unveiled authority who fails in secular modernity. This function is particularly signalled by his momentary alliance with Father Prestigne, whose religious certainty makes him the possessor of much of the detecting truth *before* Dalgliesh. Father Prestigne prioritises his values above the secular law. Where Dalgliesh cannot stop further violence and disorder, the priest can give comfort and restore moral direction to the feminine part of the murder.

James's tragic sense lies in the texture of her society that has abandoned the theological possibilities of moral order. Very much like Sayers, James advocates feminine participation in society within existing institutions, but with a far more tragic sense that viable moral structures for both sexes have been so far abandoned in secular modernity as to make society fragmented and chaotic. Whereas Sayers's novels of the feminine lean towards Shakespearean comedy, James embraces the social nightmare of *King Lear*.

An Unkindness of Ravens by Ruth Rendell (1985)[72]

This Wexford novel centres on a clash between 1980s British militant feminism (which proves rooted in the 1960s), with traditional feminine stereotypes shown to be oppressive and leaving a profound psychological legacy. *An Unkindness of Ravens* also considers society's fear of feminism as the fear of wild maenads, as female energy out of control.

The story starts with a very ordinary wife, Joy Williams, reporting the disappearance of a very ordinary husband, Rodney. However, Rodney Williams proves to have lived an extraordinary personal life, with two wives and two daughters of similar ages, Sara and Veronica. When Rodney's body is found it seems likely that a local radical feminist group with cultish overtones, Arria, are involved. Ambitious Sara, unfavoured by her mother, who adores her son, is a member of Arria, which sports a raven logo. Rumours abound suggesting that Arria encourages its members to kill a man as an initiation rite.

Meanwhile, Wexford's detecting companion, Mike Burden, is distraught. His happy second marriage to schoolteacher and feminist Jenny is unravelling, not because she is pregnant, but because she cannot bear that the baby is a girl. Jenny seems to have been driven mad by pregnancy, but the very sincere feminist ethics behind this novel do not allow the matter to rest here. The sex attribution proves erroneous and Jenny gives birth to Mark. Her restoration to psychic health confirms her commitment to feminism on the grounds that she has experienced the irrational misogyny still present in modern society as psychic residues, and *therefore* her feminism must be consciously espoused as necessary for justice.

The examples of the Williams families illustrate why the novel feels the need to endorse Jenny's moderate feminism. Joy's unstinting preference for her son is matched by the pathetic prettiness of Wendy, Rodney Williams's second wife, who was made pregnant at 16 and who then brings up her daughter in an atmosphere of immature feminine vulnerability. As a result, Veronica falls prey to her assertive, love-deprived half-sister, to nearly fatal effect.

Investigation of the ferocious-sounding radical Arria cult finds its home base in a house in which the parents inhabit the hippy, stoned world of the 1960s. Neatly representing the link between militant feminism in the 1980s and 1960s counter-culture, Arria was founded by a lesbian school teacher and proves to be advocating knife attacks on men who sexually harass young women or who appear to do so. Such actual woundings appear to back up the hints of an initiation rite involving killing a man, and the death of Rodney Williams is suspiciously in context. Also, when it seems that he had the habit of sexually abusing one daughter with grim prospects for the other, an Arria feminist revenge killing seems to be the answer. It is Wexford's daughter, Sheila, acting a role as a victim of incest, which *should* have given Wexford a clue to this, he thinks. Again, Wexford's familial psychically constructed identity becomes a vital ingredient in his detecting prowess.

Yet the fact that Wexford does not immediately make the connection between his daughter's play and his case should give the reader a clue. For, as Wexford explains, the vengeful daughter is not an incest victim driven to participation in Arria's horrible rites, but a psychopath who kills her father because this will give her the money to go to medical college. She fantasised the sexual abuse and then used it to force her half-sister to co-operate. Having read up on Freud's seduction theory, the murderer gets to a point where she does and does not believe her own fictions. The rumours of Arria advocating the killing of men prove to be fantasies also, both on the part of some wilder members but encouraged in the policemen's minds by fear of maenads, women rampaging out of control. However the fantasies haunting the very structure of militant feminism in Arria do contribute to the pathological fantasies of the killer: 'When she stabbed Rodney she was a woman out of classical myth' (p. 267). The murderer's 'acting' of abuse victim and vengeful raven takes place as a masquerade on the familial stage rather than, as with Sheila, in the literal theatre.

In showing that militant feminism can provide a space for dangerous fantasies to be rehearsed, *An Unkindness of Ravens* repudiates militancy in favour of Jenny Burden's final reasoning for social justice for women. This novel contains an ethics against radical separatism because it equates feminist militancy with the irrational, and the liberation of violent fantasies. It remains a novel promoting a feminist ethics by demonstrating that the irrational lies also in traditional privileging of the masculine, and so liberal social change is required. The crime story refuses to essentialise or sentimentalise women. *An Unkindness of Ravens* is a novel where the *process* of the detecting uncovers fears of the feminine: the reader is shown that the aesthetics of a detective novel can be understood as the ethics of a moderate feminism.

And with the inextricable conspiracy between women's crime fiction and feminism, *From Agatha Christie to Ruth Rendell* itself rests its case.

Appendix A: The Complete Detective and Crime Novels of the Six Authors

Agatha Christie (1890–1976)

Hercule Poirot

The Mysterious Affair at Styles (UK, London: Lane, 1920; US, New York: Dodd Mead, 1927).

The Murder on the Links (UK, London: Lane, 1923; US, New York: Lane, 1923).

The Murder of Roger Ackroyd (UK, London: Collins, 1926; US, New York: Dodd Mead, 1926).

The Big Four (UK, London: Collins, 1927; US, New York: Dodd Mead, 1927).

The Mystery of the Blue Train (UK, London: Collins, 1928; US, New York: Collins, 1928).

Peril at End House (UK, London: Collins, 1932; US, New York: Dodd Mead, 1932).

Lord Edgware Dies (UK, London: Collins, 1933)
as *Thirteen at Dinner* (US, New York: Dodd Mead, 1933)

Murder on the Orient Express (UK, London: Collins, 1934)
as *Murder on the Calais Coach* (US, New York: Dodd Mead, 1934).

Death in the Clouds (UK, London: Collins, 1935)
as *Death in the Air* (US, New York: Dodd Mead, 1935).

The ABC Murders (UK, London: Collins, 1936; US, New York: Dodd Mead, 1936)
as *The Alphabet Murders* (US, New York: Pocket Books, 1966).

Cards on the Table (UK, London: Collins, 1936; US, New York: Dodd Mead, 1937).

Murder in Mesopotamia (UK, London: Collins, 1936; US, New York: Dodd Mead, 1936).

Death on the Nile (UK, London: Collins, 1937; US, New York: Dodd Mead, 1938).

Dumb Witness (UK, London: Collins, 1937)
as *Poirot Loses a Client* (US, New York: Dodd Mead, 1937).

Appointment with Death (UK, London: Collins, 1938; US, New York: Dodd Mead, 1938).

Hercule Poirot's Christmas (UK, London: Collins, 1938)
as *Murder for Christmas* (US, New York: Dodd Mead, 1939)
as *A Holiday for Murder* (US, New York: Avon, 1947).

One, Two, Buckle My Shoe (UK, London: Collins, 1940)
as *The Patriotic Murders* (US, New York: Dodd Mead, 1941)
as *An Overdose of Death* (US, New York: Dell, 1963).

Sad Cypress (UK, London: Collins, 1940).

Evil Under the Sun (UK, London: Collins, 1940; US, New York: Dodd Mead, 1940).

Five Little Pigs (UK, London: Collins, 1942)
as *Murder in Retrospect* (US, New York: Dodd Mead, 1942).

The Hollow (UK, London: Collins, 1946; US, New York: Dodd Mead, 1946)
as *Murder After Hours* (US, New York: Dell, 1954).
Taken at the Flood (UK, London: Collins, 1948)
as *There Is a Tide*...(US, New York: Dodd Mead, 1948).
Mrs McGinty's Dead (UK, London: Collins, 1952; US, New York: Dodd Mead, 1952).
After the Funeral (UK, London: Collins, 1953)
as *Funerals Are Fatal* (US, New York: Dodd Mead, 1953)
as *Murder at the Gallop* (UK, London: Fontana, 1963).
Hickory, Dickory, Dock (UK, London: Collins, 1955)
as *Hickory, Dickory, Death* (US, New York: Dodd Mead, 1955).
Dead Man's Folly (UK, London: Collins, 1956; US, New York: Dodd Mead, 1956).
Cat among the Pigeons (UK, London: Collins, 1959; US, New York: Dodd Mead, 1960).
The Clocks (UK, London: Collins, 1963; US, New York: Dodd Mead, 1964).
Third Girl (UK, London: Collins, 1966; US, New York: Dodd Mead, 1967).
Hallowe'en Party (UK, London: Collins, 1969; US, New York: Dodd Mead, 1969).
Elephants Can Remember (UK, London: Collins, 1972; US, New York: Dodd Mead, 1972).
Curtain: Hercule Poirot's Last Case (UK, London: Collins, 1975; US, New York: Dodd Mead, 1975).

Miss Marple

The Body in the Library (UK, London: Collins, 1942; US, New York: Dodd Mead, 1942).
The Moving Finger (US, New York: Dodd Mead, 1942; UK, London: Collins, 1943).
A Murder Is Announced (UK, London: Collins, 1950; US, New York: Dodd Mead, 1950).
They Do It with Mirrors (UK, London: Collins, 1952)
as *Murder with Mirrors* (US, New York: Dodd Mead, 1952).
A Pocket Full of Rye (UK, London: Collins, 1954; US, New York: Dodd Mead, 1954).
4.50 from Paddington (UK, London: Collins, 1957)
as *What Mrs McGillicuddy Saw!* (US, New York: Dodd Mead, 1957)
as *Murder She Said* (US, New York: Pocket Books, 1961).
The Mirror Crack'd from Side to Side (UK, London: Collins, 1962)
as *The Mirror Crack'd* (US, New York: Dodd Mead, 1963).
A Caribbean Mystery (UK, London: Collins, 1964; US, New York: Dodd Mead, 1965).
At Bertram's Hotel (UK, London: Collins, 1965; US, New York: Dodd Mead, 1966).
Nemesis (UK, London: Collins, 1971; US, New York: Dodd Mead, 1971).
Sleeping Murder (UK, London: Collins, 1976; US, New York: Dodd Mead, 1976).

Other detectives

The Secret Adversary (Beresfords) (UK, London: Lane, 1922; US, New York: Dodd Mead, 1922).
The Man in the Brown Suit (UK, London: Lane, 1924; US, New York: Dodd Mead, 1924).
The Secret of Chimneys (Battle) (UK, London: Lane, 1925; US, New York: Dodd Mead, 1925).

The Seven Dials Murder (Battle) (UK, London: Collins, 1929; US, New York: Dodd Mead, 1929).

The Murder at the Vicarage (UK, London: Collins, 1930; US, New York: Dodd Mead, 1930).

The Floating Admiral, with others (UK, London: Hodder & Stoughton, 1931; US, New York: Doubleday, 1932).

The Sittaford Mystery (UK, London: Collins, 1931)
as *The Murder at Hazelmoor* (US, New York: Dodd Mead, 1931).

Why Didn't They Ask Evans? (UK, London: Collins, 1934)
as *The Boomerang Clue* (US, New York: Dodd Mead, 1935).

Murder in Three Acts (US, New York: Dodd Mead, 1934)
as *Three-Act Tragedy* (UK, London: Collins, 1935).

Murder Is Easy (Battle) (UK, London: Collins, 1939)
as *Easy to Kill* (US, New York: Dodd Mead, 1939).

Ten Little Niggers (UK, London: Collins, 1939)
as *And Then There Were None* (US, New York: Dodd Mead, 1940)
as *Ten Little Indians* (US, New York: Pocket Books, 1965).

N or M? (Beresfords) (UK, London: Collins, 1941; US, New York: Dodd Mead, 1941).

Death Comes as the End (US, New York: Dodd Mead, 1944; UK, London: Collins, 1945).

Towards Zero (Battle) (UK, London: Collins, 1944; US, New York: Dodd Mead, 1944).

Sparkling Cyanide (UK, London: Collins, 1945)
as *Remembered Death* (US, New York: Dodd Mead, 1945).

Crooked House (UK, London: Collins, 1949; US, New York: Dodd Mead, 1949).

They Came to Baghdad (UK, London: Collins, 1951; US, New York: Dodd Mead, 1951).

Destination Unknown (UK, London: Collins, 1954)
as *So Many Steps to Death* (US, New York: Dodd Mead, 1955).

Ordeal by Innocence (UK, London: Collins, 1958; US, New York: Dodd Mead, 1959).

The Pale Horse (UK, London: Collins, 1961; US, New York: Dodd Mead, 1962*).

Endless Night (UK, London: Collins, 1967; US, New York: Dodd Mead, 1968).

By the Pricking of My Thumbs (Beresford) (UK, London: Collins, 1968; US, New York: Dodd Mead, 1968).

Passenger to Frankfurt (UK, London: Collins, 1970; US, New York: Dodd Mead, 1970).

Postern of Fate (Beresfords) (UK, London: Collins, 1973; US, New York: Dodd Mead, 1973).

Murder on Board (omnibus) (US, New York: Dodd Mead, 1974).

Short stories

Poirot Investigates (UK, London: Lane, 1924; US, New York: Dodd Mead, 1925).

Partners in Crime (UK, London: Collins, 1929; US, New York: Dodd Mead, 1929) reprinted in part as *The Sunningdale Mystery*, Collins, 1933.

The Under Dog (UK, London: Readers Library, 1929).

The Mysterious Mr Quin (UK, London: Collins, 1930; US, New York: Dodd Mead, 1930).

The Thirteen Problems (UK, London: Collins, 1932)
as *The Tuesday Club Murders* (US, New York: Dodd Mead, 1933 selection)
as *The Mystery of the Blue Geraniums and Other Tuesday Club Murders* (US, New York: Bantam, 1940).

The Hound of Death and Other Stories (UK, London: Odhams, 1933).

Parker Pyne Investigates (UK, London: Collins, 1934)
as *Mr Parker Pyne, Detective* (US, New York: Dodd Mead, 1934).

The Listerdale Mystery and Other Stories (UK, London: Collins, 1934).

Murder in the Mews and Other Stories (UK, London: Collins, 1937)
as *Dead Man's Mirror and Other Stories* (US, New York: Dodd Mead, 1937).

The Regatta Mystery and Other Stories (US, New York: Dodd Mead, 1939).

The Mystery of the Baghdad Chest (UK, London: Bantam, 1943).

The Mystery of the Crime in Cabin 66 (UK, London: Bantam, 1943).

Poirot and the Regatta Mystery (UK, London: Bantam, 1943).

Poirot on Holiday (UK, London: Todd, 1943).

Problem at Pollensa Bay, and Christmas Adventure (UK, London: Todd, 1943).

The Veiled Lady, and The Mystery of the Baghdad Chest (UK, London: Todd, 1944).

Poirot Knows the Murderer (UK, London: Todd, 1946).

Poirot Lends a Hand (UK, London: Todd, 1946).

The Labours of Hercules (UK, London: Collins, 1947; US, New York: Dodd Mead, 1947).

The Witness for the Prosecution and Other Stories (US, New York: Dodd Mead, 1948).

The Mousetrap and Other Stories (US, New York: Dell, 1949)
as *Three Blind Mice and Other Stories* (US, New York: Dodd Mead, 1950).

The Under Dog and Other Stories (US, New York: Dodd Mead, 1951).

The Adventures of the Christmas Pudding, and a Selection of Entrées (UK, London: Collins, 1960).

Double Sin and Other Stories (US, New York: Dodd Mead, 1961).

13 for Luck! A Selection of Mystery Stories for Young Readers (US, New York: Dodd Mead, 1961; UK, London: Collins, 1966).

Surprise! Surprise! A Collection of Mystery Stories with Unexpected Endings (US, New York: Dodd Mead, 1965).

13 Clues for Miss Marple (US, New York: Dodd Mead, 1966).

The Golden Ball and Other Stories (US, New York: Dodd Mead, 1971).

Poirot's Early Cases (UK, London: Collins, 1974; US, New York: Dodd Mead, 1974).

Miss Marple's Final Cases and Others (UK, London: Collins, 1979).

Dorothy L. Sayers (1893–1957)

Detective novels (series detective: Lord Peter Wimsey in all books except *The Documents in the Case*)

Whose Body? (US, New York: Boni & Liveright, 1923; UK, London: Unwin, 1923).

Clouds of Witness (UK, London: Unwin, 1926; US, New York: Dial Press, 1927).

Unnatural Death (UK, London: Benn, 1927)
as *The Dawson Pedigree* (US, New York: Dial Press, 1928).
The Unpleasantness at the Bellona Club (UK, London: Benn, 1928; US, New York: Payson & Clarke, 1928).
The Documents in the Case, with Robert Eustace (UK, London: Benn, 1930; US, New York: Brewer & Warren, 1930).
Strong Poison (UK, London: Gollancz, 1930; US, New York: Brewer & Warren, 1930).
The Five Red Herrings (UK, London: Gollancz, 1931)
as *Suspicious Characters* (US, New York: Brewer Warren & Putnam, 1931).
The Floating Admiral, with others (UK, London: Hodder & Stoughton, 1931; US, New York: Doubleday, 1932).
Have His Carcase (UK, London: Gollancz, 1932; US, New York: Brewer Warren & Putnam, 1932).
Murder Must Advertise (UK, London: Gollancz, 1933; US, New York: Harcourt Brace, 1933).
Ask a Policemen, with others (UK, London: Barker, 1933; US, New York: Morrow, 1933).
The Nine Tailors (UK, London: Gollancz, 1934; US, New York: Harcourt Brace, 1934).
Gaudy Night (UK, London: Gollancz, 1935; US, New York: Harcourt Brace, 1936).
Six Against the Yard, with others (UK, London: Selwyn & Blount, 1936)
as *Six Against Scotland Yard* (US, New York: Doubleday, 1936).
Busman's Honeymoon (UK, London: Gollancz, 1937; US, New York: Harcourt Brace, 1937).
Double Death: A Murder Story, with others (UK, London: Gollancz, 1939).
With Jill Paton Walsh, *Thrones, Dominations* (UK, London: Hodder & Stoughton, 1998; US, New York: St. Martins Press, 1998).

Short stories (series detective: Lord Peter Wimsey)

Lord Peter Views the Body (UK, London: Gollancz, 1928; US, New York: Payson & Clarke, 1929).
Hangman's Holiday (UK, London: Gollancz, 1933; US, New York: Harcourt Brace, 1933).
A Treasury of Sayers Stories (UK, London: Gollancz, 1958).
Lord Peter: A Collection of All the Lord Peter Wimsey Stories, edited by James Sandoe (US, New York: Harper, 1972; augmented edition, 1972).
Striding Folly (UK, London: New English Library, 1972).

Margery Allingham (1904–1966) (series detective: Albert Campion, from *The Crime at Black Dudley*)

Detective novels

Blackerchief Dick: A Tale of Mersea Island (UK, London: Hodder & Stoughton, 1923; US, New York: Doubleday, 1923).
The White Cottage Mystery (UK, London: Jarrolds, 1928).
The Crime at Black Dudley (Campion) (UK, London: Jarrolds, 1929)
as *The Black Dudley Murder* (US, New York: Doubleday, 1930).

Mystery Mile (Campion) (UK, London: Jarrolds, 1930; US, New York: Doubleday, 1930).

Look to the Lady (Campion) (UK, London: Jarrolds, 1931)
as *The Gyrth Chalice Mystery* (US, New York: Doubleday, 1931).

Police at the Funeral (Campion) (UK, London: Heinemann, 1931; US, New York: Doubleday, 1932).

Sweet Danger (Campion) (UK, London: Heinemann, 1933)
as *Kingdom of Death* (US, New York: Doubleday, 1933)
as *The Fear Sign* (US, New York: Macfadden, 1933).

Death of a Ghost (Campion) (UK, London: Heinemann, 1934; US, New York: Doubleday, 1934).

Flowers for the Judge (Campion) (UK, London: Heinemann, 1936; US, New York: Doubleday, 1936)
as *Legacy in Blood* (US, New York: American Mercury, 1949).

Six Against the Yard, with others (UK, London: Selwyn & Blount, 1936)
as *Six Against Scotland Yard* (US, New York: Doubleday, 1936).

Dancers in Mourning (Campion) (UK, London: Heinemann, 1937; US, New York: Doubleday, 1937)
as *Who Killed Chloe?* (US, New York: Avon, 1943).

The Case of the Late Pig (Campion) (UK, London: Hodder & Stoughton, 1937).

Mr Campion, Criminologist (includes 'The Case of the Late Pig' and other stories) (US, New York: Doubleday, 1937).

The Fashion in Shrouds (Campion) (UK, London: Heinemann, 1938; US, New York: Doubleday, 1938).

Black Plumes (UK, London: Heinemann, 1940; US, New York: Doubleday, 1940).

Traitor's Purse (Campion) (UK, London: Heinemann, 1941; US, New York: Doubleday, 1941)
as *The Sabotage Murder Mystery* (US, New York: Avon, 1943).

Dance of the Years (UK, London: Joseph, 1943)
as *The Gallantrys* (US, Boston: Little Brown, 1943).

Coroner's Pidgin (Campion) (UK, London: Heinemann, 1945)
as *Pearls Before Swine* (US, New York: Doubleday, 1945).

More Work for the Undertaker (Campion) (UK, London: Heinemann; US, New York: Doubleday, 1949).

Deadly Duo (two novelets) (US, New York: Doubleday, 1949)
as *Take Two at Bedtime* (UK, Kingswood, Surrey: World's Work, 1950).

The Tiger in the Smoke (Campion) (UK, London: Chatto & Windus, 1952; US, New York: Doubleday, 1952).

No Love Lost (two novelets) (UK, Kingswood, Surrey: World's Work, 1954; US, New York: Doubleday, 1954).

The Beckoning Lady (Campion) (UK, London: Chatto & Windus, 1955)
as *The Estate of the Beckoning Lady* (US, New York: Doubleday, 1955).

Hide My Eyes (Campion) (UK, London: Chatto & Windus, 1958)
as *Tether's End* (US, New York: Doubleday, 1958)
as *Ten Were Missing* (US, New York: Dell, 1959).

The China Governess (Campion) (US, New York: Doubleday, 1962; UK, London: Chatto & Windus, 1963).

The Mysterious Mr Campion (omnibus) (UK, London: Chatto & Windus, 1963).

The Mind Readers (Campion) (UK, London: Chatto & Windus, 1965; US, New York: Morrow, 1965).

Mr Campion's Lady (omnibus, with stories) (UK, London: Chatto & Windus, 1965).

Cargo of Eagles (Campion; completed by Youngman Carter) (UK, London: Chatto & Windus, 1968; US, New York: Morrow, 1968).

Short stories

Mr Campion and Others (UK, London: Heinemann, 1939; augmented edition, UK, London: Penguin, 1950).

Wanted: Someone Innocent (novelet and stories) (n.p., Pony Books, 1946).

The Case Book of Mr Campion, ed. Ellery Queen (US, New York: American Mercury, 1947).

The Allingham Case-Book (UK, London: Chatto & Windus, 1969; US, New York: Morrow, 1969).

Ngaio Marsh (1899–1982) (series detective: Roderick Alleyn)

A Man Lay Dead (UK, London: Bles, 1934; US, New York: Sheridan, 1942).

Enter a Murderer (UK, London: Bles, 1935; US, New York: Pocket Books, 1941).

The Nursing-Home Murder, with Henry Jellett (UK, London: Bles, 1935; US, New York: Sheridan, 1941).

Death in Ecstasy (UK, London: Bles, 1936; US, New York: Sheridan, 1941).

Vintage Murder (UK, London: Bles, 1937; US, New York: Sheridan, 1940).

Artists in Crime (UK, London: Bles, 1938; US, New York: Furman, 1938).

Death in a White Tie (UK, London: Bles, 1938; US, New York: Furman, 1938).

Overture to Death (UK, London: Collins, 1939; US, New York: Furman, 1939).

Death at the Bar (UK, London: Collins, 1940; US, Boston: Little Brown, 1940).

Death of a Peer (US, Boston: Little Brown, 1940)
as *Surfeit of Lampreys* (UK, London: Collins, 1941).

Death and the Dancing Footman (US, Boston: Little Brown, 1941; UK, London: Collins, 1942).

Colour Scheme (UK, London: Collins, 1943; US, Boston: Little Brown, 1943).

Died in the Wool (UK, London: Collins, 1945; US, Boston: Little Brown, 1945).

Final Curtain (UK, London: Collins, 1947; US, Boston: Little Brown, 1947).

Swing, Brother, Swing (UK, London: Collins, 1949)
as *A Wreath for Rivera* (US, Boston: Little Brown, 1949).

Opening Night (UK, London: Collins, 1951)
as *Night at the Vulcan* (US, Boston: Little Brown, 1951).

Spinsters in Jeopardy (US, Boston: Little Brown, 1953: UK, London: Collins, 1954)
as *The Bride of Death* (US, New York: Spivak, 1955).

Scales of Justice (UK, London: Collins, 1955; US, Boston: Little Brown, 1955).

Death of a Fool (US, Boston: Little Brown, 1956)
as *Off With His Head* (UK, London: Collins, 1957).

Singing in the Shrouds (US, Boston: Little Brown, 1958; UK, London: Collins, 1959).

False Scent (US, Boston: Little Brown, 1960; UK, London: Collins, 1960).

Hand in Glove (US, Boston: Little Brown, 1962; UK, London: Collins, 1962).
Dead Water (US, Boston: Little Brown, 1963; UK, London: Collins, 1964).
Killer Dolphin (US, Boston: Little Brown, 1966)
as *Death at the Dolphin* (UK, London: Collins, 1967).
Clutch of Constables (UK, London: Collins, 1968; US, Boston: Little Brown, 1969).
When in Rome (UK, London: Collins, 1970; US, Boston: Little Brown, 1971).
Tied up in Tinsel (UK, London: Collins, 1972; US, Boston: Little Brown, 1972).
Black as He's Painted (UK, London: Collins, 1975; US, Boston: Little Brown, 1975).
Last Ditch (US, Boston: Little Brown, 1977; UK, London: Collins, 1977).
Grave Mistake (US, Boston: Little Brown, 1978; UK, London: Collins, 1978).
Photo-Finish (US, Boston: Little Brown, 1980; UK, London: Collins, 1980).
Light Thickens (US, Boston: Little Brown, 1982; UK, London: Collins, 1982).

P.D. James (1920–) (series detective: Adam Dalgliesh)

Cover Her Face (UK, London: Faber & Faber, 1962; US, New York: Scribner, 1966).
A Mind to Murder (UK, London: Faber & Faber, 1963; US, New York: Scribner, 1967).
Unnatural Causes (UK, London: Faber & Faber, 1967; US, New York: Scribner, 1967).
Shroud for a Nightingale (UK, London: Faber & Faber, 1971; US, New York: Scribner, 1971).
An Unsuitable Job for a Woman (UK, London: Faber & Faber, 1972; US, New York: Scribner, 1973).
The Black Tower (UK, London: Faber & Faber, 1975; US, New York: Scribner, 1975).
Death of an Expert Witness (UK, London: Faber & Faber, 1977; US, New York: Scribner, 1977).
Innocent Blood (non-Dalgliesh) (UK, London: Faber & Faber, 1980; US, New York: Scribner, 1980).
The Skull beneath the Skin (UK, London: Faber & Faber, 1982; US, New York: Scribner, 1982).
A Taste for Death (UK, London: Faber & Faber, 1986; US, New York: Knopf, 1986).
Devices and Desires (UK, London: Faber & Faber, 1989; US, New York: Knopf, 1990).
Original Sin (UK, London: Faber & Faber, 1994; US, New York: Knopf, 1994).
A Certain Justice (UK, London: Faber & Faber, 1997; US, New York: Knopf, 1998).

Other novels

The Children of Men (UK, London: Faber & Faber, 1992; US, New York: Knopf, 1992).

Ruth Rendell (1930–)

Wexford novels

From Doon with Death (UK, London: Hutchinson, 1964; US, New York: Doubleday, 1965).

A New Lease of Death (UK, London: Long, 1967; US, New York: Doubleday, 1967) as *Sins of the Fathers* (US, New York: Ballantine, 1970).

Wolf to the Slaughter (UK, London: Long, 1967; US, New York: Doubleday, 1968).

The Best Man to Die (UK, London: Long, 1969; US, New York: Doubleday, 1970).

A Guilty Thing Surprised (UK, London: Hutchinson, 1970; US, New York: Doubleday, 1970).

No More Dying Then (UK, London: Hutchinson, 1971; US, New York: Doubleday, 1972).

Murder Being Once Done (UK, London: Hutchinson, 1972; US, New York: Doubleday, 1972).

Some Lie and Some Die (UK, London: Hutchinson, 1973; US, New York: Doubleday, 1973).

Shake Hands for Ever (UK, London: Hutchinson, 1975; US, New York: Doubleday, 1975).

A Sleeping Life (UK, London: Hutchinson, 1978; US, New York: Doubleday, 1978).

Put on by Cunning (UK, London: Hutchinson, 1981; Pantheon/Random House, 1981).

The Speaker of Mandarin (UK, London: Hutchinson, 1983; Pantheon/Random House, 1983).

An Unkindness of Ravens (UK, London: Hutchinson, 1985; US, New York: Pantheon/Random House, 1985).

The Veiled One (UK, London: Hutchinson, 1988; US, New York: Random House, 1988).

Kissing the Gunner's Daughter (UK, London: Hutchinson, 1992; US, New York: Mysterious Press, 1992).

Simisola (UK, London: Hutchinson, 1995; US, New York: Crown, 1995).

Road Rage (UK, London: Hutchinson, 1997; US, New York: Crown, 1997).

Harm Done (UK, London: Hutchinson, 1999; US, New York: Crown, 1999).

Crime novels

To Fear a Painted Devil (UK, London: Long, 1965; US, New York: Doubleday, 1965).

Vanity Dies Hard (UK, London: Long, 1965) as *In Sickness and in Health* (US, New York: Doubleday, 1966) as *Vanity Dies Hard* (US, New York: Beagle, 1970).

The Secret House of Death (UK, London: Long, 1968; US, New York: Doubleday, 1969).

One Across, Two Down (UK, London: Hutchinson, 1971; US, New York: Doubleday, 1971).

The Face of Trespass (UK, London: Hutchinson, 1974; US, New York: Doubleday, 1974).

A Demon in My View (UK, London: Hutchinson, 1976; US, New York: Doubleday, 1977).

A Judgement in Stone (UK, London: Hutchinson, 1977; US, New York: Doubleday, 1978).

Make Death Love Me (UK, London: Hutchinson, 1979; US, New York: Doubleday, 1979).

The Lake of Darkness (UK, London: Hutchinson, 1980; US, New York: Doubleday, 1980).

Master of the Moor (UK, London: Hutchinson, 1982; US, New York: Pantheon/ Random House, 1982).

The Killing Doll (UK, London: Hutchinson, 1984; US, New York: Pantheon/ Random House, 1984).

The Tree of Hands (UK, London: Hutchinson, 1984; US, New York: Pantheon/ Random House, 1985).

Live Flesh (UK, London: Hutchinson, 1986; US, New York: Pantheon/Random House, 1986).

Talking to Strange Men (UK, London: Hutchinson, 1987; US, New York: Pantheon/Random House, 1987).

The Bridesmaid (UK, London: Hutchinson, 1989; US, New York: Mysterious Press, 1989).

Going Wrong (UK, London: Hutchinson, 1990; US, New York: Mysterious Press, 1990).

The Crocodile Bird (UK, Britain: Random House, 1993; US, New York: Crown, 1993).

The Keys to the Street (UK, London: Hutchinson, 1996; US, New York: Crown, 1996).

A Sight for Sore Eyes (UK, London: Hutchinson, 1998; US, New York: Crown, 1999).

Short stories

The Fallen Curtain and Other Stories (UK, London: Hutchinson, 1976; US, New York: Doubleday, 1976).

Means of Evil (UK, London: Hutchinson, 1979; US, New York: Doubleday, 1979).

The Fever Tree (UK, London: Hutchinson, 1982; US, New York: Pantheon/Random House, 1983).

The New Girl Friend (UK, London: Hutchinson, 1985; US, New York: Pantheon/Random House, 1986).

The Copper Peacock (UK, London: Hutchinson, 1991; US, New York: Mysterious Press, 1991).

Blood Lines: Long and Short Stories (UK, London: Hutchinson, 1995; US, New York: Crown, 1995).

Novellas

Heartstones (UK, London: Harper, 1987; US, New York: Harper & Row, 1987).

The Strawberry Tree (UK, London: HarperCollins, 1990).

Barbara Vine (1986–)

A Dark-Adapted Eye (UK, Harmondsworth: Viking/Penguin, 1986; US, New York: Bantam, 1986).

A Fatal Inversion (UK, Harmondsworth: Viking/Penguin, 1987; US, New York: Bantam, 1987).

The House of Stairs (UK, Harmondsworth: Viking/Penguin, 1988; US, New York: Crown, 1989).

Gallowglass (UK, Harmondsworth: Viking/Penguin, 1990; US, New York: Crown, 1990).

King Solomon's Carpet (UK, Harmondsworth: Viking/Penguin, 1991; US, New York: Crown, 1992).

Asta's Book (UK, Harmondsworth: Viking/Penguin, 1993; US as *Anna's Book*, New York: Crown, 1989).

No Night Is Too Long (UK, Harmondsworth: Viking/Penguin, 1994; US, New York: G.K. Hall, 1994).

The Brimstone Wedding (UK, Harmondsworth: Viking/Penguin, 1996; US, New York: Crown, 1996).

The Chimney Sweeper's Boy (UK, Harmondsworth: Viking/Penguin, 1998; US, New York: Crown, 1998).

Appendix B: A Conversation with Ruth Rendell/Barbara Vine

I met Baroness Rendell of Babergh at 6 p.m. on 27 July 1999 at the House of Lords in London. Lady Rendell is a working peer appointed by the current Labour Government after their election in 1997. This means that she is now a fully functioning politician who is keen to play a supportive role in the Government's attempt to reform the arcane and archaic powers of the House of Lords.

For those unfamiliar with the peculiarities of the British Constitution, the House of Lords is the second revising chamber, ultimately deferring to the elected House of Commons. Together the House of Lords and the House of Commons make up the Houses of Parliament. No members of the House of Lords have ever been directly elected to this position. Most peers take their seats (and their political role) by right of inheritance as the last bastion of *visible* aristocratic political power. Working peers such as Baroness Rendell are selected for life only, by the major political parties. Although there is supposed to be a rough parity of party nominees to be life peers, the House of Lords usually has an inbuilt Conservative majority because the hereditary peers tend 'independently' to vote Conservative. My conversation with Ruth Rendell took place on a day in which the Labour Government's project to reform the Lords on more democratic lines met strong resistance from opposition (Conservative) and hereditary (Conservative) peers. The following account is based upon my own sketchy notes and my recollections of our meeting the next day. Ruth Rendell has approved my version of our conversation.

I wanted to talk to Ruth Rendell about her development of the novel form through crime fiction and what characterises her work as a writer. Does she consciously work with political and social aims? Is she aware of addressing literary questions such as the role of romance and the Gothic both in her work and in women's imaginations? Does she have a sense of herself as a feminist exploring gender? And, more obscurely, does she see herself as possessing an imaginative vision that is hard to communicate in traditional forms of writing?

At the start of our conversation I explained that my book was to be a study of six British crime writers which would try to respect the distinctive literary visions of each. P.D. James and Ruth Rendell are friends, I was told, but the media too often assumes similarities in their writing. She was particularly pleased to hear me say that I considered her and P.D. James to be very different writers, and agreed with me that James's essentially tragic vision of secular modernity was very far from her own art, which I suggested was both ironic and utopian. By utopian, I explained, I did not mean unrealistically optimistic, but leaning in content and, more significantly, in form towards more liberal possibilities in society. As an instance of form embracing a more utopian ethics, I suggested that the most interesting developments were to be found in the Vine novels such as the refusal to name and so indict 'the mother' at the end of *A Dark-Adapted Eye* and the stress on gender, writing and reading in *Asta's Book*.

Ruth Rendell then talked about *Asta's Book* as being a study of a woman's attempt to construct her identity, in particular during earlier eras of the twentieth century when femininity was more oppressively defined. She then described a deliberate and new direction in the Wexford books. *Simisola* is the first of the consciously 'political Wexfords', examining race and exploitation in rural England. It is succeeded by *Road Rage* addressing the environment, and was joined in September 1999 by a third political Wexford, *Harm Done*, looking at domestic violence and the reaction of a housing estate to the release of a paedophile prisoner to its environs. I wondered whether the 'political Wexfords' were wholly distinctive from the earlier Wexfords and earlier non-Wexford Rendells such as *A Judgement in Stone*, since her work has always demonstrated a critical investigation of social class. Has her writing always been 'political' in this sense? I instanced *Kissing the Gunner's Daughter* as a recent Wexford permeated with a sense that class and gender structures can inflict literally 'criminal damage'.

In addition I suggested that Rendell's work should be viewed in the context of critical 'condition of England' novels of which Dickens is an exemplar. Rendell replied that she would not characterise her intentions in so 'lofty' a manner, but that she was very concerned that her writing should reflect its time and the changing moral climate. For her, *Kissing the Gunner's Daughter* was not a political novel, but she did feel strongly that Britain in the 1990s exhibited a 'pretence' that social class no longer mattered as it used to. Here in the House of Lords, little pretence was exhibited, with many members believing unselfconsciously in the rights of 'blood' to wield power far above any claims of democracy. If this was the condition of political power in the heart of London, then its effects were still potent in the English countryside. Reminding me that she has lived for much of her life in Suffolk, Rendell spoke of the inhabitants of an English country village as even now divided between 'the people and the others'. These 'others' are the middle and upper classes, who never mix socially with the ordinary working people of the village. Class remains a very real force in British society even at the millennium. For Rendell, this is a fact of contemporary English culture that needs critical examination.

Speaking of this social stratification of rural England, I speculated that the persistence of the 'country house' in such novels as *Road Rage* and *Kissing the Gunner's Daughter* could be read as also the residue of the golden age genre within her work. Could the way the country house becomes the key and the object of social critique for the detecting narrative be read as a criticism of the conservatism of the earlier form? Rendell was not keen on this approach, preferring to place the country house as an enduring aspect of her imagination as part of her fascination for houses of all kinds. Quite rightly, she pointed out the importance of the urban environment and London houses to her fictions. I received the impression that houses are the embodiments of social and domestic history for this writer; that they exist imaginatively as architectures of desire. However, that may well be to infer too much.

I then asked Ruth Rendell if she would identify herself as a feminist. She replied by telling me that upon the publication of *An Unkindness of Ravens*, MS *Magazine* in America called her 'the biggest anti-feminist there is'. Of course, that particular novel was critical of militant feminism, which does not exist in the same way today. Rendell does think of herself as a feminist, but never as one advocating separatism. Being a feminist does not mean disliking men, a sentiment with which I concurred. I added that I thought that Vine novels such as *Asta's Book* and *The Chimney Sweeper's Boy* were profoundly feminist and satisfying in looking critically at family relations. Rendell felt that writing about the family was very important to her, especially in the exploration of intense relationships often neglected by other writers. She suggested that the inhabitants of many modern novels seemed strangely bereft of families!

She then agreed with me that a feature of her work is the depiction of relationships of all kinds under stress, perhaps at the point where words have difficulty in representing feelings and emotional realities. At this point aesthetic forms such as the Gothic become valuable. 'Misunderstandings' between people passionately attached to each other was a recurrent concern in her work. Agreeing with me that mothering is also of particular fascination, Rendell emphasised that she was interested in the intensities of the mother–baby bond. Speaking more generally of the prevalence of the irrational in her work, she touched upon the limits of knowledge about hidden parts of the self. 'The point about the unconscious is that it is unconscious,' she said, yet the concealed parts of the self can manifest themselves in ways that may wholly disconcert the everyday personality. She likes 'complex and strange' characters in a world where truth *is* stranger than fiction. She used to be interested in the work of C.G. Jung but has now moved on.

I drew the topic of *Jane Eyre* into the conversation, in part because there are repeated references to the novel in Rendell's work, but in particular to open up the question of the literary heritage as a whole. Many central characters in the Rendell/Vine novels are haunted by literature. Is this understandable as a deliberate attempt to re-evaluate the social and gendered heritages of English literature? This is not how the writer works, Ruth Rendell said firmly. Writing comes through associations: literary association with other authors' plots and characters are clearly part of this writer's imaginative world. This critic would like to suggest that it is part of the mature power of Rendell's art that evocations of literature will often shape the ethical arguments of the narrative. Such conscious examples as the use of Henry James's *The Wings of the Dove* in *The House of Stairs* are exceptions to the author's typical citation of literature.

Rendell expressed enthusiasm for Henry James, having reread all his works for this particular novel. She wanted to find a way of using the plot of *The Wings of the Dove* without simply appropriating it. We did discuss *Jane Eyre* further as a favourite novel. She was conscious of its influence in originating a romance genre of dominant, sexually charismatic males and more pliant heroines. Yet to Rendell, Brontë's actual novel is important because Jane Eyre herself is an assertive woman who refuses to be defined by the masculine. I remarked that in *The Chimney Sweeper's Boy*, this was a lesson not learned until later by Barbara Vine's Ursula, who misreads Jane Eyre when falling for the egotistic male writer Gerald. Is this an example of Vine's work criticising gendered readings of romance? Rendell reminded me that Ursula is especially naive and the product of a culture promoting naivety in women.

We then briefly discussed gay relationships, which Rendell felt were well represented in her writing. I asked about her first novel, *From Doon with Death*, in which frustrated lesbian desire leads to tragedy and crime. Apparently, this work began as a character-driven situation, which preceded the detecting format.

Wexford was invented from an amalgam of other literary detectives simply as a structural device so that a genre could be fitted to the story the writer wanted to tell. It was only when the author realised that Wexford was to be a series character that he evolved into a more liberal and sympathetic figure because 'I had to live with him'. 'He is not me,' Rendell said clearly, and later, 'He is not real.' No actual policeman could operate as Wexford does.

Ruth Rendell's description of herself as a 'Christian Socialist' has always intrigued me, since she writes little about religious belief. When asked about this, Rendell said that her sense of religion was not part of what she wanted to do with her writing. She is a Christian, but not a believer in the supernatural or the 'magic' side to the doctrine. Her Christianity is continuous with her political creed because 'the basis of Christianity is Socialism'. I wondered aloud whether she had an intimation of a difficulty in writing about religious institutions with a liberal political agenda since there is a tendency (though not a necessity) for religious social structures to collaborate with conservative cultural forces. While not disagreeing with this, Lady Rendell expressed a particular dissatisfaction with the current state of the Church of England. Unhappy with the abandonment of the 1660s Prayer Book, the inauguration of the Alternative Service Book and the New English Bible (as opposed to the edition produced in late Shakespearean England which deeply influenced subsequent English literature), she sees the contemporary Church as polarised between Evangelicals, with their drift towards fundamentalism, and Catholic ritual. 'Fundamentalism is alien to me,' she said, adding that the Catholic 'Mass' is equally distant from the English tradition of the Established Church.

Taking a new tack, I wondered if Rendell ever discovered her readers to be more conservative than herself and unhappy with any direction in her work. I was fascinated to learn that she had expected some shock or adverse reaction as a result of the first 'political Wexford', *Simisola*. She was surprised that it proved fully as loved as the earlier novels. She has always aimed to do more than just tell a story but does not want to be pretentious about her art. A novel should entertain and aim to 'enthral'. Rendell believes in authenticity but not in research. While never taking notes for a project, she is still concerned to reflect cultural shifts very precisely and to record changing patterns of speech. I told her that the sprinkling of academic background in *The Chimney Sweeper's Boy* was remarkably precise in detecting shifting nuances and economies in British academia.

As we walked towards the Lords debating chamber, she showed me the signed death warrant of King Charles I. I remarked that she must recall the functioning of the death penalty for murder in Britain, and she expressed emphatic relief that it was gone. This historical fact, of course, has a profound significance for crime fiction.

Acknowledging her use of insight and intuitions, Ruth Rendell described herself as becoming more of a political and psychological novelist. One plan for the future is for a novel in which the reform of the House of Lords will provide a background. On this day, she had delivered her next Barbara Vine novel as well as taking part in the political reform of Britain. I wonder what Wexford will have to say about that?

Appendix C: A Conversation with P.D. James

Baroness James of Holland Park agreed to meet me during her working time on 16 August 1999. She has approved a copy of this interview as an accurate record of our discussion.

I started by mentioning my impression of the profound influence of the Second World War on her novels. In particular, plots making use of the legacy of Nazi atrocities such as *Shroud for a Nightingale* and *Original Sin* are supplemented elsewhere in her corpus by frequent references to war crimes. Lady James said that she had not previously been conscious of the pervasiveness of the Second World War, but agreed that it seemed to be so. She pointed out that the past, both as history and in personal lives, was very important in the understanding of the behaviour of her characters. We are what the past has made us, in both cultural and familial senses.

I had already explained the scope of my own work, and we briefly discussed the influence of the First World War on the writing of Dorothy L. Sayers. That war has deep-rooted consequences for the career of Lord Peter Wimsey and on plots such as that of *The Unpleasantness at the Bellona Club*, yet such is not the immediate impression given by Sayers's novels. I suggested that this was because Sayers was a more optimistic writer. In my opinion, where Sayers's works tend towards Shakespearean comedy in the development of marriage and romance, P.D. James's oeuvre is one of tragedy, in the mode of *King Lear*. Lady James allowed that Sayers was a more optimistic writer in the sense of having more confidence in the potential healing of society. She spoke of Sayers's belief in the near sacramental value of work. This has particular consequences for the depiction of the lives of women.

Speaking of her conscious crafting of the detecting genre, Lady James described her novels as retaining the credible puzzle inherited from the golden age writers, but reshaping it so as to be able to explore moral ambiguities in the tradition of literary realism. I did not use the phrase to Lady James in our conversation, but I think that she would agree to being identified as a 'condition of England' author in the tradition of nineteenth-century British novels. Later, we discussed her sense of herself as an author of 'Englishness' and of her concern for the potential weakening of this ethnic identity in the current political climate of devolution. Of course, the role of Englishness in Lady James's work is not primarily cast as political, but as moral and experiential through the institutions of law and justice.

Also referring to Sayers's excellent early analyses of the detecting genre, Lady James identified a key challenge to the writer as that of portraying a murderer in a fictional form that is supposed to keep the reader guessing. Such a technical problem lies at the heart of constructing a detective story. We proceeded to discuss the relationship between the detective and the murderer further. Where earlier writers apparently structured a more straightforward division between good and evil, unambiguously assigning those qualities to their respective 'homes' as 'detective' and 'murderer', Adam Dalgliesh quite often discovers aspects of himself in suspects, and even in murderers.

Shroud for a Nightingale provides an object lesson when the killer points out uncanny likeness in professional practices between the detective upholding English law and the nurse applying Nazi death. Here, Lady James brought in the crucial analogy with the medieval morality play. The detective and the murderer represent the two extremes of the moral spectrum. In real life, however, and therefore in 'moral realism', the white of the detective needs to display shades of grey, while the murderer cannot be an unrelieved demonic black.

At the mention of the morality play, I put it to Lady James that this particular traditional form is necessarily metaphysical: it presupposes a sacred dimension of reality to underpin its moral absolutes. This dimension is not represented in her work, despite her personal membership of the Anglican Communion and her interest in portraying believers in her novels. Was this part of her devotion to realism in her art (and not to the more self-referential aspects of the golden age genre)? Does it correspond to her personal religious attitude? Lady James admitted that this modification to the implications of a morality play was indeed part of her commitment to literary realism. She described her religious attitude as not one of 'certainty': no one can be 100 per cent certain of metaphysical truths. There are huge areas pertaining to faith that cannot be securely 'known'. Religious certainty can be dangerous and can lead to fanaticism, which she is concerned to avoid.

It seemed to me that whereas Lady James's absenting of metaphysical certainties in her novels was a divergence from the morality play analogy, it is wholly coherent with her art's moral focus within the detecting form. It represents the struggle for meaning in a lonely and violent universe, a struggle that is in itself a moral act for this writer. The spiritual aspect of the Dalgliesh novels makes unsurprising Lady James's stated range of influences, from Graham Greene and Evelyn Waugh to Jane Austen, with her unspiritual but firm moral code of the 'proper' behaviour between people.

I invited Lady James to give her opinion of feminism. She replied by emphasising that she liked and respected her own sex. Firmly believing in equality based upon economic liberation and the control of fertility, she did refer to a 'shadow side' to reforms. For example, easier divorce has entailed inflicting suffering upon children. In disliking 'the extremes of feminism', she said that radical feminism had done harm to relations between women and men. When I suggested that *A Certain Justice* seemed preoccupied with the problems of mothering for professional women, Lady James agreed that that was a concern in the novel, but made a crucial distinction between didacticism and literature. She was not, she said, a feminist writer in the sense of driving through a didactic project to show the problems of women in the modern world. Nevertheless, she believed that modern young women were under great strain in the effort to combine motherhood with career expectations.

Shifting the ground somewhat, I asked Lady James about her feelings for the Gothic. Certainly, she could see that the Gothic had influenced her work but she did not consider herself a Gothic writer. Lady James felt strongly that the horror element should be present in detective fiction. The finding of the body is important, and is always shown in her novels through the eyes of the actual discoverer, never a detached narrator. There are therefore significant contrasts between detective Dalgliesh stumbling upon a corpse and gruesome discoveries by gently nurtured members of the public, such as the spinster in *A Taste for Death*.

I did not say this to Lady James, but her conscious decision about the initial presentation of the dead in her plots is a vital part of her moral scrutiny of modern society. The fear of violence may be purged by the reading of crime fiction, it may even be purged by the writing of crime fiction as Lady James suggested of herself, but something of the real pain of homicide is always embedded in her reworking of golden age genres. When I tentatively placed the Gothic in Lady James's novels as a means to the representation of atrocity, often a war crime, she agreed. The Gothic usually works in detective fiction to problematise simplistic assumptions about the restitution of moral security in the identifying of a lone murderer. In P.D. James's novels, this operates by allowing the partial representation of brutalities far beyond the scope of any fictional hero to rectify.

Lady James wondered about the role of the Gothic in the other writers I am considering. We discussed the strong presence of the Gothic in the work of Ruth Rendell (and Barbara Vine) in ways that differ from her own practice. Pointing out the peculiarly inventive and grotesque murders devised by Ngaio Marsh, Lady James was interested in my citation of Marsh's account of her childhood traumas over a theatrical experience of a poisoning. Of course, Agatha Christie is the mistress of poisons and not noted for her Gothic crimes, but I sought to persuade Lady James of Christie's Gothic credentials in the later Miss Marples.

A key difference in the careers of the four golden age writers and the two contemporary authors is the effect of economic constraints. All four earlier writers began their careers with the need to earn money to support themselves and their households. Margery Allingham was haunted almost throughout her writing life by financial anxiety, and Lady James expressed considerable sympathy for her. Of her own literary career, she said that it had been her practice to continue her Civil Service profession precisely so that she would never have to compromise her artistic standards for financial reward. Since she is thus freed from immediate commercial pressures, Adam Dalgliesh and Cordelia Gray have always inhabited their author's artistic vision in ways that have empowered P.D. James's development of the literary form.

My conversation with Lady James had concentrated on the literary, moral and metaphysical dimensions of her writing. Wary of asking about her personal history, I ended by wondering if she thought that patterns in her own life had significantly shaped her work. As well as mentioning her therapeutic notion of the detective form (that reading or writing it may distance the fear of violence by giving structure to our deepest terrors), she spoke of a sense of childhood insecurity as also influential. I did not say so at the time, but it seems to me that some of the most powerfully poignant moments in Lady James's work concern lonely children. Having once read that Lady James had given birth to her second daughter in the Second World War while bombs were falling upon London, I asked about the effects of living through that assault. She corrected any wholly negative impressions of that dangerous era by explaining that living through the bombing was a time not just of fear but also of great comradeship and feeling of community. London in the Second World War was a place where Englishness was united and national identities were untroubled by difference.

If fear stalks the Jamesian modern world, it is fear of disintegrating identities in which the detective supplies a moral but pessimistic vision. I would liken the violence often accompanying Lady James's dénouements to Lear's stormy heath. Her detectives cannot redeem society. Like bare Edgar and the Fool, they suffer it on our behalf.

Notes

Novels by the six authors are cited by author, title and date unless page numbers require details of the edition used. Complete publication details are to be found as Appendix A.

1 Lives of Crime

1 Ngaio Marsh's detective, Roderick Alleyn, first appears in *A Man Lay Dead* (1934).
2 Agatha Christie, *An Autobiography* (Great Britain: Collins, 1977).
3 Agatha Christie, *The Hound of Death* (1933).
4 Agatha Christie, *The Mysterious Affair at Styles* (1920).
5 For husband Max and his extramarital relationship after World War II see Jared Cade, *Agatha Christie and the Eleven Missing Days* (London: Peter Owen, 1998).
6 Dorothy L. Sayers, *Strong Poison* (1930).
7 Barbara Reynolds, *Dorothy L. Sayers: Her Life and Soul* (London: Hodder & Stoughton, 1993; repr. St. Martins, NY, Griffin, 1997).
8 Margery Allingham, *The Crime at Black Dudley* (1929).
9 Margery Allingham, *Dancers in Mourning* (1937).
10 Margery Allingham, *Cargo of Eagles* (1968).
11 Ngaio Marsh, *Surfeit of Lampreys* (1941).
12 P.D. James, *Cover Her Face* (1962).
13 The major sources for this chapter are Cade, *Christie* and Reynolds, *Sayers*, as above, Agatha Christie's autobiography as above, Janet Morgan, *Agatha Christie: A Biography* (London: Collins, 1984), Margaret Lewis, *Ngaio Marsh: A Life* (London: Chatto & Windus, 1991), Julia Thorogood, *Margery Allingham: A Biography* (London: Heinemann, 1991), and Ngaio Marsh, *Black Beech and Honeydew: An Autobiography* (London: Collins, 1966; rev. 1981). See also my interviews with Ruth Rendell/Barbara Vine and P.D. James reproduced in full as Appendices B and C.
14 See Cade, *Christie*.
15 Marsh, *Autobiography*, p. 13.
16 See Appendix B.
17 See Appendix C.
18 See ibid.
19 For Christie's views on the genre, see her autobiography, pp. 452–3. Agatha Christie, *Hallowe'en Party* (1969).
20 For details of Sayers' introductions to the Gollancz anthologies of crime stories, see Reynolds, *Christie*, pp. 191ff.
21 Thorogood, *Allingham*, p. 324.
22 See Lewis, *Marsh*, pp. 53, 185.
23 Dorothy L. Sayers, *The Mind of the Maker* (London: Methuen, 1941; New York: Harcourt Brace, 1941).

24 Agatha Christie, *The Hollow* (1946); *Agatha Christie Sleeping Murder* (1976).
25 P.D. James, *Original Sin* (1994); *A Certain Justice* (1997).
26 Dorothy L. Sayers, *Gaudy Night* (1935); *The Nine Tailors* (1934).
27 Barbara Vine, *King Solomon's Carpet* (1992).

2 Gendering the Genre

1 The publication of Agatha Christie's *The Mysterious Affair at Styles* (1920) marks the start of the six authors' work.
2 Feminist psychoanalytic theory will be explored further in Chapter 5. Essentially it regards language as bound up with gender and the cultural privileging of masculinity because of the symbolic importance of the phallus in western society. The phallus does not simply equate to the fleshly penis, but represents masculine privilege. Due to the processes by which a small child acquires a sense of self and the entry into the language and conventions of society, rational language, rules and laws become associated with masculinity, while the feminine is structured as outside or 'other'. For the theories of Jacques Lacan, see Malcolm Bowie, *Lacan* (London: Fontana, 1991). See the revisionary treatment of Lacan given by Luce Irigaray in *This Sex Which Is Not One*, transl. Catherine Porter with Carolyn Burke (Ithaca, NY: Cornell University Press, 1985; originally published 1977 in French by Editions de Minuit).
3 Raymond Williams, 'The Metropolis and the Emergence of Modernism', in Peter Brooker, ed., *Modernism/Postmodernism* (London and New York: Longman, 1992), pp. 82–94.
4 See the Dupin stories in Edgar Allan Poe, *Selected Tales*, ed. Julian Symons (Oxford: Oxford University Press, 1980).
5 Stephen Knight, *Form and Ideology in Crime Fiction* (London: Macmillan, 1980), pp. 8–103.
6 Alison Light, *Forever England: Femininity, Literature and Conservatism between the Wars* (London and New York: Routledge, 1991); Gill Plain, *Women's Fiction of the Second World War: Gender, Power and Resistance* (Edinburgh: Edinburgh University Press, 1996).
7 See Roderick Alleyn's near hysteria when arresting villains in his debut volume, *A Man Lay Dead* (1934).
8 Margery Allingham, *Mystery Mile* (1930).
9 Dorothy L. Sayers, *Have His Carcase* (1932).
10 Agatha Christie, *The Murder of Roger Ackroyd* (1926; London: HarperCollins, 1993). All later page references will be incorporated into the chapter.
11 Dorothy L. Sayers, *The Unpleasantness at the Bellona Club* (1928).
12 P.D. James, *Death of an Expert Witness* (1977).
13 Ruth Rendell, *Put on by Cunning* (1981).
14 Inspector Fox Functions as a (m)Other to Roderick Alleyn. The relationship between 'self' and 'other' which much preoccupies feminist critics can become structured as self and (m)Other. Here the 'other' (as (m)Other) takes on a maternal function in nurturing or 'giving birth' to the self, recalling the long-forgotten psychic sustenance of the actual 'mother' before a separate consciousness was constructed. Alleyn's bond with his comforting and

never-doubting subordinate, Inspector Fox, has many of these (m)Other qualities. Indeed, given Alleyn's nervy sensitivity, Fox provides maternal affirmations of his superior's official role, thereby shoring up Alleyn's detecting and gender identity.

15 Albert Campion is distinguished by ambivalence. See Margery Allingham, *The Crime at Black Dudley* (1929); and *Traitor's Purse* (1941).
16 Dorothy L. Sayers, *The Nine Tailors* (1934).
17 Agatha Christie, *Murder on the Orient Express* (1934).
18 P.D. James, *An Unsuitable Job for a Woman* (1972).
19 Holocaust crimes particularly feature in James's plots in *Shroud for a Nightingale* (1971) and *Original Sin* (1994); but see also Chapter 6.
20 See such novels as Agatha Christie, *The Murder at the Vicarage* (1930).
21 Agatha Christie, *Dead Man's Folly* (1956).
22 Agatha Christie, *4.50 From Paddington* (1957); *Sleeping Murder* (1976).
23 P.D. James, *A Taste for Death* (1986).
24 Ngaio Marsh, *Vintage Murder* (1937).
25 Margery Allingham, *Traitor's Purse* (1941).
26 Scott McCracken, *Pulp: Reading Popular Fiction* (Manchester: Manchester University Press, 1998).
27 Jean Radford, 'Coming to Terms: Dorothy Richardson, Modernism and Women', in Brooker, *Modernism/Postmodernism*, pp. 95–106.
28 Julian Symons, *Bloody Murder: From the Detective Story to the Crime Novel: A History* (London: Faber & Faber, 1972; rev. edn London: Papermac, 1992). Symons's narrative of progress implicitly marginalises the rhetoric of self-referentiality in golden age fiction by women in ways that I want to challenge.
29 Agatha Christie, *A Murder Is Announced* (1950).
30 Margery Allingham, *Police at the Funeral* (1931).
31 Margery Allingham, *Look to the Lady* (1931).
32 Ngaio Marsh, *Tied up in Tinsel* (1972).
33 Ngaio Marsh, *Death and the Dancing Footman* (1942).
34 P.D. James, *Original Sin* (1994).
35 Dorothy L. Sayers, *Busman's Honeymoon* (1937).
36 P.D. James, *Shroud for a Nightingale* (1971; Harmondsworth: Penguin, 1989). All later page references will be incorporated into the chapter.
37 Agatha Christie, *Appointment with Death* (1938).
38 Dorothy L. Sayers, *Strong Poison* (1930; London: New English Library, 1977). All later page references will be incorporated into the chapter.
39 Margery Allingham, *Death of a Ghost* (1934; Harmondsworth: Penguin, 1942). All later page references will be incorporated into the chapter.
40 Ngaio Marsh, *Artists in Crime* (1938; London: Fontana, 1962). All later page references will be incorporated into the chapter.
41 Ruth Rendell, *Kissing the Gunner's Daughter* (1991; London: Arrow, 1993). All later page references will be incorporated into the chapter.

3 Social Negotiations: Class, Crime and Power

1 P.D. James is a Conservative peer. See Chapter 1 and Appendix C.
2 P.D. James, *Devices and Desires* (1989).

3   Ngaio Marsh, *Hand in Glove* (1962).
4   See Alison Light, who makes the valuable point that Christie is conservative, but not nostalgic.
5   Agatha Christie, *The Hollow* (1946).
6   Agatha Christie, *The Mirror Crack'd from Side to Side* (1962).
7   Dorothy L. Sayers, *Whose Body?* (1923).
8   Ruth Rendell, *A Judgement in Stone* (1977).
9   Ruth Rendell, *Road Rage* (1997).
10 Agatha Christie, *The Secret Adversary* (1922).
11 Dorothy L. Sayers, *Whose Body?* (1923; London: New English Library, 1968), pp. 122–4.
12 Ngaio Marsh, *Surfeit of Lampreys* (1941).
13 P.D. James, *Shroud for a Nightingale* (1971).
14 Agatha Christie, *The Mysterious Affair at Styles* (1920).
15 Ngaio Marsh, *A Man Lay Dead* (1934).
16 Margery Allingham, *The Crime at Black Dudley* (1929).
17 Margery Allingham, *Dancers in Mourning* (1937).
18 Dorothy L. Sayers, *Clouds of Witness* (1926).
19 Dorothy L. Sayers, *Busman's Honeymoon* (1937).
20 P.D. James, *The Black Tower* (1975).
21 P.D. James, *A Taste for Death* (1986).
22 P.D. James, *Original Sin* (1994).
23 Ruth Rendell, *The Speaker of Mandarin* (1983).
24 Ruth Rendell, *Put on by Cunning* (1981).
25 Ruth Rendell, *The Veiled One* (1988).
26 Margery Allingham, *Police at the Funeral* (1931; Harmondsworth: Penguin, 1939). All later page references will be incorporated into the chapter.
27 Margery Allingham, *The Tiger in the Smoke* (1952).
28 Agatha Christie, *Death on the Nile* (1937).
29 Dorothy L. Sayers, *Whose Body?* (1923; London: New English Library, 1968), pp. 123–4.
30 Margery Allingham, *Look to the Lady* (1931).
31 Margery Allingham, *Sweet Danger* (1933).
32 Margery Allingham, *Coroner's Pidgin* (1945).
33 Dorothy L. Sayers, *Unnatural Death* (1927; London: New English Library, 1968), p. 61.
34 Dorothy L. Sayers, *The Nine Tailors* (1934).
35 Ngaio Marsh, *Death in a White Tie* (1938).
36 Ruth Rendell, *The Veiled One* (1988).
37 Ngaio Marsh, *Final Curtain* (1947).
38 Dorothy L. Sayers, *Gaudy Night* (1935).
39 Ngaio Marsh, *Singing in the Shrouds* (1958).
40 P.D. James, *A Certain Justice* (1997).
41 Ruth Rendell, *From Doon with Death* (1964).
42 Barbara Vine, *A Dark-Adapted Eye* (1986; Harmondsworth: Penguin, 'Three Novels' edn, 1990). All later page references will be incorporated into the chapter.
43 Barbara Vine, *Gallowglass* (1990).
44 Barbara Vine, *Asta's Book* (1993).

45 Barbara Vine, *The House of Stairs* (1988).
46 Agatha Christie, *The Murder at the Vicarage* (1930; London: Fontana, 1961).
   All later page references will be incorporated into the chapter.
47 Dorothy L. Sayers, *Murder Must Advertise* (1933; London: Gollancz, 1971).
   All later page references will be incorporated into the chapter.
48 Ngaio Marsh, *Death and the Dancing Footman* (1941; London: Fontana,
   1958). All later page references will be incorporated into the chapter.
49 P.D. James, *Death of an Expert Witness* (1977; Great Britain: Sphere, 1978).
   All later page references will be incorporated into the chapter.

4   Lands of Hope and Glory? Englishness, Race and Colonialism

1 'Orientalism' is a term developed by Edward Said to indicate the way in
   which many Western identities have been formed by projecting onto the
   'dark' or Eastern 'other' the undesired qualities of irrationality, sexuality,
   criminal tendencies, unconsciousness and so on. See Edward Said,
   Orientalism (London: Routledge, 1978).
2 Agatha Christie, *The Murder at the Vicarage* (1930).
3 For Griselda's cannibal story, see Agatha Christie, *The Murder at the Vicarage*
   (1930; London: Fontana, 1961), p. 9.
4 Margery Allingham, *Look to the Lady* (1931).
5 Margery Allingham, *Coroner's Pidgin* (1945).
6 Margery Allingham, *Traitor's Purse* (1941; London: Dent, 1985). All later
   page references will be incorporated into the chapter.
7 Dorothy L. Sayers, *Clouds of Witness* (1926).
8 Dorothy L. Sayers, *Murder Must Advertise* (1933).
9 Dorothy L. Sayers, *Busman's Honeymoon* (1937; London: New English Library,
   1974). All later page references will be incorporated into the chapter.
10 Dorothy L. Sayers, *Unnatural Death* (1927).
11 P.D. James, *A Certain Justice* (1997).
12 Ngaio Marsh, *Vintage Murder* (1937).
13 Margaret Lewis, *Ngaio Marsh: A Life* (London: Chatto & Windus, 1991), p. 53.
14 Ngaio Marsh, *Colour Scheme* (1943).
15 Ngaio Marsh, *Light Thickens* (1982).
16 Ngaio Marsh, *A Clutch of Constables* (1968).
17 Dorothy L. Sayers, *Strong Poison* (1930).
18 See Alison Light, *Forever England: Femininity, Literature and Conservatism
   between the Wars* (London and New York: Routledge, 1991) on Christie's
   very limited use of racist types in marginal positions.
19 Agatha Christie, *Appointment with Death* (1938).
20 Margery Allingham, *Police at the Funeral* (1931), and see detailed study in
   Chapter 3.
21 Ruth Rendell, *Simisola* (1994; London: Arrow, 1995). All later page references will be incorporated into the chapter.
22 See Alison Light on Christie's 'hearty' femininity, which can also be
   extended to Allingham's Amanda Fitton: *Forever England: Femininity,
   Literature and Conservatism between the Wars* (London: Routledge, 1991).

23 Margery Allingham, *Mystery Mile* (1930).
24 Ngaio Marsh, *Death and the Dancing Footman* (1941).
25 Agatha Christie, *Dumb Witness* (1937).
26 Margery Allingham, *The Crime at Black Dudley* (1929).
27 Margery Allingham, *Sweet Danger* (1933).
28 Margery Allingham, *More Work for the Undertaker* (1948).
29 Margery Allingham, *Flowers for the Judge* (1936). Richie, a sympathetic member of the family firm, describes his corporate life as 'enslavement'. See Chapter 5.
30 Ngaio Marsh, *Final Curtain* (1947).
31 Ruth Rendell, *The Speaker of Mandarin* (1983).
32 Dorothy L. Sayers, *Gaudy Night* (1935); *The Nine Tailors* (1934).
33 Agatha Christie, *A Caribbean Mystery* (1964).
34 P.D. James, *Unnatural Causes* (1967).
35 P.D. James, *Devices and Desires* (1989; London: Faber & Faber paperback, 1990).
36 Ruth Rendell, *Road Rage* (1997).
37 Agatha Christie, *Why Didn't They Ask Evans?* (1934).
38 Agatha Christie, *Sleeping Murder* (1976).
39 Agatha Christie, *The Hollow* (1946). See Chapter 5.
40 Campion evades the role of colonial governor in Allingham's *More Work for the Undertaker* (1948).
41 Ngaio Marsh, *Opening Night* (1951). See Chapter 5.
42 Dorothy L. Sayers, *Strong Poison* (1930).
43 Ruth Rendell, *A Judgement in Stone* (1977).
44 Ruth Rendell, *Wolf to the Slaughter* (1967).
45 Agatha Christie, *Death on the Nile* (1937; London: Fontana, 1960). All later page references will be incorporated into the chapter.
46 Gill Plain, conference paper delivered at the 'Canonising Crime' Conference, University of Reading, July 1998.
47 Ngaio Marsh, *Photo-Finish* (1980; London: Fontana, 1994). All later page references will be incorporated into the chapter.
48 Ruth Rendell, *Simisola* (1994; London: Arrow, 1995), p. 164. Wexford quotes from Tennyson's 'Morte d'Arthur'; see Christopher Ricks, ed., *The Poems of Tennyson* (London: Longman, 1969), p. 596, l. 259–64.

5 Detecting Psychoanalysis: Readers, Criminals and Narrative

1 Scott McCracken argues that part of the appeal of detective fiction is that it raises more social questions than it is able to answer. See Scott McCracken, *Pulp: Reading Popular Fiction* (Manchester: Manchester University Press, 1998), pp. 50–74.
2 Critics who have used psychoanalysis to understand detective fiction include Dennis Porter, *The Pursuit of Crime: Art and Ideology in Detective Fiction* (New Haven, CT: Yale University Press, 1981), Sally R. Munt, *Murder by the Book? Feminism and the Crime Novel* (London and New York: Routledge,

1994), and Gill Plain, *Women's Fiction of the Second World War: Gender, Power and Resistance* (Edinburgh: Edinburgh University Press, 1996).

3 Peter Brooks, *Reading for the Plot: Design and Intention in Narrative* (Cambridge, MA: Harvard University Press, 1984).

4 See ibid. on 'eros' and the 'death drive', pp. 37–58.

5 See ibid. on 'transference', pp. 234, 320.

6 For further arguments on Jung and the entwinement of romance and tragedy, see my *C.G. Jung and Literary Theory: The Challenge from Fiction* (London: Macmillan, 1999).

7 Robin W. Winks suggests that parody is inherent in much detective fiction in Winks, ed., *Detective Fiction: A Collection of Critical Essays* (Englewood Cliffs, NJ: Prentice-Hall, 1980), p. 5.

8 Dorothy L. Sayers, *The Unpleasantness at the Bellona Club* (1928; London: New English Library, 1968). All later page references will be incorporated into the chapter. The word 'resurrection' is used to describe the exhumation of a corpse, leading to the discovery that the corpse was murdered, so rendering the death 'unnatural'.

9 Barbara Vine, *A Dark-Adapted Eye* (1986).

10 Agatha Christie, *Appointment with Death* (1938). Alison Light argues for Christie's fundamentally conservative absorption of Freud in this novel. See Alison Light, *Forever England: Femininity, Literature and Conservatism between the Wars* (London: Routledge, 1991), pp. 102–4.

11 P.D. James, *Death of an Expert Witness* (1977).

12 P.D. James, *Devices and Desires* (1989).

13 Ngaio Marsh, *Final Curtain* (1947).

14 Margery Allingham, *More Work for the Undertaker* (1948).

15 For Cosette functioning as the Jungian 'self' archetype, see Barbara Vine, *The House of Stairs* (1988; Harmondsworth: Penguin, 'Three Novels' edn, 1990), p. 783.

16 Ngaio Marsh, *Singing in the Shrouds* (1958).

17 Agatha Christie, *The ABC Murders* (1936).

18 Margery Allingham, *Death of a Ghost* (1934).

19 Ngaio Marsh, *Artists in Crime* (1938).

20 P.D. James, *A Taste for Death* (1986).

21 Ruth Rendell, *Kissing the Gunner's Daughter* (1991).

22 Gill Plain gives an invaluable analysis of the Peter Wimsey–Harriet Vane–Bunter relationship in *Women's Fiction of the Second World War: Gender, Power and Resistance* (Edinburgh: Edinburgh University Press, 1996), pp. 45–67.

23 Dorothy L. Sayers, *Clouds of Witness* (1926).

24 Margery Allingham, *The Tiger in the Smoke* (1952).

25 Ngaio Marsh, *Opening Night* (1951; London: Fontana, 1963). All later page references will be incorporated into the chapter.

26 See n. 10 above.

27 Agatha Christie, *Dead Man's Folly* (1956).

28 Agatha Christie, *The Murder of Roger Ackroyd* (1926).

29 Agatha Christie, *They Do It with Mirrors* (1952).

30 Agatha Christie, *Sleeping Murder* (1976).

31 In Freud's *Studies on Hysteria* he used the notion that actual sexual traumas caused the psychological disturbances of his patients. Later he revised this

idea to argue that many of the stories he heard were fantasy, and so inaugurated his core theories of the Oedipus complex and the sexual nature of unconscious repression. See *The Standard Edition of the Complete Psychological Works of Sigmund Freud*, translated from the German under the general editorship of James Strachey, in collaboration with Anna Freud, assisted by Alix Strachey and Alan Tyson (24 vols, London: Hogarth Press and Institute of Psycho-Analysis, 1953–74), vol. ii.

32   Dorothy L. Sayers, *Gaudy Night* (1935; London: New English Library, 1978), p. 264. Peter Wimsey persuades Harriet that celibacy does not necessarily lead to the Freudian casebook.

33   Margery Allingham, *Look to the Lady* (1931).

34   Julia Kristeva, 'Women's Time', in *The Kristeva Reader*, ed. Toril Moi (Oxford: Blackwell, 1986), pp. 187–213.

35   Ruth Rendell, *A Judgement in Stone* (1977).

36   Dorothy L. Sayers, *Murder Must Advertise* (1933).

37   Alleyn's comment 'Freud without Tears' is a pun on the popular 1930s drama, 'French without Tears'; see Ngaio Marsh, *Artists in Crime* (1938; London: Fontana, 1962), p. 131.

38   Ngaio Marsh, *Final Curtain* (1947; London: Fontana, 1956), p. 190.

39   Agatha Christie, *The Hollow* (1946; London: Fontana, 1955). All later page references will be incorporated into the chapter.

40   The title *The Hollow* must refer to Tennyson's verse drama 'Maud', especially ll. 1–4: 'I hate the dreadful hollow behind the little wood...And Echo there, whatever is asked her, answers "Death" '. See Christopher Ricks, ed., *The Poems of Tennyson* (London: Longman, 1969), p. 1040.

41   Margery Allingham, *Flowers for the Judge* (1936; Harmondsworth: Penguin, 1944). All later page references will be incorporated into the chapter.

42   P.D. James, *Original Sin* (1994).

43   Freud proposed a myth of the founding of civilisation upon the guilt incurred by the murder of the 'primal' or first father by his sons: see *Totem and Taboo* (1938; London: Ark, 1983).

44   P.D. James, *An Unsuitable Job for a Woman* (1972; London: Sphere, 1974). All later page references will be incorporated into the chapter.

45   Shakespeare's Cordelia says that she will 'love, and be silent' in *King Lear* I, i. 61; see Arden edn, ed. Kenneth Muir (London: Methuen, 1972), p. 7.

46   Ruth Rendell, *The Veiled One* (1988; London: Arrow, 1989). All later page references will be incorporated into the chapter.

47   C.G. Jung, *The Collected Works of C.G. Jung*, vols i–xx, A and B, ed. Herbert Read, Michael Fordham and Gerhard Adler, trans. R.F.C. Hull (London: Routledge & Kegan Paul, 1953–91), vol. vii, p. 92.

6   Gothic Crimes: A Literature of Terror and Horror

1   Alleyn suggests a werewolf identity in Ngaio Marsh, *Vintage Murder* (1937; London: Fontana, 1961), p. 135.

2   Ruth Rendell, *No More Dying Then* (1971; London: Arrow, 1994), p. 29.

3   Emily Brontë, *Wuthering Heights* (1847; Oxford: Oxford University Press, 1995). For crime novels explicitly echoing the Brontë text, see Dorothy

L. Sayers, *Clouds of Witness* (1926; London: New English Library, 1978). All later page references will be incorporated into the chapter. See also P.D. James, *The Black Tower* (1975).

4 For a detailed analysis and history of the Gothic, see Fred Botting, *Gothic* (London and New York: Routledge, 1996). For a study of the 'female Gothic', see Avril Horner and Sue Zlosnik, *Daphne du Maurier: Writing, Identity and the Gothic Imagination* (London: Macmillan, 1998), pp. 1–30.

5 Gothic 'terror and the sublime' were described in the eighteenth century by Edmund Burke in *A Philosophical Enquiry into the Origin of Our Ideas of the Sublime and the Beautiful* (1757; Oxford: Oxford University Press, 1990), pp. 36, 53–79.

6 See Botting, *Gothic* on the Gothic sublime, terror and horror, pp. 9–12, 74–7.

7 Arthur Conan Doyle, *The Hound of the Baskervilles* (1902) in *The Complete Works of Sherlock Holmes* (London: Magpie, 1993), pp. 669–766.

8 See the opening of Dorothy L. Sayers, *The Unpleasantness at the Bellona Club* (1928).

9 Dorothy L. Sayers, *Gaudy Night* (1935; London: New English Library, 1978), p. 250.

10 Dorothy L. Sayers, *Busman's Honeymoon* (1937; London: New English Library, 1974), p. 82.

11 Ibid. pp. 374–7.

12 For an exploration of the 'comic Gothic' see Avril Horner and Sue Zlosnik, *Comic Gothic* (University of Salford, European Studies Research Institute, 1998), pp. 4–5.

13 Margery Allingham, *The Crime at Black Dudley* (1929).

14 Margery Allingham, *The Tiger in the Smoke* (1952; Harmondsworth: Penguin, 1957).

15 Ngaio Marsh, *Final Curtain* (1947; London: Fontana, 1956), p. 29.

16 Ngaio Marsh, *Death and the Dancing Footman* (1941; London: Fontana, 1958), p. 62.

17 Barbara Vine, *Gallowglass* (1990; Harmondsworth: Penguin, 1990), p. 30.

18 P.D. James, *Shroud for a Nightingale* (1971; Harmondsworth: Penguin, 1989), p. 50.

19 P.D. James, *Devices and Desires* (1989; London: Faber & Faber paperback, 1990), p. 87.

20 P.D. James, *The Black Tower* (1975; London: Sphere, 1977).

21 First reference to the 'black tower' as a phallic symbol is on a map, p. 12; as an explicit sign of suffering and death, p. 212.

22 Ruth Rendell, *The Veiled One* (1988).

23 Agatha Christie, *The Murder at the Vicarage* (1930; London: Fontana, 1961), p. 118.

24 Agatha Christie, *Nemesis* (1971).

25 Ngaio Marsh, *Vintage Murder* (1937; London: Fontana, 1961), p. 45, for Alleyn's familiar daemon. See n. 1 to this chapter.

26 Ngaio Marsh, *Overture to Death* (1939).

27 Ruth Rendell, *A New Lease of Death* (1969; London: Mysterious Press, 1988), p. 171.

28   Ruth Rendell, *No More Dying Then* (London, Arrow, 1994), p. 29.
29   Ruth Rendell, *The Speaker of Mandarin* (1983; London: Guild, *The Fourth Wexford Omnibus*, 1990), pp. 427–30.
30   Ruth Rendell, *The Best Man to Die* (1969; London: Arrow, 1994), p. 170.
31   Ruth Rendell, *The Veiled One*, (London: Arrow, 1989) pp. 237–932.
32   P.D. James, *An Unsuitable Job for a Woman* (1972; London: Sphere, 1974), pp. 106–7.
33   Barbara Vine, *Asta's Book* (1993).
34   Barbara Vine, *A Dark-Adapted Eye* (1986).
35   Barbara Vine, *A Fatal Inversion* (1987).
36   Agatha Christie, *The Sittaford Mystery* (1931).
37   Dorothy L. Sayers, *The Nine Tailors* (1934; London: New English Library, 1982), p. 271.
38   Dorothy L. Sayers, *Murder Must Advertise* (1933).
39   Ibid. (London: Gollancz, 1971), p. 189.
40   Margery Allingham, *The Case of the Late Pig* (1937).
41   Ngaio Marsh, *Death in Ecstasy* (1936).
42   Ngaio Marsh, *Dead Water* (1963).
43   Ngaio Marsh, *Spinsters in Jeopardy* (1953).
44   Ngaio Marsh, *Photo-Finish* (1980; London: Fontana, 1994), p. 254.
45   P.D. James, *Devices and Desires* (London: Faber & Faber, 1990), p. 133.
46   P.D. James, *The Skull Beneath the Skin* (1982; London: Sphere, 1983).
47   Ibid. p. 154.
48   Ibid. pp. 270–1.
49   P.D. James, *An Unsuitable Job for a Woman* (London: Sphere, 1974), p. 105.
50   P.D. James, *A Taste for Death* (London: Faber & Faber, 1986), p. 349.
51   Margery Allingham, *Police at the Funeral* (1931; Harmondsworth: Penguin, 1939), p. 215.
52   For a corpse as the 'lady in the lake', see both P.D. James, *Original Sin* (1994) and Ruth Rendell, *The Best Man to Die*, p. 23.
53   Ngaio Marsh, *Final Curtain* (London: Fontana, 1956), p. 172.
54   Charlotte Brontë, *Jane Eyre* (1847; Harmondsworth: Penguin, 1966).
55   Agatha Christie, *Dead Man's Folly* (1956); Jean Rhys, *Wide Sargasso Sea* (1966; Harmondsworth: Penguin, 1968).
56   Ngaio Marsh, *Death in a White Tie* (1938; Harmondsworth: Penguin, 1944).
57   Ibid. p. 179.
58   Ibid. p. 285.
59   Ibid. p. 290.
60   Ruth Rendell, *A Judgement in Stone* (1977; London: Arrow, 1978).
61   Ibid. p. 64.
62   Ibid. p. 107.
63   Ruth Rendell, *Simisola* (1994; London: Arrow, 1995), p. 322. Cookie Dix asks Wexford if he is searching for a 'madwoman in the attic' when in fact he is looking for a black slave.
64   P.D. James, *The Black Tower* (London: Sphere, 1977), pp. 12, 212.
65   Ibid. p. 219.
66   Ibid. p. 285.
67   Margery Allingham, *Mystery Mile* (1930).
68   Margery Allingham, *Look to the Lady* (1931).

69 Margery Allingham, *Sweet Danger* (1933).
70 Margery Allingham, *More Work for the Undertaker* (1948).
71 Margery Allingham, *The Beckoning Lady* (1955; Harmondsworth: Penguin, 1960).
72 Ngaio Marsh, *Dead Water* (1964; London: Fontana, 1966), p. 95 for a 'nuclear' corpse.
73 Agatha Christie, *They Do It with Mirrors* (1952; London: Fontana, 1993). All later page references will be incorporated into the chapter.
74 Jane Austen, *Northanger Abbey* (1818; Harmondsworth: Penguin, 1972).
75 See Sayers's remark on her anti-Brontë cast of mind as she is finishing *Clouds of Witness*: *The Letters of Dorothy L. Sayers 1899–1936: The Making of a Detective* Novelist, chosen and ed. Barbara Reynolds with a preface by P.D. James (1995; London: Sceptre, 1996), p. 215.
76 Ngaio Marsh, *Off with His Head* (1957; London: Fontana, 1959). All later page references will be incorporated into the chapter.
77 P.D. James, *Original Sin* (1994; Harmondsworth: Penguin, 1996). All later page references will be incorporated into the chapter.
78 James uses Mersea Island as the scene of final confrontation, a bleak landscape also associated with the work of Margery Allingham.
79 Barbara Vine, *The House of Stairs* (1988; Harmondsworth: Penguin, 'Three Novels' edn, 1990). All later page references will be incorporated into the chapter.
80 Henry James, *The Wings of the Dove* (Harmondsworth: Penguin, 1976).

7 The Spirits of Detection

1 Dorothy L. Sayers, 'Salute to Mr Chesterton: More Father Brown Stories' (review), *Sunday Times*, 7 April 1935, 9.
2 Agatha Christie, *The Mysterious Mr Quin* (1930; London: HarperCollins, 1993), p. 24.
3 W.H. Auden, 'The Guilty Vicarage', in Robin W. Winks, ed., *Detective Fiction: A Collection of Critical Essays* (Englewood Cliffs, NJ: Prentice-Hall, 1980), p. 24.
4 For P.D. James, see Appendix C. For Margery Allingham, see Richard Martin, *Ink in Her Blood*: *The Life and Crime Fiction of Margery Allingham* (Ann Arbor, MI: UMI Research Press, 1988), p. 14.
5 For a study of Spiritualism in relation to literature and the feminine, see Diana Basham, *The Trial of Woman: Feminism and the Occult Sciences in Victorian Society* (London: Macmillan, 1992).
6 Agatha Christie, *The Sittaford Mystery* (1931; London: Fontana, 1961).
7 Ibid. p. 83.
8 Agatha Christie, *The Hound of Death* (1933; London: HarperCollins, 1993).
9 Ibid. pp. 184–99.
10 Ibid. 'The Hound of Death', pp. 7–25, 'The Red Signal', pp. 26–47, 'The Fourth Man', pp. 48–65, 'SOS', pp. 200–18.
11 Margery Allingham, *Blackerchief Dick: A Tale of Mersea Island* (London: Hodder & Stoughton, 1923). For details of its uncanny composition, see

Julia Thorogood, *Margery Allingham: A Biography* (London: Heinemann, 1991), pp. 75–8.

12 Dorothy L. Sayers, *Strong Poison* (1930).

13 Dorothy L. Sayers, *Gaudy Night* (1935).

14 Dorothy L. Sayers, *Strong Poison* (1930; London: New English Library, 1977), pp. 158–92.

15 Dorothy L. Sayers, *Gaudy Night* (1935; London: New English Library, 1978), p. 250.

16 Marion Shaw and Sabine Vanacker, *Reflecting on Miss Marple* (London: Routledge, 1991).

17 Miss Marple as 'Nemesis' announces herself as such in *Nemesis* (1971; London: Fontana, 1974), p. 172. She is an 'avenging fury' in *A Pocketful of Rye* (1953; London: Fontana, 1958), p. 89.

18 Agatha Christie, *Hallowe'en Party* (1969).

19 Ibid. (1969; London: Fontana, 1972), pp. 177–89.

20 P.D. James, *An Unsuitable Job for a Woman* (1972; London: Sphere, 1974), p. 191.

21 Ruth Rendell, *Wolf to the Slaughter* (1967; London: Arrow, 1982), p. 21.

22 Ruth Rendell, *Murder Being Once Done* (1972; London: Arrow, 1973), p. 84.

23 Ruth Rendell, *A New Lease of Death* (1969; London: Mysterious Press, 1988), p. 160.

24 Agatha Christie, *The Mysterious Mr Quin* (London: HarperCollins, 1993), p. 24.

25 Ibid. p. 7.

26 Agatha Christie, *Murder on the Orient Express* (1934; London: Fontana, 1955), p. 22. Poirot muses upon the future victim: '[t]he body – the cage … through the bars, the wild animal looks out.'

27 Dorothy L. Sayers, *Whose Body?* (1923; London: New English Library, 1968), p. 129.

28 Ibid. p. 147.

29 See Wimsey's exposition to Hilary Thorpe on the role of the writer in *The Nine Tailors* (1934; London: New English Library, 1982), p. 106.

30 Dorothy L. Sayers, *Unnatural Death* (1927).

31 Margery Allingham, *Traitor's Purse* (1941).

32 Ngaio Marsh, *Death in Ecstasy* (1936; Harmondsworth: Penguin, 1940). All later page references will be incorporated into the chapter.

33 Ngaio Marsh, *Singing in the Shrouds* (1958; London: Fontana, 1962), p. 105.

34 Dorothy L. Sayers, *Gaudy Night* (London: New English Library, 1978), p. 64; P.D. James, *An Unsuitable Job for a Woman* (London: Sphere, 1974), p. 66.

35 Ruth Rendell, *A New Lease of Death* (London: Mysterious Press, 1988), p. 28.

36 Ruth Rendell, *No More Dying Then* (London: Arrow, 1973), pp. 102, 143.

37 Ruth Rendell, *Simisola* (1994; London: Arrow, 1995), p. 5.

38 Margery Allingham, *Look to the Lady* (1931).

39 Margery Allingham, *Sweet Danger* (1933; Harmondsworth: Penguin, 1952). All later page references will be incorporated into the chapter.

40 Margery Allingham, *The Tiger in the Smoke* (1952; Harmondsworth: Penguin, 1957).

41 Margery Allingham, *Hide My Eyes* (1958).
42 Margery Allingham, *The Tiger in the Smoke* (Harmondsworth: Penguin, 1957), p. 197.
43 Ibid. p. 198.
44 Ibid. p. 198.
45 Ngaio Marsh, *Spinsters in Jeopardy* (1953).
46 Ruth Rendell, *The Veiled One* (1988).
47 Barbara Vine, *A Dark-Adapted Eye* (1986; Harmondsworth: Penguin, 'Three Novels' edn, 1990).
48 Ibid. p. 18.
49 W.H. Auden, 'The Guilty Vicarage', p. 21.
50 Agatha Christie, *Appointment with Death* (1938; London: HarperCollins, 1993). All later page references will be incorporated into the chapter.
51 See John G. Cawelti, *Adventure, Mystery and Romance: Formula Stories as Art and Popular Culture* (Chicago: University of Chicago Press, 1976).
52 Compare Yeats's famous poem 'The Second Coming': 'Turning and turning in the widening gyre': *The Collected Poems of W.B. Yeats*, 2nd edn (London: Macmillan, 1950), pp. 210–11.
53 Dorothy L. Sayers, *Unnatural Death* (1927). The novel condemns a lesbian killer but presents a wholly admirable portrait of two elderly ladies as mutually devoted. See further Chapter 8.
54 Ngaio Marsh, *Artists in Crime* (1938).
55 P.D. James, *A Taste for Death* (London: Faber & Faber, 1986). All later page references will be incorporated into the chapter.
56 Ruth Rendell, *A Judgement in Stone* (1977; London: Arrow, 1978). All later page references will be incorporated into the chapter.

8 Feminism Is Criminal

1 Agatha Christie, *The Murder of Roger Ackroyd* (1926; London: HarperCollins, 1993), p. 10.
2 See Appendices B and C for Ruth Rendell and P.D. James and feminism.
3 Dorothy L. Sayers, *Have His Carcase* (1932; London: New English Library, 1974), p. 9.
4 Margery Allingham, *The Beckoning Lady* (1955). For Barbara Vine on mothering, see *A Dark-Adapted Eye* (1986) and *Asta's Book* (1993).
5 Agatha Christie, *Partners in Crime* (1929; London: HarperCollins, 1995).
6 Ibid. p. 224.
7 Agatha Christie, *The Hollow* (1946).
8 Agatha Christie, *4.50 from Paddington* (1957).
9 Dorothy L. Sayers, *The Documents in the Case* (1930).
10 Dorothy L. Sayers, *Strong Poison* (1930).
11 Dorothy L. Sayers, *Gaudy Night* (1935; London: New English Library, 1978). All later page references will be incorporated into the chapter.
12 Margery Allingham, *The Beckoning Lady* (1955; Harmondsworth: Penguin, 1960), p. 178.
13 Ngaio Marsh, *Spinsters in Jeopardy* (1953).
14 Ngaio Marsh, *Death and the Dancing Footman* (1941).

15   Ngaio Marsh, *Final Curtain* (1947).
16   Ngaio Marsh, *Death in a White Tie* (1938).
17   P.D. James, *Cover Her Face* (1962).
18   Barbara Vine, *Gallowglass* (1990).
19   Barbara Vine, *The Chimney Sweeper's Boy* (1998).
20   Agatha Christie, *Nemesis* (1971; London: Fontana, 1974), p. 69.
21   Agatha Christie, *By the Pricking of My Thumbs* (1968).
22   Dorothy L. Sayers, *Clouds of Witness* (1926).
23   Margery Allingham, *Look to the Lady* (1931).
24   Margery Allingham, *Flowers for the Judge* (1936).
25   Margery Allingham, *Dancers in Mourning* (1937).
26   Margery Allingham, *Coroner's Pidgin* (1945).
27   Margery Allingham, *Mystery Mile* (1930).
28   Margery Allingham, *More Work for the Undertaker* (1948).
29   Ngaio Marsh, *Dead Water* (1964).
30   Ngaio Marsh, *Overture to Death* (1939).
31   Ruth Rendell, *A Sleeping Life* (1978).
32   P.D. James, *Original Sin* (1994; Harmondsworth: Penguin, 1996).
33   Ibid. pp. 259–60.
34   Ngaio Marsh, *False Scent* (1960; London: Collins, 1961), p. 40.
35   Dorothy L. Sayers, *Unnatural Death* (1927; London: New English Library, 1968).
36   Ibid. p. 177.
37   Ibid. p. 131.
38   Margery Allingham, *Death of a Ghost* (1935).
39   Margery Allingham, *The Fashion in Shrouds* (1938; Great Britain: Dent, 1986). All later page references will be incorporated into the chapter.
40   Ngaio Marsh, *Photo-Finish* (1980). See Chapter 4 for a full study.
41   Ngaio Marsh, *Grave Mistake* (1978).
42   Ngaio Marsh, *Vintage Murder* (1937).
43   Ngaio Marsh, *Hand in Glove* (1962).
44   P.D. James, *Shroud for a Nightingale* (1971). See Chapter 2 for a full study.
45   P.D. James, *Death of an Expert Witness* (1977).
46   Ruth Rendell, *From Doon with Death* (1964).
47   Margery Allingham, *Coroner's Pidgin* (1945; Harmondsworth: Penguin, 1950).
48   Agatha Christie, *Appointment with Death* (1938).
49   Agatha Christie, *Murder in Mesopotamia* (1936).
50   Dorothy L. Sayers and Jill Paton Walsh, *Thrones, Dominations* (London: Hodder & Stoughton, 1998).
51   Margery Allingham, *Police at the Funeral* (1931).
52   Ngaio Marsh, *Opening Night* (1951).
53   P.D. James, *Devices and Desires* (1989).
54   P.D. James, *The Skull Beneath the Skin* (1982).
55   Ruth Rendell, *Simisola* (1994).
56   P.D. James, *Cover Her Face* (1962; London: Sphere, 1974), p. 156.
57   Agatha Christie, *The Mirror Crack'd from Side to Side* (1962).
58   Agatha Christie, *Murder on the Orient Express* (1934).
59   Margery Allingham, *The Mind Readers* (1965).

60 Margery Allingham, *Traitor's Purse* (1941).
61 Ngaio Marsh, *Artists in Crime* (1938).
62 P.D. James, *Unnatural Causes* (1967).
63 Ruth Rendell, *Wolf to the Slaughter* (1967).
64 Ruth Rendell, *Kissing the Gunner's Daughter* (1991). See Chapter 2.
65 Barbara Vine, *The House of Stairs* (1988).
66 Barbara Vine, *Gallowglass* (1990; Harmondsworth: Penguin, 1990), p. 261.
67 Agatha Christie, *Sleeping Murder* (1976; London: Fontana, 1978). All later page references will be incorporated into the chapter.
68 Dorothy L. Sayers, *The Unpleasantness at the Bellona Club* (1928).
69 Ngaio Marsh, *Singing in the Shrouds* (1958; London: Fontana, 1962). All later page references will be incorporated into the chapter.
70 Ruth Rendell, *The Veiled One* (1988).
71 P.D. James, *A Certain Justice* (1997; London: Faber & Faber, 1998). All later page references will be incorporated into the chapter.
72 Ruth Rendell, *An Unkindness of Ravens* (1985; London: Arrow, 1986). All later page references will be incorporated into the chapter.

Select Bibliography

Critical works on detective and crime fiction

Auden, W.H., 'The Guilty Vicarage', in Robin W. Winks, ed., *Detective Fiction: A Collection of Critical Essays* (Englewood Cliffs, NJ: Prentice-Hall, 1980), 15–24.

Bell, Ian A. and Graham Daldry, eds, *Watching the Detectives: Essays on Crime Fiction* (London: Macmillan, 1990).

Benstock, Bernard, ed., *Essays on Detective Fiction* (London: Macmillan, 1983).

Binyon, T.J., *Murder Will Out: The Detective in Fiction* (Oxford: Oxford University Press, 1989).

Bloom, Clive, ed., *Twentieth-Century Suspense: The Thriller Comes of Age* (London: Macmillan, 1990).

—— *Cult Fiction: Popular Reading and Cult Theory* (London: Macmillan, 1996).

Carr, Helen, ed., *From My Guy to Sci Fi: Genre and Women's Writing in the Postmodern World* (London: Pandora, 1989).

Cawelti, John G., *Adventure, Mystery and Romance: Formula Stories as Art and Popular Culture* (Chicago: University of Chicago Press, 1976).

Craig, Patricia and Mary Cadogan, *The Lady Investigates: Women Detectives and Spies in Fiction* (Oxford: Oxford University Press, 1986).

Irons, Glenwood, ed., *Feminism in Women's Detective Fiction* (Toronto: University of Toronto Press, 1995).

Knight, Stephen, *Form and Ideology in Crime Fiction* (London: Macmillan, 1980).

McCracken, Scott, *Pulp: Reading Popular Fiction* (Manchester: Manchester University Press, 1998).

Munt, Sally R., *Murder by the Book? Feminism and the Crime Novel* (London: Routledge, 1994).

Murch, A.E., *The Development of the Detective Novel* (New York: Philosophical Library, 1958).

Nichols, Victoria and Susan Thompson, *Silk Stalkings: More Women Write of Murder* (Lanham, MD: Scarecrow Press, 1998).

Ousby, Ian, *The Crime and Mystery Book: A Reader's Companion* (London: Thames & Hudson, 1997).

Porter, Dennis, *The Pursuit of Crime: Art and Ideology in Detective Fiction* (New Haven, CT: Yale University Press, 1981).

Rader, Barbara A. and Howard G. Zettler, *The Sleuth and the Scholar: Origins, Evolution and Current Trends in Detective Fiction* (New York: Greenwood Press, 1988).

Reilly, John M., ed., *Twentieth-Century Crime and Mystery Writers* (London: Macmillan, 1980).

Symons, Julian, *Bloody Murder: From the Detective Story to the Crime Novel: A History* (London: Faber & Faber, 1972; rev. edn. London: Macmillan, 1992).

Walker, Ronald G. and June M. Frazer, eds, *The Cunning Craft: Original Essays on Detective Fiction and Contemporary Literary Theory* (Chicago: Western Illinois University Press, 1990).

Winks, Robin W., ed., *Detective Fiction: A Collection of Critical Essays* (Englewood Cliffs, NJ: Prentice-Hall, 1980).

Critical works on individual authors

Acheson, Carole, 'Cultural Ambivalence: Ngaio Marsh's New Zealand Detective Fiction', *Journal of Popular Culture*, 19(2) (1985), 159–74.
Bakerman, Jane S., 'Cordelia Gray: Apprentice and Archetype', *Clues: A Journal of Detection*, 5 (1984), 101–14.
Bargainnier, Earl F., ed., *10 Women of Mystery* (Bowling Green, OH: Bowling Green State University Press, 1981).
Barnard, Robert, *A Talent to Deceive: An Appreciation of Agatha Christie*, revised and updated with a complete bibliography by Louise Barnard (London: Collins, 1980).
Birch, Helen, 'P.D. James's Stylish Crime', *Women's Review*, 10 (1986), 6–7.
Brown, Janice, *The Seven Deadly Sins in the Work of Dorothy L. Sayers* (Kent, OH: Kent State University Press, 1998).
Clark, Susan L., 'A Fearful Symmetry: An Interview with Ruth Rendell', *Armchair Detective*, 22(3) (1989), 228–35.
Hall, Trevor H., *Dorothy L. Sayers: Nine Literary Studies* (London: Duckworth, 1980).
Hannay, Margaret P., ed., *As Her Wimsey Took Her: Critical Essays on the Work of Dorothy L. Sayers* (Kent, OH: Kent State University Press, 1979).
Knepper, Marty S., 'Agatha Christie: Feminist', *Armchair Detective*, 16 (1983), 398–406.
Light, Alison, *Forever England: Femininity, Literature and Conservatism between the Wars* (London: Routledge, 1991).
Martin, Richard, *Ink In Her Blood: The Life and Crime Fiction of Margery Allingham* (Ann Arbor, MI: UMI Research Press, 1988).
Moggach, Lottie, 'How I Write: An Interview with Ruth Rendell', *Times*, 13 September 1997, 23.
Pike, B.A., *Campion's Career: A Study of the Novels of Margery Allingham* (Bowling Green, OH: Bowling Green State University Popular Press, 1987).
Plain, Gill, *Women's Fiction of the Second World War: Gender, Power and Resistance* (Edinburgh: Edinburgh University Press, 1996).
Rahn, B.J., 'Ngaio Marsh: The Detective Novelist of Manners', *Armchair Detective*, 28(2) (1995), 140–7.
Sanders, Dennis and Len Lovallo, *The Agatha Christie Companion* (London: W.H. Allen, 1985).
Shaw, Marion and Sabine Vanacker, *Reflecting on Miss Marple* (London: Routledge, 1991).
Siebenheller, Norma, *P.D. James* (New York: Frederick Ungar, 1981).

Biographical and autobiographical works

Cade, Jared, *Agatha Christie and the Eleven Missing Days* (London: Peter Owen, 1998).
Christie, Agatha, *An Autobiography* (London: Collins, 1977).
Lewis, Margaret, *Ngaio Marsh: A Life* (London: Chatto & Windus, 1991).

Marsh, Ngaio, *Black Beech and Honeydew: An Autobiography* (London: Collins, 1966; rev. edn. 1981).

Morgan, Janet, *Agatha Christie: A Biography* (London: Collins, 1984).

Reynolds, Barbara, *Dorothy L. Sayers: Her Life and Soul* (Great Britain: Hodder & Stoughton, 1993, repr. St Martins, NY, Griffin, 1997).

Thorogood, Julia, *Margery Allingham: A Biography* (London: Heinemann, 1991).

Index

Numbers in **bold** indicate separate studies of those novels or separate biographical sketches. Where a particular chapter is indicated, it means that the entry forms a main subject of the whole chapter.